WITHDRAWN

THE COFFEE CLUB
MYSTERIES

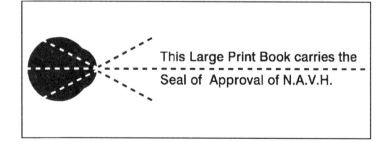

This Large Print Book carries the
Seal of Approval of N.A.V.H.

THE COFFEE CLUB MYSTERIES

6 WHODUNITS ARE BREWING IN SMALL-TOWN KANSAS

DARLENE FRANKLIN, CYNTHIA HICKEY,
ELIZABETH LUDWIG, DANA MENTINK,
CANDICE PRENTICE, JANICE THOMPSON

THORNDIKE PRESS
A part of Gale, a Cengage Company

Farmington Hills, Mich • San Francisco • New York • Waterville, Maine
Meriden, Conn • Mason, Ohio • Chicago

LIBRARY OF CONGRESS CIP DATA ON FILE.
CATALOGUING IN PUBLICATION FOR THIS BOOK
IS AVAILABLE FROM THE LIBRARY OF CONGRESS

ISBN-13: 978-1-4328-6306-7 (hardcover)

Published in 2019 by arrangement with Barbour Publishing, Inc.

Printed in the United States of America
1 2 3 4 5 6 7 23 22 21 20 19

CONTENTS

■ ■ ■ ■

Coffee, Tea, or Murder

BY CYNTHIA HICKEY

■ ■ ■ ■

ONE

The store definitely needed a new sign. I stared up at the faded plastic rectangle with the hand-painted words THE COFFEE PERK across its surface. If I wanted folks to come in and sit a spell, I'd need to pretty the place up. But the inheritance I received from Aunt Edna was almost gone. It had to be all about priorities.

I sighed and unlocked the front door. The shop would open in half an hour and my regulars would come in for java and free Wi-Fi. A light May breeze blew a color-printed flier down the street.

Inside, I put my light brown hair up under a cap and stared at my baby. Cozy and welcoming with mismatched tables, chairs, and tablecloths, it invited a person to settle in for a while. A bookcase held books for sale by local authors and a magazine rack held donated magazines and copies of the weekly paper. I kept the counter polished to a high sheen and the floors clean enough to eat off of, so to speak. The Coffee Perk was everything I'd dreamed of.

"Are you open?"

I turned and stared into the blue eyes of Dean Matthews. I knew him by name and face only because I consumed his crime novels as if they were a box of the finest chocolates I couldn't get enough of. "Oh yeah, uh, the coffee isn't made yet."

"Not a problem. Wi-Fi isn't set up at my place yet, and I really need to work." He flashed the same killer smile from his book jackets and took a seat in the farthest corner of the store.

"Sure, come on in," I muttered the moment I could speak again.

"I noticed when I drove by last night that the *P* letter is out in your sign," he called out while opening his laptop.

New sign was definitely on the to-do list. I booted up my five-year-old computer and found the nearest installer. Billy Bob Rankins. Ugh. I'd gone to high school with the man, and let's just say, we weren't exactly bosom buddies. Since I needed the bulb replaced right away, I dialed his number on the shop phone.

"Well, if it isn't Morgan Butler."

"I need my sign fixed. It needs a new bulb. Do you have time today?"

"Yeah, I can come over later today, but it'll cost you."

I closed my eyes. "How much?"

"A date. Let's put the past behind us."

"Not a chance. I'll never go out with you, so stop asking. Do you want the job or not?" I leaned against the counter and turned my back to Dean. I didn't want him to see how blotchy my face got when I was angry. "I really need the job done today, Billy Bob. Can you come around three?"

"Yeah, I can be there around three." *Click.*

I hung up the phone and turned to see Mrs. Hudson talking to Dean. I frowned. Was everyone going to start coming in before I flipped the sign from Closed to Open?

I started several brews from unleaded to strong. Some of my customers liked blended, but there were plenty of the old-fashioned kind who wanted plain, simple black java.

I took another peek while waiting for the coffee to brew. Dean sat back in his chair and ran his hands through his thick hair. He frowned, then started typing again as the bell over the door jingled.

"If not for those big ears, that man would be too perfect." Harper Daggett, my best friend since forever, leaned on the counter.

"You think he has big ears?" I glared.

"Don't look at me like that. I know you're a big fan of his, but yes, his ears are a bit large."

"Maybe." I didn't care. He was eye candy and could use my Wi-Fi anytime. Of course,

11

it was Tuesday, and I closed the shop early for the book club. I didn't think I could cancel the opportunity to hang with friends, even for Dean Matthews. I eyed the clock.

"Yeah, I need to get to work." Once Harper got her favorite vanilla latte, she sailed out the door with one last look at Mr. Handsome and a big grin at me.

Throughout the day, I wasn't the only one sneaking peeks at the author. Almost everyone in Oak Grove knew the man's name and face. Would he let me sell his books in my store? Of course he would. It wasn't as if he could stop me from ordering them.

Closing time. The only customer left in the store was Dean, who typed blissfully away, unaware of my cardinal rule about Tuesdays.

"Excuse me, Mr. Matthews?" I approached his table.

"Dean." He continued typing, not looking up from his keyboard.

"Oh, uh, okay. I'm Morgan. I'm closing."

That got his attention. He glanced up. "It's only five o'clock."

"I close early on Tuesdays for book club."

"I won't bother you."

How did I get out of this one? Would the ladies care? They ranged in age from my twenty-eight to Jo's seventy-five. Of course, none of them was past giving a good-looking man a glance. "Can you come back in an hour then? I close shop for supper."

"Great. I'm starving. Can I buy you a burger?" He stood. "I'll run out and buy two cheeseburger baskets from the Sunflower Diner and be right back."

The man must be used to people doing his bidding because he didn't wait for an answer. Before I could say no onions, he darted outside and down the street.

I eyed his computer. Would he care if I took just a — Wait a minute. Billy Bob was supposed to have been here by three. I headed to the phone behind the counter and dialed his number. No answer.

Dean returned within fifteen minutes during which time I'd restrained myself from taking a peek at his current novel. I flipped the sign to Closed and joined him at one of the tables.

"So, Morgan," he said, dipping a french fry into ketchup, "how long have you owned this place?" His sharp blue gaze never left my face.

"A year. It sat empty for quite a while until I bought and renovated it." Gracious, the man was actually interested in what I had to say. I asked my own nosy question. "Why would a bestselling author move to Oak Grove?"

"For the peace and quiet. Something that's hard to find in a big city."

I forgot the time until someone tapped on the window. I turned to see Jo Anderson and

13

Harper staring in. Jo had her hands cupped around her eyes and her gaze locked on Dean. Harper had a bit more finesse and just grinned in at me.

"Excuse me," I said, standing. "You might want to melt into the floorboards before the others arrive." Too late. By the time I reached the door, Penny Parson, Evelyn Kliff, and Jeanine Gransbury had joined the group on the sidewalk. Harper animatedly told the others who the handsome man was.

"Is he joining the book club?" Jo asked. "Because I don't mind."

"No, he's writing. Shh." I ushered them inside and locked the door before leading them to the farthest table from Dean.

"Here's a jar of honey." Penny handed me a blue-and-white crock.

"And some herbs," said Evelyn. "Rosemary and basil. You really should start buying scones from Jeanine. They go quite well with coffee."

I glanced at our resident baker. "That would take customers from her shop. I'm just fine, thank you." My mouth practically watered over the book-shaped cookies Jeanine set in the center of the table.

"I'm taking one to our guest." Harper snatched up a cookie and a pink napkin and sashayed — there was no other word to use — over to his table.

He grinned, proving the killer grin was

actually his real one and not one he used just for publicity. "Thank you." He glanced at our table, winked, stuck a set of earbuds into his ears, and turned back to his laptop.

Our latest book club choice, a cozy mystery involving a crime-solving cat, sat untouched on the table in front of us. We did not talk books that night. How could we when a much more interesting topic sat at a different table?

I sent Billy Bob a text before I climbed into bed, telling him that if he showed up in the morning, I'd give him all the coffee he wanted.

Billy Bob arrived the next morning just as the store opened along with a handful of other customers. But no hunky author. Oh well. It was nice while it lasted. Billy Bob smirked at me. "Sorry. I fell asleep; then I had a customer first thing this morning."

"You're over sixteen hours late, Billy Bob." I turned to start a fresh pot of coffee. "I'll bring you out a cup when I'm done. I sent you the link to the new sign I want. This original sign left by the previous owners has definitely seen better days."

"Thanks. I'll check it out and replace the bulb for now." He left the shop and banged a metal ladder against the outside wall.

I'd poured him his first cup just as my phone rang. I glanced at the next customer, Mrs. Hudson.

15

"Go ahead, dear. I'm in no hurry." Mrs. Hudson, one of the town's wealthiest citizens, smiled and waved a manicured hand. While she had to be in her midseventies, she always dressed as if she were going to an important event, complete with sky-high heels and full makeup.

I took a coffee order for ten people attending a business meeting then hung up and rushed outside to give Billy Bob his coffee. "Keep 'em comin'," he said. "I had a late night."

Rolling my eyes, I returned to my customers. When the line slowed, I poured another cup for the bossy handyman and set it on the counter. "Billy Bob can wait another minute," I muttered. My stomach rumbled from having no breakfast, and I dug under the counter for a granola bar.

I glanced around the room as I ate. Gratefulness filled my heart to see a customer at every table. *Thank you, God, for this blessing.*

I tossed the granola bar wrapper into the garbage and snatched Billy Bob's next cup of coffee from the counter. I moved toward the door just in time to see the ladder fall sideways, hitting the sidewalk with a loud clatter.

I dashed outside as everyone in the shop converged at the front window.

Two

When I reached the sidewalk, I stumbled backward, hand over my mouth, and tripped over a toolbox. My fingers loosened, and the coffee mug shattered on the cement. I landed hard on my backside and screamed. Billy Bob lay crumpled on the sidewalk, his legs twisted in the rungs of his ladder, and stared at me with wide, dead eyes.

Once I was over my initial shock, I scurried over and felt for a pulse in Billy Bob's neck. Nada. The man was definitely dead.

I glanced up, catching sight of a very stern-looking man in a sheriff's uniform staring down at me. "He's dead, I think. Were you patrolling the town? You must have seen him."

"Yep. Something I figure might need doing on a regular basis." He put his hand on the butt of his gun. "I need you to step away from the body, ma'am."

I wasted no time in following orders. "Are you the new sheriff?"

He jumped back as if I'd started to attack.

"Keep your hands up."

"Okay." Up they went. "My name is Morgan Butler, and I'm the owner of the Coffee Perk. I hired Billy Bob Rankins — that's him — to fix my sign. He was supposed to come yesterday afternoon but came this morning instead." I squinted to read his name tag. "Sheriff Hayden."

"Giving information without being asked, Miss Butler?" His eyes narrowed. "You act as if you've done this before."

"Nope. Just watched lots of movies, and I love to read crime novels." Uh-oh. He got a spark in his eye at that. Would he think I'd gotten nefarious ideas from books?

"Let's step inside." He jerked his head toward the door and spoke into his radio for an ambulance and crime scene investigators.

"Aren't you going to check if Billy Bob's dead?" I walked inside and plopped into a chair. My customers were still gawking out the window. "I mean, he is. I checked, but shouldn't you?"

"He's dead." He stood over me, doing his best to look taller than his five-foot-sixish. "Start from the beginning."

I repeated what I'd told him, adding, "I'm sure any of the people here will confirm what I've told you."

Making guttural sounds in his throat, Sheriff Hayden wrote down everything I said into a little black notebook. When the ambulance arrived and poor Billy Bob was loaded onto a gurney, I was given the order not to leave town.

Where would I go?

"This shop is now a crime scene until we get an autopsy. You will not be allowed to reopen until we've cleared it." He jerked his head toward the door.

His head jerk was starting to become annoying. "I can't afford to close up shop."

He raised his eyebrows.

"Fine." I stomped out, tears welling in my eyes. I trudged upstairs to my apartment and called Harper from the cell phone I'd left charging on my nightstand. "Billy Bob is dead. He fell while fixing my sign." I fell backward onto my bed.

"Hold up. Start over."

I recapped finding Billy Bob. "They're going to close my shop. What am I going to do?"

"Well, book club can be held in your apartment."

"I'm talking about money, Harper." I closed my eyes. "I'm barely squeaking by as it is. The new sheriff is horrible."

"It'll work out. You know the ladies from the book club will help where we can."

I knew that, but they couldn't pay my bills. "I just needed to vent. Thanks."

"I'll say a prayer for a quick reopening to your shop and for justice regarding Billy Bob."

We hung up, and I went back downstairs. Word must've spread like wildfire, because there were at least twenty or thirty people waiting for me. All of a sudden everyone in town was dying for a cup of coffee. Well, figuratively speaking anyway.

After the police cleared out my shop and hung yellow tape everywhere, I spent the rest of the day trudging all over town trying to find an alternate location to serve coffee. No luck. It seemed, for the moment at least, that I was *persona non grata* as far as the respectable businesses in town were concerned. You know, the ones who didn't kill people.

I didn't have much time to figure things out. If the police kept me shut down more than a couple of days, the residents of Oak Grove might learn to make their own coffee, and then where would I be?

The next morning, I stood on the sidewalk and stared at the yellow crime scene tape forming a giant X over my front door. Through the window my coffee urns beckoned. Maybe if I could sneak in the back —

"What happened?" Dean stood next to me and stared at the door. In one hand he held a briefcase, in the other a bag from the local bakery, the Mad Batter. "I brought bagels."

"They closed me down because of the death."

His mouth dropped open. "The one day I

go to Vicksville, and you have a death in your shop without me? This is a story I want to hear. Where can we eat?"

"My apartment."

"Excuse me?"

"I was thinking out loud about how I could keep my business going. All I need to do is sneak in the back door of the shop and grab a few things. It's a large apartment, just a big room, really. I think it'll work."

"Whoa. Let's think this through. Follow me." He led me to a small green area next to the library. We sat at a picnic table. "I know I write fiction, but I'm pretty sure it's against the law for you to enter the shop until it's been cleared."

"But I need my coffeepots, my tea-kettles . . ." I folded my arms on the table and laid my head down.

"Have you considered renting what you need?"

"In Oak Grove?"

He chuckled and tapped me on the head. "Chin up. We'll think of something. Here's your bagel. Multigrain with strawberry cream cheese. The baker — Jeanine, right? — told me what you like."

I perked right up. "I'll do some research once I stop feeling sorry for myself."

"You make me smile, Morgan."

My face flushed. The feeling was definitely mutual.

When we returned to the shop, Sheriff Hayden stood outside. His stony countenance sent ice water trickling down my back. Instinctively, I stepped closer to Dean.

"Ms. Butler, I'd like to question you further on the death of Billy Bob Rankins. Please come to the station with me."

My eyes widened. "Why?"

"Are you resisting?"

"No, I just . . . Oh, never mind." I glanced up at Dean. "Will you put a sign on my shop door that says I'll open for business as soon as I can?"

"I will." He leaned close. "It'll be fine, Morgan. Don't worry."

"Thanks." Without a backward glance, I slid into the back seat of the sheriff's car. I missed our old sheriff. He would never have treated me as a person of interest. Why was this one treating me like a criminal?

At the sheriff's office, I was led to a room containing a metal table bolted to the floor and four chairs, two on each side. "Do I need to get a lawyer?"

"I don't know, do you?" Sheriff Hayden motioned for me to sit.

I did, nervously crossing and uncrossing my arms. I wasn't quite sure what I was doing there, but it couldn't be good. I struggled to stop squirming in an attempt to look more innocent.

"The M. E. had a bit of time early this

morning to do the autopsy on our dead guy."
He paused. When I refused to squirm, wrapping my ankles around the legs of the chair and gripping the seat with both hands, he continued. "The fall wasn't the cause of death."

"Oh?" Good. That meant it must have been a heart attack or something, and it wouldn't be a crime scene anymore, right? Wrong.

"He was poisoned by your coffee first. How do we know this? Well, Ms. Butler, we analyzed the mug that the victim drank from and left on your sign." He slid a cell phone across the table. "This is Rankins's phone. Guess what the last text to him said."

Uh-oh.

"You offered him lots of coffee. Remember that?"

I nodded. "The coffee was fine when I brewed it."

"How long have you known the victim?"

"Since high school."

"Friends?"

"Not really."

"Enemies?"

"No!" I frowned. "He wanted me to date him. I said no."

"Why?"

"Uh . . ." I lowered my voice. "I didn't particularly like him."

"Hmmm." He sat back. "Do you know the agonizing way poison works?"

"Not really." My shoulders slumped. I was in hot water. "What happens now?"

He folded his hands on the tabletop and leaned forward. "I will keep a very close eye on you, Ms. Butler. I'll be questioning the people of Oak Grove. I'll be calling in the Kansas Federal Bureau of Investigation. We'll find out who killed Rankins."

"Good. Then you'll find out it wasn't me. I'm not stupid enough to leave a traceable trail telling him I'm making coffee and then poison him with it."

"We'll see. You're free to go, but be aware I am keeping a close eye on you."

I couldn't get out of there fast enough. Outside, I stood on the sidewalk wondering whether I should walk home or call one of my friends. Oak Grove wasn't that big and I needed time to clear my head, so walk won out.

It still rankled that I was considered a suspect. Oh, Sheriff Hayden hadn't said the words outright, but I knew the lingo. Until someone else looked guiltier than me, local law enforcement wouldn't look any further.

The tears I'd held at bay all morning turned traitor and ran down my face. I swiped the back of my hand across my eyes and hoped, no prayed, no one would see me. No such luck.

As I passed the Pump and Go, red-haired Billy Tanker looked up from spraying the dust off the concrete. "Hey, Morgan!"

I waved a hand and kept going.

He turned off the water and jogged to catch up. "You look like your dog died."

"No, just Billy Bob Rankins."

"Really?" His eyes grew big. "Was he a good friend of yours?"

"Not really."

"You're acting very strange." He hurried back to his job, leaving me to my miserable mood.

I couldn't help but glance up at the shop sign as I passed before heading to my apartment. I needed a plan to clear my name, and I knew just the person to help me.

THREE

"I need you," I said the moment Dean walked in my door the next morning. I'd put a sign on my shop door telling my customers to walk up the stairs to my apartment for their coffee. I'd arranged some card tables and folding chairs around the spacious living room. Those, along with my own couch and armchairs, would accommodate the regulars. Unfortunately, the only coffee I had available was from my Keurig.

Dean grinned. "That's the best offer I've had in a long time."

"Oh hush. I need you to help me clear my name."

That halted his humor. "Excuse me?"

"Billy Bob was poisoned by my coffee, so I'm suspect number one."

He cut a quick glance at my Keurig.

"I didn't kill him!"

"Uh, did they arrest you?"

"No."

"Then you're a person of interest. No big

deal." He set his laptop bag on my table.

"You'd think differently if you were the one being harassed by Deputy Dunderhead."

"Sheriff."

"I know." I groaned. "Sheriff isn't alliterative though, is it?" Ugh. I plopped onto a kitchen chair and huffed. "My shop is closed, bills are due, and I really don't think the sheriff's department is looking any further than me."

"Why do you need me helping you?"

"You're the most qualified person I know."

"Because I write crime novels?"

"Yes." I stared at him. "You've done a ton of research about crime, right?"

"Well, yes, but —"

I reached over and gripped his hand. "Please, Dean. I can ask the ladies of the book club, but it might be dangerous. In fact, they've promised to question the folks they run across, but . . . what if it's dangerous?"

He laughed. "So, you'll risk me."

I shrugged, not having anything to say to dispute his words. "I'll give you free coffee for life."

He thrust out his hand. "Deal. We'll start working once you close up."

"Awesome." I returned his shake then sprang to my feet to get him the first of his free cups of coffee. Once I had him settled with his laptop and happily typing away, I moved on to my second plan of the day.

Some might consider it breaking the law, but paying my bills trumped just about anything at this point.

As I approached the back door of the Coffee Perk, I said a quick prayer of forgiveness. Surely God understood my need to grab just a few things. I inserted my key into the lock and stepped into eerie silence. I shivered. I didn't believe in ghosts, but it sure felt as if someone's spirit still lingered with harm on their mind.

Pushing aside foolish thoughts that went against everything I knew of God and death, I headed for the supply closet where I kept extra percolators and supplies. I started filling boxes with everything I thought I'd need in order to run my business. When I'd finished, three large boxes sat on the floor in front of me. I'd have to make three trips. Choosing the most important supplies, should I not have the opportunity to come back before being arrested, I hefted that box into my arms and headed out the back door.

"Ms. Butler."

Uh-oh. Busted, but not by our new sheriff. I turned and glared at the man who very much wanted to buy my shop right out from under me. "Roy Collins."

The man looked every bit the evil banker he was. Expensive suit, high-priced haircut slicked back from his face. Beady brown eyes peering above pudgy cheeks. He gave me the creeps and, ever since he foreclosed on my grandmother's house, thus causing me to live above my shop, I harbored a deep dislike for the man. "Sell my family home yet?"

"I've had several offers, actually." He straightened his red power tie. "Looks like you've run into a spell of bad luck. Ready to sell yet?"

I narrowed my eyes. "You wouldn't be so low as to kill someone, make me look like the guilty party, then waltz in and take what you want, would you?"

He laughed without humor. "It's cute how you live in a fantasy world. Take care of yourself. You know who to call when you're ready to sell." He strolled away, whistling the tune to the *Andy Griffith Show,* which was the creepiest thing the man had done yet.

I set the first box outside the door to my apartment so Dean wouldn't feel obligated to keep me from retrieving the others, then headed back to the shop. By the time I carried up the third box, my arms and thighs ached. I really needed to work out more.

I carried the box inside and noted I had several people sitting around my kitchen table, cups of coffee in hand. Frowning, I retrieved the other boxes.

"I made them coffee," Dean said, glancing up from his laptop. "I hope you don't mind, but they were hanging out at the bottom of the stairs. I had to persuade them your sign

29

was for real."

"I hope you charged them." I needed every dollar I could get.

"They said they knew your prices and put the money in that jar next to the refrigerator." He eyed the boxes near the door. A light of understanding dawned in his eyes. He shook his head and returned to his work.

"Back in business, I see." Mrs. Hudson leaned on my kitchen island. "A bit unorthodox, opening shop in your private residence, but to each his own."

"I need the money. Give me a few minutes and I'll have fresh coffee on."

"I had a French vanilla from that contraption over there." She lowered her voice. "Did you know that's the author, Dean Matthews?"

"Yes, ma'am."

"Oh. Sometimes I'm the last to know. I spoke to him downstairs, but thought he was just another businessman. I saw Collins talking to you in the alley. Is he still pressuring you to sell?"

"Yes." I measured out the required amount of fresh-ground coffee.

"Well, if you do sell, consider me first. I'd like to open a used-clothing boutique of more upscale clothing than the one on Main. This place might hold bad memories for you now, you know, with you being a suspect in that poor man's death." She flashed a coral-colored smile and sailed out my door.

Why did so many people want my simple little shop?

Within the hour word had spread that I was back in business and every spot at the island, card tables, and couch was taken up by customers. One gentleman even took the liberty of turning sports on the TV.

Dean heaved a dramatic sigh and pulled a set of earbuds from his bag. With a glare around the room, he stuck them in his ears.

Poor guy. I was pretty sure he was praying for his own Wi-Fi more with every passing minute. While I suspected most of the customers were there out of curiosity, I'd guessed right that some regulars would still get together to gossip. I was blessed to have the business. Things would return pretty much to normal by morning when I had my supplies set up.

Later that night, my friends and book club members tromped up the stairs and into my apartment. Harper took one look at the mess left behind from the day's customers. "You must be desperate." She plopped a twenty-dollar bill on the counter. "No arguments. Pay me back when you can."

The other sweet women followed suit, giving however much they could afford. It wouldn't pay all the bills, but it would give me coffee for the week. I'd take things one day at a time.

I sniffed back tears. "You ladies are the best."

"We all need help sometimes," Jo said.

"This is your time," Harper said, taking a seat on the sofa. "Have you thought of offering tea? Some folks don't like coffee. How about different versions of lemonade, fruit drinks, smoothies?"

I hadn't considered expanding, but now in this time of need might be the right time. "I'll seriously consider that."

"You know where you can get organic honey." Penny smiled.

Jeanine took a seat in one of my wing chairs. "I heard you were questioned about Billy Bob's death."

"I heard he was poisoned by your coffee," Evelyn said, glancing toward the kitchen. "Which makes it surprising that you had so many customers today. I also heard your apartment was filled to capacity. Were people buying?"

"Keurig." I sighed and took a seat on a kitchen chair. "I just recently got the percolators back up and running."

"So, what are you going to do?" Harper asked. "Can we help?"

"Your support is all I need." My face heated. "I've asked Dean Matthews to help me find the real murderer."

"There's no such thing as a fake murderer, dear," Jo said. "You either kill someone or you don't."

"True." I nodded. "I need to find out what kind of poison was used to kill Billy Bob."

"Here." Harper scribbled a name on a slip of paper and handed it to me. "Don't lose this. That's my cousin, Ruth. She works at the M. E.'s office. Tell her I told you to call. She'll tell you what you need to know."

"Can we call her now?"

Harper shrugged. "I can try." She dug her cell phone out of her purse then pressed a button. "Hey, Ruth, it's me. Can you tell me what was used to kill Billy Bob Rankins? Really? Where would one find something like that?" Harper pressed her lips together. "Thanks." She hung up. "Death camas. It's a type of lily that grows around water. Highly toxic."

"Won't she get into trouble for telling you that?" I frowned.

"Nah. She practically runs the place. Just don't tell anyone where you got the information."

I needed to find out whether there was any death camas growing around the nearby lake. I typed the name into the search bar of my phone. "When not in bloom, it looks like a green onion."

"It won't smell like one," Evelyn said. "It's also not real common around here. You'll find it more in the western US, but it can grow here. Every bit of it is toxic. It's also called the death lily."

I shuddered and read the symptoms. Spasms, rapid breathing, low heart rate, diarrhea, deep tendon reflexes, coma, abdominal pain, to name a few. Billy Bob did not die peacefully. How long had he tried to hold on to the ladder before falling to his death? I actually felt sorry for the guy even though he'd been a thorn in my side for a long time. I not only needed to clear my name, but find justice for his death.

"His funeral is tomorrow, visitation tonight," Jo said. "The family wants it over and done with so they can return to their lives. Someone has already offered to buy the business."

"That sounds cold-hearted. The rushed funeral, not someone buying the business." I glanced at each of the dear faces around me. "I do not want any of you involved in this. I mean it." I cleared my clogged throat. "I couldn't bear for any of you to end up like Billy Bob."

"I think we can help without making it obvious," Harper said, smiling. "There are gossipers in this town. All we have to do is listen and maybe do a little prodding."

Despite my reservations about their involvement, I couldn't help but feel loved. "Then let's attend the visitation together. I'm sure my presence will create a buzz for the rest of you to follow."

FOUR

I stared out the front window of Harper's vehicle. Without getting out of the car, I was made aware that people didn't really want me there. "Ladies, this is not going to be easy for me. For your sakes, split as soon as we're out of the car."

"Don't be ridiculous," Jo said. "All for one and one for all."

"We are not the Three Musketeers." Actually, there were only three of us in the car. The others chose to come separately.

"There are the others." Jo pushed her door open.

The rest of the book club clustered in front of the funeral home. I took a deep breath and exited the vehicle. Glares burned holes right through me. I'd had no idea Billy Bob was so well-liked.

"Don't worry," Harper whispered in my ear. "That's his family. No one else liked him."

I might survive the night after all. Keeping

far away from the pack of Rankinses, I entered the plantation-style building and followed the signs to Billy Bob's service. My friends did as we'd agreed and split off to mingle.

Ignoring the whispers, I approached the casket and stared into the face of the man who had died on the sidewalk outside my shop. I sighed. "Goodbye, Billy Bob. I wish we could have gotten along better."

"Not friends with the victim, Miss Butler?"

I turned and stared into the sheriff's cynical eyes. "How many times are you going to ask that question? I will state again that I did not kill him. Just because we didn't get along doesn't mean I would commit murder."

"We'll see. We have help with our investigation arriving tomorrow. We will get to the bottom of this."

I rolled my eyes and headed to a side table filled with punch, cookies, and coffee. It didn't look as if anyone had taken even a sip of the coffee I donated.

As I nibbled, I scanned the room, honing in on a red-faced Harper. That conversation promised to be interesting. I sidled around the edge of the room and did my best to hide behind a silk ficus tree.

"I'm telling you, that woman had every reason to kill my cousin."

"I've heard silly things come out of your mouth before, Renee, but this one takes the cake." Harper laughed. "Do you really think Billy Bob was murdered because of a broken date?"

"Well, why else? Everyone loved him."

"Nobody liked him except his family. And even then, not all of them. People put up with him because he was good at his job and reasonably priced."

Renee Rankins snorted. "Oh, there's Mrs. Hudson. She was very close to Billy Bob."

I came out from behind the tree once I knew the woman was gone and tapped Harper on the shoulder. "Hey."

She shrieked and whirled. "What are you doing back there?"

"Eavesdropping." I grinned. "Go see what you can find out about Billy Bob and Mrs. Hudson." Why would a thirty-year-old man be close to a seventy-five-year-old woman he wasn't related to?

"That'll be a waste of time, but I'll see what I can do." She headed across the room.

I started to join a couple of my other friends who clustered around the sheriff until I spotted Roy Collins making a beeline toward Mrs. Hudson. When Roy reached the older woman before Harper and pulled the woman aside, Harper glanced at me and shrugged.

I shook my head. We'd dig in that sandbox later.

Trying to be as invisible as possible, I skirted the edges of the room until I reached a group of whispering women. I hated resorting to gossip, I really did. It wasn't an action God approved of, but I didn't see any other way of learning who might have killed Billy Bob and why.

"I heard he was in debt to his eyeballs," one woman said. "Had a gambling problem."

"No, he didn't, he just overpaid for things. The man was big on himself," another corrected. "Bought his groceries online, of all things." She glanced up and noticed me. "Why, hello, Morgan."

"Mrs. Boothe." I smiled and continued on my way. If you were going to talk about someone, at least have your facts straight. Billy Bob was so tight with his money he squeaked when he walked. Having known him for so long, friends or not, I knew for a fact that he made the women he dated pay for their own meal. That's why he was still single.

I spotted a tall red-haired woman standing off to the side who seemed very interested in those attending the visitation. I'd never met the woman before and was pretty sure she didn't live in Oak Grove. I approached her and held out my hand. "I'm Morgan Butler. I don't think we've met."

She gave a thin-lipped smile. "You're the suspect." She returned my shake. "KBI Agent Sheila Waters."

"I'm a suspect? I thought a person of interest was a notch above a suspect."

"Person of interest, but since we have no other suspects, Ms. Butler, that leaves you."

Wonderful. The female version of Sheriff Hayden. "I'm glad you're here to find the true criminal, Agent Waters. You'll soon realize it wasn't me. I had no reason to kill Billy Bob. He was fixing my sign." I whirled and rushed outside, doing my best to keep the tears from spilling down my cheeks.

If I really was the one and only suspect, I couldn't show weakness. If I did, those who thought me guilty would swoop in like vultures and tear me to shreds. I hurried to Harper's car and shut myself inside.

My phone vibrated in my purse. I dug it out and read a text from Harper. SPARE KEY IN RIGHT WHEEL WELL. GO HOME. I'LL CATCH A RIDE LATER.

I didn't need to be told twice. I climbed from the car, found the key, and sped from the parking lot. I didn't want to go home, though. I needed a quiet place to think and devise a plan.

The lake was the perfect spot. Fifteen minutes later, I sat on a wooden bench near the boat dock and stared at the water lapping against the pilings. I didn't see anything that looked like green onions growing near the water's edge.

I asked myself the question everyone else

was asking. Why would someone kill Billy Bob?

The man had been an arrogant jerk on his best days, but everyone knew exactly where he stood on any given topic or person. He was the least false person I'd ever met. Unlikeable, a big jerk, but honest to the point of rudeness.

Most murders, at least according to television or books, were about love or money or the love of money. Some were crimes of passion, but I doubted that would happen in my humble coffee shop.

I laid my head back and closed my eyes. They snapped open at the sound of footsteps coming my way. I turned to see a smiling Dean.

"I thought you were at the visitation." He sat next to me.

"I left. I'm glad you're here. Will you walk through what might have happened to Billy Bob with me?"

"Sure. I was going to go fishing, but I'm always up for helping a friend."

I'd never had a close male friend before. Either they or I ended up wanting more. In this case, it would most likely be me wanting more than friendship. Still, one day at a time.

"The morning before he died, I called Billy Bob to set a time to fix my sign."

"I remember. The shop isn't that big. I could hear everything you said, including you turning him down for a date and the time he was supposed to have arrived."

My eyes widened. "Did you tell the sheriff that? He might add it to the list of reasons why I'm a cold-blooded killer."

"He didn't ask. Go on." He leaned against the back of the bench, stretching his arms wide. One settled behind me, his fingertips lightly touching my shoulder and threatening to distract me.

"He was supposed to be there at three. He didn't come until the next morning. I texted him that I would give him all the coffee he wanted if he showed up." That made me the primary suspect.

"Which someone poisoned him with."

"Yes."

"Someone in the shop that morning had to have slipped the poison into his coffee. Someone is framing you." He pulled a small notepad from inside his jacket. "Who was in the shop that morning?" I listed the names I could remember, and he wrote them down. "The name of the guilty person should be on this list." He handed the list to me.

"Thanks." I frowned. "Why would someone want to frame me?"

"You tell me."

My blood ran cold. Someone wanted to frame me for murder. Who hated me that much?

"A few people want to buy the shop. Not

for the coffee, but for the space." I picked at a cuticle. "But why kill Billy Bob and not me? Killing him doesn't guarantee I'd sell."

"Opportunity?"

"Perhaps." I shuddered. *Why my shop?*

"Could something be in the crawl space?" I murmured to myself.

"What? There's a crawl space?" Dean's eyes sparkled.

"Yes." I hated closed-in, dark places.

"Have you been down there before?"

"No, and I'm not excited about the idea now."

"Let's go look right now."

My legs felt like Jell-O. I could no more explore that crawl space right now than fly to the moon. "As much as that's not tempting, I need to wait until after work tomorrow. I'm exhausted."

"Sorry." He reached out and brushed the skin under my eye.

I had an immediate waking-up reaction and knew for sure I was falling for him. Probably not the wisest thing under the circumstances. I mean . . . he was a famous author, and I was . . . me.

"You have pretty bad circles under your eyes. I should have noticed. I can be intense."

"Yes, you can." I laughed.

"I'll plan for tomorrow evening, because you have my curiosity piqued."

Mine was too. I could sleep better knowing

I'd found the next step in the process to clear my name, even if it did involve getting dirty.

FIVE

A sharp rap sounded on my door. I glanced at the clock. Eight a.m. I'd overslept.

The knock sounded again. Turning on the coffeepot, I marched to the door and slung it open, pasting a smile on my face. My smile faded. Looking more official than she had at the viewing stood Agent Waters.

"May I come in?" Her tone didn't really sound like a question.

I opened the door wider and motioned my arm in what I hoped was a welcoming gesture. "I've just put coffee on. Would you like a cup?"

"No, thank you. This isn't a pleasure visit." She glanced around the room.

"Have a seat at the kitchen table. I'll get dressed and join you in a second." What had Sheriff Hayden told the agent? Why couldn't anyone see I was incapable of the act they accused me of?

With shaking hands I got dressed, poured my coffee, then joined the agent. "What can I help you with?"

She stared at me long enough that I started to feel uncomfortable. She took a deep breath through her nose, then said, "The sheriff isn't being very cooperative, Ms. Butler, and your friends are interfering too much by asking questions all over town. But I've also spoken to everyone who was in the shop that morning, and they all said they drank from the same pot the victim did and suffered no ill effects."

"Yes!" I jumped to my feet and did a fist pump. "Finally. Someone with reason."

Agent Waters's eyebrows rose. "Please sit down, Ms. Butler."

I did so, grinning. "I bet the sheriff loved hearing that news."

She gave a thin-lipped barely-there smile. "While you are no longer a person of interest in my eyes, it was not a smart thing to do to attend the visitation last night. Why were you there?"

"To find clues about who the real murderer is and clear my name."

She narrowed her eyes and sat back in her chair. "That is dangerous and irresponsible. Is that why your friends are nosing around?"

"Possibly." I lifted my cup to my lips, took a sip, then set it on the table before speaking. "Somebody is trying to frame me for a reason. I have the right to find out why."

"What reason would that be?"

"I don't know, but I intend to find out."

"How do you propose to do that?" She crossed her arms. "I will arrest you if you impede my investigation."

"I promise to stay out of your way." To the best of my ability, anyway. I glanced at the clock again. I'd hoped to crawl under the building before business started for the day, but that wasn't going to happen. I should have already set out the Open sign.

I glanced up as an elderly couple walked in, took their seats on my sofa, then called out, "We'll take the regular." A second later Dean strolled in, flashed me a smile, and took his seat on the other side of the table.

Clearly shocked, Agent Waters stiffened. "Are you doing business out of your home? Is that legal here?"

"I need the money." I shrugged. "Some people say it's better to ask for forgiveness than to get permission. At least when it comes to permits."

She shook her head. "Not sure that's an accurate statement. I'll see about releasing your place of business today." She stood. "Please stay out of trouble, Ms. Butler."

"To the best of my ability, Agent Waters." I grinned. Soon, no more people trooping through my private abode. When she'd gone, I turned to Dean. "That is one smart woman. She knows I didn't kill Billy Bob. No one else died from my coffee."

"That's good news, right?" He opened his laptop. "Unless they think you had an accomplice who poisoned Billy Bob before he got to your store."

"Shh." I glanced around the room. "Not funny at all." I'd guess Sheriff Hayden would think that a possibility, but I prayed the agent wouldn't. I felt as if she and I were sort of working together. "We still need to find out who really killed Billy Bob."

"Why? You're cleared."

"Not really. I mean, yes, but no. You're right. They might think I'm an accomplice and this whole 'we are no longer looking at you as a suspect' could be a ploy to trip me up." My mouth dried up. "I need to find out why someone tried to frame me. I can't let that go."

He sighed. "This could be very dangerous."

"Most likely."

"We might be killed ourselves."

"Strong possibility." I grinned. "Just kidding. Think of the material you'll be gaining for your books."

He laughed. "There is that."

By noon the yellow tape was gone from the front door downstairs and I was again open for business in my shop. The placed filled within the hour. The residents of Oak Grove seemed genuinely happy that I wasn't a murderer, or so the rumors said. I wished that every day could be that profitable.

I thought again of replacing my sign, because it seemed in bad taste to leave it up. But it played a huge part in drawing in customers. Had Billy Bob ordered the new one before meeting his demise? I couldn't order another one until I found out.

I dialed the office number of Rankins Handyman. A woman's voice I didn't recognize answered. "Rankins Handyman, this is Vicki, how may I help you?"

"I wasn't aware the business was still open."

"Then why did you call?"

"Oh, this is Morgan Butler and I was wondering —"

"How dare you call here after murdering my cousin. Of all the nerve." *Click.*

Well, pooh. I guess it didn't matter whether Billy Bob placed an order for the sign or not. I'd order from someone else.

"What are you going to do with the sign once you replace it?" A man leaned on my counter, a wicked twinkle in his eye. "I bet you could sell it for a good price to the Rankinses. You know, as a memento."

"Can I get you a coffee?"

"No, I'm here on behalf of my client."

My welcoming smile faded. "What kind of client?"

"Someone who's going to make you very happy. He's offering to purchase this property for this amount." He slid a piece of paper across the counter. "It's more than fair market value."

One-and-a-half-million dollars. I almost accepted on the spot, but something didn't feel right. "I purchased this shop for half a million."

"We are quite aware of what you paid, Ms. Butler. Think about it. Here's my number." He plopped a business card next to the outrageous offer and left my store.

My weak knees barely carried me to the table where Dean sat. "Look at this." I handed him the paper.

His eyes widened. "Are you going to accept?"

"Doesn't it raise any questions in your mind? Why pay so much more than the market value?"

"That's a good question. What are your thoughts?"

"It has something to do with why some mystery person is trying to buy up whatever property he can in Oak Grove."

"It must be someone with a great deal of money."

I shook my head. "I don't know anyone like that." Not yet, I didn't. But make no mistake, I would, and soon.

Once I closed shop at six, I dressed in my grungiest leggings, which meant they had a hole in one knee, and a ratty T-shirt. Dean waited for me in faded jeans and a tight black

T-shirt that left me speechless. The man looked good on a book cover, but in person he could stop a girl's heart. The fact that he didn't try to look drop-dead gorgeous only made him more appealing.

"You sure you don't want to wait until dark?" he asked. "You crawling around under your shop is bound to raise questions."

"It'll be dark enough under there in the daytime, thank you very much." Snakes, spiders, other sorts of creepy-crawler thingies. Ugh. No, I couldn't do it at night. I wasn't that insane. Thank the good Lord above I had a bright flashlight.

I took a deep breath, squared my shoulders, and turned on my flashlight. "Here goes nothing." Really, it was nothing. I had no idea what I was looking for. I could only hope I'd know it if I saw it. The Bible said God looked out for the foolish, right? Then I should be safe. I removed the wooden square serving as a makeshift door to the crawl space and set it against the back wall of the building.

I got on my hands and knees and then lowered to my belly to army crawl under the floorboards. The dank smell of dirt and I didn't want to know what else wafted up my nose and made me sneeze.

"God bless you," Dean called. "I could do that for you."

"As I've said before, I don't want the building to fall on you." I didn't want it to fall, period, but this was my mystery to solve. If someone got injured or killed it should be me.

I wiggled in deeper. My breathing quickened. I shined the light from one corner to the other. There was nothing under there but dirt. I scooted out backward. "Not a thing. It was a total waste of time," I said, brushing the dirt off me.

"What did you expect to find, Ms. Butler?" Sheriff Hayden stood next to a stony-faced Dean.

"Anything that would help me know why someone wants to frame me." Wasn't it obvious? Did the man think I crawled under there for fun?

He shook his head. "The gall of some people."

I crossed my arms and glared. "Are you here on official business or just to irritate me?"

"Just checking to make sure you aren't plotting to kill someone else." His mouth twisted and he headed down the sidewalk.

"I'm sorry, Morgan. He saw me standing here and said I looked suspicious. Then he looked under the building and, well, you know the rest. The man said my presence confirms his suspicions that you had an accomplice."

"Don't worry. You get used to being a suspect. Let's head inside and discuss our next move over coffee."

"I can't. I have a video call with my literary agent in . . ." He glanced at his watch. "Half an hour. She'll be shocked if she sees me like this."

Like what? His hair a bit mussed? "I'll get the book club ladies together. They'll have some ideas. Thanks."

They didn't. While everyone was pleased I was no longer a suspect in Agent Waters's eyes, they didn't take the sheriff's accusations seriously and told me to just let things go until they caught the real culprit.

I stared at each face around my kitchen table. "Sheriff Hayden isn't looking any further."

"But the agent is," Harper said.

"Someone offered me one point five million dollars for this building."

Shock and wide eyes followed my statement. "That makes things a little different," Jo said. "Why? This building is barely worth what you paid for it."

"I know, right?" I leaned my elbows on the table. "Something is horribly wrong in Oak Grove. We've a weasel in our midst, and I need help flushing him or her out. Are you with me?"

Heads nodded.

"Great. How do we do it?"

No one had a clue.

"In the movies," Penny said, "they lay a trap."

"That's right. A stakeout," Jeanine added. "We could do that. I'll supply the baked goodies."

"While that sounds wonderful, who would we be watching?" I shook my head. "I think I need to turn down the offer, say I'll never sell, even at double that amount, and see what happens. That ought to draw someone out from under their rock."

"It could get you killed," Evelyn said, twirling her coffee mug on the tabletop.

"Not to be a wet blanket," Jo said, "but have you considered praying about this and letting God handle the outcome?"

"I can't sit back and possibly be arrested or killed. I'm being proactive. Besides, I pray every time before doing something."

"Something . . . foolish?" Jo smiled.

"Yes. Does anyone think one of Billy Bob's cousins might have killed him?" I asked. "They had the funeral lickety-split and plan on selling the business just as fast."

"It's sold. Someone purchased it," Penny said. "I heard the person offered more than market price. Just like someone offered you."

I rubbed my palms over my face. "Someone wants to own this entire town. The question is, why?"

Six

After the morning rush the next day, when the only person left in the shop was Dean, I called the number on the business card and declined the outrageous offer. Let the fun begin.

Dean looked up from his laptop. "You're sure?"

"I'm sure. I've got to shake things up to get to the bottom of Billy Bob's death." My stomach was twisted in knots at the thought of turning down a fortune. I could have expanded with that money, started somewhere else. But nothing said I couldn't make some improvements in what I had. I called Jeanine and offered to sell baked items on consignment. She agreed.

Satisfied I'd accomplished something, I turned to Dean. "Why is it taking so long for your Wi-Fi to be hooked up? Where did you do the video call?"

Dean grinned. My heart leaped. "It's on. I like coming here more than sitting at home.

Life isn't boring in your little corner of the woods. Besides, I'm writing about this mystery when I finish word count on my contracted novel. My agent loves the idea, so I need to be where things are happening."

My heart didn't leap that time, it danced. I couldn't help but wonder how I would be portrayed in the book. I seriously hoped it wasn't as one of those empty-headed heroines in a B horror movie that ended up dying because of her stupidity. Dean hadn't actually said he came because of me, more like because of helping me and writing, but I'd take what I could get.

Uh-oh. The man from the previous day, the one with the business card, entered the shop.

"What do you mean you turned down the offer?" He scowled, his eyes flashing above reddened cheeks.

"I don't want to sell." I tilted my head. "What's so important about this place?"

"Not just this place, but all the shops on Main Street. The person I work for has more money than he knows what to do with and wants more than that. They'll pay you up to two million."

My knees threatened to give way. Temptation grabbed hold of me and squeezed. But if I gave in, justice might never be served. Billy Bob died because of . . . well, I didn't know, but I would find out. "I think the person you work for is doing something illegal." I turned my back to him and started a fresh pot of coffee.

I glanced up again as Mrs. Hudson strolled in.

"Good afternoon, Morgan."

"Mrs. Hudson."

She cast a glance at Dean then leaned closer to me. "That man is in here every day."

"He's using my free Wi-Fi."

"Have you given any more consideration to my offer of purchasing your shop?"

"No, but I just turned down a very large offer. I'm not selling." My welcoming smile faded. "First Roy Collins, then some mystery person, and now you. I do wish people would stop harassing me."

Her eyes flashed. "I do not harass." She took a deep breath. "I'm here when you change your mind, dear. Oh, I'm having a garden party next Friday. I'm inviting all the business owners in Oak Grove. Bring a friend." She winked and motioned her head at Dean before pulling a glossy flier from her bag. "Do be sure to come." She turned and glided from my shop.

It never failed to impress me how a woman her age could still walk in heels without looking like a drunken cow. I set the flier under the counter. I'd be sure to attend, not because I had any interest in gardening, but because all the bigwigs of Oak Grove would be in attendance. It was quite possible one of them killed Billy Bob.

Who better to want to buy up the shops along Main if not one of the owners of said shops?

When the workday ended, I decided a stroll along Main Street was in order. Our little business district looked stuck in the fifties with red-brick storefronts and electric street lights designed to look like gas lanterns. I loved Oak Grove and hated that the shadow of death hung over the peaceful town.

At the end of the street was the sheriff's office. Sheriff Hayden stepped out onto the sidewalk. I ducked into the hair salon before he could spot me.

"Are you here for a haircut?" A teenager beamed up at me from behind the counter.

"No, just hiding out."

She peered out the window. "From the sheriff? Oh, you're the one they say killed Billy Bob." She paled. "Are you here to kill someone?"

"For crying out loud." I slammed open the door and stepped back outside. How many people in town actually thought I was guilty? Maybe I should sell and move. My shoulders slumped. No, I loved it here. I wasn't going anywhere. Except to the Sunflower Diner. My stomach made it loud and clear that I hadn't eaten lunch.

Heads turned as I entered and a middle-aged woman approached me, a wary look in her eyes. They acted as if I were going to commit mass murder or something.

"Booth or table?"

"Booth," I said. I rarely ate out alone, but I had some thinking to do and nothing to eat at home. I followed the waitress to a booth for two and took a seat with my back against the wall.

The waitress handed me a menu. "Are you and your book club ladies trying to solve Billy Bob's murder?"

"How did you hear that?" Seriously. Were there no secrets in this town?

"Someone I know heard it from someone they know." She clutched another menu to her chest. "Granted, I don't believe you killed anyone, but you all can't go around asking everyone personal questions."

"How else will we find the killer?" I raised my eyebrows and glanced at her nametag. "Look, Missy. I need to clear my name. No one else has a more vested interest in doing that than I do."

"I say it was one of Billy Bob's cousins. They're hanging out at his shop living it up on his dime. If you really want to know who killed him, you should look there." She whirled and went to another table.

Missy had a point, but how could I get any of the Rankins family to talk to me? Last time I'd tried, I'd gotten yelled at and hung up on. I guess I could go there in person to check on my sign. I picked up the menu.

Someone slid into the booth across from me. "Ms. Butler."

"Agent Waters." I cringed and closed the menu.

"Tell me more about the offer you received for your shop."

"How did you know about that?"

"Nothing is sacred in this town, Ms. Butler. Word spreads faster than a cold, I've discovered." She motioned for the waitress to bring a menu. "I hope you don't mind if I join you."

"I . . . guess not." I waited until she had the menu in front of her before speaking again. "Roy Collins and Mrs. Hudson are very bent on purchasing my shop. Then I got that offer yesterday from an anonymous buyer who's trying to buy up Main Street. I'm not sure what Mrs. Hudson hopes to gain by buying me out. The woman has plenty of money and lives in that big house out by the lake."

"How did she make her money?"

I shrugged. "Husbands? She's been widowed twice."

Agent Waters nodded. "I'll look into her background. I'm not foolish enough to believe you haven't been snooping around. Learn anything interesting?"

"Just that Billy Bob's cousins didn't like him and that there are actually people in this town that think I killed him. I find that ridiculous since I didn't even have a motive, but the cousins want his money. Murder always seems to be about money."

The waitress returned and we both ordered cheeseburgers and fries. Afterward, Agent Waters straightened against the back of the booth. "Would you like to hear my theory?"

"Absolutely, although I'm surprised you'd tell a civilian."

"I don't think you'll talk to anyone other than the crime author guy and your book club ladies."

She really didn't miss much.

"I agree with you that money is at the root of this case. I believe the victim was either poisoned before arriving at your shop or that someone managed to slip poison into his cup of coffee while you weren't looking." She crossed her arms. "That's nothing you don't already know or suspect. But what you probably haven't thought about is the fact that Billy Bob was in the wrong place at the wrong time, and you were the intended target. I'm not married to that idea, but it is a possibility."

"Me?" My stomach dropped to my knees. "Why would anyone want me dead?"

"If you're right about someone buying up the shops on Main, and no one is selling, what would cause them to change their minds?"

"Fear." I swallowed past the mountain in

my throat. *Dear God, I should have prayed to You more. Please don't let me get killed.*

"Yes." She almost looked pleased that I knew the answer. "If you were killed, it would serve as a warning to the other business owners."

"Billy Bob was a business owner."

"Nobody liked the man, and everyone thinks his cousins did the deed. With you, there'd be no other motive but a show of force." She shrugged. "That's one theory, anyway. You should be very careful, Ms. Butler."

SEVEN

After a mostly silent meal with my thoughts whirling around my head, I told Agent Waters good night and headed home. Seeing a light on inside the gift shop, I made a detour. I had some questions, and perhaps the older woman who owned the shop could enlighten me.

A bell jingled over the door when I stepped inside, despite the closing time listed on the front door. The smell of roses and cinnamon greeted me from a large bowl of potpourri near the door. My gym shoes made little sound on the worn wooden floors.

A gray head popped over the counter. "Morgan." Mrs. Ethelridge grinned, her ill-fitting dentures slipping a bit. "Looking for a gift?"

"No, ma'am, I have some questions. You should lock the front door when you aren't open."

"I know, but I hate to let down a customer who might be running late." She went to the door and locked it. "I've just made tea. Hold on and we'll step into the back and have a conversation." She bustled away then returned to wave me into a crowded back room. We sat at a small folding table on which sat a silver teapot and mismatched cups. Once we both sipped our mint green tea, she asked, "What's your first question?"

I set my cup carefully onto its chipped saucer. "Have you been approached by anyone offering an astronomical amount to buy your store?"

"Oh yes." Her eyes lost a bit of their twinkle. "Some man came in here and offered me quite a bit of money to sell. He wasn't very happy when I refused. This shop is the only legacy I have to leave to my grandchildren. It has been in the family for three generations."

"Have the people offering to buy bordered on harassment?"

She shook her head. "Just said they'd find a way to change my mind." Her forehead creased. "I think someone was snooping around my home last night. My cat, Herbert, was quite agitated, and there were footprints by my rosebushes."

"Did you call the sheriff?"

"That numbskull? No."

"Maybe you'd have better luck with one of the deputies coming out and looking around." It scared me that she lived alone on the outskirts of town. Her murder would be as convincing, if not more, than mine at frightening the business owners. I almost told her about Agent Waters's theory, but bit my tongue. I wouldn't want to scare her if it wasn't true. "Is there anywhere you can go stay for a while? It might be dangerous being alone."

"I will not be forced out of the home I've lived in for fifty years, Morgan."

If she wasn't careful, maybe the person would find a way to foreclose on her shop, just as Roy Collins had on my family home. "Have any of the other owners said anything about selling?"

"The man who owns the florist shop is selling, I think, but they haven't been here long enough to set down roots." She poured more tea into her cup.

I finished my tea and left the store. Outside, I glanced up and down the street. The back of my neck prickled as if eyes watched my every move. Shaking off the feeling, I marched to the florist's shop.

I'd never met the owner so I was surprised to see a large man delicately arranging baby's breath in a crystal vase. "Are you the owner?"

"Yes, I am. What can I do for you?"

"I'm Morgan Butler, owner of the Coffee Perk. I heard you were selling your store."

"I don't see how that concerns you, little lady, but yes, I am. I was offered quite a bit of money for this place. I can now retire in comfort." He set the vase into a cooler behind him. "Mind if I ask why you're so interested?"

"Just curious if you know who you sold it to."

He frowned. "A broker stopped by and made the offer. I have no idea who the purchaser is." He pulled a card from under his cash register. "Here's the guy."

I recognized the same number as the card I'd been given. "Thank you for your time." I left and contemplated going to the nearest motel on the freeway and hanging around to see whether this broker had checked in. I seriously doubted he'd tell me who he worked for, but it might be worth a shot.

The streetlights flickered to life. The street was virtually empty of cars and pedestrians. If I wanted to hunt the man down, I'd have to wait until tomorrow.

An engine revved behind me.

I turned as headlights blared to life, getting bigger as they sped toward me. I shrieked and ran. The sheriff's office loomed ahead. I ducked into the alcove and watched as a dark sedan sped past.

The door opened behind me and I stumbled inside. Strong hands caught me and pulled me close.

I glanced up into the concerned eyes of Dean. "Someone tried to run me over." I forced the words past a clogged throat.

"Are you sure?" He steadied me.

"Pretty sure."

"Making more accusations, Ms. Butler?" Sheriff Hayden glared from the doorway of his office.

"Someone tried to kill me." I glared. "That is a fact."

" 'Pretty sure' doesn't make anything a fact."

"Wrong choice of words. Someone did try to run me over. They drove a dark sedan. I also just came from Mrs. Ethelridge's shop, and she said someone was snooping around her house. I want to speak with Agent Waters."

"She's out following up on a lead." He smirked. "That's all you got? No license plate? No physical description of a Peeping Tom?"

"No." I sagged. I'd been so concerned about not being killed, I hadn't thought to try and get the license number. Knowing it would be useless, I asked to fill out whatever I needed to file a complaint. When I finished, Dean offered to walk me home.

Once we reached my apartment, I turned at the bottom of the stairs. "Thank you. Why were you at the sheriff's department?"

"Someone broke into my house and stole my computer."

"Your books!" I covered my mouth with my hand.

"I back everything up on a jump drive and an external hard drive, both of which I keep locked up. Unless they're a good hacker, they won't get anything." He took me by the arm and led me up the stairs. At the top, we stepped into my apartment, and he closed the door. "Morgan, I think they took the computer because they know I'm writing a book based on Billy Bob's murder. They want to know what we've discovered."

I fell into a kitchen chair. "It has to be one of my customers. Anyone could have overheard us talking. They might assume you'd written down our conversations."

"Things are getting dangerous." He pulled out a chair and sat. "Even though I don't think we're any closer to figuring this out than we were a couple of days ago."

"I wish I knew as much as the thief thinks I do." I leaned my elbows on the table and put my head in my hands.

"This is what we know. Someone is offering large sums of money to purchase shops along Main Street. There doesn't seem to be any reason other than for money." Dean got up and paced.

"Agent Waters thinks I was the target." I explained her theory. "Someone trying to run me over tonight kind of confirms it."

Dean grabbed me by the shoulders and pulled me to my feet. "This has gone far enough. You can't stay here, Morgan. Call one of your friends and see whether you can stay with them."

I thought of Mrs. Ethelridge's bravery. "No, I won't be run from my home. I've already been kicked out of one house. I'm staying."

He made a noise of frustration in his throat and released me to run his hands through his hair. "I don't want anything to happen to you."

"That makes two of us, but God is my protection. I'll keep my doors locked at all times."

"Call me every morning when you wake up and every evening when you go to bed." Grave lines appeared around his mouth. "I mean it, Morgan. If I don't hear from you, I'll be banging your door down."

I had my very own knight in shining armor. "I promise."

He placed a tender kiss in the center of my forehead and headed for the door. He kept his gaze on me until it was closed.

I fell onto my sofa and called Harper. "Dean kissed me."

"What?"

"Well, on the forehead, but it's a start." My skin tingled where his lips had lingered. "Someone tried to run over me with their car and someone stole Dean's laptop."

"What?" she said louder.

"Can you hear me?"

"Of course I can. I just don't believe what

I'm hearing. Are you all right?"

"I was shaken up, but Dean calmed me down." I propped my feet on the coffee table then, realizing I hadn't locked the front door, jumped back up and slid the chain into place. "Dean wants me to call him every morning and night until the killer is caught."

"Smart man. I can't believe you aren't falling apart right now."

"What good would that do? Someone thinks I know something. I have to find out what that something is."

"Without getting killed."

"Right. That's the tricky part." I headed for my bedroom and toed off my shoes. "If you get any brilliant ideas that would help, don't hesitate to share. Agent Waters and I are actually working together."

"Really?"

I told Harper about my dinnertime conversation with the agent.

"Wow. I mean . . . wow."

"Don't sound so shocked. I'm not an idiot incapable of digging up clues. Anyway, it's more to annoy Sheriff Hayden than anything, I think." I shimmied out of my jeans and lay across the bed. "I'm exhausted. Come by the shop on your lunch break tomorrow. I'm going to start having baked goods."

"Think about having sandwiches for the lunch crowd. 'Bye." She hung up.

I lay on the bed and stared at the ceiling.

Sandwiches were a great idea. I could make up several kinds fresh each day from a cookbook my mother gave me before she died. I could even name them after customers. I could call one the Billy Bob Big Boy. I grinned and kicked my legs to roll off the bed.

I had nothing more on my agenda than a shower and sleep. I turned the water to hot and finished getting undressed. After adjusting the temperature to just shy of too hot, I stepped under the spray and bowed my head. I often spent time in prayer in the shower. No distractions, no sound other than the water cascading around me. I prayed for wisdom and protection and for a quick end to the mystery before someone else died.

My thoughts flickered from the mystery buyer to the Rankins family. All seemed motivated by the love of money. One of them killed Billy Bob. That meant there were at least ten suspects, maybe more.

Back in the bedroom, I grabbed a baggy pair of cotton shorts and a tank top, my normal sleepwear. I climbed under the sheets and reached up to turn off my lamp.

Several hours later came the unmistakable sound of glass breaking in the front room, then something banged against the door with enough force to shake the floor.

EIGHT

I slid out of bed and with the speed of a worm creeping across concrete, closed my bedroom door and locked it. Then I grabbed my cell phone and squeezed under my bed and dialed a number I'd never had to dial before.

"911, what's your emergency?"

"I think there's an intruder in my apartment," I whispered. I rattled off my name and address.

"Are you somewhere safe?"

"For the moment."

"Help will be there in five minutes. Do not hang up the phone. Are you calling from the Coffee Perk?"

"Yes. The upstairs apartment." I strained my ears for the sounds of someone in my home. All remained silent until someone pounded on the door.

"Sheriff's department."

"They're here." I wiggled from my hiding place.

"You're free to hang up. Stay safe."

I hung up, shrugged into a robe, and stepped into my living room. The window next to the front door had been shattered. The front door stood open two inches, all that was allowed because of the chain. An old-fashioned method of security had possibly saved my life.

"Ms. Butler?" Sheriff Hayden peered through the crack. "Let us in."

I slid the chain off and opened the door. "Thank you."

He eyed the broken glass. "Stay here while I check out the apartment."

"There's nowhere else to go except the bedroom where I locked myself in and the bathroom, also in the bedroom." I waved my arm around the great room. Once used as storage space above an old-fashioned hardware store, what wasn't cut into rooms was cavernous.

"Let me do my job."

I shrugged and went to the closet to get a broom and dustpan. I swept up the pieces of glass then set the dustpan next to the wall. It was then I noticed a small rolled-up slip of paper wedged in the glass remaining in the window.

Considering myself knowledgeable from the many books I'd read, I used the corner of my shirt to pull the paper free and placed it on the kitchen table. I used a napkin to smooth it out. Words written in bold black letters said, "Stop snooping and sell. Now you know we can get to you. Consider this your last warning."

"What's that?" Sheriff Hayden peered over my shoulder.

"A note left in the window." I stepped back. "I didn't touch it with my fingers."

"Hmm." He pulled a pair of rubber gloves from his pocket and lifted the note. "Do you have somewhere you could stay tonight?"

My legs gave out, and I leaned against the table. "You think they'll come back?"

"You shouldn't take any chances, Ms. Butler."

"The chain kept the intruder out once, it will do so again. The window is too small for anyone to squeeze through, unless you're a cat." I shuddered. "I guess you believe I'm innocent now."

"Possibly." He stuck the paper in a small bag he pulled from his pocket then shoved the lot back into the same spot. "Come to the office in the morning to give your statement. Lock your door."

I nodded and saw him out. I closed the door and slid the chain back in place before leaning my back against the wood. Whoever wrote that note was worried I was going to find out something from my "snooping." I needed to find out what that something was before whoever killed Billy Bob succeeded in silencing me. I propped a kitchen chair under the doorknob and curled up on the sofa to try and sleep.

Monday morning, I stared out the window of my shop and thought about the many unanswered questions I had. Who would have known the coffee on the counter was meant for Billy Bob? Or did they think it was my cup and I was the target? Was someone trying to scare me into selling? Or were they trying to force me out of business by scaring off my customers?

Dean strolled down the sidewalk and through the open door of the shop. He took one look at my face, set down his briefcase, and pulled me into his arms. "You look like you're ready to cry. Are you still shook up about the break-in?"

I hadn't felt on the verge of tears until I'd seen his smiling face. "I just wish this were all over."

"You should have asked me to come over yesterday after church. Part of why I'm calling you every day is so you can tell me if you need something. Come on." He led me to a table. "Do you have any plans for today?"

"I want to visit the Rankinses that are left in town." I told him what I'd been thinking earlier. "It could easily have been one of his relatives who wanted him dead. They could have given him the poison before he even showed up here."

Dean sat silent for a moment then gave a quick nod. "I'll go with you. Close the shop. Put up a sign saying you'll return in two hours."

"Folks won't be happy about missing their morning coffee. We'll go after the rush. Nine o'clock?"

"Sounds good." He gave a lopsided smile. "This book better be a bestseller with all the danger knocking on your door. Is someone coming to fix your window?"

I laughed. "Personal research. How many authors can claim that? And yes, they're up there right now replacing the glass."

The last morning customer left a little after nine, and I flipped the sign to CLOSED, taping a note next to it that said I'd return after lunch. Folks would understand. Oak Grove was a small town. Shops opened and closed at odd hours on a regular basis.

"I'll drive," Dean said. "I'm parked around the corner. You just tell me where to go."

I stopped at the corner and stared wide-eyed at the car. "You own a Jaguar?"

He grinned. "My dream car."

"Wow, then why drive that old truck I've seen you in?"

"The old truck is like an old friend."

I was afraid to touch the silver paint job. Dean opened the passenger door for me. Leather seats. I settled into buttery softness.

This was the life. I could have this if I sold my shop.

The temptation didn't last long. To sell would be to give in to bullies, something I wouldn't do. I gave Dean instructions on how to reach our destination and settled back to enjoy the ride.

Ten minutes later, we parked in front of a square cement block building painted a blinding white. An obscenely large sign the size of Rhode Island stated we'd reached the right place. Four cars in the lot had out-of-state plates, so I figured some of the family must have stuck around to finalize the details of the sale.

Dean walked in first, probably as a shield. When the three men and one woman seated in the office caught sight of me, pandemonium burst forth.

"Hold on." Dean held up his hands. "We're here to talk. You cannot honestly believe Morgan killed Billy Bob."

The woman wrinkled her nose. "Maybe she hired someone."

"For what purpose?" I asked. "I hired him to do a job that hasn't been done. Why would I kill him to keep him from doing the job?" I lifted my chin. "Speculation around town is that one of you did it."

"She has a point, Michelle." A man standing in the back motioned to some empty chairs. "Sit down and tell us why you're here."

I glanced at Dean, who nodded. I chose a chair close to the door in case I needed to make a fast getaway. "I'd like to ask you a few questions."

"We might answer," Michelle said. "These are my brothers, Don and Ron. Danny is around here somewhere. Billy Bob was our cousin."

"Friend as well?"

She rolled her eyes. "Not hardly. The man was as cold as an Alaskan glacier. Still, he was family."

I leaned forward. "Why the rush to sell his business?"

"For the money." She laughed and glanced at her brothers. "He named us all as beneficiaries. Some man came and offered two million dollars. We'd be stupid not to accept. That's half a million for each of us."

I could do the math. "Who was this man?"

She handed me a business card. Same number as before. No name, just the phone number. "Did you see this man in person?"

"Only when he made the offer shortly after we heard about Billy Bob," Don, or Ron, said. "All other business was done via email or over the phone. Why?"

"He's offering other business owners the same deal."

"So?"

"So, what if Billy Bob had dealings with these people outside of selling his business?"

I glanced from face to face. They all looked puzzled.

"I'm sure he did." A wiry young man entered from a side door. "I'm Danny Rankins. Billy Bob told me he was going to make a lot of money and asked if I wanted to join him. I said no. You couldn't trust my cousin when it came to get-rich-quick money schemes. All he saw was dollar signs and didn't think any further. I thought he was pulling my leg to get me to give him money."

Excitement rippled through me, raising the hair on my arms. Really, that had been a shot in the dark. "Did he say what this opportunity was?"

"No, but he gave me a phone number. Hold on." He riffled through some papers in a folder on top of a filing cabinet. "Here you go."

Again, no name, but this time it was a different number. I slipped the piece of paper into my pocket. I'd be making a phone call as soon as we left the building.

"Oh, and your sign came in. What do you want me to do with it?" Danny raised his eyebrows. "It isn't paid for."

"No, it isn't." Since I still hadn't ordered a replacement, I decided I'd take the sign. "Any idea who can install it for me?"

Danny laughed. "I can, but I'll bring my own beverage."

"Yeah," Don or Ron said. "We don't want

him drinking any of your coffee."

"Good grief. I did not poison the coffee." I stood and glanced at Dean.

He unfolded his long frame from the folding chair and stared pointedly at everyone except me and Danny. "The rest of you don't seem a bit surprised to hear that Billy Bob had an idea to make a bundle of cash."

Really? I thought they'd all looked as ignorant as I felt.

"In fact," Dean went on to say, "you all had the exact, practiced expression of surprise. I think the only person being honest in this room is Danny."

"Fine," Michelle huffed. "He came to us with the same deal. We all turned him down." She cut a dirty look to Danny. "We don't know anything more than that except for the fact he mentioned there was a 'he' and a 'she' in it with him."

Finally, some clues. I thrust out my hand. "Thank you."

The only one to move to return my gesture was Danny. "I'll be over in an hour to hang your sign, no charge."

Michelle rolled her eyes so far back in her head they almost disappeared.

"I'll put the coffee on." Danny, Dean, and I were the only ones who laughed at my joke.

Outside, Dean took me by the elbow and led me to the car. He opened the door for me and I slid in.

I pulled the paper and my phone from my pocket. "We have a couple more clues: this number, and that we are possibly dealing with a man and a woman." I dialed the number on the paper.

"Roy Collins here."

NINE

I hung up. "That number belongs to Roy Collins. Which means . . ."

"Collins and Billy Bob Rankins had some kind of questionable business together." Dean turned the key in the ignition. "Something that promised a big reward."

I clicked my seat belt into place. "So, we have our 'he.' I wonder who the 'she' is?"

"Well, we have to prove that Collins is the man we're looking for. I just don't see him trying to break into your apartment."

I shrugged. I couldn't envision the man doing that either, but it wouldn't be the first time someone was hired to do a job. "Now what?"

"We shadow Roy, I guess. In fact, I think I have a check to deposit." He winked.

"I'm calling the girls." I dialed Jo's number. "Can you get the ladies together and do some questioning of the bank employees?" I explained about Billy Bob and Roy being in cahoots about something. "We're going to the bank now, but they might be more willing to talk to you gals rather than me."

"Sure. I'll call them right now. Be careful, Morgan."

"I will, thanks."

Dean parked in a spot near the front of the bank. "I'm not sure what we'll say if we see him," he said. "Maybe nothing. Follow my lead."

All right, but that came very hard for me. If I saw the man, I'd want to ask straight out what kind of deal he'd offered Billy Bob.

I hung off to the side while Dean approached the teller. Through the glass pane of his office, I could see Collins on the phone. From his dark face, I guessed it wasn't a pleasant conversation. When he glanced my way, I wiggled my fingers in a little wave.

His brows drew together. He said something into the phone then hung up. Straightening his tie, he headed my way. "Ms. Butler. Have you changed your mind?" His smile seemed strained.

"Nope. I'm here with Dean." I bit my lip to keep from asking questions and glanced around the bank. Very quiet for a weekday afternoon. "I've actually expanded the products I offer. Stop by sometime and enjoy a scone." I smiled and joined Dean before I did something stupid. Like confront Collins about Billy Bob.

"Good afternoon, Morgan."

I spun around. Mrs. Hudson grinned at me. "You startled me." Normally the woman could be heard coming miles away in her heels. Today, she wore silk flats. "Nice slippers."

"They are shoes, dear." She showed me the rubber soles. "A woman has to give her feet a rest once in a while. Are you here to sell?"

I exhaled in a huff. "I. Am. Not. Selling."

Dean bumped me with his elbow. It could have been an accident, but most likely it was his way of telling me to take it down a notch.

"Sorry. No, Mrs. Hudson, I am not selling. Thank you for asking." I forced my smile back into place.

She twisted her lips and muttered something that sounded like "This is harder than it should be" as she walked away.

Roy watched her go then returned to his office.

I stared from one to the other. An idea was forming in my head, but I didn't have all the pieces yet.

"So only Billy Bob and the florist have sold so far?"

I yanked myself from my thoughts to focus on Dean's question to the teller. Smart man. No young woman could keep from answering any question that came from such a handsome source.

"Yes, sir. We're the only bank in town. If someone else sold out, we'd know." She grinned as if she were the source of all information. "In fact . . ." She leaned closer. "Mr. Collins just bought a brand new Mercedes. Yep, we know everything that goes on around here."

Gossipy little thing. So far, except for the new car, she hadn't told us anything we didn't already know. I spotted Sheriff Hayden strolling down the sidewalk and realized I hadn't filled out a report on the attempted break-in.

"That was a waste of time," Dean said as we headed back to his car.

"I need to go to the sheriff's office and fill out the report."

"Right. The more I think about what Shelly said —"

"Who's Shelly?"

"The teller. Anyway, I think the fact Collins bought a new vehicle is important somehow. Didn't he drive a Kia before?"

"You pay attention to what people drive?"

"Yeah, don't you?"

I shook my head. "Not unless it's a red convertible or a Porsche, and I still have to look at the name on the back. Why is it important?"

"Do you think he's come into some of that windfall already? From their get-rich-quick scheme?"

"We seem to be in agreement that Collins is guilty." I hoped we had enough information to cast suspicion on him so that Agent Waters would take a closer look.

At the office, I filled out the necessary report and asked to speak with the agent. The receptionist told me, without looking up, that Agent Waters was out and she didn't know when she would return.

"I'm not out." Agent Waters stepped from a side room.

The receptionist jerked. Her face reddened and she mumbled, "That woman scares me."

"Come with me, Ms. Butler." Agent Waters turned and walked away without waiting.

I motioned for Dean to follow and joined the agent in a room containing an oblong table, eight chairs, and a whiteboard on a swivel, which the agent quickly turned over. But not before I saw that it had pictures and index cards pinned to it. "Can I see that?"

"You may not. Have a seat." Agent Waters sat in a chair at one end of the table. "What do you want to see me about?"

"Did you hear about someone trying to break into my apartment early Sunday morning?" I sat in a chair next to Dean. "I'm here to fill out the report."

"No." She darted a look toward the door before handing me a form to fill out.

I wished I could witness when she confronted the sheriff. "I'm fine. All that happened was a broken window and a warning note. Dean and I paid a visit to the Rankins family this morning."

Her eyes narrowed. "I told you not to snoop."

"No, you said I could get information if I passed it on to you." I crossed my arms. "I was in no danger. Dean was with me."

She stared at Dean. "Do you happen to be Superman in disguise and able to stop bullets, Mr. Matthews? Are you as strong as the Hulk and can overpower anyone wanting to kill you or Ms. Butler?"

High spots of color appeared on Dean's cheeks. "No, ma'am."

She transferred her attention back to me. "I told you to keep your eyes and ears open. That does not mean to actively pursue questioning potential suspects."

"So, they are suspects!" I grinned. "Well, I'm pretty sure you can mark them off your list. Roy Collins killed Billy Bob, and he has a woman accomplice."

"Explain."

I did. I told her about Danny Rankins telling us about an opportunity presented to Billy Bob, how he said there was a he and a she, etc. "If you bring Roy Collins in for questioning, you can force him to tell you who his female accomplice is."

"Are you trying to tell me how to do my job?" Agent Waters raised her eyebrows.

"No, just making a suggestion." I grinned, refusing to be intimidated.

She scribbled something on a notepad. "I'll be right back." She marched from the room.

I jumped from my seat and slipped behind the whiteboard. My picture was there under persons of interest. Next to mine were the Rankinses'.

"She's coming," Dean hissed.

I glanced across the board one more time before dropping to my knees, pulling my earring from my ear, then getting back to my feet. "Found it."

Agent Waters sighed. "You're a terrible actor, Ms. Butler. If you have no more information for me, then I have work to do."

I put my earring back in my ear. "You can take my name off the suspect list. You said you knew I couldn't do it."

"I said *I* knew. Unfortunately, the sheriff is of a different mind. Good day, Ms. Butler. Mr. Matthews."

Dean took me by the elbow and practically dragged me to his car. "She could have arrested you for obstruction of justice."

"I didn't do anything wrong. If she didn't want me to see the whiteboard, she wouldn't have left me in the room with it. I told you, we're working together."

"You seem to believe that more than she does."

"Sometimes an ordinary citizen can see what law enforcement can't." I plopped into the passenger seat.

"Did you see anything?"

I blew out a frustrated breath. "No."

He frowned. "She has nothing more to go on than we do. We're all missing something simple."

Danny Rankins sat on the curb waiting for us when we arrived. "Pretty sure you were gone longer than an hour," he said, getting to his feet. "I could use some help getting the sign out of the truck and hoisted up."

"I'll help." I stepped onto the curb.

"Right. You couldn't lift a corner. I'll take pretty boy here." Danny jerked a thumb at Dean.

I unlocked the door to my shop and left the men to their own devices.

After waiting on a couple of customers who wandered in, I dialed Jo. "Could you get the tellers to talk?"

"Not a one of them. Those two girls' lips were tighter than the lid on a pickle jar." Jo sighed. "But we haven't given up. See you at book club tomorrow night."

The next day passed with nothing new happening. Customers entered and exited my shop for baked goods and coffee. Many of them commented on my stylish new sign. I kept my eyes and ears open as instructed and learned absolutely nothing new.

I decided to come at this from a different direction. Instead of the motivation, I would think about the means. Billy Bob had been poisoned with a lily. I booted up my computer and typed in *death camas.* Without the bloom, it looked just like a green onion. The blooms looked like tiny lilies. So pretty for something so deadly.

I drummed my fingers on the counter. Back to motivation. Roy and . . . ? I couldn't remember ever having seen him with a woman for any length of time. Not that I kept close tabs on him, but gossip was the favorite pastime in town. Someone would have mentioned a woman.

If he had a serious relationship, he'd have a photo on his desk, right? Maybe it was time to see if I qualified for a mortgage. I called the bank and set up an appointment for the last spot of the day tomorrow.

At precisely five o'clock, I locked the door and set the sign to CLOSED. I only stayed open later on Friday and Saturdays, and definitely not on book club night. The ladies would be over in an hour, and I had a few things to get done.

I grabbed a couple of boxes that had been delivered that afternoon and carried them to the supply closet. I unpacked the coffee beans and stored them in airtight containers. When I finished, I stacked the boxes in a corner.

The door slammed closed. I grabbed the door handle and tried to turn the knob. Locked. From the other side.

My breathing quickened. My heart raced. I was locked in a closet. Where was all the air? I couldn't breathe.

Settle down, woman! You're in your shop. The closet isn't airtight. I concentrated on slowing my racing heart. The book club gals would be there by six. By six fifteen, they would start to worry. They'd want to look for me. They wouldn't find me in my apartment, nor would they find me in the shop. I'd locked the doors.

Suddenly the closet door opened and Harper peeked in. "What time is it?" I asked her.

"Ten after six. What happened?"

"How did you get in?"

"The back door was open."

I stepped out of the closet and took deep breaths. "Someone locked me in."

She stared at me and scratched her head. "Are you sure? Isn't it possible the wind blew the door shut because the back door was open?"

"It was closed, Harper. I was locking up for the book club." I rushed to the back door and locked it — again. But then I saw that the door didn't latch completely. "You're right. It's rusted out."

"Well, that's good news, right?" Harper said. "No one snuck in here and deliberately locked you in the closet."

"Yes, I suppose so," I said, weary of the paranoia and fear that had begun to dog my every step. When would my home feel safe again?

TEN

As was the norm now it seemed, book club was more about what was happening with me in relation to Billy Bob's murder and less about what we'd read. By the time I went to sleep that night, my brain whirled with possibilities that had no answers.

I woke the next morning with things no clearer in my head. In hopes of figuring out something, anything, I poured a cup of coffee, went to stand on the sidewalk, and stared up at my new sign. I loved the tipped cup with coffee splashing out to spell the words THE COFFEE PERK.

I turned to see Sheriff Hayden coming my direction, thunder on his face.

I pasted on my brightest smile. "Hello, Sheriff. Would you like some coffee?"

"Nope. The only thing I want is for you to stop meddling before you get killed. Tell your friends to stop calling me for updates every day." He stormed down the sidewalk.

I vowed right then and there not to vote for

him in the next election. The man couldn't see the truth of my innocence when it was right in front of him. I turned the sign in the window to OPEN and started my workday.

"Good morning." Dean came up behind me and planted a kiss on my cheek. "What have you been up to?"

We were the only ones in the shop, so I got two cups of coffee and followed him to his usual table. "Not a whole lot," I said. "But I'm getting tired of looking over my shoulder all the time." I told him about the night before and fearing I'd been locked in the closet.

He sat back in his chair. "Did you listen to the pastor's sermon on Sunday?"

I glanced over my shoulder. We were still alone. "Of course. He spoke about waiting to hear from God before making a move. Oh." My shoulders slumped. I tended to forget to stop and pray. When my mind fixed on something, I raced full speed ahead and threw caution sky high.

I was actually having fun trying to pin down Billy Bob's murderer, in between someone trying to run me down and breaking into my apartment, that is. What if God told me to stop? "I thought you wanted us to solve this for your book."

"I do, but not at the expense of your life. What if someone really did lock you in that closet and then did something like set fire to the shop? You wouldn't have gotten out alive."

That was scarily true. "I have an appointment with Roy Collins at four o'clock today," I said, my voice barely above a whisper. "Should I cancel?"

"He can't try anything in the bank, but Morgan . . . every step you get closer to proving who the guilty person is raises the risk to your life." He stood and came to my side, cupping my face in his hands. "I couldn't bear for —"

A group of elderly women trooped through the front door. Dean and I sprang apart as if we were guilty of something naughty.

My face heated. He winked. The women giggled. Four o'clock seemed days away.

When it finally came, I was more than ready to lock the door early. Still embarrassed about getting caught in an almost embrace with Dean, my emotions were muddled. Oh, I liked him — a lot — but things were still too new for us to become an item in people's minds.

I headed down the sidewalk in the opposite direction than Dean, but couldn't help casting another look over my shoulder. He did the same. We both smiled and stood there staring at each other like a couple of teenagers.

Finally, I pulled away and floated to the bank. Who would have thought that I, Morgan Butler, would attract the attention of

Dean Matthews?

I still soared in the clouds when I stepped into the bank. Grinning, I glanced at the few people doing business inside then headed to the back toward Roy's office.

My grin faded. He seemed to be in a heated conversation with Mrs. Hudson. The office door was cracked open, just a bit. I ducked behind a pillar and strained my ears to hear.

Someone cleared their throat behind me. "May I help you?"

"Nope. Found it." I pointed to my earring. Losing an earring seemed to be the best way to stop people from thinking I was eavesdropping.

Unfortunately, Roy spotted me and the teller. He shoved the door closed the rest of the way before I could hear a single word. I stood outside the window and pointed at my watch. It was four o'clock.

He scowled and yanked the door open. "Reschedule." The door slammed.

I shouldn't have expected rudeness from him to be a surprise, but it was. I fought back the ridiculous urge to stick out my tongue.

What could Roy and Mrs. Hudson have between them to warrant such a heated discussion? Roy flailed his arms around. Mrs. Hudson crossed her arms and leaned forward. It wouldn't have taken much for fire to come out of her mouth.

Roy glanced my way and said something

very mean. I could read his lips clearly. He picked up the phone, punched in a number, and within seconds the bank security guard escorted me from the building.

It had all happened so fast I hadn't had time to feel insulted. Now, I whirled to reenter the bank, only to find my way blocked by the guard.

"No, ma'am. I was told you are not to come back in here today."

"Come on, George. I had an appointment."

"The entire bank heard Mr. Collins tell you to reschedule."

I smiled. "I need to go inside to do that."

"Use your phone." White teeth flashed in an ebony face.

"Fine. I'm charging you extra on your coffee next time." I stomped away to the sound of his deep laugh.

Despite not having my chat with Roy, I felt as if I knew who the "she" was Danny Rankins was talking about. Good thing her garden party was coming up soon. I wouldn't have to wait long to do a little snooping.

I couldn't help the feeling of accomplishment that put a bounce in my step. I was good at this mystery solving if I did say so myself. I turned and made a beeline for the sheriff's office and asked to speak with Agent Waters.

"What now?" she grumbled the moment I stepped through the small room designated as her temporary office.

Without waiting to be asked, I sat in the chair across from her. I tapped my forefinger against my lips. "I still think Billy Bob's death has everything to do with two people wanting him to join them in some kind of get-rich-quick scheme. We know that one of those people is Roy Collins. I think the other person is Mrs. Hudson. She's the wealthiest person around. How did she get her money, you ask? She's lost a couple of rich husbands." I leaned forward. "What if they didn't die by natural causes? Hmmm?"

Her face went stony. I thought she'd argue but instead she surprised me with a nod. "Sit tight." She typed something into her laptop then pursed her lips. "Mrs. Hudson's husbands made their money from real estate. They both died of heart attacks in their sleep." She met my gaze. "I suppose you got an invitation to the garden party?"

I nodded. "Did you?"

"No. Without doing anything, saying anything, or getting yourself into trouble, keep your eyes and ears open for evidence that Mrs. Hudson is our killer. Keep my number on speed dial." She pierced me with a steely gaze. "Call at the slightest hint of a threat. Don't be a hero."

Eleven

When I woke Friday morning, every ounce of enthusiasm I had about maybe being a good detective vanished. If I was right about Mrs. Hudson, then I was walking right into the spider's web.

I stared into my closet. What did someone wear for such an occasion? I reached for a sky-blue sheath dress, the same color as my eyes, and some low-heeled white sandals. If I died, I'd at least look good.

After closing the shop once the morning rush was over, I headed outside of town to the red-bricked mansion Mrs. Hudson lived in. I parked at one end of the curving driveway and strolled up a flagstone walkway. The front door opened before I could ring the bell.

A woman in a black dress motioned for me to go through the french doors on the other side of the room. "The party is just starting."

"Thank you." I squared my shoulders and marched outside.

The yard teemed with every business owner in Oak Grove, plus other pillars of the community. The mayor was there; Roy Collins, of course; the school principal, etc. It was like a listing of Who's Who in Oak Grove. Nothing could possibly happen to me with that many people around.

"Hey, gorgeous."

I turned and smiled at Dean. Of course he would have been invited. Anyone who wanted to make a statement of importance would invite the most famous person in town. "Hey back."

"There's a buffet table over there that could feed a small country. Are you hungry?"

Since I'd skipped breakfast in anticipation of a lunch buffet, my stomach chose that moment to loudly complain. "Definitely."

He chuckled and put his hand on the small of my back. I reveled in the warmth of his touch and the envious glances cast our way.

I filled a china plate with tiny pastries then grabbed a flute of orange juice. One sip told me it also contained champagne. I wrinkled my nose and set the flute on a side table with other used dishes on it. "Have you figured out the purpose for this party yet?"

Dean shook his head. "I think it's an opportunity to schmooze the business owners with the pretense of a party. There's also been some whispering about a charity Mrs. Hudson is rallying for."

"The Charity of Hudson's Bank Account." My gaze fell on the hostess as she strolled and smiled through her guests as if she were the queen of England. My gaze dropped to her feet. Heels today.

I waved at Jeanine, who hovered next to the pastries. I was pleased she'd been the one to make the delectable treats. I popped a lemon-cream-filled pastry into my mouth. "I suppose I should mingle. Agent Waters asked me to be her eyes and ears today. Uh-oh." I squeezed the small purse on my arm. "I forgot to put my cell phone in this purse. She told me to put her on speed dial."

"Then I guess we're mingling together, because I'm not letting you leave my side." Dean gave a thin-lipped smile.

"All right, but try to be subtle about eavesdropping. Some of these people still think I poisoned Billy Bob."

"When they sink their teeth into something, they're like a terrier tugging on the end of a tied sock."

"You have no idea." We strolled to where a path meandered through flowering bushes. Mrs. Hudson really did have a lovely garden. "Stop. In here." I pulled Dean behind a bush when I spotted Mrs. Hudson clip-clopping her way to Roy. I put a finger to my lips and listened.

"You're as guilty as I am, Roy Collins!" Mrs. Hudson practically spit the words.

"You lured me in like a starving dog." He plopped down on a carved marble bench and put his head in his hands. "Just finish what you started and leave me alone."

"Oh no, you don't. You wanted in. You like the money as much as I do." She tapped his foot with the toe of her shoe. "Someday, you'll have such a padded bank account, you'll thank me."

"When's enough, Irma?" He glanced up, his face red. "You already have more money than Solomon."

"Who's that? The king in the Bible?"

"Never mind." He sighed and got to his feet. "Six more months, and then I want you out of my life."

The woman laughed, the sound sending a chill down my spine. "Not as long as you're useful, dear." She turned and headed our way.

Dean grabbed me close and kissed me. Wowza. Not how I envisioned our first kiss, but I wasn't one to complain about something that gave me tingles all the way to my toes.

Mrs. Hudson cleared her throat. "Morgan and Mr. Matthews, there are more suitable places to carry on. Try the other side of the garden, away from the guests." Her eyes flashed.

I got the impression she didn't buy our ruse. I swallowed past the lump in my throat. "Okay, we will." I grabbed Dean's hand and pulled him down the path. "That was close."

He tugged me closer. "I'd like to kiss you again when we aren't playacting." His eyes smoldered.

Speechless, I nodded. It still amazed me that Dean seemed to enjoy my company. When I found my voice again, I asked, "What now?"

He shrugged. "We keep circling the party, maybe follow Roy around."

Hands still linked, we strolled along the path, ending up where we'd started. A small orchestra played softly from a secluded gazebo. The day was too perfect.

A small cloud floated across the sun, casting sinister shadows across the lawn. Then the sun came back out, and I shook off the feeling of foreboding.

I stood and studied the crowd. Didn't people usually smile at parties? Those smiles I did see seemed forced. It was time to take action. "Come on." I tugged Dean to Mrs. Ethelridge.

"Hello, Morgan." She smiled, a genuine one this time.

"Hello." I gave her a quick hug. "Can I ask you something?"

"Just as soon as you tell me who this handsome young man is."

"This is Dean Matthews, the author."

"Romance?"

Dean laughed. "No, ma'am. Crime thrillers."

She put a hand to her chest. "I'm afraid those are too scary for me. What's your question?"

"People seem frightened. What's going on?"

She leaned close. "Supposedly, there's going to be an announcement made today."

"About what?" I frowned.

"I have no idea, but it has everyone nervous. Remember how the florist sold out? Well, he decided to do a little investigating into the man who visited him and actually made the offer. That man doesn't exist. No such person."

"But I saw him."

She shrugged. "He told the florist his name, but he thinks now it must have been made up."

"Does anyone know who's supplying the financing?" Dean asked.

"No, but further investigation showed that the 'buyer' often files bankruptcy in order not to pay the promised amount and only after the papers are signed. There's a special clause in the contract that makes it binding." She cut a sharp glance at Mrs. Hudson. "Irma is the only one not on pins and needles. I find that very strange, don't you?"

"Yes." I glanced at Dean then back to Mrs. Ethelridge. "Have you been approached again?"

"No. I'm not one to gossip, Morgan. I know what the Bible says about such things, but I heard tell that Irma isn't as wealthy as she once was. Rumor says she has a gambling habit. So does Roy, so did Billy Bob."

"How do you know this?"

She tapped her temple. "I've been in this town for a long time. Not much gets past me." She giggled. "Well, all right, I'll admit it. I see them at the high-stakes tables at the casino in Oklahoma. Me, I stick to the slots. I'm going to go sit for a while. Good luck finding answers."

"We can't take what she said as truth," Dean said, leading me to a small round table with two chairs. "Not without evidence."

"I know." I sat and slipped my feet out of my shoes. A gambling addiction wouldn't necessarily lead to murder, but if the three were working together to make money to pay off gambling debts, and had a falling out . . . More speculation. "We need to ask Roy outright."

"Too dangerous. They'll know for sure you're on to them."

"They already know, Dean. Remember the car and the break-in?" I stared at Roy downing one mimosa after another. "It's time to end this."

"We'll call Agent Waters, tell her what we know, and let her handle the rest."

Sound advice, but Roy seemed to be growing more tipsy with each minute. I needed to question him before he was too far gone.

Mrs. Hudson seemed to be of the same mind. She motioned for a man in black pants and a white shirt to escort Roy away from the drinks. Roy put up a bit of a fight before falling into a chair two tables away from where Dean and I sat.

"See?" I flashed Dean a grin. "It's a sign from God that we're to question him. He's right there."

"I'm pretty sure God didn't put a drunk Roy in front of us." Dean stood and offered a hand to help me to my feet. "If I find things getting out of hand, I'll drag you away."

"Deal."

Roy groaned when we sat down, Dean pulling up a third chair. "Go away."

"Nope. I'd like to ask, what's between you and Mrs. Hudson?" I folded my hands on the table. "Did you kill Billy Bob, or did she?"

He scowled and glanced to where the older woman watched them. "You're asking for trouble, Ms. Butler. Believe me. The last thing you want is to get mixed up with that, that, devil."

"If you'd tell us what's going on, maybe we can help. I have connections with the sheriff's department." I elbowed Dean when he snorted.

"The only connection you have," Roy said, "is one of annoying the sheriff. Him and I go way back."

"Roy, just tell us whether you know anything or not and how Mrs. Hudson plays into all this so we can go home." I crossed my arms.

"Do you know what killed Billy Bob?" Roy asked.

"Death camas."

"Which grows where?"

"In marshlands or near water."

"Where are you now, Ms. Butler?" He stood and planted his hands flat on the tabletop.

"A garden party." My eyes widened. "Is there a pond?"

"Not as dumb as you look." He strolled in the opposite direction from where Mrs. Hudson stood.

"I didn't see a pond." I stood and glanced around the area.

"I spotted a gate near where Mrs. Hudson and Roy argued." Dean gave a crooked smile. "I saw it over your shoulder right before I kissed you."

My face heated. "Let's go take a look. Do you have your cell phone with you?"

He pulled it from his pocket and typed the name of the plant into his search engine then held the phone up where I could see the screen. "Is this what it looks like?"

I nodded. "Between the two of us, we should be able to find the plant if it's here."

We skirted around Mrs. Hudson so as not to alert her then rushed toward the place we'd taken refuge earlier. Sure enough, a wrought-iron gate sat partially covered by vines.

The gate creaked as Dean pushed it open. A small koi pond with a gurgling fountain sat at the feet of a marble statue. This was clearly a sanctuary with trimmed bushes and exotic plants.

"Look." I pointed to a cluster of death camas.

"That isn't all." Dean directed my attention to the bottom of the pond. "I'm pretty sure that's my laptop."

TWELVE

Mrs. Hudson came up behind Dean and knocked him out cold with the butt of a pistol. "You're quite clever, Morgan." She turned the gun on me. "Too clever. Grab your sweetheart's feet. We can't leave him here to be found."

Keeping an eye on the weapon in her hand, I grabbed Dean's feet. "Where to?"

"I have a car waiting on the other side of that wall."

Roy, head hanging, stepped from behind the weapon-wielding woman and took Dean by the shoulders. "I'm sorry, Ms. Butler."

"Stuff it, Roy."

We carried Dean to the waiting car. Tears blurred my vision as we put him in the trunk of a Cadillac. I had just enough time to reach in and check for a pulse before I was pushed toward the driver's seat of the car. Thank God, he was breathing.

"You're driving, Morgan." Mrs. Hudson smiled over the roof of the car. "That way I can keep an eye on you from the back seat. Roy, you're in front. Try anything, either of you, and I'll shoot you." She slapped her hand on the rooftop. "Let's go. Head to the east side of the lake."

There were so many questions swimming around in my head, but I still didn't speak. Whatever I said could, and most likely would, get me in deeper trouble. I followed Mrs. Hudson's directions and pulled onto a dirt road near the lake.

"Park at the water's edge, Morgan. Roy, get out of the car."

"What are you planning, Irma?" Roy stumbled out of the car. "No more killing."

"Oh, dear Roy, don't you know I do exactly what I want?" She aimed the weapon at him and fired.

He spun like a puppet and dropped.

My eyes widened, and a squeak escaped my lips. I clamped a hand over my mouth. "You brought us here to die," I forced between my fingers. I clenched my fists at my sides. "You won't get away with it. Agent Waters knows Dean and I are at your party. She also knows we were going to question you."

"Unfortunately, you never got around to that." She smiled and tilted her head. Leaning against the car, she crossed her ankles. "Ask away."

"Did you kill Billy Bob?"

"You know I did. You're a smart girl."

Oh, I wish I had my phone so I could record her. "Why?"

"Billy Bob didn't feel right about working with me to convince the other business owners to sell. Since he knew too much after my telling him all about the riches he'd make, I didn't have a choice but to silence him." She grinned like a skinny shark. "We tried coercion, blackmail . . . too many people in this town are as stubborn as you."

"So it is about money."

She shrugged. "Isn't it always? I've run through my late husbands' money quite quickly. I do love my poker. Roy was more than willing to be my partner when he learned how much money he could make." She twisted the pearl necklace she wore around her finger. "I'm not getting any younger. I have five, maybe ten years left of my life, and I intend to live it to the fullest."

"By ending the lives of others." Without asking permission, I sat on a boulder, my legs refusing to hold me any longer. "How did you get the poison in his cup?"

"Darling, I poured some in when you went to answer the phone. No one pays any attention to what an old woman is doing. Especially if the poison looks like creamer you're adding to your coffee.

"But Roy knew you killed Billy Bob."

She shrugged. "He put the pieces together,

I expect."

"You're sick." Nausea rose in my stomach. "What are you going to do now to get money?"

"I'll sell my house and move somewhere else. It's simple, really. That house is worth a fortune. I'll have plenty to live on until I make a new plan." She pulled away from the car. "I need you to get back into the driver's seat, dear, and drive into the lake."

"No." I took a step backward. "Nobody will believe I did that on purpose."

"Of course they will. We're going to get your unconscious boyfriend into the seat next to you. I'll say how you couldn't keep your hands off each other and ducked out of the party to be alone. I had this car at the mechanics a few days ago because of a faulty brake. I've thought of everything."

"Not everything." A bullet in my body would ruin her plan of a couple necking and rolling into the lake. I turned and darted into the woods.

A manic scream chased me, then silence.

I stopped and strained my ears to hear. The only sound was the whisper of the tree branches and the serenade of birds. Mrs. Hudson might be light on her feet, but she was still an old woman, and I'd know if she were coming after me. I couldn't go too far and leave Dean in her hands, so I kept to the shadows and went in the direction I thought would circle me around to the other side of the clearing where we'd stopped.

There was no sign of Mrs. Hudson, and the trunk of the car stood open. I swiped away the tears running down my face. What had she done with Dean?

I found myself torn between wanting to collapse in a weeping heap and racing through the woods to the water's edge to see whether Dean floated among the foliage growing there.

A groan came from Roy. He wasn't dead. At least not yet. Keeping low and casting glances left and right, I rushed to his side and turned him over on his back.

The bullet had taken him low on his left side. "Good thing for you she's a bad shot," I said. Must be why the woman chose poison to kill Billy Bob. I glanced in the empty trunk and found a clean towel. I stuffed it in the waistband of Roy's pants and tightened his belt a notch.

He groaned again.

"Sorry, but this will slow the bleeding. Where did she take Dean?"

"I didn't see." He clutched my hand. "Go. Run. She's crazy."

"I know." I needed to formulate a plan. She couldn't have carried Dean by herself, which meant he'd escaped. Did I dare hope?

Roy wasn't looking good at all. I fished in his pockets for a cell phone, apologizing for getting personal. I didn't find one. I sighed and hunkered down against the car's bumper, feeling very much like a sitting duck.

Where was Mrs. Hudson? I slowly scanned the trees forming a half-circle around us then, not finding anything to cause alarm, pushed to my feet and approached the water's edge again. Small footprints and large ones marred the damp dirt. I wasn't a detective, but this looked as if Dean had escaped the trunk and confronted Mrs. Hudson. Then, they'd both left.

Not one to be idle for long, especially when every nerve was strung as tight as a clothesline, I searched the trunk. The only thing of value was a tire iron. I set it on the ground and moved to the front seat. Bingo. Roy's phone.

I sat on the front seat, dialed 911, and told them about the situation. Then, despite an order not to hang up, did so and pressed the numbers for the sheriff's office. Calling both might get someone to the lake quicker.

"Sheriff Hayden."

I spoke as rapidly as I could. "This is Morgan Butler. Dean Matthews and I were abducted by Mrs. Hudson. She made me drive to the lake where she intended to kill us. I escaped, but Roy Collins has been shot. I don't know where Mrs. Hudson or Dean are." I took a ragged breath. "We need the police and an ambulance, now. I need to go find Dean."

The sheriff was silent for a very long moment. "You're serious?"

"Very. Look. I know we've had our differences, but if you don't come to the east side of the lake right away, I'll have to call Agent Waters, and there might be nothing more than three dead bodies when you get here."

"Be there soon." *Click.*

Some people's ego could definitely be an asset to others. I pressed the number for Agent Waters.

"Agent Waters."

Mrs. Hudson stepped from the trees with her gun aimed at me. "Put the phone down, Morgan."

I put the phone on the driver's seat, but left it connected. "Mrs. Hudson, what did you do with Dean?"

"He leaped out of the trunk when I opened it and took off after you." She shrugged and walked up to the car. "At least I think that's where he went. I truly wanted to shoot him in the back, but a bullet would mean your deaths weren't an accident." She nudged Roy with her toe. He groaned. "He's still alive, I see. You've also administered rough medical aid. Unfortunately, that was a wasted effort." Her finger twitched.

"No, wait. Don't shoot. I'm still unclear about your motive."

"You must really think I'm stupid." She

leaned into the car and pulled the trigger, blowing the phone to pieces and putting a hole in the car seat next to me.

I screamed and rolled into a ball. "You're certifiable."

"Maybe so. Get into the driver's seat, Morgan."

"No." I curled tighter into a fetal position. "You're just going to have to shoot me."

"Stop being so dramatic." She grabbed my hair and yanked.

"Ow!" I slapped at her hands. "Let go of me."

She jabbed me with the pistol. "Women are too much trouble. That's why I've always partnered with a man. Get out of the car."

With the painful aid of her dragging me out by the hair, I did. *God, please let me live long enough for help to arrive.* I was pretty sure Agent Waters would put the facts together after hearing Mrs. Hudson's voice. Especially if she spoke with the sheriff.

Roy groaned again.

Mrs. Hudson glanced down.

That was my chance. I sprang, knocking her arm to the side and pulling my hair free of her grip. Screaming like a Viking, I tackled her to the ground. The gun flew into a pile of decaying leaves.

The woman was remarkably strong for someone her age, but I was younger and fueled by anger. I straddled her waist and held her hands over her head. Jutting out my bottom lip, I blew my hair out of my face.

She snorted. "Now what? If I get an arm free, I'll scratch your eyes out."

"Then I guess we sit here until help arrives." My arms were already cramping. I really needed to start a workout routine.

I shifted position.

She bucked under me.

I tightened my legs and squeezed. "I can do this all day." Not really. My muscles were screaming. "Did you really think you could own all of Main Street?"

She narrowed her eyes. "Why couldn't I?"

"What about the land the buildings sit on? That belongs to the city."

"Minor detail. I'd own the buildings and could charge whatever rent I wanted."

"Charge too much and the buildings would be empty and you'd get nothing. Greed is a sin, Mrs. Hudson."

She rolled her eyes. "As if murder and theft aren't. Don't preach to me, little girl. I could sell this entire town to a developer and be richer than you ever dreamed a person could be. Now, shut up."

"I could, but talking would make the time pass faster until the sheriff gets here. I did manage to place a call before you shot the phone."

She cursed. "Just let me go. I never had any intention of killing you. It was all an act."

I laughed, surprised I could find humor in the situation. "You would have sent me and Dean into the water without hesitation if we'd given you just a bit of cooperation."

"My heart. I'm dying. Get off me."

"Nope." My fingers were growing numb. "While we're having such a lovely conversation, I want to know if you're the one who tried to run over me in your car and broke into my apartment?"

"Of course not. I hired someone to do those things." She bucked under me.

"Why?"

"To frighten you into selling. You aren't bright enough to back away when danger approaches."

"I was smart enough to figure out you killed Billy Bob." I squeezed her wrists harder until she winced.

"I've got it from here, sweetheart." Dean lifted me off Mrs. Hudson then aimed the woman's gun at her.

Thirteen

I leaned into Dean. "Where did you go?"

"After you. I followed the same circle you did and came up on the two of you. I'll never forget the sight of you sitting on top of Mrs. Hudson. Thankfully, I stepped on the gun, thus locating it easily in the leaves, and ended up being your knight in shining armor." He grinned.

"I'm going to be sick listening to such drivel." Mrs. Hudson crossed her arms. "What now?"

"We wait for the sheriff. Morgan is going to remove my belt and use it to tie your hands behind your back. Then, you're going to sit in the car."

"I cannot go to jail, young man. I would never survive without certain luxuries. You might as well shoot me."

It wasn't easy removing Dean's belt and staying out of his way while doing so, but I got it free from the loops. I admit I got a great deal of satisfaction as I pulled Mrs. Hudson's arms behind her and tightened the belt as much as possible. Then I shoved her toward the car.

"I lost a shoe." She glared.

"I don't care."

She kicked me in the shin with the other shoed foot. "Seriously." I pinned her against the car and took off her shoe. I tossed it as far as I could. "What size shoe do you wear?"

"Eight and a half. Why?"

"Because those were Jimmy Choo, and I love them. They happen to be just my size. I'm keeping them." I shoved her onto the back seat and slammed the door.

"They cost me eight hundred dollars," she screamed through the window.

"I earned them." I marched to Dean's side and slid my arms around his waist. "I really dislike that woman."

"That makes two of us." He kissed me then knelt next to Roy. "He's lost a lot of blood."

"Yeah, but —" Movement to my right caught my attention.

Through the back window, I caught sight of Mrs. Hudson's skinny hiney hanging over the back seat as the car rolled into the water. "Dean!" I grabbed the tire iron from the ground and darted after the car.

Dean splashed in seconds after I did. He worked on bashing in one window with a rock, while I worked with the tire iron. I'd just managed to shatter the window and knock out a good portion when the car sank, dragging me with it.

Mrs. Hudson glared in my direction, not fazed in the slightest that my arm was tangled in the seat belt. I took a deep breath and submerged. I freed myself and removed the rest of the window as Dean did the same on the other side. The car filled with water.

I stretched my arm inside, grabbed a fistful of Mrs. Hudson's hair, and dragged her to freedom. Oh, sweet vengeance. I didn't let go until we crawled on shore.

Agent Waters helped me to my feet as Sheriff Hayden took possession of the wet and sputtering Mrs. Hudson. "I have a feeling you've had an interesting day, Ms. Butler," Agent Waters said.

"Very interesting." I closed the trunk and sat on it. I watched as Roy was strapped to a gurney. "How is he?"

"He's lost a lot of blood, but I think he'll survive long enough to go to jail."

"Mrs. Hudson is the one who killed Billy Bob." I shoved my wet hair out of my face.

A paramedic draped a blanket around my shoulders. "Do you need to be checked out?"

"No. I'm just wet and tired."

"Roy knew who killed Billy Bob, though, am I right?"

I nodded. "Mrs. Hudson had quite a tight hold on him. He does deserve jail, but she needs a life sentence. No remorse with that woman."

"Come down to the station when you've dried off and give us your statement." Agent Waters's mouth twitched. "As hard as it is for me to say, you did a good job, Ms. Butler."

"Thanks." My grin was three times as big as hers. I had done well. But not without the help of one very special man. I glanced to where he spoke with the sheriff.

Dean winked over Sheriff Hayden's shoulder then joined me a few minutes later. "The sheriff will give us a ride to Mrs. Hudson's to retrieve our cars."

I nodded and hopped off the car trunk. "It's been a long day. Let's go home."

I slept in the next morning. Every muscle in my body ached from wrestling with an old woman. I glanced at the clock. Dean would pick me up in thirty minutes to go to the sheriff's office.

While I waited, I stood at the front window of my apartment and stared at the main street of the town I loved. It had almost been changed forever because of the greed of one woman. Strange how one person can have so much of an effect on others. I vowed right then to make sure any ripples I left behind only widened to do good to others. Dean's car pulled to the curb and I hurried down.

"I could get used to this," he said as I got in the car. He leaned over and kissed me.

"Maybe now that someone isn't trying to kill me, we'll have time to focus on us."

"That is a great idea."

"You'll get one heck of a book out of this."

He laughed. "A bestseller, I hope. I'll change the names, of course, but put in a note that it's based on the crimes of the Oak Grove Widow."

"That's what you're going to call her?"

"Like it?"

"Definitely, because Mrs. Hudson will hate it." I clicked my seat belt into place and slipped my hand in his.

At the sheriff's office we were ushered right into the conference room where Agent Waters and Sheriff Hayden waited. They both glanced up with no expression on their faces. This couldn't be good.

"Mr. Matthews, please wait until we call you. We'd like to speak with you each individually."

Dean's eyes widened, but he nodded, gave my hand a squeeze, and left, closing the door behind him.

I sat across from the two stony-faced law enforcement officers. "What?"

"Mrs. Hudson claims you and Mr. Matthews tied her hands and tried to kill her. That you threw her to the ground and beat her." Sheriff Hayden flipped through some papers in front of him.

"She's lying. She tried to kill me."

"Tell us in your own words what happened at the party," Agent Waters said. "We'll determine who's at fault afterward." She shot the sheriff a sharp glance.

I explained about my conversation with Mrs. Ethelridge and overhearing the argument between Roy and Mrs. Hudson. "Then we found the pond with the death camas. I knew then we'd found the person responsible for Billy Bob's death. Mrs. Hudson put the poison in the coffee while I was on the phone." I waved my hand. "Write that down, Sheriff."

He made a face and scribbled something in his notes.

"All right, move on to how you and Mr. Matthews got to the lake." Agent Waters held my gaze. How did she go so long between blinks?

"She hit Dean over the head and had Roy and me put him in the trunk of her car. Then, at gunpoint, she made me drive us all to the lake. Her intentions were for me and Dean to stay in the car and drive it into the lake." I huffed. "As if I'd do that on purpose. She wanted it to look as if Dean and I were so crazily involved in making out that we didn't notice the car rolling into the water. No one is that stupid."

"Questionable," Sheriff Hayden said. His look clearly said he meant me.

I turned slightly to ignore him. "She shot

Roy as soon as he got out of the car. I got away and ran then circled back around to the car. I didn't know where Dean and Mrs. Hudson had gone. I helped Roy the best I could until Mrs. Hudson came back. We fought, and I pinned her to the ground until Dean arrived. I tied her hands with his belt, and we put her in the car. She shoved it into neutral and tried to commit suicide by rolling it into the water. I did not try to kill her. I saved her."

"By pulling her hair?" Agent Waters's brows almost disappeared in her hair.

My face heated. "That was payback for her pulling me from the car by my hair."

Her lips twitched. "You have got to be one of the luckiest people who walk this earth."

"Nope. Only blessed." I smiled. "I did have fun digging into the truth, though. Despite the danger, it was quite an adventure."

"Oh no you don't." Sheriff Hayden slapped the table. "You will not think of yourself as some kind of gumshoe who interferes with police investigations. I'll lock you up faster than you can say 'the Coffee Perk.' "

"I guess you need to pray for no more mysteries in Oak Grove, Sheriff." I tilted my head. "Am I done?"

"Yes," Agent Waters said. "The questions were a formality. This can count as you giving your statement." She stood and offered her hand. "Have a good day, Ms. Butler. You

124

have an insatiable curiosity. Take care with that."

"I will." I returned her shake and tossed the sheriff a wave. It was finished.

I waited while Dean went through the same questioning. His took less time. Soon, we were back at the lake, in the same spot as yesterday. My skin crawled. We sat on an old blanket he kept in the trunk of his car and stared at the water. The noonday sun sent a path of sparkling gold across the placid surface.

"It could have ended here," he said, sliding his arm around my waist. "I finally found the woman I want to call my girl and I almost lost her."

"God was with me every step of the way." I rested my head on his shoulder.

"Shaking His head at your foolishness."

"Yep." Life could now go back to normal. Dean could write in my coffee shop. Tuesdays could go back to the book club actually talking about books. I could devise ways of expanding the products I offered my customers. "Things might be a little boring after all the excitement."

He gave me a squeeze. "We'll make our own excitement."

"You'll have to find other subjects for your books."

"The news supplies plenty of resources."

I sighed. "It will be nice not to have a killer

after me.”

“Life can’t be boring with you around, Morgan Butler.” Dean shifted to face me. “But a little less dangerous will be nice.” He leaned his forehead against mine. “If you do find yourself in the middle of a murder again, I hope it’s me you want by your side.”

I pulled back and cupped his face. “I wouldn’t want anyone else. Just don’t tell Harper.” I smiled.

“She can find her own partner.” He lowered his head and kissed me.

It was good to come back to a place that could have held bad memories. Wonderful, sweet Dean now gave me something much better to remember this spot by.

ABOUT THE AUTHOR

Cynthia Hickey grew up in a family of storytellers and moved around the country a lot as an army brat. Her desire is to write about real, but flawed characters in a wholesome way that her seven children and nine grandchildren can all be proud of. She and her husband live in Arizona where Cynthia is a full-time writer.

■ ■ ■ ■

THE HONEY HIVE
MYSTERY

BY DANA MENTINK

■ ■ ■ ■

ONE

The noise intruded into my dream, like an enemy wasp invading a honeybee hive. In my dream we'd been cooking potato pancakes, Rick's specialty. He fried and flipped, and I cuddled up to his side, feeling the warmth of my husband right down to the bump on his left shoulder, a souvenir of the time he'd tumbled off a ladder while grinning at me instead of attending to the apple tree he was trimming. Rick was my security, my courage, my perfect life partner.

The dream retreated along with the phantom scent of the frying food, leaving behind the cold truth. There was no Rick anymore, this side of heaven, and there hadn't been for almost eleven months now. My brain knew he was not here, but my heart, oh how my heart simply would not get the message.

Rick, my college sweetheart, the dreamer who made me believe we could leave Philadelphia for a small town we'd never clapped eyes on before. Rick, my husband and business partner for four years, now gone just shy of a year. When I was younger, a year seemed like a very long time. I'd since realized it was only a blink. Widow was my new identity, and I detested it.

I sat up in the fragrant darkness, inhaling the sweet smell not of potato pancakes, but of apple blossoms. Same blossoms, same tiny town of Oak Grove, Kansas, where we'd moved three years before. Even the same warped ladder leaned against the gnarled tree trunk where I'd left it. Same everything, but a completely different life, since Rick died of an aneurysm. One moment I had a soul mate, the next he was gone.

The pain throbbed strong. I ached to call my friend Evelyn Kliff. Evelyn understood, having lost her own husband three years ago. We meet with the other women, the book club ladies who keep me anchored to this earth, every Tuesday at the Coffee Perk to talk about books and life and whatever else God lays on our hearts. I longed for the solace of that weekly gaggle fest, but, as Robert Frost put it, there were miles to go until Tuesday since the clock by my bed proclaimed it was only two thirty a.m., hours before sunup, on a cool Wednesday in June. Whatever had awakened me did me no favors.

Anger broiled inside me, or perhaps it was just foolishness. "So what if it's early?" I said, voice loud in the darkness. "Might as well dive into the day." There was plenty to be done. The first ever Spring Fling Festival was only a few days away, and there were labels to be affixed to jars, honey to be extracted, and lip balms to be made with my honey and Evelyn's organic lavender. If work was the key to getting through life without my husband, I would dive in with both feet. God had allowed Rick and me to find a passion for each other and our bees. I resolved to cling to the latter as long as He let me. Ju Ju twitched one satiny ear and wriggled her long Slinky of a body, as if to say, "You gotta be kidding me. It cannot possibly be morning yet."

I stroked her graying muzzle. Technically, I rescued Ju Ju the dachsie right after Rick died, from a shelter where she was dumped after a family replaced the old dog with a younger model, but in truth, I am fairly certain I am the rescuee. God sent me a life preserver dressed in a furry coat. When I would spew out my anger and loss to Him, there was my sweet old dog to catch my tears and lie with me as I prayed. At this very moment, Ju Ju, eyes still closed, snaked out a tongue and licked my wrist. I scratched her long flanks and kissed her bony head before I shoved my chilled feet into a pair of old boots. *Ready or not, morning, here I come.*

Crunch. I froze, boots planted.

I knew the sound. It was the noise of feet

crossing the trail I'd painstakingly covered in gravel before winter to keep the mud down. Feet? At this hour?

Another crunch. I stiffened.

Pulse skittering, I reached for my phone. Should I call Sheriff Hayden, the town cop? I tapped in the number and waited longer than I should have before I realized my phone was dead. I'd forgotten to charge it. Typical Penny Parson move. I was probably being silly anyway. I had nothing worth stealing unless you counted the bees, and they were hard to snatch.

Should I run to get help?

The double-edged sword of living in a trailer on the edge of town was . . . plenty of lovely peace and quiet for my bees . . . and the nearest neighbor lived more than a mile away. Not to mention that this neighbor, crotchety music teacher Rocky Dickerson, despised me, my dog, my bees, and my deceased husband. After our previous altercations, he'd probably plunk out a celebratory tune on his piano if he knew there was an intruder on my property, rather than offer any assistance.

I sneaked to the window, lifted the shade a fraction, and peered out into the night. Nothing. Could it have been a coyote? A dog? Maybe even a cow or horse escaped from a nearby farm? The smart thing to do would be to wait it out, safely locked in my trailer, but outside were my precious beehives, my only asset, the sixty thousand insects that kept me together body and soul, the only thing I had left of Rick.

"We're going to make it, Pen. You, me, and our bees are gonna live the life we always wanted."

We'd craved a simple existence. A country life, close to the land, toiling side by side, far away from the city . . . and we'd had it, for a while. We'd built it together, with plenty of blood, sweat, and tears. The memory goaded me into action, and I stood up, ready to rumble.

Ju Ju periscoped her head out of the blankets to watch. She was essentially a coward at heart, but stronger than her fear was her love for me. I tucked her under one arm. Swallowing hard, I flicked on a flashlight and crept out into the dark.

Cool air chilled me, teasing goose bumps from my flesh. Over the soft murmur of a spring breeze, I heard it again, the crunch of feet on gravel, which abruptly stopped when the trailer door snapped shut behind me.

"Who's . . . who's there?" I called out.

No answer. My unsteady flashlight beam picked up nothing but the shadows of my Langstroth hives arranged near the border of the old apple orchard. The Pink Lady apples were untended, available for any and all who wished to pick them, but no one would be helping themselves to the fruit at night.

"I'm armed," I shouted bravely. *With a thirteen-year-old dachshund and a flashlight,* but no need to disclose that.

Ju Ju barked, to enhance my credibility. I clutched her close.

Another scrape and a thud, and my heart was hammering in my throat. A shadow detached from the pool of darkness. The beam of my flashlight caught the back of someone running into the orchard, head ducked low. Man or woman? A sluggish trickle of bees danced against the moonlight. Bees aren't nocturnal, and they don't appreciate being disturbed. Whoever it was must have knocked against the wooden hives as they passed through.

Why? Who? My thoughts were as scattered as the bees. I ticked off the points in my mind. There had been an intruder on my property and I had no way to call for help. Town was too far away to reach on foot, and my old clunker of a truck rested on a flat tire I'd intended to replace in the morning.

An owl exploded from the apple trees and rocketed away in the night. I swallowed a scream, clutching the dog. Was the trespasser coming back? My courage drained away and I lugged Ju Ju back to the trailer where I'd parked my old red Schwinn bike that Rick had always called the Red Rocket. I plopped Ju Ju in the basket he'd rigged up on the handlebars, and she barked once more, as if to encourage me to hurry.

I didn't need the urging. Feet to the pedals, pulse slamming against my throat, I pushed as hard as I could for Rocky Dickerson's house.

Two

Long days tending my bees left me in pretty good shape for my thirty-two years, but thanks to the steep slope, it still took me nearly fifteen minutes to pull up, chest heaving and sweaty, at Rocky Dickerson's front door. His house was grand, by Oak Grove standards, a two-story Victorian with brick facing and a gabled roof. The front patio was covered, the slanted roof supported by white pillars. Rocky, the town gossips whispered, had inherited his grandfather's old home, and his equally aged grand piano. Music ran in the family. Charm did not.

As I got off my bike, I considered our last face-to-face meeting. Rocky had called the police after he'd been stung by my bees.

"You were trespassing," Rick had told him. *"On our property."*

"No it's not." Rocky waved an old deed like a war flag. *"Says right here, my property line extends five hundred yards into that orchard."*

"That's an old deed," Rick proclaimed in

triumph. *"Your granddad sold off the orchard in the fifties, and it's ours fair and square. I did my homework at the county records office."*

The conversation deteriorated from there until Sheriff Card had sent us on our separate ways with dire warnings about any further disturbances.

Rick had been furious, anger flaming his cheeks, so unusual for my good-natured hubby. A month later he was dead. It wasn't Rocky's fault, of course. Rick was living on borrowed time, unbeknownst to us, but still . . . the bitter part of me couldn't help but wonder if the angry altercation had sped up my husband's demise. It didn't help that Rocky accused me of everything from stealing his mail to littering on his property to whoever would lend him an ear.

I muttered a prayer that Jesus would tread hard on my tongue as I hurried up the drive.

If you're going to wake the guy up at this hour to ask for help, a little honey in your attitude won't hurt. After all, Proverbs was clear about pleasant words being like honeycomb and all, so I tried to wipe the scowl from my face and plaster on something less sour. It was probably a wasted effort, as my hair was blown into a frightening puff and my face was shiny with perspiration.

Holding the dog, I raised my knuckles to knock. I'd just grazed the wood when the door swung open with a squeal that made Ju Ju hide her snout under my armpit. I would have done the same if there had been another armpit handy besides my own.

"It's okay," I whispered. "Uh, he probably just didn't shut the door properly." I had read my share of romantic suspense novels where the heroine commits one of those "too dumb to be believed" moments, walking into a spooky old house by her lonesome without so much as a cell phone in her pocket. I had no intention of being one of those ditzy types. Backing away slowly, I figured I'd go back to my trailer. No way the intruder would still be there. As soon as the sun made an appearance, I'd fix my tire and head straight for the police station. Ju Ju seemed to read my mind and approve because she took her face out of my armpit and offered an anemic tail wag.

During my retreat, the steps creaked under my weight. I'd gotten to the bottom when I heard it.

A male voice, thin as paper, a half moan. "Help."

The little hairs on the back of my neck elevated, and Ju Ju returned her head to its spot under my armpit, small body trembling.

I was hearing things. Had to be. Too many late-night Alfred Hitchcock movie marathons. I crept down one more step.

"Please, help," the voice called, fainter now.

I gulped. Well, there was no choice, really,

was there? I was taken right back to the car wreck when I was seventeen. Pinned behind the wheel, terrified out of my mind until a stranger had stopped, an angel from God in the form of a truck driver named Earl John Warren. Earl John held my hand in his big calloused one and spoke softly to me until the medics arrived. He told me all about his family and asked about mine, shared his favorite knock-knock jokes and his thoughts on the New York Yankees. Earl John, with a truck full of eggs to deliver and a wife and six kids to go home to, had not turned his back on me, so how could I walk away from that voice crying for help?

On shaking legs, I tiptoed back up the stairs and through the front door. It creaked, of course, like a tortured soul, as I pushed it open.

"Mr. Dickerson?" I whispered. "It's Penny Parson. Do you . . . I mean . . . was that you who called for help?" There was no answer. I fumbled for the light switch, finally finding it. A small pool of light issued forth from a stained-glass lamp on the sideboard. The room was a mess. Drawers open, music magazines tossed on the floor, the piano bench lying on its side.

Robbery? I sucked in a breath.

I opened my mouth to call out again when a figure appeared on the stairs. Rocky. Relief washed through me. He was ambulatory, so things weren't as bad as I'd thought. He hadn't fallen or broken a limb or anything.

"Mr. Dickerson. I'm really sorry to bother you at this hour."

No answer.

"Mr. Dickerson?" He didn't respond, but it could be no one else, silhouetted against the upstairs hall light. Rocky Dickerson was what my grammy would have described as a bean pole, over six feet tall with a head of unkempt black hair and not an ounce of fat anywhere on him. From what I could see in the dim hall light, he was dressed in a bathrobe knotted around the middle, concealing his jammies. At least, I hope the man wore jammies to sleep. I tried again.

"I, uh, I came to use your phone and I heard a call for help. Was that you?"

He didn't answer, just clutched the bannister.

A strange feeling twisted up my stomach, the sensation that something was about to change, like a time bomb ticking down the final seconds, like an aneurysm starting to rupture.

But that was silly, wasn't it? Time to switch my movie viewing from Hitchcock to the Home and Garden Channel.

I must have imagined the plea for help, because there was Rocky, large as life, probably trying to wake up from a nightmare only to find there was another nightmare in his front parlor in the form of a half-crazy woman who'd just barged into his house. A woman he didn't like. And her dog. At an hour that normal people did not come calling. It was a lot to process.

"Very sorry to ask, but may I use your phone?" I said.

He made a sort of noise, a half squeak, part grunt.

"I know it's late, or early." I started again. "It's an emergency or I wouldn't ask. Believe me."

He was silent for a moment, then he toppled down the stairs in a whirl of gangly limbs.

I screamed as he landed, sprawled across the bottom steps, awkward, like a department store mannequin. Putting Ju Ju down, I sprinted over to him. Ju Ju danced a panicked rhythm on the hardwood floor, whining.

"Oh Mr. Dickerson, are you hurt?" Hurt? The guy had probably just sustained a major head injury, broken bones, or worse, thanks to my shocking him awake.

His eyes were closed, mouth open. I leaned my cheek close and detected no puff of air. I felt the same panic, awful and black, that I'd felt when I found Rick. Helpless, frantic, paralyzed with shock.

CPR, CPR. The directive floated into my consciousness. *Check for a pulse.* Ignoring Ju Ju's whines, which had turned to plaintive yips, I touched Rocky's throat, praying there would be a flutter of life there. There wasn't, but my fingers came away sticky. Yanking them back, I stared at the blood staining my fingertips. Bleeding, I had to stop the bleeding, start compressions.

I pulled the top of his robe open, then screamed and crab-walked backward, sending Ju Ju into a frenzy of barking.

Dead center in Rocky's chest was a hole. A very neat, round hole, oozing blood.

A bullet hole.

THREE

I must have sat there for a while, blood on my hands and a frantic dog burrowing in my lap, though I could not say exactly how long. When I was able to pull in a shuddering breath, I realized that I was sitting with a dead body, a murder victim yet, and no one had any idea what had happened except me and the person who shot him. That was enough to send me stumbling in search of a phone, but first I slammed on every light switch I could find. I avoided looking at what lay at the bottom of the stairs, but when I drew up opposite the stainless-steel refrigerator door, I almost screamed again at my horrifying reflection.

Streaks of blood painted my face. I ran to the kitchen sink, yanked on the tap, and washed, wiping my face and hands dry with my T-shirt. Sucking in breaths to try and steady myself, I scanned the tidy tile countertops until I found what I was looking for — an avocado-green phone, the old-fashioned kind with an actual dial and a twirly cord.

Snatching it up, I dialed the only number I had memorized besides Rick's cell phone. Evelyn answered on the fifth ring.

"This better be good."

"Evelyn, it's Penny. There's a . . . I mean . . . I'm in trouble." At that point my voice stopped working.

After a three-second pause, my friend leaped into the void, peppering me with questions and ending with the words I most needed to hear.

"I'll call the police from my truck. Hold tight. I'm on my way."

I stayed in the kitchen in the pool of golden light that did not comfort, clutching my dog, both of us shivering. Perhaps I should have been more worried about the killer still roaming the house, but Ju Ju has a nose for people and she would have let me know. Plus, I had a sinking certainty that whoever had killed my neighbor was the same person I had encountered on my property who had sent me running to Rocky's in the first place. Still, I kept near the phone and opened the back door in case I had to flee, mumbling incoherent prayers.

Minutes? Hours? Some interminable interval passed before I heard Evelyn's rumbly truck pull into the drive. And then she was there, wrapping me in her strong arms, her gray hair tickling my cheek as she tucked me close. The barking outside indicated she'd brought a couple of her rescue dogs.

"Bon Bon and Mervin are in the back of the truck but they'll be out in a flash if I call them." Little Bon Bon, the Chihuahua mix, and Mervin, an attractive blend of pit bull and shepherd, would be listening eagerly for the sound of Evelyn's whistle. Smart, devoted, faithful. Canine backup was better than the National Guard.

She pushed me to arm's length. "Are you hurt?"

I shook my head.

"But you're coming apart at the seams?"

I nodded.

She squeezed my arms. "We'll get through this together, don't worry. I'm just going to . . . um . . . check on the patient. I'm sure Sheriff Hayden is taking his sweet time lugging his useless carcass out of bed."

I gulped, and she left me, returning in a moment with a face a shade paler than it had been a moment before.

"Dead?" I whispered.

"Thoroughly," she said.

I gulped again, and Bon Bon started up a barking that set Ju Ju to wriggling. My head spun.

"Just breathe. In with the good air, out with the bad," she said. "Talk when you can."

I did a fair amount of breathing and crying and blowing my nose and such, interspersed with facts. She listened gravely. Evelyn is the best listener I've ever met.

Oak Grove's newly appointed sheriff pulled up behind Evelyn's truck. We watched through the kitchen window as he unloaded his small frame, taking a moment to stretch his limbs and smooth his full head of hair. It was still dark, but there was enough moonlight to detect his look of annoyance as he strolled into the house and met us.

"I was off duty. I got a call that you two found a body." He shook his head. "What is it, really? Some sort of old carpet rolled up? A bag of laundry you two amateur sleuths decided was a corpse?" He huffed out a breath. "You Coffee Perk gals think because you solved that sign hanger's murder, that made you some kind of sleuths."

And it had made him look inept. I was still struggling for words when Evelyn chimed in with a single pointed finger.

"Go look for yourself," she snapped.

He did, returning with a slightly cowed demeanor. "Okay. Sit down you two, and let's have it," he commanded.

We did, and the questions commenced. I related the whole story of the stranger on my property and the discovery of the body. All the while, Ju Ju curled on my lap and Evelyn clutched my cold fingers.

The sheriff listened, scrawled in his tiny

notebook, and then shot me a calculating look.

"You and Rocky didn't get along, did you?"

"We had a disagreement but . . ."

"And you show up here in the wee hours, at his house."

"Yes, but . . ."

"With some story about a stranger on your property."

"There *was* a stranger on my property. It's not a story."

"Of course there was," Evelyn said. "If you think she had anything to do with this —"

"I don't think anything," he said.

You can say that again. Mercifully, the words stayed inside my mouth. Score one for Jesus.

"But as soon as Sheila gets here . . ."

He referred to Sheila Waters from the Kansas Bureau of Investigation, the officer he would no doubt stick with all the paperwork, if he could get away with it.

"We'll take a trip over to your property and see if we can substantiate your claim."

Claim? I felt like slamming a palm onto the tabletop. How had I become the bad guy here? "And if not?" I squeaked. "What then?"

He raised a shoulder. "Maybe nothing, but you've got blood streaked all over your shirt, which I'm assuming is the victim's blood, and I'm betting your fingerprints are all over this house."

"Well I don't have a gun on me," I fired off.

"Easy to discard that nearby, maybe drop it in a field or throw it in the creek. Got an alibi? Anyone who can corroborate where you've been for the last few hours?"

"Only a dog." Ju Ju aimed her nose in his direction and growled. *Good dog.*

"Dogs don't count."

I could not believe what I was hearing. "Are you seriously saying that you think I shot Rocky Dickerson?"

He smiled again. "Not saying anything, just collecting evidence. But this is a small town, honey, and Rocky didn't have any enemies that I'm aware of . . . except you and your husband."

"This is ridiculous," Evelyn said. "And her name is Penny, not honey. Why would she stay here and phone the police if she'd just killed the guy?"

"She didn't. You did. The perfect way to divert suspicion."

Evelyn gaped. "Where did you get your police badge? A box of cereal?"

He cocked his head at me. "Did you know that Dickerson just hired a lawyer to look into the property-line dispute?"

"There was no dispute," I said. "His grandfather sold the land."

"Uh huh, but maybe that property line wasn't drawn up quite perfectly. Maybe you wound up with an extra helping of Dickerson's acreage. Maybe you didn't want to give up any of your ill-gotten gains and decided to do something about it."

"This is lunacy." Evelyn stood, dragging me to my feet. "I'm taking Penny home."

"Not yet you're not. Not until we get a team out there in the morning to investigate, photograph, etc. Right now she's got to come down to the station to give a statement, and we'll need those clothes for evidence."

"Fine," Evelyn said. "After that, she'll come home with me, and we'll be at her property by nine sharp to supervise the investigation."

I marveled at the courage in her words. She'd been so strong for me after Rick's death, and she was a rock again now. *Thank You, God, for Evelyn.*

"You'll stay out of the way or you'll both be arrested," he snapped.

She was about to fire off a retort, but I grabbed her hand. "We won't get in the way, Sheriff."

"Don't worry," Evelyn whispered to me as Sheriff Hayden got busy on his cell phone. "We'll tell the girls at the Perk. They'll know how to handle this."

The sheriff held the phone away from his mouth. "And don't get your busybody ladies down at the Coffee Perk muddling about in this situation. I'll arrest any of them who stick their noses into this investigation."

"I'd like to see him try," Evelyn said in my ear.

FOUR

Hours later, I stared at the ceiling of Evelyn's spare bedroom. Her home was nestled on the organic farm she used to tend with her husband of twenty years until his death. Now Evelyn raised organic herbs and cared for her brood of chickens and dogs, and we exchanged our honey, herbs, and prayers back and forth as needed. It was the perfect partnership for our businesses and souls.

In spite of Evelyn's hospitality, the idea of getting any sleep was a fantasy. After hours at the police station, she'd loaned me some clothes to replace the police department sweats I'd been given in exchange for my sweatpants and T-shirt and put clean sheets and a handmade quilt on the bed, but as I lay there with Ju Ju, my mind would not allow any rest. No amount of prayer could banish the horror from my mind. Evelyn and I are both early risers in our lines of work, hopelessly wired to awaken with the roosters.

By the time I got settled, it was after seven,

which in my book was past getting-up time. Ju Ju, had no such rigid sleep rules, nestling between my legs under the blankets and snoring fit to beat the band. When Rick and I were first married, living in a cramped apartment in Philly and working corporate jobs we despised, we had taken in a stray cat that snored louder than we ever thought possible. Fortunately, Puffers fell deeply in love with the building custodian and promptly took up residence with the delighted gentleman. Ju Ju's snores were at a lower decibel level, for sure.

I finally gave up, sliding her to one side and heading to the kitchen to push the button on Evelyn's ancient coffeemaker. The cozy space was redolent with the scent of herbs drying on racks in tidy rows.

Evelyn found me there. As I suspected, she'd been up for a while.

I pointed to the delicate fronds of thyme and lemon oregano. "For the Spring Fling?"

She nodded. "I'm going to make another batch of lotion and the bath scrubs. Those went over big at the Christmas church bazaar. Probably won't bring in much profit, but it might keep the dogs in kibble a while longer." She frowned. "I already texted Morgan, Harper, and Jeanine. I woke them up. Harper wasn't thrilled about my timing, but she saw reason when I explained the circumstances. They'll meet us at the Coffee Perk later this afternoon. Jo's out of town."

She took the mug I offered her and slugged down some of the hot brew, wincing. "They've already started brainstorming a list of who to ask who might know anything and everything about Rocky Dickerson."

I poured myself some coffee with a hand that didn't even shake, I am proud to say. "That's a comfort. I mean, it's all going to be fine anyway, I'm sure, right? The sheriff can't really think I'm a suspect."

She shook her head at that notion. "You know what kind of cop he is. Vindictive for one, and we showed him up helping Morgan solve the murder of her sign hanger last month. Second, he's incompetent. He never would have been given the position if he hadn't called in favors to snag the job after Sheriff Card died from that heart attack. He is an imbecile of epic proportions." She drank some coffee. "Blech. This is terrible, isn't it?"

"Well . . ."

She sighed. "Hubby always made the coffee, and I never got the knack for it."

I squeezed her hand. Rick had been hopeless in the kitchen too, but I missed all the ways he'd cared for me. Little ways, like keeping a sweater for me in his truck because he knew I'd forget one, or buying up extra cartons of Edna Orkin's cherry ice cream from the Fourth of July festivities to squirrel away in the freezer for me. Just for me. Rick didn't even like cherry ice cream. I blinked hard.

This wasn't making me feel better, the coffee or the conversation. Evelyn read the look on my face.

"Sorry, honey," she said, patting my knee as Bon Bon and Mervin galloped near, hoping to wake up Ju Ju. My current situation made me feel like one of Evelyn's rescue dogs. I just wanted someone to feed me, pat me on the head, and tuck me underneath a warm blanket. I wanted Rick. *Lord, please help me have the strength to face this alone. Not alone,* I thought suddenly. There was Evelyn and my Coffee Perk gang to help me. I felt momentarily bolstered.

We toasted bread and spread on some of the apple blossom honey I traded her for a glorious bunch of basil a while back. I scrambled an egg for Ju Ju. Yes, I know that's not traditional dog food, but she is missing a few teeth and she's ninety-one in dog years. That's my excuse anyway, but it's really because the act of caring for her, babying her, made me feel a little less the pain of being alone. Evelyn, being the incredible friend that she is, didn't say a word as Ju Ju lapped up her scrambled egg, though she got a questioning look from Bon Bon and Mervin about a possible breakfast upgrade.

Then Evelyn drove me and Ju Ju back through town.

"Let's stop at the Coffee Perk," she suggested.

"Great idea. I need all the caffeine assistance I can get." We entered the glorious comfort of mismatched chairs and tables. Morgan was filling a cup for Dean Matthews. The blue-eyed charmer was a writer, and handsome to boot, and was as close to exotic as we got in Oak Grove. He and Morgan were testing the dating waters, so all the Coffee Perk gals tried to be on their best behavior when they saw him. Morgan came around the counter and hugged me close and pressed a kiss to Ju Ju's head. My dog was tucked neatly inside my borrowed jacket since Morgan's place was a dog friendly establishment.

"Terrible," Morgan said. "Just terrible."

The mail carrier, Ralph Wessex, dropped a stack of envelopes on the counter and tugged at the front of his postal carrier uniform, which fitted a bit too snugly around his wide middle. He sent me a doleful look, the bags under his eyes probably matching my own, though he was in his midsixties at least.

"I heard," he said. "Hope it wasn't too awful for you, finding him like that. I was the first to come upon Mrs. Noble after she died of a heart attack and I sure won't ever forget it. Dead people are memorable, so murdered ones must be even more so."

I swallowed. "How did you get the news so quickly?"

He grinned. "Postal carriers hear more gossip than the village pastor. We know everybody's secrets." He lowered his voice. "For instance, I happen to know that Rocky's twin brother, Charles, is coming to town to settle up Rocky's affairs. They weren't exactly bosom buddies. He came before, in the winter, remember? Only stayed for two days."

I didn't remember. The winter was a blur, as was everything since Rick died.

"How did Charles hear so quickly?" Evelyn wondered.

Ralph shrugged. "Police, I guess. They share information faster than my two ex-wives."

Morgan sniffed. "Maybe Sheriff Hayden's finally accomplished something besides scrounging free coffee and pastries."

Ralph patted my arm as he went by. "Don't worry, Penny. Nobody thinks you had anything to do with Rocky's murder."

Except the police.

"The gals will all be here later after the lunch rush," Morgan said. "We'll put on our thinking caps." Something dancing in her eyes made me wonder if she was enjoying the thought of diving into another murder . . . or maybe it was the fun of a budding romance with Dean Matthews. My heart squeezed. Did she know how blessed she was to have the possibility of love in her life?

I remembered my wedding day. We'd opted

for a civil ceremony and a backyard barbecue celebration. I might not have had the romantic white dress moment, but I had never felt happier in my life than when we ate barbecued chicken and cherry ice cream while the bees buzzed around my parents' patio flowers. Maybe my dear friend Morgan would find a love like that.

Hang onto it with both hands, I thought, squeezing back an unexpected rush of tears. This would all be so much easier with Rick. Life was so much easier with Rick. Our years together were proof of how richly God had blessed me. With the bitter pain, came the sweet memories. Evelyn and I took our coffee to go and rattled our way back to my property, my nerves doing the rhumba all the way.

FIVE

Sheriff Hayden's squad car was joined by a KBI vehicle. A woman in her fifties leaned on the hood, poking notes into her cell phone. Sheila Waters, red hair threaded with silver, wore a jacket and slacks with her Kansas Bureau of Investigation badge clipped to her belt.

My heart thwacked against my ribs.

"It's good they've brought in the KBI," Evelyn said to reassure me as we climbed out of the car. "Sheila will figure out in no time that you had nothing to do with Rocky's murder."

Sheila nodded at us, but I noticed she was not smiling.

"Ladies, we'll need you to stay back here, behind this yellow tape, until we finish up."

"Did you find anything to prove there was an intruder?" I blurted.

She held up a palm. "Nothing so far, but we've just started, and, well, Hayden's gone and upset the bees."

I almost laughed out loud when I saw the sheriff crouched on my porch with an ice pack pressed to his cheek.

He scowled at me. "I can see why Dickerson wasn't thrilled to have you for a neighbor."

My amusement flipped to irritation. "Bees aren't aggressive unless you threaten them. If you had told me you wanted to disturb the hives, I would have helped you and you wouldn't have gotten stung. So don't blame the bees."

"I wasn't disturbing anything, just walking along taking pictures." Now I could see the swollen stings on his face too. I scanned the property. Odd. If Hayden really had been only walking and taking pictures, the bees shouldn't have attacked him.

I looked closer at my tidy hives, neatly spaced out near the trees that sheltered them from the wind and harsh sunlight. A cloud of bees zinged around hive number two, which Rick had dubbed Honey Hideaway. He'd given all the hives silly names.

The other hives were quiet, with only a few bees launching from the hives to start their work. "The bees in that hive are irritated," I said, pointing to Honey Hideaway.

"So am I," Hayden said.

Sheila eyed me. "Can you help us get a better look at that hive? Suit us up or whatever?"

"I can, but I'll have to go with you if you want to touch it at all."

Hayden waved a hand. "You go ahead, Waters. I'll stay here and make some phone calls."

Sheila shot him a look that said, *"Coward."* I handed Ju Ju over to Evelyn.

"Are you sure you should be doing this?" she whispered. "Isn't it kind of like helping them tie a knot in your noose?"

I gulped. "There's something wrong with my bees, and I need to find out what it is. Maybe it will clear up this mess in short order."

Or maybe I was about to give the police more evidence that I'd concocted the whole intruder story to cover up a murder.

Teeth gritted, I marched to my tidy shed with the KBI agent trailing right behind me.

Sheila looked a bit unsettled as I handed her the bee suit and netted hat.

"Do these things really help?"

"Absolutely, and I just laundered them, so the bees won't detect the smell of any previous stings."

Her eyebrows went up. "Bees can smell?"

"Not exactly like we do, but they can detect pheromones, especially the 'alarm' pheromone they give off when they sting. If they get wind of that scent, they spread the word, and you've got yourself a problem."

She paled a bit. "Ah. I was hoping they'd be asleep or something."

"Not likely. It's our peak time of year. Bees

and beekeepers are busiest in the spring. The queen is a machine this time of year, laying more and more eggs. Drones reappear and the hive is really hopping. Nectar and pollen are coming into the hive thick and fast, so there's no rest for any of us, insects or humans."

I'd already done my spring inspection and was pleased to note that the colonies had weathered the winter just fine. Each hive had its queen safely enthroned and they had enough honey for feeding. Sugar syrup laced with fumigilin to prevent the Nosema parasites had been offered and accepted a few weeks earlier, so the hives were brimming with healthy bees. The top and bottom deep hive drawers in each Langstrom structure had been reversed, ready for a new season, and my little critters were busy at work, collecting nectar from the nearby apple blossoms. I could not help the swell of pride that surged through me.

"I don't really like insects," Sheila said, donning the white suit. I assisted her with her hat and netting before I pulled on my own.

"Well you should like bees," I said. "They're the reason we can grow anything on this planet. What's more, they are the only insect that manufactures a food that we eat." That fact completely dazzled me. God's little bee creations were breathtaking in so many ways.

However, Sheila did not look the least bit impressed.

I was used to the irrational fear and general ignorance. I'd started out that way myself, and it was now my self-proclaimed mission to teach people that bees were one of the earth's biggest assets. I launched in on the incredible abilities of my buzzing friends, the same talk I gave to school groups that visit my apiary, but she stopped me with a raised finger.

"Do you mind if we skip the lesson and get on with this?"

Trying not to be insulted, I zipped up my suit and grabbed the smoker.

"Smoke will mask the alarm pheromones," I couldn't help adding. "Interrupts their defense response."

I took a moment to light my smoker by cramming in some newspaper and wood shavings that Herb at the carpentry shop supplied me with, and set it aflame. A few pumps of the bellows had the smoke percolating nicely.

"Lead on, Ms. Parson."

Sheila held a camera in one gloved hand as we made our way around the hives. My bees were busily doing their thing, the field bees scooting out from the brood box and scuttling back and forth, bringing the precious nectar they'd collected back to the honey super. I'd just completed a harvest of several of the hives, so my work shed was crammed with newly filled bottles of honey, and the bees were back at it, feverishly working on filling the newly emptied super with more golden treasure. I had a feeling I was going to have to order more of the glass jars to hold the loot. Bees have an amazing work ethic.

Sheila's eyes were on the ground, looking for some sign of the intruder I'd heard. I scanned as well, but saw nothing other than the graveled paths, with green grass poking through here and there, and the clumps of flowering mustard that dotted my fields.

The Honey Hideaway still caught my attention, the bees appearing agitated. I strode over and applied gentle puffs from the smoker.

"Are you going to open it?" Sheila asked, her voice high.

"The outer cover isn't closed properly."

"But . . . isn't that going to make them mad?"

"That's what the smoke is for." I puffed the bellows, sending wafts around the hives. Sheila took a step back as I opened the outer and inner covers. My instincts were buzzing louder than the bees. The covers weren't on properly, and there was no way the wind or a raccoon had unsettled them and slapped them back on in such a haphazard fashion.

"Did you leave it all cockeyed like that?" Sheila asked.

I didn't dignify that with an answer. The bees were bumbling about. They'd already made good progress in starting to refill the cells with their precious sweet elixir.

I blinked and peered closer through the netting. My interest fueled Sheila's courage as she pressed close to look over my shoulder.

"What's that brown stuff?"

I swallowed, eyeing a weird ten-inch blob. "It's propolis."

"What's it for?"

"It's an incredibly sticky glue the bees make. They use it to seal cracks," I managed. "It's antibacterial."

"Uh huh."

"And sometimes . . ." I gulped. "Well, they can use it to seal something off that might harm the colony."

"Like?"

"Um, well, one time, uh, um, my husband's glasses fell off and he didn't notice. The next morning the bees had completely covered it over with propolis. They'll encase anything that could be a threat to the hive."

"I see."

We both stared at the object, perfectly silhouetted and unmistakable, mummified in the sticky, green-brown bee glue.

"So what you're saying is, the bees covered that object to protect the hive from contamination?"

The words dried in my throat. "Yes," I

whispered.

Sheila turned a calculating expression on me. "I guess the question is, who put a gun in your beehive, Ms. Parsons?"

SIX

No matter how much I talked, I simply could not explain how a gun had come to rest inside Honey Hideaway.

"It had to be the intruder," I insisted. "Whoever it was dumped the gun there when they ran away from Rocky's place."

Sheriff Hayden attempted a smile, but his cheek was too swollen. "So someone murders Rocky Dickerson, walks a mile to your property, drops a gun in your beehive, and makes a clean escape without being seen by anyone."

"Yes," I said, chin up. "I think that's exactly what happened."

"Right, well, as soon as we get the gun cleaned up and checked for prints, we'll know more."

"You won't find my prints on it, that's for sure."

Hayden looked down his nose at me. "That doesn't preclude you from having worn gloves."

I rolled my eyes and so did Evelyn. "This is

ridiculous."

Sheila finally made it back to the car with the entombed gun in a gummed-up evidence bag. Her bee suit was smeared with the stuff and, though she'd kept the hat on until a few moments before, she'd gotten a glob of the propolis in her hair and on the back of her hand.

"Man, this stuff's sticky," she said, trying to detach her fingers from the bag.

"Unbelievably so," I said automatically. "Rubbing alcohol will get it off, mostly, but it pretty much ruins clothing."

"The guys at the tech lab are going to have a good laugh over this one," Hayden said. "I'll be in touch, Ms. Parsons. In the meantime, don't make any sudden plans to leave town."

He drove off followed by Sheila Waters after she stripped off her bee suit.

My mouth was dry, my muscles tense. A gun, no doubt the gun that had killed Rocky Dickerson, had been lying right there in my beehive all night. Panic gnawed at my stomach.

"Evelyn," I said. "What am I going to do?"

She blew out a breath. "You're coming back to the Coffee Perk with me, and we're going to fill in the girls like we planned."

"But what can they do?"

"Never underestimate the power of a caffeinated woman," Evelyn said. I tried to hold

169

on to her positive attitude as we drove into town and parked outside the Perk.

After we settled Ju Ju on the dog bed in a lovely spot of sunshine by the front door, we joined the ladies. The women were indeed fully caffeinated, judging from the mugs in their hands. Morgan ushered us right over to a table tucked into a quiet corner. Since it was late morning, there was a lull in the coffee-seeking throngs. I settled in next to Jeanine Gransbury, who smelled comfortingly of scones.

I sniffed her sleeve. "Lemon scones today?"

"Apricot and white chocolate. I'm experimenting on a new flavor for the Spring Fling." She opened a treat-filled bag and we all dived in except Harper Daggett, who was extracting something from her purse. Since Harper was a first-grade teacher, her purse was always crammed with everything from extra socks to stickers, from granola bars to safety pins. If you ever got lost in the wilderness, Harper was the person you wanted standing beside you.

"Here's what I know so far," she said in low tones, reading from her tiny notebook. "I've been conducting interviews when I'm not helping organize the rummage sale stuff for the Spring Fling."

"Interviewing whom?" Evelyn said around a bite of scone. I noticed she'd sequestered another in her tote bag for later. I would keep her secret. All's fair in love and scones.

"Betty, of course."

"Ah," everyone said at once. Betty, the postmistress of the tiny Oak Grove post office, was the clearinghouse for the local news. It was positively mystifying how she collected gossip and information. If there was anything to be gleaned about Rocky Dickerson and his enemies, it would be from Betty.

I scooted to the edge of my chair. "What did she say?"

Harper cupped the mug of coffee in her hands. "She said Rocky's twin brother, Charles, was here in town a couple of weeks ago."

"Ralph told me he was here last winter, but I didn't know about the recent trip."

"It wasn't common knowledge, according to Betty. She couldn't be specific about the exact date, but she said the visit didn't go well and he left abruptly."

Hmmm. Perhaps twin brother Charles was an avenue to be explored.

"And," Harper said, eyebrows arched for the coup de grace, "while he was here, he visited Lola Collins on a number of occasions. He was even spotted having dinner with her at the Lobster House in Vicksville. A candlelit dinner, complete with a shared flourless chocolate torte for dessert."

I let that settle in my mind. Lola Collins ran an antiques appraisal business, and she was also known for being especially charming with her male clients. She was the closest Oak Grove came to having a town bombshell.

"Charles and Lola," I murmured. "I guess that gives me a place to start."

"And we'll poke around on our end," Harper said. "Rocky was a frequent flyer at the library, and you can tell boatloads about a person from their search history."

"Can you get your hands on that?" Evelyn said.

Harper offered an elaborate wink. "I have my ways."

We parted with hugs all around.

As I gathered Ju Ju and stepped outside into the June sunshine, I spotted Lola a couple of doors down, festooning her shop window with a tissue-paper garland and a hand-lettered sign.

THE TREASURE TROVE
COME VISIT DURING THE SPRING FLING
YOUR TRASH MAY BE TREASURE!

I thought about the papers and belongings flung all over Rocky's living room. Whoever had killed him was looking for some kind of treasure.

Perhaps Lola could point me to some answers.

I left Evelyn, who headed to the hardware store to purchase more twine for her herb bundles. Ju Ju and I approached Lola's store.

Lola brushed back a section of her long blonde hair and fired a lipsticked smile at me that faltered for a moment like a light bulb flickering on and off. "Hi, Penny. Do you, uh, I mean, I heard you found Rocky."

News traveled at the speed of light in Oak Grove. "Yes." I cuddled Ju Ju closer and wrestled up my courage. Normally, I was not the prying type, content, like my worker bees, to focus on my own business, but with Sheriff Hayden convinced I was a murderer, it was time to put on my big girl pants.

"I heard you know his brother, Charles."

She blinked and wandered inside her shop. I followed. I'd never actually been inside. I expected some kind of a museum archive, stuffed with dusty relics, but the interior was chic, housing a tidy mahogany desk, two leather chairs, recessed lighting, and a tasteful area rug.

"Yes, I know Charles. I met him when he came to visit Rocky a few weeks ago."

"He visited your shop?"

She smoothed the silk tunic over her dark slacks. "Yes."

I waited a few beats. "Why?"

"Why does anyone visit an antiques appraiser?" I thought her laugh was a tad on the nervous side.

"What did he want appraised?"

She cocked her head. "That seems like private information, Penny."

"Normally, I wouldn't pry, but the police think . . ." My face went hot. "I mean, I'm just trying to figure out what happened to Rocky."

A man stepped through the open door into the shop, his face so like Rocky's my arms tightened and Ju Ju let out a yip.

"And you think I might have killed him?"

SEVEN

My mouth went dry as I looked at Charles Dickerson. The man I'd practically just accused of murder was tall and lanky like his brother, but a good deal handsomer with black hair nicely cut, blue eyes, and a dimple on one side of his smile. "Well, no, but I . . . I mean . . . well . . ." *Smooth detective work, Parson.* "I–I'm very sorry about your brother."

He raised a hand and smiled. "Thank you. We weren't close, but it's a shock. And never mind about insinuating I had something to do with his death. I suppose it's natural to suspect the next of kin, but I can assure you, I didn't kill him." He arched an eyebrow at me. "You don't look like much of a killer either. I heard the police were questioning you."

Questioning? I cringed, wondering what he'd think when it became public knowledge that the killer's gun was found in my very own beehive number two. "I discovered your brother's body."

He nodded. "The killer was probably some random maniac. My brother was careless, absentminded. During my last visit I cautioned him about leaving his doors unlocked, but Rocky never listened to anyone except our father. Pops died of a stroke when we were twelve. Rocky got his musical talent from Pops and Grandpa. I admit I was always a tad jealous about the connection they had." He winked at me. "Jealous, but not in a murderous way, just your run-of-the-mill sibling rivalry."

I returned his smile.

"Rocky always griped that he would've been some sort of musical prodigy if he'd gotten his big break. Instead he taught lessons in his dusty crypt of a house and collected as much musical junk as he could, just like our grandpa. That's why I'm back. Took a few weeks off to clear out the house before it's sold. It's the last thing I can do for my brother now."

So he was passing himself off as the loving brother now? Cleaning out the house as an act of good will? Yeah, right, and I was the queen of England.

I saw Lola's gaze flick quickly to Charles and then away. "He's going to donate most of it to the Spring Fling rummage sale," Lola said quickly. "That's why he's here. So we can sort through the items and price them."

"What kind of things?"

Charles sighed. "Old instruments of all kinds. Boxes upon boxes of sheet music. Dusty books that no one on earth would want to read except my brother. Most of it best suited for the incinerator." He shrugged. "It's the proverbial dirty job that somebody's gotta do. Rocky had already started boxing up some things to donate to the sale, I understand. I guess even he could see that his house was turning into a self-storage locker."

Ju Ju wriggled to be put down. "I'd better get going and let you get to your work."

Charles nodded. "Nice to have met you, Ms. Parson."

He gallantly pushed the door wide for me and Ju Ju.

"It was great talking to you, Ms. Parson, and I'm sorry that you had to get involved in my brother's mess. I guess we're sort of neighbors, at least for a while."

"Call me Penny." I cleared the door and let Ju Ju down. She scampered up to Charles and sniffed his shoe. When he bent to pet her, she backed away and returned to me. Ju Ju loves all people but new males require some extra vigilance. She fixed me with those brown eyes and shook her wiry little body as if to send me a message. *Have courage.* Courage was something I thought I'd possessed until my husband died. Now, it was all I could do some days to force my body out of bed. If it weren't for Ju Ju, my Bible, and my bees, I would probably cower under the covers on a daily basis. Ju Ju poked her nose into my calf.

All right. Courage. "So, er, why were you here before, Mr. Dickerson, if you don't mind my asking?"

"Please, call me Charles," he said. "Before? In Oak Grove?" He frowned. "I visited briefly in the winter."

"No, I mean, you came to the Treasure Trove a couple weeks ago." *And you and Lola enjoyed a romantic dinner.* "What brought you to the store?"

Something flickered in his eyes before he shut it away, all smooth confidence behind an easygoing smile. "Oh, no mystery there. I'm a real estate guy. I own an office in Clarksville and another in Plains, about fifty miles from here. I was thinking about expanding to Oak Grove and I thought I'd talk to some of the locals." He grinned at Lola and gave her a mischievous wink. "I always look for the pretty ones first. That's why I came back today too. This lovely appraiser and I are heading out for lunch. Ready to go, Lola?"

Lola looked at her black pumps and then shot a side-eyed look at him. "Yes. Sure."

Lies. I might be an inept detective, but my instincts were shouting loud and clear.

Charles Dickerson was lying. Maybe Lola was too.

As I waved and walked toward the hardware store to meet Evelyn, my nerves were buzzing louder than my bees.

Why had Rocky's brother really sought out Lola Collins?

I felt him watching me as I walked away, wondering how I'd managed to land in the middle of such a sticky mess.

Beehives take a great deal of care, murder or no murder, and I needed to return to my property and see to my afternoon chores. Since Evelyn was still busy in the hardware store, probably collecting the current gossip along with the twine, I sent her a text, took a shortcut through town, and headed home with Ju Ju. The full-on sunshine thrilled us both, and we stopped for sniffing on her part and soaking in a sky of pure sapphire on mine.

We passed Mrs. Milkburn, who always reminded me of my aunt Martha, my mother's sister, with her puff of white hair and vibrant green eyes. She was in her front yard hosing down a card table. We exchanged a greeting.

"They need my table for the rummage sale. I'm going to decorate it real cute with these pink plastic flowers I ordered. They should be here in today's mail, but that no-good Ralph is late delivering the mail again. He's stopped to talk, no doubt. What a gossip."

I edged away. "It certainly is going to be a great Spring Fling," I said. "I'm off to harvest some honey."

"Are you still able to do that with the police on your property?"

Good to know Mrs. Milkburn didn't partake in the gossip she accused Ralph of enjoying, I thought sarcastically. I plastered on a smile. "Why, sure. Why wouldn't I be?"

She lifted a shoulder. "No reason. I just happened to be at the grocery store this morning, and I heard talk that the police found a gun on your property."

I sighed. "I, um, can't talk about that, but it will all be cleared up soon. I'm still making my honey. Don't you worry." I edged farther away.

"Oh, try not to fret, Penny," she said. "No one suspects you. We know it was probably Rocky's brother. I saw him lugging a big black case into his trunk when he was in Oak Grove a few weeks ago. He was in a real hurry to close it up so I couldn't see."

"What kind of case?"

"A musical case. For a violin or viola or something. I bet he was stealing antique instruments from Rocky and things went bad." She shook her head. "What's the world coming to when brother sins against brother?"

In my Bible it had been like that since Cain and Abel, but I didn't see much benefit in contradicting her. "I don't know, Mrs. Milkburn. Sorry, I've got to dash."

The sun warmed my back but did nothing to calm my jittery nerves for the rest of the long walk. So Charles was taking instruments from Rocky's home? That was probably the real reason he'd gone to see Lola — for an appraisal of a stolen instrument. He'd probably had to sneak it out of Rocky's house. How much would a valuable violin be worth, anyway? It was time to do some cybersleuthing.

As I hurried onto my property, the needs of my business trumped my detective urges. The plentiful spring apple blossoms and wildflowers had provided my bees with sweet nectar for abundant honey making, and hive number three was filled to bursting. I donned my beekeeping suit and grabbed the smoker, putting the drama of the past twelve hours behind me. I pulled the honey-laden frames from the hive and carefully brushed off the milling bees. Back in my workshop, I sliced off the wax comb caps with a heated knife and set the frames in the spinner, which would whirl away the honey from the wax using centrifugal force. Then it was into the sieve for straining before the liquid gold went into the little glass jars with our Parson's Honey label, complete with an embossed bee.

As always when I surveyed the boxes filled with our quality honey, I felt a terrible ache in my heart that Rick wasn't there to see the fruits of all his hard work. How many nights had we lain side by side brainstorming solutions to our various problems: absconding, chilled brood, and the dreaded robbing of our hives? They had all seemed like enormous problems at the time, but thanks to Rick's resourcefulness and undying optimism, we'd overcome every one.

Until he was gone and I was left behind to carry on alone.

I didn't feel at all optimistic at the moment, in spite of my tidy jars of honey. I knew my fingerprints would not be on the gun they'd found, but that didn't mean I was in the clear. Tongues were wagging all over Oak Grove, and I had a feeling they'd continue to do so until Rocky's killer was caught.

No, I thought, heaving out a sigh that sent Ju Ju scurrying to my side to check on me. Rick would have wanted me to go forward boldly and do whatever I had to in order to clear my name. He'd always said all we need is faith and fortitude.

Encouraged, I dug out my newly charged cell phone and did some quick research.

The answer came quickly. Violins, it seemed, could be treasures in their own right. A rare instrument made by Antonio Stradivari in the 1700s had recently been auctioned for . . . I almost dropped the phone. "For sixteen million dollars," I said aloud. Sixteen million dollars was plenty of motive.

Had Charles found such a treasure in Rocky's house?

And had he killed to take it for himself?

EIGHT

It was not until the next afternoon that I got the flat tire on the truck fixed, grateful that my grease monkey of a dad taught his only daughter how to take care of her vehicles. I knew more about cars and engines than Rick had, and I'd not been above teasing him about it.

"It's okay, Rick. I'll take care of the vehicle maintenance."

"Awww, that's why I married you, Pen. You've got more talent than Juilliard."

The memory made me smile and tear up at the same time.

As I was wiping the grease from my palms, a KBI police car pulled up. I swallowed down a gush of panic as Sheila Waters stepped out.

"Hello, Penny."

"Hi," I squeaked, while Ju Ju pranced over for an ear rub. I had not yet explained to her that the police were not exactly our bosom buddies at this point, but Ju Ju never met a stranger, so it would have been pointless anyway.

"I wanted to come by and give you an update."

My own breathing sounded loud in my ears. "Yes?"

"Once the tech guys finally managed to get that goo off the gun, they confirmed it is a nine-millimeter Smith and Wesson, the same one used to kill Rocky."

"Oh."

"And there are no prints on it at all."

I wasn't sure whether to be relieved or disappointed. No prints meant they couldn't identify the real killer, at least not that way, and it sure didn't deflect suspicion from me.

"I see."

"And no sign of forced entry to Rocky's home, but that's not surprising, since the brother says Rocky never locked his doors."

"Dead ends," I sighed. "Where does the investigation go from here?"

She shifted, smoothing her already smooth blazer. "We're following some leads."

"May I ask if any of them involve me?"

"Now that you mention it, I spoke to John Lemmon, the lawyer recently hired by Rocky, regarding your land dispute."

"Oh." The twinge in my stomach told me there was another body blow coming. "And?"

She looked apologetic. "Seems the lawyer felt there was enough of a case to go forward with a lawsuit against you. Lemmon believes the land deed is nebulous enough that Rocky could have claim to the acreage on the east side of your property."

I groaned.

"And the lawyer also said he spoke to your husband about it, and Rick said something to the effect that you two would do whatever you had to in order to keep the land."

My eyes went wide. "Well he didn't mean murder, for goodness' sake."

She nodded. "Listen, I'm just telling you what I've heard. Of course, we'll continue to investigate. I hate to ask, but we are going to need to search your trailer and workshop."

"For what?" I demanded.

"Just routine."

I tried to breathe down the anger that burned inside. Insinuating we'd made threats against Rocky? Now they wanted to paw through my home? "You'll need a warrant to do that," I heard myself say.

With an apologetic shrug, she held up a document. "Got one right here."

It felt like a nail hammering into my coffin. Not that they would find anything, but it was unsettling, knowing they would pry into all the corners and root through all the belongings, my whole life, without my husband there to console or defend me. It was a violation, pure and simple. "Okay," I managed. "I'll show you around."

"I'm sorry, Penny, but I can't have you on the premises while I'm conducting the search."

Barred from my own home? I had done nothing, and now I was being treated like a criminal. It was more than I could bear. With all the dignity I could muster, I swooped up my dog. Ju Ju licked my chin. "Well then," I said fighting tears, "I guess you can start pawing through our personal business. I'm going to take my dog for a drive."

"I'll be careful not to disturb anything," Sheila said, a bit sympathetically, I thought.

I responded by slamming the car door and holding back tears as I rattled off my own property, leaving the police to turn what was left of my life upside down.

I drove. My gut whispered to me to head right out of Oak Grove and drive until my heart stopped thumping like a bass drum, but I found myself pulling to a stop where it had all fallen apart, across the road from Rocky Dickerson's house. His property was set under a thicket of oak trees. The nearest neighboring house was only just visible across a broad swath of grass, behind a thicket of unkempt elderberry bushes.

Ju Ju whined in that way that meant, "I need to go. Now."

I carried her over to the wide scalp of grass surrounding Rocky's house. I figured he wouldn't be able to complain about me anymore, so Ju Ju's reconnoitering would go unnoticed. Ju Ju finished her sprinkling and hopped off in pursuit of a swallowtail butterfly.

There were no vehicles belonging to the police or Charles Dickerson outside Rocky's place. The big old house was silent and still. A stack of flattened cardboard boxes stood ready on the porch, presumably for Charles to continue boxing up the donations for the rummage sale. I wondered what Rocky had decided should be donated. He and his brother would probably have disagreed strongly on what was junk and what wasn't. One man's trash and all that.

Something caught my eye — movement. I jerked my head toward the scrap of white lace that covered the tiny attic window. It was still.

Had I imagined it?

Ju Ju chased the butterfly closer to the house and I followed, listening, scanning. No movement. No sound but the breeze in the oak leaves and the occasional clatter of a squirrel chasing his buddy around the scarred trunks.

Thunk.

I straightened. I had not imagined the sound, a hollow thump, but my senses could not believe the place from which it had emanated.

The sound had come from Rocky Dickerson's attic.

Okay, I told myself. Don't go all to pieces. Charles probably had car trouble and he got a ride over here from Lola. He was probably busily packing things up in the attic so he could get out of Oak Grove.

"Ju Ju," I called, as she pawed at the bottom of the tree where the squirrels were frolicking. "Come here. I don't know why I drove us here anyway. Let's go."

The sound came again, low and soft from the attic.

Ju Ju barked at the squirrel, and the sound stopped.

My phone trilled in my pocket. I answered in hushed tones.

"Guess what?" Harper's breathy voice filled the line.

"What?"

"I happened to stumble on a little drama here. Charles came to the library this morning asking about the donation items his late brother delivered for the rummage sale."

"Really?"

"Really. Louise told him they were stored in the church basement and that they'd been donated fair and square and she didn't think he ought to be digging through them."

"Really?"

"Really. And he got a bit huffy and said he thought Rocky had put an item in there by mistake and he was jolly well going to get a look."

Another violin, like the one Mrs. Milkburn had mentioned? "Really?"

"Would you quit saying that?" Harper huffed. "Yes, and off he went to the church. I'd love to follow him, but I've got to prep the kids' activities for the fun zone."

"Wait, where are you now?"

"Right where I told you. I'm getting in my car to drive back home and get my supplies. I've got three hundred sheets of origami paper to be sorted to make the hopping frogs."

"So you mean Charles just left the library, like right now?"

"Yeah, like two minutes ago. Listen, I've gotta go. Talk to you soon."

I disconnected, staring up at the Dickerson house.

If Charles was currently storming over to the church . . .

My gaze wandered up to the scrap of lace curtain.

Then who, exactly, was prowling around in Rocky's attic?

NINE

I should phone the police.

The thought banged around my mind for a good thirty seconds before I discarded it. Sheila was currently tearing my trailer apart, and Sheriff Hayden would be more trouble than he was help. Besides, there was probably a perfectly simple explanation for the prowler in Rocky's attic. Maybe Charles had asked Lola to come over and peruse the rest of Rocky's belongings while he stayed to look through the rummage sale boxes. Or maybe Rocky had a housekeeper that I didn't know about, or he'd hired a local kid to assist with the house packing.

It was time to put on my detective hat and at least try to solve the puzzle without getting myself into more trouble. There was no way I was going back in Rocky's house, invited or not (see earlier rule about "too dumb to be believed" moments), but there was no law that said I couldn't meander around the rear of the property. If it was somebody up to no good, they would probably sneak in and out through the back door. Since there was no fencing, I could easily pass for an innocent woman out taking her dog for a walk if someone emerged from the house to question me. Phone in hand, ready to dial Evelyn if anything strange occurred, I strolled as casually as I could manage past the brick side of the old place then past the overgrown elderberry shrubs, which Ju Ju nosed every few feet.

I'd just about made it to the corner when my phone rang. I'd forgotten to put it on silent. Nancy Drew would never have made such an error. To make matters ever so much worse, the ringer scared me so badly I dropped the phone. Flailing, I finally scooped it up along with some dried leaves and a chewed pine cone.

"Yes?" I half-whispered.

"What's the matter?" Evelyn demanded. "You sound funny. Where are you?"

"I was out driving and I landed at Rocky Dickerson's house. There's someone in the attic, and it's not his brother."

"Well, what do you think you're doing skulking around there? Get back in your truck this minute and call the police."

Ju Ju stiffened, the hairs on the back of her neck bristling.

My stomach squeezed. "Evelyn, I think someone is coming."

"Get out of there, Penny," she all but shouted.

"I will. Right now." I shoved the cell phone in my pocket.

"Come on, Ju Ju," I stage whispered.

But Ju Ju had another idea. She exploded into action, running flat-out like a heat-seeking missile, around the corner to the back.

"Ju . . ." I managed before I caught my foot on an exposed sugar maple root. I hit the ground with such force the breath was knocked out of me. A mop of hair covered my eyes and I pawed it away, sucking in oxygen to refill my lungs.

Heart thundering, I scrambled to my feet, elbow stinging, and scurried around the corner. Probably not the smartest move if there was a murderer lurking but, killer or no killer, I wasn't leaving my Ju Ju alone in the woods. Was there someone waiting just around the corner with a gun? A brick? Even a good-sized library book would be enough to take me out in my present state.

Another piercing bark marshaled my courage.

I'm coming, Ju Ju.

I did a quick dodge around the corner of the brick wall. I emerged onto the overgrown lot, crowded with flowering shrubs that my bees would have waggled their behinds about. No sign of my lionhearted pipsqueak of a dog. The glass patio doors were closed, no indication of movement anywhere. I pressed on until I noticed the root cellar at my feet. One of the warped doors was not quite secure, and I could feel the faintest gush of cold air emanating from below. Surely Lola or the housekeeper would not have entered the house through the root cellar. It was time to collect my dog and get out of Dodge.

Ju Ju's barking was still shrill and excited, but now it sounded farther away from somewhere in the screen of leaves. I called to her again, louder this time.

Another bark and the sound of a body thrashing through the woods, moving at a good clip, made my skin prickle. Ju Ju must have taken off into the woods after the intruder.

"Ju Ju," I yelled again. What if the prowler injured my little baby? My sweet girl, my best friend? I lurched forward in a panic. "Ju —"

And then suddenly she popped back through the wall of bushes, tail wagging and something clasped between her teeth.

I didn't wait to investigate. Relief swirled through me along with the fear, and I tucked her under my arm like a quarterback toting a football. I ran back to my truck, hopped in, and locked the doors. I gunned the engine. Lead-footed and Nascar worthy, I drove in crazy fashion until I was halfway home and my phone rang. I pulled to the shoulder, the engine still running, and answered.

Evelyn's voice was high and strained. "Are you dead? Are you murdered? Speak to me."

After I assured her that I was not in the process of dying, I told her what had happened.

She blew out a breath. "I got hold of Deputy Davis and he's coming to Rocky's house."

"Whoever it was will be long gone," I said, stroking Ju Ju's heaving side as she flopped on the passenger seat.

"Never mind that," she said. "I am going to meet you at your place in fifteen minutes and give you some information and a severe tongue-lashing about your foolish, risk-taking behavior."

"That sounds nice," I said with a laugh. "I'll see you there." Since my legs were still shaking a bit, I sat there for a minute, listening to my dog panting and gumming something at the same time. I suddenly remembered that Ju Ju hadn't gotten away empty-handed . . . er . . . empty-jawed.

Gingerly, I plucked the torn material from between Ju Ju's teeth. She rolled an eye at me but did not protest.

It was a torn bit of fabric, heavyweight but not exactly denim. Its color had probably been dark blue before so many washings.

"Looks like you found yourself a clue," I told her, wrapping the bit of cloth in a tissue.

"You've earned a piece of cheese for a reward."

She smiled in that doggie way of hers and closed her eyes to finish her snooze.

Sheila was loading my computer into her trunk when I arrived.

"Hey, what are you doing? I need that for my honey orders."

"You'll get it back," she said, eyeing me. "I got a call that I'm to head to Rocky Dickerson's and meet Deputy Davis."

"Well, if you're finished tearing my house apart," I snapped. Not her fault, I knew, but my self-control was fraying around the edges. I thrust the wadded-up tissue at her.

She examined it. "Is my nose running?"

"No. It's a scrap of cloth from an intruder at Rocky's place. My dog obtained it," I said stiffly.

Sheila grilled me for the particulars, scribbling notes on a small pad. When she was finished, I raised my chin. "Now, if you'll excuse me, I have a business to try and run, and since I'll be writing up orders on clay tablets and sending smoke signals to my customers, I'd better get started."

She laughed. "Okay. I'm sorry to cause you trouble. You have a good sense of humor, Ms. Parson. Hang on to it."

As she drove away, I considered. Rick always said no one could make him laugh like I did. I tried to recall some of the times I'd cracked him up. When I attempted to learn to hula hoop, when I lost my car keys in a vat of honey, the funny-face pancakes I'd made for his birthday.

"Oh Rick," I murmured. "It's so hard to laugh without you."

But Rick would have seen the humor in Ju Ju's detective work and maybe even in our bees packaging up the murder weapon. I said a silent prayer to thank God for the memories He'd given me, sweet memories of Rick that would help me through the quiet, lonely days without him.

"But Lord," I added, "if You could lend me a few sleuthing skills to help me solve this mystery, I'd sure appreciate that too."

TEN

Evelyn arrived with reinforcements and refreshments around dinnertime. "Here," she said, toting a thermos. "Morgan sent coffee and hugs. I told the girls about your latest adventure."

Jeanine uncovered a tray of lasagna. "And I brought the carbohydrates."

"And I'm here to supply some juicy gossip," Harper said with a mischievous twinkle in her eye. She brushed back her curly hair and settled into a chair at my kitchen table, eyeing the premises. "Doesn't seem like the cops messed it up too much."

"No," I admitted. "Sheila was careful." She hadn't even displaced my mama's antique salt and pepper shakers on the table, salt in the little porcelain hive and pepper in the cheerful bee. "So what's the gossip?" I put out paper plates and napkins and handed Ju Ju the promised bit of smoked Gouda. She scurried away to tongue-swab it thoroughly before she gulped it down. That animal is passionately devoted to cheese.

"Well," Harper said around a bite of sumptuous noodles and marinara, "Rocky's grandfather was a collector of music memorabilia."

"What kind of music memorabilia?" Evelyn said.

"All kinds. Instruments, concert posters, records, etcetera. He was a musical pack rat."

"That explains the boxes of stuff Rocky was packing up for the rummage sale." Jeanine poured herself some coffee. "Charles was still over there pawing through the junk when I put in the last batch of scones to bake. Louise came over from the library on her afternoon break for a cookie fix."

I smiled. Louise Applewhite, the librarian, was a devotee of fitness, but her sweet tooth would not be denied. Hence, she was a frequent visitor at the Mad Batter, Jeanine's bakery. Currently she was in charge of donations for the rummage sale and thus they were well organized and efficiently done.

"Louise told me she wanted to lock up the church basement after she closed up the library, but Charles was there looking through his brother's boxes. He's getting on her nerves. All style and polish on the outside, but something different underneath, she said."

I thought about those treasured Stradivarius violins I'd researched. "So maybe there's some sort of priceless instrument lying around that house? Something Rocky was killed for?"

Harper frowned. "Maybe, maybe not. Unfortunately, when Rocky's granddad fell on hard times, most of it was sold."

I wrapped my fingers around the hot mug. "That must be why he sold part of his land too."

"Makes sense," Jeanine said.

Evelyn drummed her fingers on the table. "But maybe Charles has hope that the treasure is still hidden there in the house or in the boxes for the rummage sale. He must have gotten an idea like that when he last visited Rocky."

"But there's still the problem of who was in the attic," I mused. "It wasn't Charles. He was in town at the time."

"Could have been Lola," Jeanine put in.

I surprised myself with my own statement. "That's my next lead."

Harper raised an eyebrow. "Your next lead?"

I nodded, the idea crystallizing in my mind. "I'm going to talk to Lola and see what she has to say. We're both scheduled to set up tables and chairs tomorrow morning for the Spring Fling."

"Well I'm going with you," Evelyn said. "You get into plenty of trouble when I'm not around."

I didn't argue. I was secretly relieved to have her watching my back. The idea of fetching chairs from the creepy church basement didn't thrill me either.

The knock at the door startled us all. I opened it to allow in a nervous-looking Deputy Cameron Davis. At the arrival of this young, good-looking man in uniform, the gals all sat up a bit straighter, I noticed. Harper smoothed her hair.

Davis swiped off his hat. "Good afternoon, ladies," he said. He glanced at all of us, but I thought his gaze lingered for a moment longer on Harper. Interesting.

"I just uh, well, we just finished the sweep of Dickerson's house and the woods behind. We found nothing except that the root cellar was open like you said, Ms. Parsons."

Finally. Maybe the police actually believed me this time. "So someone got in via the root cellar to search the house. Any idea who? Clues from the scrap Ju Ju collected?"

"Um, no, ma'am. Not yet. We sent —"

"It to the lab for testing," I finished, suppressing a groan. "Right. And now we wait for results. I'm getting good at this."

He chuckled. "Police work is a lot of hurry up and wait."

"Did you happen to see Lola in town, Officer Davis, a few hours ago, when Penny was at Rocky's place?" Harper said, twirling a strand of hair around her finger. "We were thinking maybe she's in on whatever's going on."

"No, ma'am, but I was busy helping secure Blevins, so I was preoccupied."

"Why Blevins?" I wondered aloud. That old print shop had been empty for going on a decade. Even the local teens were tired of sneaking into the abandoned structure.

"With this crime wave going around, Sheriff Hayden asked me to check the building, since we have the extra rummage sale donations stored there."

All four of us stared at him. "We do?" Jeanine said. "I thought all the donations were in the church basement."

"Ran out of room. Pastor Barney said last week he needed the space to store the canned donations for the food drive, so we moved a bunch of the stuff over to Blevins."

"What kind of stuff?" I asked.

He shrugged. "Boxes. Some heavy, some not. I didn't look inside."

"Were they labeled?"

"A few, but like I said, I was more concerned about the security situation."

Harper smiled at him. "Say, Deputy . . ."

"Yes, ma'am?"

"Would you mind letting me in to take a peek at those boxes tomorrow morning? I'm helping Louise organize the rummage sale, so I should sort them before the sale starts. I promise I won't take anything."

He nodded. "Sure thing. How about we meet there at seven a.m.?"

"All right." Harper nodded at him, and he bid us good night and left.

"Well, well," Jeanine said. "Looks like Harper has a date."

Harper shot her a sour look. "He's just unlocking the door for me."

Jeanine lifted a shoulder. "Who knows? Maybe he's got the key to your heart along with the one to Blevins."

We all laughed at that one. The sound of their mingled chuckles soothed my heart. No matter how much I had lost, I still had these ladies in my life and in my heart. *Thank You, God, for my Coffee Perk sisters.*

ELEVEN

The normally sleepy town of Oak Grove didn't usually kick into high gear until nine-ish, but this Saturday, at the tender hour of six a.m. the day of the Spring Fling, the place was busier than a hive full of worker bees. I waved to Ralph, who was helping to inflate a giant bouncy house on the library lawn presumably before he started on his rounds. Judging by the level of shouting and the billowing plastic, Mrs. Milkburn would once again be complaining that her mail delivery was late.

Ju Ju took one look at the rising frog-shaped inflatable and leapt into my arms. Her occasional spurts of courage did not extend to bouncy houses, apparently. I figured seeing an amphibian a bazillion times its normal size could do that to a small dog. In front of the church, Louise had already begun unfurling a huge white tent that would shelter guests from the sun while they listened to tunes from the Oldtimers Band, featuring two banjos, one snare drum, and, when the cardiologist brass player was not called away on an emergency, a trombone.

I waved across the street to Harper, who was walking with Deputy Davis to Blevins Print Shop now turned rummage sale warehouse. She waved back. They would make a handsome couple, I thought, and again I felt the pang of loss at my own uncoupling.

Evelyn toted a box of her lip balms and lotions. "I'm just going to take this to my booth, okay? Can you stay out of trouble for five minutes?"

I gave her my solemn Girl Scout promise as she walked away. Lola emerged from the church in neat slacks and a soft blue sweater. All of a sudden I felt frumpy in my jeans and oversized T-shirt from which I'd spot-cleaned a sticky splat of honey that very morning. She cooed a bit to Ju Ju, and we made our way into the church and down the steps to the basement. The place was stacked to the rafters with boxes. It was going to take a Herculean effort on the part of the rummage sale committee to get all these items displayed for the sale set to begin in a matter of hours.

"Chairs are beyond that last stack," I said to Lola.

The space was cool, with a damp feel and the strong smell of mildew. I imagined the spiders that might be lurking about in the dark corners. Bees gave me not the slightest

205

qualm, but spiders were a whole different kind of bug. I shivered.

Lola was about to head in the direction I'd pointed when we both froze. There was movement from somewhere behind the boxes. Ju Ju's scruff went up.

"Maybe someone from the rummage sale committee?" I whispered to Lola.

"Pastor Barney said they weren't showing up until seven thirty, after we moved out all the chairs," Lola whispered back.

Round-eyed, we stood like statues. Then came the swell of a man's voice, cussing up a storm. Ju Ju barked and raced around the boxes before I could stop her. The swearing stopped but the barking didn't. We both drew back a bit as Charles stalked around the closest pile of boxes. His mouth opened in an *O* of surprise when he got a look at us.

Immediately he flashed a smile. "Oh, uh, didn't think anyone would be here so early."

"We didn't either," I said, blowing out a breath. "How did you get in?"

He brushed a cobweb from his hair. His jeans were torn at the knee and a smudge of dirt marked his unshaven cheek. "I convinced the janitor to let me in since the librarian is getting tired of me poking around these boxes. I figured I'd be out before the troops arrived for this spring thing."

I noticed Lola had not joined in the conversation, so I kept going. "What are you looking for, Charles?"

He eyed me for a moment as if weighing whether or not to answer. "Whatever it was my brother was so secretive about, he squirreled away somewhere. I've torn the house apart, and there's no sign of anything worth much except some cheap secondhand instruments, so either he was lying or he accidentally boxed up the supposed treasure for donation. He called me in a panic the day before he died, accusing me of breaking in and stealing something while he was away, so I think the dunce lost track of it."

"Did he give you a hint about what it could be?"

"Something of our grandfather's. He uncovered it when he was checking for a leak in the attic. Called me to brag about it a couple of months back."

"An instrument maybe?"

"That was my guess," Charles snapped. "But I know it's worth a mint. Rocky waxed eloquent about how it would keep him in comfort the rest of his life." He smacked his hand on a box hard enough to make Ju Ju jump. "My idiot brother might have stuck my fortune in a rummage sale box."

His fortune?

Charles must have read my look.

"Just because Gramps doted on Rocky and fawned over his so-called musical talent doesn't mean I shouldn't have my share.

Rocky's dead, and whatever Gramps left comes to me. I've checked, and Rocky didn't make a will, so I'm the next in line." His eyes flashed fire, and he pushed by us and up the basement steps, pausing only to throw a comment over his shoulder. "If you find anything in one of Rocky's boxes that looks valuable, call me. That treasure is mine."

His steps were heavy as he trod up the stairs.

After a moment of silence, I turned to my companion. It was time to pull out all the stops. "Lola, how exactly did you get involved with Charles Dickerson? And don't give me the same story Charles did. I know he's not interested in opening a real estate business in Oak Grove."

I thought at first she wouldn't answer. Her brow was furrowed, her lower lip caught between her teeth.

"I inherited my appraisal business from my great uncle. I worked with him, sort of interned, if you will, all through high school and college. He taught me everything about antiques." Lola bent to pick up Ju Ju, absently rubbing my dog's ears. "Uncle Hal kept meticulous records."

My stomach tightened with anticipation.

"He appraised something for Charles and Rocky's grandfather."

"What kind of something?"

She sighed. "That's the mystery. The records were damaged in a fire. I only know whatever it was, was worth close to a million dollars."

I blinked, trying to recall from my economics class exactly how many zeroes were in a million. "What's your guess? Was it a violin? A cello? What?"

"The likeliest answer is it was a small instrument like a violin, since it was little enough to be misplaced. Charles said Rocky called and wrote letters to some appraisers in New York about whatever it was. He kept telling Charles that he had this treasure, sort of lording it over him without giving away any details, until it made Charles crazy. When he came to my shop one day and asked for help, I . . . I shared what I knew from my uncle Hal." She pressed Ju Ju close, a furry security blanket. "It was exciting, you know? To think that I might help uncover a long-missing treasure? Every appraiser's dream come true."

I waited, letting her spool out the story.

"But . . . I mean, I didn't like the way Charles was pressuring Rocky, bullying him almost, into telling about the treasure. Charles would call me up and ask me to spy on Rocky, to go talk to him and try to wheedle information out of him. I . . . I wanted to step away from the situation, but Charles kept strong-arming me."

I surveyed the pile of boxes. "He is deadly determined, all right."

She sighed, ruffling the fur on the top of Ju Ju's head. "It's not here in these boxes, whatever he's looking for."

"How do you know that?"

Her face suffused with color. "I . . . I mean, Rocky wouldn't have been that careless, would he?"

I didn't buy her answer. Her blush told me she'd been pawing through the boxes without Charles's knowledge. "You've already checked them, haven't you? Were you going to tell Charles if you found it?"

She looked me full in the face. "Like I said, it would be an appraiser's dream to find a million-dollar treasure, wouldn't it?"

"Were you looking in Rocky's attic yesterday?"

Her eyes slitted. "No. Why would you ask that?"

I shrugged, noncommittal, while I turned the facts over in my mind. "Rocky was absentminded, flighty, some might say. He could have packed away the treasure unknowingly."

She didn't answer, placing Ju Ju back on terra firma. "Guess we won't know until we find it, if we find it."

I looked her dead in the eye. "Do you think Charles killed his brother?"

"I don't know."

The cold of the basement seeped into my bones as the thought rose unbidden in my mind. *Did you?* "What does your gut say? Is Charles capable of murder?"

"My gut says a million dollars is a pretty good motive for Charles to commit murder." She piled a half-dozen chairs onto a dolly and lugged them to the church's rickety elevator. "We'd better get our job done."

I gathered up another armful of chairs and added them to the dolly.

A million dollars was a decent motive for Charles to kill Rocky.

And it was a plenty good reason for Lola to commit murder too.

TWELVE

Hours later, sweaty and hot, I was grateful to take a break. Evelyn helped arrange the chairs around the long folding tables while Louise unfurled pale green tablecloths decorated with tulips, bees, and clover. The frog bouncy house was fully deployed. Ju Ju gave it a suspicious bark. Pastor Barney tended to the charcoal in a big outdoor grill and started roasting hotdogs, hamburgers, and veggie burgers to go alongside the slices of cherry and peach pies offered by the Farm Aid Society.

The thought of all that delicious food made me hungry so I convinced Evelyn we needed a couple of scoops of banana nut ice cream over at the Double Dipper for a pre-lunch snack. Ice cream had milk and eggs, and that practically counted as an honest meal. We polished ours off in record time (minus the tiny spoonful I saved for Ju Ju). I ordered a strawberry swirl to go for Harper, confirming first that there were no nut ingredients, on account of her allergy.

We headed over to help Harper with the snooping at Blevins's shop. The interior was dark except for the sunlight that streamed in from the front glass windows. We found her near the back counters, frowning at a box into which she aimed her cell phone flashlight.

"Hey," I said, and she jumped.

"You scared me. There's no electricity, so it's plenty creepy in here."

"Sorry, let me make amends with an ice cream offering."

She accepted gratefully, and Ju Ju stuck close by her side in case Harper had the yen to share her last bite. Ju Ju is an equal opportunity freeloader.

Evelyn peered into the box. "What have you found?"

"Plenty, but none of it worth much. There are more boxes in the storage room I haven't even touched yet." She gestured to a yellow ceramic beehive teapot peeking out from its box. "Thought you'd like that, Penny."

"I'd like a priceless violin more."

"The bigger things are in the storage room, but I haven't gotten to that yet." She scooped some half-melted ice cream into her mouth before she continued. "The boxes are all jumbled together, but this one is definitely Rocky's." She gestured to the other items set out on the counter. There was a pile of records, some dusty old books, and a silver triangle complete with dinger. I'm sure there's a technical term for the little stick that hits the triangle, but dinger is the only thing that comes to mind.

"Would it have killed the guy to label the boxes?" Harper's face pinched as she considered what she'd said. "Oh. Uh, that wasn't the greatest choice of words."

Evelyn shuffled through the records. "Top Tunes from 'The Lawrence Welk Show' I don't think that's exactly a million-dollar prize."

"I'm going to check out the storage room." Ju Ju gave up on her ice cream quest and trotted along behind me. I activated my cell phone flashlight to avoid tripping on the uneven floor. The building had probably been erected in the 1940s, and the tiles were warped and cracked. I pushed open the storage room door and mechanically groped for the light switch.

"No . . ." Harper called out.

"Electricity," I finished. "Thanks for reminding me."

There was a small window set high into the wall and a back door that opened to the parking lot.

"It's a mess back here," I said. "I . . ." Without warning, a tower of stacked boxes came crashing down. I screamed as a heavy box slammed into me, knocking me to the floor.

Someone ran for the back door, holding what looked like an instrument case. Springing to my feet, I gave chase. "Stop right there," I shouted, leaping over the fallen boxes. The intruder tossed more boxes down as they went, causing me to leap and twist. Something clattered to the floor and there was a muttered exclamation. I heard the door open. A shaft of daylight blazed through and I had to shield my eyes against the sting as I tumbled over another box. Managing to keep my footing, I pushed ahead, my foot crunching through something on the floor.

I freed my shoe and reached the back door, flinging it open. Stacks of wooden pallets dotted the weedy lot. An ancient pickup truck that probably hadn't run in twenty years perched there on flat tires. As my eyes adjusted, I listened for the sound of movement, shoes on the blacktop, anything over my own raspy breaths. I heard only the small squeak from the far end of the fenced lot. My heart fell. Whoever it was had escaped. Again.

As I trudged back to the storage room exit, my stomach clenched. Ju Ju! She'd been right behind me when the boxes had fallen. I sprinted and nearly ran into Evelyn. Tears blinded me as I saw Ju Ju huddled in her arms, ears down in fear, but in perfect condition.

"Oh baby," I sobbed, swooping her into my arms. "You could have been squashed."

Harper appeared behind Evelyn. "Are you okay? Who was it? Did you get a look?"

"No. It could have been anyone."

She sighed, and we made our way back inside. "What do you think the person was after?"

"Same thing we are."

"A valuable instrument?"

"Yes, and I think he found one. I saw him carrying something like that, but I think he dropped it. Or she — I couldn't tell."

Evelyn stopped so suddenly that I almost plowed into her.

"Ummm," she said, pointing to the floor. "Like that instrument, maybe?"

I looked down. Her cell phone light revealed an open violin case, the instrument lying next to it where it had fallen just before I'd crushed it under my foot.

Deputy Davis arrived with Sheila Waters right on his heels. They shone their Maglites on the broken bits of instrument.

"Someone was in here and found it," Evelyn said. "Penny startled them and they took off out the back door, dropping the instrument, and then —"

"And then I stepped on it," I said mournfully. Even Ju Ju's affirming nose-pokes to my shin did not cheer me. "I'm so sorry. I can't believe I pulverized it."

Sheila bent closer. "I don't know anything about instruments. We'd better get Lola in here to take a look."

Deputy Davis went to fetch her while Sheila took my statement. She'd have to believe me this time, wouldn't she? After what seemed like a very long time, the deputy returned. "Had to look all over," he said. "Her shop was closed up. Finally found her in the field helping with something. She'll be here in a minute."

The field was close by, close enough that it might have been a convenient place to land after breaking into the storage room. My suspicions were starting to turn into paranoia. Surely it hadn't been Lola who'd toppled the boxes on me.

"Any sign of Charles around town?" I asked.

"Not that I've seen," Sheila said.

Lola arrived, slightly breathless. Was it a sheen of sweat I saw on her brow?

"Sorry, I was helping in the kids' tent. It's hard work."

Sheila directed her to the ruined instrument. "Don't touch it, but can you give us a quick appraisal?"

"What's going on?" Charles demanded from the doorway, making us jump. "I saw the cops running over here."

"Mr. Dickerson," Sheila said, "I'll need you

to wait outside for a moment."

"I just wanted to be sure everyone was okay," he said. His smile was charming enough, but his eyes combed the floor. Where had he been? Was it a man or a woman I had been chasing?

Charles squinted at the mess that Lola was now examining. "Is that . . . a violin?"

I nodded.

"Did it come from one of Rocky's boxes?"

"There's no way to tell that," Sheila said. "If you'll please wait —"

"I'm not leaving," he said. "If that is a Stradivarius, it sure as shootin' came from one of my brother's boxes." He groaned as he saw it. Genuine emotion or great acting? "It's mangled. What happened to it?"

"I . . . I stepped on it."

He stared. "A Stradivarius is worth upward of sixteen million dollars."

And I had just ruined it. The guy was now left with a triangle and an ugly beehive teapot. "I'm sorry," I said.

"No need to be too sorry," Lola said, straightening. "This violin isn't a Strad."

"How can you tell with such poor lighting?" Charles demanded. "Without enough time to examine it properly?"

She pointed to the ruined innards. "Because it says 'Made in New Jersey.' "

I gaped.

"This is a cheap student violin, probably

not worth more than thirty bucks." She smiled. "Guess this isn't your missing treasure, Charles."

He smiled too, but his expression was still dark as he scrubbed a hand over his face. "Good. That means Penny here doesn't owe me sixteen million dollars."

I gave him a weak nod. "I'll second that."

THIRTEEN

That night thoughts kept prodding me, questions that I could not answer. I woke repeatedly, once to the cadence of a barn owl hooting over the passing hours.

Had it been Lola or Charles who tried to swipe the violin thinking it was a Stradivarius? Both were in the vicinity, and both wanted that treasure. Could they have been working together? And if the two of them were in cahoots, who was prowling around Rocky's attic? This case had more twists than a box of licorice.

The uncertainties kept me tossing and turning until sunup. Staggering through my chores, I loaded up the last batch of honey and drove back to town. The sun was warming up a perfect Kansas morning, and people were beginning to arrive for the Sunday festivities. Pastor Barney obligingly delivered an early sermon to accommodate the congregation.

After church, I was happy to see a line out

the door of the Mad Batter. There was certainly no better way to start the morning than with a hot cup of coffee and a warm scone. Mouth watering, I shored up my inner resolve. Business first. Threading my way through the early birds, I again admired my pretty booth decor: the honey lip balms and lotions displayed in bushel baskets lined with bee-print fabric, and the yellow mini-shelves that displayed the iridescent jars of honey. The containers of whipped honey had their own basket. Rick would have been proud to see it.

In the tent and behind the table, two young high school students practically vibrated with enthusiasm. I'd hired seniors Becky and Rhonda to run my Parson's Honey booth in exchange for a share in the profits. To their credit, they'd studied all the info I'd given them on the qualities of my apple blossom and wildflower honeys and the chunks of natural honeycomb packed in plastic boxes.

The process to create the whipped honey, always a crowd favorite, they could recite by memory. I heated the raw honey to 120 degrees and strained it before it was reheated and restrained. Then I added a tiny bit of finely crystallized honey. After a week, I ran it through the grinder to break up newly formed crystals, which ironically, prevented the formation of larger crystals, leaving creamy-smooth whipped honey.

A slathering of the finished product on a buttered biscuit was a joy to be savored. It was Rick's favorite, and as I stood in front of my booth, I smiled to think of it. For the first time since Rick's death, I didn't cry over the memory.

Was I gradually surrendering my grief like the rigid combs surrendered their precious liquid? No, not surrendered, I decided, but maybe the grief was tempering a bit, melting into a dull, ever-present ache. God's grace and healing were slowly bringing me back to life.

"You okay, Ms. Parson?" Rhonda asked, her multiple earrings glinting in the sunlight.

"Yes," I said, blinking away the reverie. "Are you ready for the last day?"

They both nodded vigorously. Newly minted experts, Becky and Rhonda were chomping at the bit for more customers, so I handed over the last box of honey and the cash box, replenished with change. Ju Ju greeted each girl in turn and accepted their affection in regal style.

"Did you get breakfast?" I fished in my pocket for a couple of extra bucks so they could buy themselves some scones.

"Oh, no need, Ms. Parson," Becky gushed. "We each had a soda and three donuts for breakfast."

Ah, youth, I thought. At thirty-two, I felt eons older than these young girls. Had I ever been so young? So heedless of the hardships life could offer? "Any customers yet?"

"No, but there are some people heading for the rummage sale already. Better get over there if you want any good stuff," Rhonda said.

"Sound advice. I'll check in with you later."

I whistled to Ju Ju, and we approached the long tables crammed with glassware, old books, and sets of teacups. Louise waved at me. "I was right to start the rummage sale early," she crowed. "Look at all these customers."

A dozen or so visitors scanned the tables intently, holding items up in the sunshine to get a better view. Lola was there with Charles, I noted, heads together, chatting. He saluted me with a cup of coffee. Ralph sauntered up and spoke softly.

"He's still convinced he can find his brother's treasure."

"I'm beginning to wonder if there is one," I said.

He winked at me. "Heard you busted up a violin pretty good. Smashed it to matchsticks."

I laughed. "I'm just glad that wasn't the treasure."

"Doesn't have to be an instrument," he said. "That treasure could be something different, hiding in plain sight." He picked up an ugly ceramic ashtray and wiggled his eyebrows in comic fashion. "How about this thing? Maybe it belonged to the king of England."

"Only if the king went to Vegas," I said, pointing to the Viva Las Vegas lettering.

Leaving him chuckling, I made my way along the tables, stopping at the lonely beehive teapot Harper had unboxed the day before. It looked so pathetic sitting there, and I pictured Rocky all alone in his great big house with this silly yellow teapot. We hadn't been friends, more like enemies, but he was sequestered in that drafty house, without even a satisfying relationship with his brother. Guilt pricked at me. I should have tried harder to extend the hand of friendship.

"Love thy neighbor," the Bible said, not just the ones that are easy to get along with. I hadn't worked to get past Rocky's difficult exterior.

My eyes filled and I resolved to ask God for forgiveness. In the meantime, I picked up the teapot. Louise swooped down on me in a moment.

"Three dollars," she said promptly. "Do you want it? Comes in the original cardboard box."

I looked at Charles. "He's okay with selling it?"

She nodded. "He checked, of course. It's mass produced and cheaply made. No one's treasure there."

Thinking of Rocky, I handed over the three bucks and accepted my teapot. For some odd reason, it made me feel better to know that something Rocky left behind would be taken care of.

After the last full day of Spring Fling activities, my feet were complaining big time and Ju Ju could barely drag one teeny paw after the other. As self-appointed Spring Fling ambassador, she had attempted to personally greet each and every visitor. One had to admire her enthusiasm.

My booth inventory was happily depleted. Becky and Rhonda helped me pack up the remainders and received their share of the profits, which thrilled them.

Evelyn was also pleased as she joined me, heading to the Coffee Perk for a decaf and some friendly chatter. The place was packed with Oak Grove regulars who had spent the day manning the Fling activities.

The smiles were tired and welcoming as I eased up to a table with Harper, Jeanine, and Evelyn. Even Morgan took a moment to join us. I plopped my boxed teapot on the table and hoisted Ju Ju on my lap where she fell into a snooze.

"Where are you going to put that in your tiny trailer?" Jeanine said, eyeing the teapot.

I shrugged, too tired to answer.

"We've been packed all day," Morgan said

triumphantly. "I don't know if it's all this talk of treasure and the murder, but something is bringing people to our Fling in droves."

"It's not our impeccable planning?" Ralph said. He sat with his boots slid off, uniform pants rolled up to show his hairy ankles, and his socked feet propped up on an empty chair. He looked all in. He'd been manning the bouncy houses before and after his delivery routes. That was the kind of people that inhabited our small town, I thought, surveying the gathering with a swell of emotion. The small-town heart. It was one of the reasons Rick and I had picked this hole-in-the-wall place in the middle of Kansas.

We did well, Rick, I thought. *This place really is home.*

Harper yawned widely. She'd spent the day lugging rummage sale boxes to and fro, refilling the tables, and zipping around the kid activity zone. An origami frog poked out from her shirt pocket. She'd probably put in more miles than my busy bees.

"Find anything — ?" I started.

Harper waved a hand. "I asked Lola to look at each and every dented, rusty instrument I came across. Not one of them was worth a plugged nickel, so to speak."

Louise sailed in, appearing not the least bit fatigued. "Hey, all. Isn't it fabulous? The rummage sale is bringing in buckets. We'll be able to buy at least fifty new books for the children's collection."

That statement was met with wide smiles.

"We put out every last thing from both the church basement and Blevins," Harper said. "Whatever's on the rummage tables is all that's left. It'll be packed up for donation tonight."

I sighed. "No treasure after all."

"I guess not." Harper stood and squeezed my shoulder.

Dean Matthews approached our table. "Too bad you didn't find a handwritten symphony score."

Ralph slugged some coffee. "Is that like a baseball score?"

Dean laughed. "No, it's the written-out sheet music, all the parts together. Mozart's nine complete handwritten symphony scores went to auction in the late eighties. They brought a pretty sweet sum."

"How sweet?" Jeanine asked.

"One and a half million dollars."

Our mouths dropped open and our gazes swiveled to Harper.

"Did you examine all that sheet music, Harper?" I forced out.

"Well there was that one handwritten manuscript by Igor Stravinsky in the old tattered cover we sold for a quarter."

Evelyn put down her coffee so fast it sloshed on the table.

Harper broke into a hearty laugh. "Kidding."

Evelyn gulped. "Not funny."

"I looked through all the music and there was nothing there but modern-day photocopies and tattered books. Trust me. There are piles of it left if you don't believe me. You can look through it yourself."

I stretched my stiff back. "I trust you. Rocky's treasure will just have to remain hidden, though I imagine Charles will keep looking for it."

As if on cue, Charles strolled past the window, head down and frowning. On his way to Lola's shop for a meeting? Judging by his expression, he had not found what he desperately sought in the town of Oak Grove.

I looked around the table at my friends who'd tried to help me every step of the way, with Rick's death, with my brush with murder, with the precious gift of connection at a time when the whole world seemed to be falling away from me. Impulsively, I got up and gave each of them a squeeze.

They squeezed me back. Even without a whiff of treasure, I felt very richly blessed indeed. I toted my sleeping dog to the truck and headed back to my property.

FOURTEEN

I showered and fed Ju Ju, and we sat down to our nightly ritual, a cup of tea with a tiny squeeze of apple blossom honey for me and a doggie dental chew for Ju Ju. I'd started the ritual after Rick passed, as a way to eat up some of the long, dark hours until morning. Now Ju Ju and I had come to welcome the routine. It was a sweet way to retreat from the day's work and worries and ease our way into a good night's sleep.

I gazed at the teapot still boxed up in the middle of my table. What was I going to do with the ungainly thing, I wondered.

I pulled it free from the Styrofoam packing. Yep, it was just as odd a decoration as I'd thought at first glance — lumpy and squat, the spout sporting a hairline crack.

"We'll figure out what to do with it in the morning." I swept up the pot and the box to move them off the table. Odd, I noticed, how the teapot was so lightweight, made of cheap porcelain, yet the box had some heft to it.

Pulling the box closer, I examined the inside. The white Styrofoam walls that surrounded the empty space inside were in pretty good shape, but they didn't weigh much, so what accounted for the unexpected mass?

My heart beat a pulse faster as I pulled the Styrofoam out and peered inside.

Time stood still, and my pulse hitched. Neatly lining the walls of the box were two fat envelopes, tied closed with string.

"Ju . . ." I breathed. "You don't suppose . . ." I pulled the package free and untied the nearest one with shaking fingers, freeing the yellowed papers inside and laying them carefully on the table. I've never had a jot of musical talent, but I knew enough to recognize that the blobs and lines were musical notes, handwritten, old. They flowed across the paper like tiny bees, flying along the lines of the music staff. Ju Ju cocked her head.

"Am I really seeing this, or is this a dream?" Ju Ju barked.

I ignored her, pulling the other envelope from the container. More music, yellowed and brittle. Another treasure, right there, sharing table space with a worthless old teapot.

Ju Ju's barking reached ear-splitting decibels, but I could not look away from the music, not until a deep voice startled me.

"So that's where it's been all this time. I

should have guessed."

I bolted out of my chair, hands pressed to my chest.

Ralph Wessex stood across from me, still in his uniform shirt and rolled-up pants.

Hairy ankles, I thought as the pieces fell into place.

Rolled-up pants.

Rolled up . . . to conceal the tear where Ju Ju had clamped on.

"You were searching Rocky's house," I said. "That's why Mrs. Milkburn complained about the mail being late."

He frowned. "She's always complaining about something, the old crony. Never content with anything."

"Ralph, what are you doing here?"

"Looking for the treasure, like everyone else. During my route one day, I heard Rocky spouting off to his brother on the phone about a treasure. The window was open so it wasn't like I was eavesdropping. Anyway, I heard him talk about this windfall, and it got me to thinking. I opened his mail."

I gasped. "But you're a postal carrier. That's a crime."

"So was killing him, but I did that too."

He was so matter of fact about it, like he was chatting about the weather. I realized my mouth was hanging open so I closed it. "Oh Ralph. Why would you do that?"

"I've got two ex-wives and three kids, and they all suck up money like Hoovers. I'm sick of this town, this job, this life." He waved a weary hand in the air. "After I heard Rocky blabbering on about his treasure, I opened the mail he got from New York, read it, and sealed it shut again. The appraisers he wrote to were cagey, didn't come right out and say what they'd evaluated, but they made it clear it was worth a bundle. The night I decided to search, I thought he was away, out of town. He surprised me, and I shot him. Didn't plan it. Just happened. Messed up the place to make it look like a robbery and to hide my searching. Never did find diddly-squat in his wreck of a house."

He looked at the teapot. "I figured he must have hidden the treasure inside something else, maybe something he'd donated to the Spring Fling, which is why I swiped the violin from the storeroom. Good thing it wasn't the treasure, since you crushed it." He laughed. "It was about the only thing I hadn't searched . . . except the teapot." He chuckled. "That old, ugly teapot. Rocky was smarter than I thought, hiding it there. The box must have gotten inadvertently mixed up with the rummage sale donations. Must have driven him nuts."

"Take the music, Ralph," I said, forcing the words past the terror in my throat. "Take it, leave town, and I won't tell anyone."

He smiled, almost sadly, I thought, as he pulled a gun from his pocket. "My spare," he said. "Your bees did a number on my other gun after I put it in your hive."

My hands began to shake. "Please. You don't have to kill me."

"Let's walk to your work shed."

"Why?"

He didn't answer, and I understood. He would kill me there and lock me inside, stuff me behind one of my shelves, where it would take longer to find me. He'd be long gone when my body was discovered. I tried to scoot Ju Ju behind my leg.

"Dog's going too," he said. "Won't do for her to be charging around loose. It'll bring people running."

That did it. The fear that bubbled like a fountain slowly drained away and anger took its place. I'd lost Rick, but he'd left me with a heart filled with love and a gut full of determination. No one was going to take away my life without a fight, and absolutely no living creature was going to harm Ju Ju if I had anything whatsoever to say about it. I made my plans and hoped my expression did not telegraph my internal rage.

"Go on," he said, gesturing with the gun. "Walk to the shed. Now. Tell the dog to come with you."

"Come on, Ju Ju," I said. Confused, she trotted after me out toward our workplace, our solace. I pushed open the door and clicked on the light switch.

"Inside," he said.

Ju Ju scampered in next to me. I gestured to the small stove setup. "I left some honey on the stove. Let me take it off the burner at least."

"No way," he said.

"Fine, then the whole place could catch fire before you have a chance to cross the state line. That's going to bring a lot of attention that you don't want."

He considered. "All right. Do it fast."

I walked to the little stove. I hadn't left it on, of course, but there was a pot of honey there, a leftover gallon or so that I'd intended to bottle until my supply of jars ran out.

One chance was all I would get.

My back to Ralph, I grabbed the pot, whipped around, and flung it at him with all my might.

The vessel hit him in the chest, knocking him backward where he smacked his head hard against the floor. The sticky mass covered his face and ran down his torso. The gun, jarred loose, skittered under the cabinet. Ju Ju alternated between wanting to chase the weapon and barking at Ralph, whom she suspected was playing a wonderful new game.

He wasn't. His eyelids flapped as he struggled in and out of consciousness. I pulled the cell phone from the pocket of my robe and dialed the police. Then I grabbed an empty cast-iron pot to clobber him with, in case he decided to try anything. Scooping Ju Ju up, I sat on the old, worn wooden chair to wait for the police.

Ju Ju still didn't understand what had happened, and I was still processing too, my heart thundering hard against my ribs. Ralph, the genial, smiling postal worker, was a cold-blooded killer.

I cuddled Ju Ju close. "It's all right, baby," I crooned, kissing her head. "I promise I'm never going to let anything hurt you. Ever."

That said, I thanked God for His protection and cried tears of relief, which Ju Ju licked up, one by one.

The girls gathered around at the Coffee Perk to hear the incredible tale that I'd already repeated again and again for Sheriff Hayden and Sheila Waters.

"I just can't believe it," Morgan said. "No way would I have suspected Ralph could do such a thing."

I sipped my coffee. "Like Lola said, a million dollars is a lot of motivation."

Janine clucked. "Craziness, pure and simple. What's going to happen to the music now?"

"It's the property of the police for a while." Harper reached over to scratch Ju Ju where she sat curled on my lap. "Then the lawyers will figure out if Charles really does have rights to it or not."

"But really," Evelyn said, "who would pay a million bucks and change for an old piece of music?"

"An old piece of music which happens to have been handwritten by a Russian composer named Rimsky-Korsakov way back in 1899." I shook my head. "If Rocky hadn't been so absentminded, it would probably already have been sold and he'd still be alive."

Morgan put another stack of napkins on the table and joined us. "What was it, anyway? This priceless music. Anything we'd recognize?"

"Yeah." Jeanine quirked a brow. "I mean, what score would cause all this chaos?"

I chuckled. "You'll never believe it."

"Try us," all three women said at once.

I leaned back in the chair to enjoy the moment. "I did some research. It's actually a musical interlude, part of an opera."

"Uh huh," Evelyn said.

"Korsakov meant to evoke the seemingly chaotic and rapidly changing flight pattern . . ." I took another sip of coffee.

"Of . . . ?" Morgan pressed.

"You'll never guess," I teased.

"What?" they all but shouted in unison.

"He meant to replicate the amazing energy of the bumblebee."

Now their mouths dropped open, much as

mine had when I read the title.

"Are you saying . . . ?" Evelyn said.

"I am saying," I pronounced, "that the name of the piece is the famous 'Flight of the Bumblebee.' "

After a moment of stunned silence, they broke into peals of laughter, as comforting to me as the hum of my precious bees. These amazing women of all ages and life situations had once again seen me through an epic crisis.

Morgan raised her mug in salute. "To the magnificent bumblebee," she said, "and the ladies who solved yet another mystery."

"Hear, hear," we all said, clinking our glasses together. Their laughter was sweet as honey to my soul.

ABOUT THE AUTHOR

Dana Mentink is a two-time American Christian Fiction Writers Carol Award winner, a *Romantic Times* Reviewers' Choice Award recipient, and a Holt Medallion winner. She is a national bestselling author of over thirty-five titles in the suspense and lighthearted romance genres. She is pleased to write for Harlequin's Love Inspired Suspense, Harlequin Heartwarming, and Harvest House. Dana was thrilled to be a semifinalist in the Jeanne Robertson Comedy with Class Competition. Besides writing, she busies herself teaching third grade. Mostly, she loves to be home with Papa Bear, her teens fondly nicknamed Yogi and Boo Boo, and various pets including a nutty terrier, a chubby box turtle, and a feisty parakeet.

■ ■ ■ ■

CHILI CON CARNE
MURDER

BY CANDICE PRENTICE

■ ■ ■ ■

ONE

Humming a mindless tune, I washed my empty oatmeal bowl in the sink and stared out the kitchen window. In the backyard, two squirrels played like kittens, tumbling over each other in the grass. I smiled and reached for the empty coffee carafe from my ancient coffeemaker, but I missed and knocked it off the counter. It hit the old wood kitchen floor and shattered. Shards of glass flew everywhere. So much for making a post-breakfast cup of coffee. After a moment of shock, I shooed my four dogs from the room to avoid injury.

I tried to sweep up all the pieces of glass, but that only worked for the bigger pieces. I got down on my hands and knees with a wet dishrag and made a microscopic search for more shards. All the while, my dogs whined at me, probably thinking I was having fun playing on the kitchen floor without them. When I was done, my kitchen floor was cleaner than it had been for years.

I stood in the middle of the room and put my hands on my hips. Penny Parsons, one of my best friends and a member of my Tuesday night book club, was always talking about my really bad coffee. Perhaps it was time to invest in a new kind of coffeemaker. Maybe one with little pods. Or a french press. I'd think about it later. Meanwhile, I needed to update some financial files on my laptop before I tackled the rest of my day.

My dogs pranced at my side as I walked into the family room off the kitchen. I dropped into my late husband's favorite recliner. After George's unexpected death, I'd curl up in a ball in this chair and cry. We'd never had children, so I was alone. I'd taken to sitting here. I could close my eyes and imagine him in it, reading and glancing at me over his glasses. But now, after three years, the already old chair was growing threadbare. Perhaps the time had come to buy a replacement. My husband remained alive in my memories. A tattered recliner wasn't necessary.

I opened my old laptop. The ancient machine took longer than normal to boot up. Finally, a blue screen appeared with a bunch of gobbledygook words and symbols. The only phrase I clearly understood was "A problem has been detected and Windows has been shut down to prevent damage to your computer."

I poked around, pressing keys, trying to fix it, but I had no idea what I was doing. Fortunately, I'd had enough foresight to keep my files on an external drive. Still, that meant I had to get this machine fixed or buy a new one, and fast. I needed a computer this coming weekend when I went to the farmers' market to sell soaps, herbal teas, and eggs, among other things. One of my friends from church owned a computer shop. Perhaps I'd ask his advice.

I sighed and glanced at my to-do list on my cell phone. I wouldn't have time to shop this morning, for a laptop or a coffeemaker. Today I was helping prepare a lunch for the needy that my church hosted weekly. Normally, I looked forward to it, but our regular organizer was away on vacation, and the man filling his position, Kirk Philips, challenged the command "Love thy neighbor" to my core. Fortunately, he was only temporary. So, instead of thinking about Kirk, I'd concentrate on someone else. Jonathan, George's cousin. He always showed up early and quietly drank coffee while I helped prepare the food. I enjoyed seeing him.

I jumped up from the chair and headed upstairs to get ready for the day. In the bathroom, I stood in front of the mirror and developed a sudden, intense dislike for my thick hair. After George died, I'd stopped going to the salon because I didn't care. My hair had gone gray. I used sewing shears to trim it. Now, I liked the color, but I was no hairdresser, and my attempts at trimming made me look like I'd stuck my fingers into an electric socket. As I applied mascara, I had an insane thought that I should do something drastic, like dye my hair auburn and add bright blue highlights. *Widow goes wild.* My friends would laugh themselves silly.

I smiled. Things weren't bad, really. I'd look into my computer options this afternoon. And maybe I could make an appointment to get a nice haircut. Meantime, I would run by the Coffee Perk and see the owner, Morgan Butler. She'd give me hugs and I'd get my post-breakfast cup of coffee. Then the rest of the day would be perfect.

I stepped into the Coffee Perk, Oak Grove's best coffee shop, inhaling the fragrance of freshly ground coffee beans, and immediately relaxed. Morgan, who hosted our weekly Tuesday evening book club meetings, looked up as I hustled to the counter.

"Evelyn! Good to see you. What's up?"

"I need a hug and a cup of coffee. It's been a rough morning. My coffee carafe met its doom on my kitchen floor this morning, among other issues."

She giggled. "You mean the carafe from that ancient coffeemaker that wheezes while it drips?"

"Yes, that one."

Morgan's face grew serious. "Was there glass all over the place?"

"Yes."

"Are the pups okay?"

"They were more entertained than anything else, watching me crawl all over the floor. In fact, they thought I was playing and wanted to join in. But losing my carafe is a bit of a tragedy."

"Based on what Penny says about your coffee, I'm not sure about that. Still, I'm sorry." She danced around the counter, full of her usual energy, and drew me into a comforting hug.

"Thank you," I whispered.

"You're welcome." She returned to her spot behind the counter. "I hate to take advantage of a friend, but your loss could be my gain. I just got in an order of french presses. I wanted to see if people would be interested in buying them." She pointed at a display in the corner. "You could be the first. You might find your coffee becomes excellent. Buy one, I'll give you a discount on some ground coffee to try out, and I'll throw in a free cup of Columbian to soothe your woes."

"I can't think of anyone else I'd rather buy something from. That takes care of one of my problems, anyway." I went to the corner and picked up one of the presses then I returned and watched while she worked.

"What else happened this morning?" she asked. "You said there were other issues?"

"There were. I got the blue screen of death on my laptop. Not a good time for that to happen because the farmers' markets are in full swing right now and I need to access my records."

Morgan snapped a plastic lid on my coffee cup. "Knowing you and your precise ways of doing things, you have a backup."

"I do, thank goodness."

"I have a thought." Morgan slid the cup across the counter to me and bagged my new press. "You know Danny Kaplan from your church? The EMT with the computer business on the side? This morning he came by to update my computers. He was on his way to your church. Says he's building them a new system. He actually mentioned you."

"Aw. That's nice. We've been in Bible study together for the last several years."

"Maybe you could ask him to help you with your computer."

"I'd already thought of that. I was going to call and ask his advice this afternoon."

"He's super nice. For a man his age, he's pretty good looking — in an Irish kind of way, with that reddish hair and green eyes. He's tall. And he's single."

"Hey! He's *my* age. Are you saying I'm old?"

"Nope. What I *did* say is that he mentioned

you. And he's single. And nice looking." She gave me an exaggerated wink.

I realized what she meant and blushed. "No way! I'm not looking for a man."

"I think he likes you."

"Of course he does. We're friends. Besides, he says he's content being a bachelor."

"Someone can be content but still want something more in life." She chuckled.

What I didn't tell Morgan was that lately I'd been noticing Danny more often than I wanted to, and I'd been avoiding thinking about it.

"I can tell by your expression that I should change the topic." She grinned and rested her hip against the counter. "You headed off to the Tuesday lunch program at your church?"

"Yes. That's another issue. Honestly, I'm not looking forward to it as much as I usually do. The guy who normally heads up the program is away, so Kirk Philips is filling in. He's a bit of a dictator."

"Kirk Philips . . . I've heard that name."

"He grew up around here then moved away, but he recently returned."

Morgan's brow wrinkled in thought. "Isn't he related to someone at your church? And to Hazel Prescott? The woman who recently passed away?"

"Yes. He's related to Carrie, the church administrative assistant. They're cousins, so

Hazel was aunt to both of them. She never married and treated her nieces and nephews like her children. I don't know Kirk well, but Jonathan, George's cousin, was friends with him growing up."

"How is Jonathan doing? Is the PTSD still under control?"

"Yes. And he's been living in his trailer now for almost six months. That's a record."

The bell on the front door rang as Morgan slid me the cup of coffee. She glanced over my shoulder and waved. I turned. Vernon Benson, a local contractor and member of my church, strode across the shop. He'd been hired as general contractor for our church fellowship hall redo. He huffed and puffed as though he'd been running, and his bald head was as red as his cheeks.

"Hey, I need coffee." He drew in a deep breath and blew it out. "The usual."

"Sure thing," Morgan said. "Would you like some water as well? You look like you've had too much sun or too much exercise."

"No, I'm fine. Just coffee." He paid for his coffee and Morgan handed him some change.

"You working at the church this morning?" I asked.

He glanced at me. "I'm, uh, no. I just ran by there to check a few things before ordering supplies. Why?"

I smiled. "It's lunch day. I was going to offer you a free lunch."

"Got another place to be." He scurried from the shop.

I perused some muffins stacked under the glass of the display case.

"Vernon was brusque this morning," Morgan murmured. "Unlike him. Usually he's whistling and singing scripture songs, although he has been getting grumpier lately. Maybe it's just all those little kids he has."

"I'd noticed that too." I pointed at the glass case. "I think I want a couple of those for Jonathan. He always comes to eat lunch at the church on Tuesdays."

Morgan pulled two from the display case, bagged them, and handed them to me. "I know you care a great deal about him. That means I do too. Consider these a gift for him."

"Oh, that's so sweet, hon." Tears sprang to my eyes. "George loved Jonathan. I'm doing what I can to help him, but I'm not close to him."

"You probably can't be, with all those issues he has. Still, I'm sure he knows you care."

"I hope so." I counted out money from my wallet to pay for my french press.

"You're coming to book club tonight, right?"

"Yes." I handed her exact change.

"I'll pray for you today and see you tonight."

"I appreciate it." I waved over my shoulder as I left the shop.

My church was on the outskirts of town. To get there, I passed acres of cornfields and orchards, but not many cars. I was singing along with a worship CD I'd recently bought, not paying close attention to the road, when another car came barreling toward me, halfway in my lane. I barely had time to head for the shoulder to avoid being hit.

I recognized the car and the driver. It was Jonathan.

After he roared by, I pulled back onto the road, shaken by the near miss, and squinted into the rearview mirror. Jonathan was traveling so fast, I could barely see him anymore. I wondered why he was in such a hurry and whether he'd come back that way to the church lunch. I hoped so. While he sat drinking coffee, I'd sometimes meet his gaze and see a glimpse of my husband in his eyes. It used to make me want to cry. Now, I was just glad for the reminder . . . and also grateful that the man my husband loved so much had at least a semblance of fellowship.

I parked in the lower church parking lot, next to Kirk's car, near the door to the fellowship hall in the basement of the building. After breathing a prayer for Jonathan and for myself to have strength to deal with Kirk, I stuffed my keys into my purse. As I exited my truck, I grabbed the bag of goodies for Jonathan.

The upper parking lot held the usual cars, minus the youth pastor's. He was on vacation. Carrie and the pastor were here. Her little Honda and his Chevy truck were parked in their usual spots. Velma Johnson's car was there as well. Velma acted like she was staff, even though she didn't hold any official position.

Danny Kaplan's truck was in the lot too. Morgan was right. He was working on the church computers today. Maybe I'd have a chance to run upstairs and talk to him about my ailing laptop.

I hurried to the door of the fellowship hall, heels of my sandals clicking on the pavement, purse banging against my hip. The August sun beat on my head. Stifling heat made me feel smothered. According to the weather report, today would be a scorcher. Unfortunately, Kirk had decided to serve chili con carne. As far as I was concerned, the choice was horrible for a hot summer day. Besides, I believed a dish like chili con carne was better aged for a little while, so the flavors had time to meld. But Kirk had been adamant, and one just didn't argue with Kirk. Some people tried, of course. Like Velma Johnson. But she argued with everyone, including the pastor.

I took a deep breath to prepare myself for Kirk's snappish orders and opened the door.

Then I stopped in surprise. The fellowship hall was quiet. Kirk usually blasted worship music so loud it was hard to hear him barking orders over the chaos. But today I heard nothing. No music, no noise of dishes and pans. The metal curtain that covered the serving window was still shut tight.

"Kirk?" No answer. Perhaps he'd gone to get more ingredients.

I crossed the room and opened the swinging door to the kitchen. The room was dark. I groped for the light switch and turned it on. The kitchen came into clear focus. The first thing I noticed was a puddle of red on the tan tile floor next to a massive upended pot. An opened, industrial-sized can of tomato sauce lay next to it. Then I saw Kirk, lying in the midst of the sauce, legs and arms at weird angles.

"Kirk?" I hurried across the room and knelt next to him. Perhaps he'd had a heart attack. His personality certainly lent itself to that possibility.

He didn't respond. That's when I noticed he had a fading black eye and a bleeding gash in his temple. His blood mingled with the sauce. I felt sick. I stood, dizzy, and backed out of the kitchen, tracking tomato sauce across the tile. With trembling hands, I rummaged through my purse, finally finding my cell phone. I called 911. After I explained what I found, they ordered me to stay where

I was and to keep people away from the body. I sat hard on a chair and called upstairs to the church office to break the news.

Ironic that I'd just told Morgan that I was prepared to work with Kirk today. I hadn't been prepared to see him dead.

Two

Danny, in his role as EMT, had rushed downstairs. After checking Kirk per instructions of the 911 operator, he waited with me for the police to arrive, talking in a soothing voice. The pastor appeared as well, pale and shaken. He'd ordered Velma and Carrie to stay upstairs.

I wondered what had happened. Initially I thought perhaps Kirk had had a heart attack and hit his head on the counter, but then the police descended on the church like a swarm of bees. Apparently, Kirk's death was suspicious. I'd had a disturbing initial interview with a deputy, who seemed to view me as a potential murderer. If I were honest, I was slightly incoherent, so I could see why he was suspicious.

Thirty minutes later, I still waited in the room, watching a hive of activity. Danny was making rounds, talking to people. Deputies and other people trooped in and out, but it was all a blur to me. I clenched my jaw to stop my teeth from chattering. My insides felt as cold as if it were ten degrees outside. I desperately wanted to go out into the heat, but I'd been ordered to sit and stay. Was it just this morning that I'd thought the rest of the day would go perfectly?

Danny zeroed in on me again, concern wrinkling his forehead. "You're shaking."

"I feel cold even though it's warm." I clenched my damp hands on the bag of muffins in my lap. "I think the air conditioning is set too low."

"Could be anxiety or a stress reaction that's making you hyperventilate, and your body is responding by lowering its temperature."

"I don't understand why. I saw another dead person not too long ago, and I didn't get all anxious and stressed out."

"Different situations bring on different reactions. I'm going to ask the sheriff if you can leave. It's ridiculous that you have to sit here like this."

He crossed the room and engaged in a rather hostile conversation with the sheriff. Sheriff Hayden wasn't a very nice man on a good day. He tended to treat everyone like a criminal, even when they were buying a cheeseburger at the local diner. I knew I should cut him some slack. A police officer's job could no doubt lead to cynicism, but feeling good about him, especially right now, was difficult.

Finally, the sheriff threw up his hands and marched across the room toward me, coming to a stop one foot in front of me. I could see the hairs in his nose. Danny hurried behind him.

The sheriff opened his notebook. "Evelyn Kliff, right?"

"Yes."

"You made these tracks?" He pointed his pen at the tomato footprints leading from the kitchen to where I sat.

"I did. I got tomato sauce on my shoes when I was checking Kirk's pulse." I swallowed hard.

"What's in that?" He jabbed at the bag in my lap containing Jonathan's muffins.

"Just some baked goods I brought to give to someone." I offered it to him.

He opened the bag, sniffed, then handed it back to me, eyes narrowed. "I recognize you. You're friends with some of those ladies that have the weird reading club at the coffee shop, right? The ones who fancy themselves Sherlock Holmes pretenders?"

"I'm friends with them, but I wouldn't say our club is weird or that they think they're Sherlock Holmes."

"Right." He snorted. "What time did you say you got here?"

I shrugged. "Around ten, I guess."

"And who was here when you arrived?"

"I don't understand, Sheriff. A deputy

already asked me these questions."

"I want to hear the answers myself," he snarled.

I recoiled. "Well, I didn't see anyone, just their cars."

Sheriff Hayden snapped his fingers in front of my face. "Are you being a hostile witness?"

I felt like crying. "No, sir. I have this roaring in my ears, so it's hard to hear, and I'm feeling confused."

Danny made a very peculiar sound, almost like a growl. I looked up at him. He was glaring at the sheriff, who was glaring at me.

"I'll clarify for you then." The sheriff spoke very slowly, like I was an idiot. "Whose cars did you see in the parking lot?"

"Okay . . . um . . . Velma's, Carrie's —"

"Last names and what they do here," he barked.

Danny shifted at my side and growled again.

"Mark Sheldon, the pastor. Carrie Prescott, the church secretary. Velma Johnson the, uh, person who does a bit of everything."

"Busybody," Danny murmured.

"What?" the sheriff snapped.

Danny shrugged.

"Um, Danny's car too."

Sheriff Hayden's attention turned to Danny. "You were here?"

"Yes, I was."

"You work here?"

"No. I'm building them a new computer system."

"Were you alone?"

"Part of the time. We all were, at least part of the time. And, yes. I could have come down here and killed Kirk without anyone else knowing."

The sheriff grunted, and his gaze whipped back to me. "Did you see anyone else? Anywhere around here? Driving away, maybe?"

My stomach clenched. *Jonathan.* I wanted to lie, but then I remembered a verse in Proverbs 12 about being an honest witness. I opted for the truth. "Yes. Jonathan Kliff."

"Kliff. Relation of yours?"

"My late husband's cousin."

The sheriff scratched his head. "You mean that crazy Marine dude living out in the middle of nowhere in the trailer?"

"I wouldn't say he's crazy."

"No? The guy used to live on the street. He talks to himself and shakes. I arrested him a couple of times for loitering earlier in the summer."

"He's much better now. He's gotten medication."

"Crazy is as crazy does," the sheriff muttered then his eyes lit up. "You say he was driving away?"

I reluctantly nodded. I'd just made Jonathan suspect number one.

Sheriff Hayden smirked at me. "One of my deputies will be here in a minute to get more details from you."

Danny rested his hand lightly on my shoulder. "I'm taking Evelyn home. She's having a reaction to the stress of finding Kirk's body. Have you noticed her appearance? White face? Breathing hard?"

Sheriff Hayden opened his mouth to argue, but Danny squared his shoulders and stood nose-to-nose with him.

"If she collapses, it won't look good for you."

The sheriff's eyes snapped with irritation, but he waved in my direction. "Go on, then. I'll be in touch. And remember, I know your friends. You're all troublemakers. Leave this alone. We don't need your help." He glowered at Danny. "I'll have more questions for you as well. You better not disappear." He turned and stalked away.

"Mercy!" I said under my breath.

"He definitely needs some of that." Danny squeezed my shoulder then let go. "That man is uptight and needs an ego adjustment. Still, there's always a reason people act like that. Maybe he's unhappy at home. At the very least, given his personality, his wife might be. Ignore him and his rude comments about your friends. Let's get out of here."

I stood, willing my legs to behave. Danny took my elbow. I was thankful for his support and smiled up at him. He smiled back then guided me across the room and out the door. Gratefully, I stepped outside and took a breath. The heat that had seemed so stifling earlier now felt like a warm embrace.

I fumbled in my purse for my keys. Danny took them from my hand, opened my truck door, and helped me inside.

"You okay driving?" he asked.

"Yes. I already feel better. I slowed down my breathing. That helped."

"That's good, but how about I follow you home?"

"That isn't necessary. I'm sure you have other things to do."

Danny shook his head. "I finished working on the church computers. I was headed back to the shop to do some repairs and updates. I don't have another appointment until after lunch. So unless I get a call to attend to an emergency, I'm free. I'd feel better knowing you're okay."

"All right." Despite telling him I didn't need the company, I felt relief.

I rounded a curve in my long, tree-lined driveway, and my white farmhouse came into view. The soothing sight of home helped clear the image of Kirk and his blood from my mind. When Penny Parsons had discovered Rocky Dickerson's body, I'd gone to the scene to be with her. At the time I'd been too concerned about her well-being to feel ill over his body. But now I'd gotten the full brunt of a dead person. It didn't help that blood from his head mingled with tomato sauce.

Poor Kirk. I hadn't liked him. In fact, no one I was acquainted with who had known him had much good to say about him, which was unfortunate. And now he was dead, with no chance of changing people's opinions. Flawed as he was, Kirk didn't deserve to die like that.

Danny pulled up beside me, and I forced myself to move, although my body felt stiff, like I'd been picking beans for hours. Perhaps a bracing glass of iced tea would help. I'd just made my favorite herbal blend that morning. I grabbed my purse, Jonathan's goodies, and my new french press, and exited the car.

Danny jumped out of his truck and looked around. "I've known you for a couple of years, but I've never seen your house until now. It's awesome. You've talked about living on a farm, but I didn't realize it was such a large spread. It's like a, uh, a real farm." He grinned.

I laughed, and it felt good. "It is a real farm, or at least it was. Back in the day, my husband and I raised organic produce, chickens, and eggs, and sold them to markets and restaurants. We also raised grass-fed beef. I had to stop after he died. I couldn't keep up, physically or emotionally. Now I rent out a lot of the pasture to other farmers, keep an herb garden for my products, and chickens for eggs."

Danny nodded. "I've heard farming is a tough job."

"Yes, it is. And it's a difficult way to make a living. Early in our marriage, before we were established, I had to take temporary jobs to fill the income gap."

"And now you make a living with herbs?"

"Not much of a living, to tell you the truth, but we had quite a good nest egg, George had life insurance, and now I have the rental money from the fields. Fortunately, this was his family's farm, so I don't have a mortgage, just taxes and insurance." I shrugged. "That's probably too much information."

"Not at all. My apologies for asking a personal question."

I patted his arm. "It's no problem. We've talked about plenty of other things just as personal during Bible study. I'm going to have some iced herbal tea to settle my stomach. I need it after finding . . ."

My throat closed and for just a minute I fought my stomach to stay still. Danny reached over and patted my arm.

"I'm sorry you're going through this."

"Me too. Hey, I could use some company for a few minutes, if you have time. I can offer you a drink — the tea, or perhaps lemonade? It's homemade."

"Of course I'll stay. Besides, who can turn down homemade lemonade?" He smiled at me, and I felt a little niggle of attraction, which I promptly pushed to the back of my mind.

As we approached the front porch, a cacophony of barking greeted us.

"You've talked about your dogs. Four of them, right?"

"Yep. My husband and I used to do dog rescue." I pointed at the front porch, which ran the length of the house. "Do you mind if we sit out here? I find it peaceful. I can turn on the fans overhead, if you're too hot."

"That would be fine. It's shady. And you could probably use the warmth."

He followed me as I trotted up the porch stairs. Four brightly painted rocking chairs — red, blue, green, and yellow — sat in a row, interspersed with tables in the same bold colors.

"Please have a seat. The rocking chairs are more comfortable than they look."

"Hmm. Which color shall I choose?" He walked up and down, pausing in front of each one. "Green doesn't go with my complexion. Makes my skin sallow." He patted his cheeks and a grin played on his lips. "Blue feels moody — I'm not in a blue mood." He pointed at the yellow chair. "I think you should sit in this one. It might help you warm up. Besides, yellow reminds me of you. Bright and cheerful. I'll take the red one. A ruddy color suits. I'm feeling flush with health. Besides, they're right next to one another."

I chuckled and opened the door, greeted by my dogs. The tails on three of them moved like frenzied metronomes and they pushed their heads past my legs to see who was with me. The fourth just sat and watched me. "Quiet!" I ordered. The dogs stopped barking. "Now, all of you, sit." They did.

"Well behaved." Danny stood behind me, peering down at them.

"Yes, for the most part. But for someone new, four dogs can be overwhelming, despite their good behavior. BonBon, the smallest, is quite demanding."

"I can deal with it. We'll get acquainted while you're inside."

"Okay, guys." I motioned for them to come outside. BonBon bounced around my legs then Danny's. Diggy, a collie mix, ran circles around BonBon, but ignored us. Mervin, my stately pittie-shepherd mix, sniffed Danny with calm dignity. And KC, the oldest, shuffled over to Danny and sat at his feet.

"Have fun!" I disappeared into the house.

As I poured my tea, a sudden flash of memory of Kirk brought a tremor to my hand. Poor man. To see him dead like that was awful. The gash on his head and blood on the floor, mingling with tomato sauce, was a picture I was sure I'd never be able to forget. I pressed my hand on my stomach and willed my mind back to the drinks.

Minutes later, I carried my tea and Danny's lemonade outside, plus a plate holding the muffins I'd bought for Jonathan. I didn't want them to go stale. I placed everything on the table between us. BonBon had settled in Danny's lap. Diggy lay at the head of the stairs, staring out into the distance. Mervin watched to see what I was going to do. And KC rested at Danny's feet.

"Thank you. Looks good." Danny rubbed his hand on the arm of the chair. "These really are more comfortable than they first appear."

"They are." I settled against the yellow rocker's high back and sighed. Mervin ambled over and dropped at my feet. I pointed at the plate. "As I told the sheriff, these muffins were supposed to be for George's cousin, Jonathan, but obviously I wasn't able to deliver them."

"I'm sorry he missed out, but I'm glad to help you by eating one." Danny took one and began removing the paper. "Tell me more about your dogs."

"Trying to distract me?"

"A little. Is it working?"

"Actually, yes." I took a sip of tea then I began while he ate. "BonBon, that little bundle in your lap, is a tiny mix of Chihuahua and who knows what else. She thinks she's the boss of the world. She joined us as a pup right before George died. Diggy, the one staring over the front yard, is a collie mix, and he's young. I got him last year from a dog rescue that was desperate to place him. He and BonBon play and fight like siblings, but he's never attached to me. In fact, he's never shown interest in any person. I wondered at first if it was because I have too many dogs. Or if maybe I didn't have the emotional bandwidth for another, but now I think it's just him." I shrugged. "Anyway, then there's Mervin." The big dog at my feet lifted his head at the mention of his name. "He's my baby — has been since I got him. He's very smart."

Danny reached down and stroked KC's head. "And this one?"

"That's KC, who's a mix of who-knows-what. He was George's dog. He's getting on in years now."

Danny nodded thoughtfully, and KC snuffled against his hand. "Losing a spouse is hard."

I ducked my head. "It's very difficult, particularly when it's unexpected. George was young, as age goes. We had so many plans and, suddenly . . ." I felt tears in my eyes. The emotions of the morning were catching up.

"Oh man!" Danny slapped his forehead.

"I'm sorry. Wow. Talk about insensitive. Really, really bad timing on my part."

I smiled and sniffed at the same time. "It's fine. My tears are probably more stress related than anything else. In fact, just this morning I realized I'm ready to get rid of George's old recliner. That's not to say I won't always miss him. Just that the grief that made me want to curl up and die has passed."

"I lost someone too, a long time ago. The raw emotion passes, but there's always an ache."

I glanced at him in surprise. "You've never said anything about that."

He shrugged. "I wasn't ready. It happened in my twenties — another lifetime ago. I lost my wife. We'd only been married a year. To be honest, I was angry at God for a long time. That's why I never discussed it. I shut my heart up really tight. But in the last year, God has been dealing with me about letting go of emotions like fear."

"Fear?"

"Fear that if I open my heart to someone else, I might lose them."

"Oh! I do understand that as well. Sometimes that thought strikes me when I'm worried about my good friends."

"Exactly." He finished the last bite of his muffin. "Watching you work through your grief process the last few years in Bible study helped me a lot."

I felt a slight blush on my cheeks. "I'm glad God could use that. Grieving is so complicated." I sipped my tea. "I don't . . . didn't . . . know Kirk that well, but I wonder who will be grieving for him."

"That's a good question." Danny rocked slowly and wrapped his hands around his glass. "He's a mystery to me, but I'm not from around here. And frankly, his personality didn't lend itself to friendship."

"That's the truth," I said. "He and Carrie were cousins. Their aunt Hazel recently passed away. Kirk was also friends with Jonathan when they were younger. I've wondered why Kirk came back."

"Jonathan is an interesting fellow too. How is his PTSD? I've been praying for him."

I nodded. "He's doing well. He still refuses to come to church, but he shows up every Tuesday to the lunch. In fact, he comes early for coffee while we prepare food."

"You were pretty riled up when Sheriff Hayden talked about him."

"That man!"

Danny pointed at me. "You're baring your teeth. Not that I blame you. He made me pretty mad the way he was lighting into you."

"You were sort of growling when he was badgering me."

"I was, wasn't I? Better than decking him." Danny made fists and hit at the air. "Anyway, back to Jonathan. I haven't seen him around as much as I used to."

"He's doing better now. He has a trailer outside of town." I put my glass hard on the table. "And now because of me telling Sheriff Hayden about him driving away so quickly, he's a suspect."

Danny wagged his finger at me. "I hear what you're saying, but it might not be good to jump to conclusions. Yet."

"I suppose you're right. My emotions are stretched thin right now. Like the top of a drum."

"It's not every day you find someone dead," Danny said, matter-of-factly.

"Yes. And the day started badly as it was. I dropped my coffee machine carafe and it shattered all over the floor. Then I got the blue screen of death on my old laptop. And while I was getting ready to go, I decided I really hate my hair and considered blue streaks." I yanked at a hunk of my hair. "But I solved one problem. I bought a new french press."

"Blue streaks, huh? That would be a statement. I'm not sure what it would state, but it would be one." He chuckled. "I'm not an expert on the topic of women and hair color, and you didn't ask my opinion, but I think your hair color looks just great as is. However, when it comes to computers, I *am* an expert. I can help you with the laptop. Want me to take a look at it?"

"I was going to ask your opinion. I would pay you, of course."

Danny finished his lemonade. "I would be glad to look at it. And we'll see about paying. Depends on what's wrong." He set his glass on the side table and glanced at his watch. "I should head back to the office. This has been a pleasant interlude. It's very peaceful here. I'm sorry about how it began, but I'm glad we had time to talk without the hustle and bustle of people at church."

"Me too." I had enjoyed our time maybe too much and wished he didn't have to leave so soon.

He stood after gently putting BonBon down. "Why don't you get me your laptop. I'll take it to the shop and see what's up."

I put my glass on the table, went inside, retrieved the machine, and brought it to him.

His brows raised as he took it from my hands. "You didn't mention its age. This poor fellow is a dinosaur in the world of electronics. I'm surprised it was still running."

"The computer's name is Fred. He's very old." I grinned. "George used it for a long time, and he's been gone for three years."

"Well, I might be able to get old Fred up and running temporarily, but after seeing his condition, I can't promise anything. It might be terminal."

I put my hand on my heart and sighed with mock grief. "I'll prepare myself."

272

Danny laughed again then narrowed his eyes. "I hope you had a backup. I can't guarantee I'll be able to access all the information on the hard drive."

"I do. I have one of those secondary hard drive thingies because the hard drive on this one was so small. I keep all my business records in digital format and print them out once a month, so I had to make sure it was safe."

"Good for you! Most people don't think ahead like that." He tucked the laptop under his arm. "I'll call you with the diagnosis. And I can help you buy a new one, if you need it."

"Thanks, Danny." The relief and happiness I felt seemed out of proportion to the situation. I was fully capable of buying a computer, and I was sure some geeky young person at an electronics superstore would help me, but it was nice to have someone offer to help that I knew. Particularly Danny. That emotional revelation disturbed me as much as it intrigued me.

Danny patted my arm with his free hand, jogged down the stairs, and headed across the yard to his truck. As he pulled away, I waved.

I picked up the dishes from the table. Danny *was* a nice-looking man, but he acted like a big brother to all the women in the church, including me, never showing particular interest in anyone.

I shook my head like a dog to rid my head of thoughts of Danny Kaplan and took the dishes to the kitchen.

My cell phone, which I'd left in my purse, buzzed with a text message. It was from Penny. We'd grown close after she lost her husband not too long ago, plus we both farmed, in a manner of speaking. She raised honeybees and sold the honey. Our jobs complemented each other.

HEARD ABOUT KIRK. YOU OKAY?

I texted back. I'M OKAY, BUT I THINK JONATHAN MIGHT BE A SUSPECT.

After a pause, I received another text from her.

THAT'S TOO BAD. MAYBE YOU'LL HAVE TO SOLVE THE MYSTERY? CALL IF YOU NEED TO TALK. OTHERWISE I'LL SEE YOU TONIGHT.

YES, I'LL BE THERE. THANK YOU, HON. LOVE YOU.

She texted me back a smiley face.

Penny did understand, as would Morgan, as soon as they heard. Both of them had experienced similar incidents.

My cell phone rang in my hand. I didn't recognize the number, but I answered it anyway. Call it instinct or perhaps discernment.

"Hello?"

"Uh, is this, uh, Evelyn?"

"Yes, who is this?"

"It's, uh, Jonathan. I need you to come and get me. Please. I'm at the sheriff's office."

He hung up before I could say a word.

At the sheriff's office, I parked my truck in the lot next to the building and rushed inside. Jonathan sat in a chair in the small, bare waiting area and jumped up when he saw me. His raggedy blond hair stood on end.

"Sorry to bug you, Evelyn, but I need to get out of here. They drove me here. I need to get my car. I . . . I'm going to fly apart." He started to grab at his hair then took a deep breath and stopped.

"Please don't apologize, hon. Let's get going." We headed for the door.

Then Sheriff Hayden burst through a door and strutted toward us. "Wait!"

"Yes, what?" I snapped.

Jonathan edged toward the door.

"You!" the sheriff barked at Jonathan. "Don't leave town. And you" — he waved his index finger in my direction — "we need to interview you. Now would be a good time."

Sheriff Hayden reminded me of a banty rooster. I avoided roosters in general because I'd been attacked by one once, and they intimidated me. I wished I could avoid the sheriff as well, but I refused to let him browbeat me. I had to get Jonathan somewhere safe before he flew apart.

I drew myself up to my full height, which

wasn't very tall. "I'll come back, if you'd like me to, Sheriff. Right now, I'm taking Jonathan to his car so he can go home."

The sheriff opened his mouth to speak, but a tall, red-haired woman followed him through the door. I recognized Agent Waters of the Kansas Bureau of Investigation. She'd been assigned here when Morgan and Penny had been involved with murders.

"Conrad, who is this?" she asked.

"Evelyn Kliff. The one who found the victim. I . . . er . . . we need to talk to her."

"I'd be glad to come back and speak with you, if you'd like, but right now I'm going to take Jonathan to his car." I pushed my purse strap firmly on my shoulder.

Jonathan paced behind me.

Agent Waters's gaze fluttered from me to him and back again. "Evelyn, we do need a further interview with you; however, I'm sure it's been a difficult morning. How about I just come to your house this afternoon? In an hour? Would that be convenient?"

Sheriff Hayden grumbled something under his breath that didn't sound nice.

"Yes." I glanced at my watch. "That works." Talking to her at my house would be preferable to coming back here. I sincerely hoped the visit wouldn't include the sheriff.

When Jonathan and I reached my truck, he crawled inside, folding his lanky frame into the passenger seat.

"Thanks." He slouched and plucked at his jeans.

"It's no problem at all. Where is your car?"

"In the parking lot at the grocery store."

I started the truck and headed out to the street.

Jonathan's right leg started jiggling. "They think I did it. They think I killed Kirk."

"That doesn't surprise me, hon. You were driving away from the church like you were being chased by wolves. You almost ran me off the road."

"Sorry . . . sorry. It's just that I saw him. Dead like that. Blood . . . I hate blood . . ."

"You mean, you found his body and ran?"

"I couldn't stay. Dead bodies make me crazy."

"Oh Jonathan! Why didn't you just call the police?"

"Are you kidding?" He snorted. "Because they'd blame me. Plus, bodies just make me forget everything."

"But you had no reason to kill him."

"I did," he muttered.

"What?"

"I did have a reason, but I'm not going to talk about it." He plucked at his pants again.

"Okay, okay," I said in a soothing voice that I used to use to calm rescue dogs. "Do you want to talk to the pastor?"

"No! I don't believe in that stuff." Both his

legs jiggled now. "I just need to get home."

"Okay. I'll get you to your car as fast as I can." I decided the best thing to do was distract him. "Have I told you that I've started making soap to sell at the farmers' market? It's fascinating, really. I use goat's milk, which probably sounds weird."

I continued, and as I did, he calmed down.

By the time we reached the parking lot, he was no longer bouncing both legs or picking at his pants. He grasped the door release. The door swung open and he climbed out. But before he slammed it shut, he bent down to look at me. "Thanks, Evelyn. You're the best. You always have been. George was a lucky guy."

"I was the lucky one, Jonathan."

"You both were." He slammed the door and walked away.

An hour later, I paced my living room, waiting for Agent Waters to get to my house. When she arrived, my dogs ran to the door. I pulled it open and told the dogs to sit. She smiled as she looked at them, her face softening.

"I can lock them away, if you'd like."

"No. I love dogs. I have two of my own. I miss them when I'm gone."

I opened the screen door, and she walked in.

"Okay, guys. Have at her."

All the dogs except Diggy circled around her until she'd greeted each one personally.

"Let's go to the family room." I figured my favorite room would make being interviewed easier. "Would you care for anything to drink?"

"No, thanks. We should get business done. I have some other things to do."

I led her to the family room and motioned toward my large leather couch. I sat in the recliner.

"This is lovely." She motioned toward the sliding door that overlooked the large, tree-shaded backyard. "You must enjoy the peace."

"I do. My husband inherited the place from his grandfather. We put a lot of work into it."

"What does your husband do?"

"He was a man of many jobs, including farming. He passed away three years ago."

A spasm crossed Agent Waters's face as she settled on the couch. "I'm sorry to hear that."

BonBon jumped up next to her and rested her head on the agent's thigh. Agent Waters put her hand on BonBon's head and glanced at the other dogs.

"All mixed breeds, I see."

"My husband and I used to do dog rescue — mostly mixed breeds. After he died, I turned the business part of that over to a good friend, and I'm only partially involved at this point."

"A worthy cause. Good for you." She pulled a notebook and pen from her pocket. The turned wood barrel of the pen caught my eye.

I pointed at it. "That is gorgeous."

Her eyes softened, and she held it up. "It is, isn't it? My brother made it for me from a tree that was in our parents' backyard. They are both deceased."

"What a nice gift."

She nodded then her eyes hardened. "I have just a few questions to get started. First, you look familiar. Have I seen you before?"

"Yes. I'm friends with Morgan Butler and Penny Parsons."

Her lips thinned. "Ah, yes. I remember your friends. Well, then. You're familiar with the drill. I won't waste any time with explanations of procedure."

She asked me about my job at the weekly church lunch then about the discovery of Kirk. The way she did it made the experience more clinical, and I appreciated the lack of emotion.

"Did you know the victim?" she asked.

"Not well. Though he was from this area, he was relatively new at the church. I only moved here after I married George. Kirk was filling in for one of our church members who runs the lunch program. He wasn't well liked. He was, um, difficult."

"I see." She asked me questions about the church and the staff. I filled her in the best I could, realizing as I spoke that any of them could have been guilty.

"Jonathan Kliff is related to you, I assume, by marriage?"

"Yes."

"In your initial interview, you said you saw him driving away. Tell me about that, please?"

"He was driving down the road at a fast clip, away from the church." I swallowed. "When I drove him back to his car, he told me he found Kirk, but then he ran away because the blood freaked him out. He has PTSD."

She made a note.

"This past year, doctors have gotten his treatments balanced. Before that, he sometimes slept on the street. Sheriff Hayden doesn't have anything good to say about Jonathan. I know that PTSD might somehow make people think he's violent and deadly. But the thing is, Jonathan isn't like that. He's a gentle guy." I paused. "There was some sort of awful bombing that injured him and killed his buddies. He told George, my husband, about it, but neither ever told me. Whatever it was, it made him turn inward."

"I'm familiar with PTSD. I've seen it in law enforcement. The diagnosis certainly isn't an automatic guilty verdict. I look at facts." Agent Waters's face was expressionless. "Are you aware of any ties between him and Kirk?"

"They grew up together. Hung around

together when they were teenagers." I clasped my hands in my lap.

She stared at me. "Are you aware that Jonathan and the deceased recently had a violent altercation?"

"No, I wasn't," I whispered, wringing my hands, thinking about Jonathan's confession. "Perhaps that explains Kirk's black eye. I saw it and wondered."

"It does." Agent Waters shut her notebook and stood. "Thank you for your time. I may have more questions later."

I walked her to the door where she abruptly turned to face me.

"Just in case you get it in your head to investigate like your friends did, please understand that I can't keep you safe. But if you do decide to do it, I'd like to know anything pertinent that you discover." She paused. "That is not my permission for you to become a sleuth. It is my acknowledgment that your friends were nosy. And foolish."

I gulped. "I understand."

Agent Waters leaned down and patted each one of the dogs on the head. Then she grinned for the first time since she'd arrived. "My dogs will smell your dogs and think I'm two-timing."

I laughed. As I shut the door behind her, I knew for sure that Jonathan was a viable suspect. My heartbeat quickened. I would have to follow Morgan and Penny's example.

I needed to find out who had killed Kirk before Jonathan was arrested.

That evening, I drove to town and parked along the street in front of the Coffee Perk. The shades in the windows were drawn and the closed sign showed on the door. Besides discussing our latest book, I was sure that one of tonight's topics would be the mystery of who killed Kirk, and that was good. I needed their help.

When I stepped inside, everyone had already arrived.

"Am I late?"

"No," Morgan said. "We're early. We've been discussing your mystery."

"You are going to investigate, aren't you?" Penny asked. "I told everyone that Jonathan might be a suspect."

"After an interview with Agent Waters, I'm pretty sure of it."

"So she's here. That's good." Morgan patted the chair next to her. "Sit! We want to hear all the details." She poured a cup of coffee from a carafe on the table and slipped it in front of me.

I dropped onto the chair. "I'm going to try to investigate, but I have no idea what to do. I'm good with chickens, herbs, and organizing, but solving a crime?"

"I run a coffee shop, and I did it," Morgan said.

"And I raise bees." Penny chuckled. "Although I guess that sort of made it easier to handle the sheriff. He's a bit like an angry bee."

"That's the truth," I murmured.

"Courage." Jo patted my arm. Her fluffy white hair glimmered in the lights.

Harper leaned toward me. "Tell us everything."

I began with a description of the scene in the church fellowship hall. I gulped. "Finding Kirk like that was . . . well, it's just awful to think about, especially knowing it was deliberate. At first I thought he'd had a heart attack and hit his head."

"Some kind of powerful emotion led to his murder, that's for sure," Morgan said.

Harper shook her head. "I happened to see Cameron . . . er . . . Deputy Davis today."

"Oh really?" Morgan chuckled. "Pray tell, what was that about?"

Harper smacked Morgan's arm. "Stop! I know what you're insinuating. You're looking to set me up. Just because you've found love with Mr. Good-Looking Book Author."

Morgan smiled. "I believe I have. Anyway, I'm sorry. Do go on." She didn't look the least bit sorry.

Harper rolled her eyes then turned apologetically to me. "I'm afraid Jonathan *is* a suspect, Evelyn. Deputy Davis says he and Kirk had a blowup over the weekend that ended in fisticuffs. Kirk ended up with a black eye."

"Agent Waters told me about that. And I saw Kirk's black eye at the scene. All Jonathan admitted to me was that he had reason in the cops' eyes to kill Kirk."

"I don't want to be the negative voice here," Jo said, "but are you absolutely positive he didn't do it?"

My common sense warred with my emotions. I wanted to defend Jonathan, just like I had when I was talking with Agent Waters, but did I know for sure? "I guess I can't be absolutely positive he didn't. He did run, but he told me seeing Kirk gave him a flashback."

Morgan nodded. "You might be able to determine that just by talking to him, if you can. Ask him point-blank. Then look for signs of lying. You've probably been around him long enough to be able to tell if you watch closely."

"I guess I can do that."

"You need to find out more about Kirk," Jo chimed in. "And the other people who had access to him." She knit her brow. "He's related to that woman who works at your church. The secretary. The one whose aunt just passed away."

"Yes. Carrie Prescott." I leaned back in my chair. "They were cousins."

"I know her family," Jeanine said. "That aunt of hers, Hazel Prescott, just died recently. Boy, that woman could cook! Her potato salad was outstanding, and her eggplant Parmesan was to die for. Her baked goods out of this world. I would love to see some of her recipes."

"That's the truth." Harper nodded.

"She said she was going to write a cookbook." Jo rubbed a finger on her coffee cup.

"I can see why," Jeanine murmured.

"Carrie is a puzzle," Penny said thoughtfully, wiping a strand of brunette hair from her eyes.

"She's one of those people who tries to be everything to everybody," Jo said. "But she's a little slow on the draw, if you get my drift. Like she's not altogether there sometimes."

"Head in the clouds." Harper tapped her temple.

"That's how she acts," Jo said, "but I'm not sure if that's how she really is or if it's just covering up other things. She seems a bit self-centered to me."

"Good point." Morgan tapped the table. "So, she's definitely a suspect. Who else?"

"Who was there at the church that morning besides Carrie?" Penny asked. "It almost had to be someone there. The building is kind of out in the middle of nowhere."

I frowned. "Wow. I really hate to think it's anyone from my church, but, okay, here's a list as far as I know. The pastor, Carrie, Velma Johnson —"

"Velma?" Morgan snorted. "That woman is a thorn in my side when she comes in here. Always complaining about my coffee and telling me how to run my business."

Penny rolled her eyes. "She bought honey from me and brought back an almost empty jar, demanding I refund her money because the honey made her sick. Then she proceeded to tell me how to raise bees."

"Maybe she ate the whole jar at once," I said. "You know Proverbs says something about getting sick if you eat too much honey. 'Hast thou found honey? eat so much as is sufficient for thee, lest thou be filled therewith, and vomit it.' "

Everyone laughed.

"If I mention how irritated she makes me, I'll have to go home and repent," Jeanine said.

"She is difficult," I admitted.

"What about your pastor?" Penny asked. "Any link between him and Kirk?"

"I have no idea. I guess I need to find out. But I can't imagine him or Carrie killing Kirk." I set my elbows hard on the table. "Really, I can't imagine *anyone* killing Kirk. Maybe the police are wrong, and he really did have a heart attack and hit his head."

Everyone stared at me like I'd grown an extra arm.

I waved my hands in the air. "Okay, okay! Just call me naive."

"Naive." Morgan laughed.

"You hate seeing the bad in people," Penny said.

I sighed. "George used to say, 'Evelyn, you can't just see the good in people, because they'll blindside you.' I've always wondered about that. Aren't we supposed to see the best in people? How can I reconcile people's bad behavior with that? Like the sheriff's ill temper, for instance."

Jo crossed her arms on the table. "God wants us to love people despite their flaws. He never said ignore the flaws. When you see people through a lens of only good, then you can't see the real person. And when you don't see them as real, you can't pray for them like you ought to."

"That's a good point," I said.

Everyone nodded.

I scratched my chin. "You know who else was at the church earlier this morning? Vernon Benson, the construction guy. He's helping with the fellowship hall redo." I glanced at Morgan. "Remember? He came in the Perk this morning."

"He did!" Morgan said. "And he looked like he was stressed, like he'd been exercising or something."

Harper pursed her lips. "Right place, maybe right time."

"Does that cover suspects for now?" Penny asked.

"I think so." I tapped the table with my

fingers. I was forgetting something.

"I'll listen for gossip while I work," Morgan said.

"Me too." Jeanine grinned.

"How about snacks, everyone? Then we can discuss our book." Morgan jumped up and headed for the counter. "Jeanine brought a new cookie she's experimenting with."

"Sounds great to me!" Penny patted her stomach.

"We're quality control." Harper chuckled. "Testing the products."

"I can always count on you guys." Jeanine smiled. "And I brought a lot of them, so how about you take some to Jonathan, Evelyn. You know what they say about men and their stomachs. Might make the conversation flow when you see him."

"That reminds me of something." Morgan placed a large basket of cookies on the table. "Before we tackle our book, we need to cover one more topic."

"What's that?" Jo asked.

"Danny Kaplan."

My stomach flip-flopped.

"Why would we talk about Danny?" Penny asked. "I know he's a great guy. Really good with computers, but . . ."

Morgan winked at me. "Because I think Evelyn likes him."

Everyone's eyes fell on me.

Penny's mouth fell open. "Seriously? You

never said a word."

"Do tell!" Jo said.

"Yes, please do." Jeanine giggled and put her chin in her hands.

I blushed. "Morgan, I can't believe you even said that! And the rest of you, stop right now. I do not like him like that." I paused. "Well, honestly, I've avoided thinking about it. But even so, he's a confirmed bachelor."

"So, you do like him," Penny said.

My mouth flapped like a goldfish's.

"You're young," Jo said. "Remember what the Bible says about younger widows. They should marry again."

"I'm not *that* young."

"Well, you're not as old as I am."

The prospect sounded more appealing than I thought it would. And that reminded me of what I'd forgotten. "You know what? Danny was there that morning too. He was fixing the church computers."

"Well then, you must investigate him as well," Morgan said. "Personally."

"Morgan! Really."

She snickered. Grins spread over everyone else's faces. Penny wiggled her eyebrows.

"Now I don't feel so alone," Harper said, referring to Morgan teasing her about Deputy Davis.

"Have mercy on Evelyn," Jeanine said. "And why don't we pray for her right now. For her safety and for success. And discernment about a certain man."

We all joined hands. Jo led the prayer. When we were done, I felt better. I could do this.

"We're going to help you." Morgan jumped up to get more coffee before we began discussing our book.

"We will," Penny said. "We'll all ask questions too."

Everyone else nodded.

Jo reached across the table and grabbed my hand. "I know bad things have happened. A man was murdered. But I have a good feeling about how it's all going to turn out. Just go slow and keep praying."

I would go slow. I was in no hurry to jump into danger.

THREE

On Wednesday morning BonBon woke me by jumping in the middle of my stomach. I groaned and gently pushed her away. "Get off, you little hairy beast. Haven't I told you that you aren't my alarm clock? Not that you ever listen."

Her skinny tail beat the air. She climbed back on top of me and licked my chin. I looked at the clock. Six-thirty. I knew I wouldn't get back to sleep. I had too much on my mind. Too many questions to answer. I crawled out of bed and threw back the curtains. The sky was so blue and the air so clear, it seemed like God had taken a paintbrush and covered everything with a fresh coat of color. I watched the two squirrels playing in the yard, and I smiled.

Perhaps the freshness of the day had nothing at all to do with the weather. Maybe with the passing of the worst of my grief over George's death, a film had been lifted from my eyes, and I'd gone from being depressed and seeing muted shades in nature to being alive again and noticing bright, bold colors. I knew without a doubt that George would approve. He would never have wanted me to grieve forever.

The dogs snuffled around while I dressed. I tucked my phone into my pants pocket, and we all jogged down the stairs. I grabbed my egg basket and trotted outside. The dogs did their business and started to play, rolling around the grass like happy children.

I went to the chicken coop to check for eggs. I had five. I put them in my basket. Henry, a buff-colored Brahma Bantam hen, pecked at the ground around my feet. She was a recent addition from a chicken rescue and the sweetest bird I'd ever owned. She liked to cuddle, and I'd gotten into the habit of carrying her while I walked through the herb beds in the morning.

I picked her up and tucked her under my arm like a football, put the basket on my other arm, and went to a large patch of dirt containing a dozen raised beds.

While Henry made her little contented chicken purrs, I admired the plants. Chamomile, lavender, mints, oregano, basil . . . so many. Once the dew dried, I'd come out and clip some. Meantime, I needed to eat breakfast and determine my course for the day. If I was going to solve this mystery, I had work to do.

I put Henry back with her flock in the pen and headed toward the house.

"Come on, kids!" I called to the dogs.

Inside, I fed the pack and made oatmeal with golden raisins, a sprinkle of homemade granola, and a drizzle of honey. With some apprehension, I made my first cup of coffee in the new french press using the ground coffee from the Perk. It looked good and smelled good, but that meant nothing. I added cream. Then I grabbed my Bible and headed to the family room.

Ensconced in the chair, I opened my Bible in my lap and absentmindedly sipped the coffee. I gasped and took another sip. Then I stared at the liquid in my mug. It was the best coffee I'd ever made! I took another sip to make sure I wasn't imagining things. I wasn't. Not only was it the best coffee I'd ever made, the taste rivaled Morgan's brew. I couldn't wait to tell Penny!

I ate while I did devotions, going through the last of the Bible study questions for tonight's service at church. I jotted notes in a small spiral notebook I always carried with me. When I was done, I leaned back.

"Okay, Lord. I need guidance." I thought about my friends' words the night before.

Jo was right. Jonathan could be guilty. If he was, I wanted to find out myself rather than hearing a guilty verdict from a jury. And then I could encourage him to come clean, and I would no longer be involved with the mystery. But, if he wasn't, then I would help clear him. Agent Waters had reluctantly listened to Morgan and Penny when she was investigating their mysteries. Based on what the agent said when she interviewed me, she might listen to me too. I flipped to a new page in my notebook and printed SUSPECTS at the top and underlined it. Then I began my list.

Jonathan
Carrie Prescott
Velma Johnson
Vernon
Benson

I tapped my pen on my lower lip. I'd better add my pastor, even though I couldn't imagine what he'd have against Kirk.

Pastor Mark Sheldon

And last I wrote *Danny.* Oh, how I hoped it wasn't Danny.

I needed to be methodical about this. First, I would talk to Jonathan. Then I would try to determine if any of my suspects had motivation. I could begin that process at church tonight. I also needed to find out more about Kirk. I wasn't sure how to do that, but I'd go see Jonathan as soon as I was done with my morning chores. The best approach was to show up unannounced. That way he wouldn't be able to weasel out of the visit to avoid me, which he'd done in the past.

I leaned back and scraped the last of my

oatmeal from the bowl and swallowed the last of the perfect coffee. Then I ran my fingers through my raggedy hair. Perhaps I should get it cut this week. I pulled my phone from my pocket and dialed the salon from my contact list. They had an opening the next day, and I took it.

As I hung up, I assured myself that my sudden desire to get a haircut had nothing to do with a certain computer guy/EMT that my friends had been teasing me about. Danny was personable and lots of fun, but as far as I knew, he was unavailable. Besides, he was so opposite George. Danny was a button-down, geeky kind of guy who always looked put together. George had been a white socks, worn boots, jeans, and flannel shirt kind of guy. When George dressed up, it meant unstained blue jeans and polished boots. Danny regularly wore suits to the Sunday service. George had been very laid back. Danny's personality had more than a touch of effervescence. But the things they had in common — intelligence and humor, plus core values of godliness and kindness — were the same.

My cell phone rang. There, on my screen, as if my thoughts had somehow encouraged him to call, was Danny's name.

"Hello." Awkwardness made my voice squeak.

"Evelyn, hello! You sound funny. Are you

okay? Are you having side effects from yesterday?"

My awkwardness fled at the cheerfulness of his voice. "No. In fact, I'm doing surprisingly well, considering."

"That's good to hear. Please know I'm here if you need to talk about any of it."

"Thank you."

"All right. To business. I'm calling about your laptop. I'm not going to beat around the bush."

"I can tell by the tone of your voice it's terminal."

He chuckled. "That's about it in a nutshell. I'm glad you have everything backed up. I won't have to attempt to scrape together information from your hard drive."

"I guess it's time to think about a new one, and quickly. I need it for my records. I have a farmers' market this weekend. I use my laptop to keep track of inventory, as well as my finances."

"What else do you use your computer for? I know you're not a hard-core gamer. This old laptop would have barely survived a lively game of solitaire."

I giggled. "No games. I don't want to start a habit like that. Too addicting. Aside from business, I do online research, some advertising, and I sometimes engage on social media."

I heard him shuffling things around. "I have

some used laptops that might be suitable, but really, if you can afford it, I'd recommend something brand new and shiny."

"That sounds good. I've never bought a computer on my own, but brand new and shiny sounds enticing. Do you have any suggestions about brands? I'm pretty clueless."

"Besides the basic hard drive, speed, and memory sizes, it's probably down to how you feel about the way the keys work; how the machine looks, if that matters to you; and what you really want to do." He paused. "Say, how do you feel about a field trip? We could drive to that big-box store a couple towns over and maybe a brand name computer store. You can get a feel for what you like. And if you don't find anything that seems right, I can give you a loaner for the weekend."

I had a sudden urge to cry at his kindness. I wasn't sure where it came from, but it was a good feeling. A warm feeling. "That would be perfect."

"I can skip out of work this coming Friday afternoon. Would that work for you? Then you'll have a laptop in time for Saturday morning."

"That sounds perfect. Thank you so much, Danny."

"My pleasure."

We exchanged a few more pleasantries then he hung up.

I sat there with my cell phone in my hand, staring at the screen. Was Danny just being nice? Did he help everyone buy new computers? He was content being a bachelor. I'd heard him say so at Bible study when he'd first started attending the church. I shook my head. *Evelyn, you just settle down right now. You don't need to get emotional. You've had enough emotions to last a lifetime. Besides, he could be a murderer.*

But my heart wasn't listening. It was feeling something it hadn't felt in quite a while.

After chores, I grabbed the bag of cookies that Jeanine had given me the night before for Jonathan and headed down my tree-lined drive. On the spur of the moment, I had decided to take Diggy with me. The dog liked nothing more than a truck ride. In fact, he liked it better than anything else except Bon-Bon.

Jonathan's trailer was on the back of an acre, miles out of town. His elderly car sat in the driveway out front. I parked next to it. I knew he might chase me away. He didn't like people coming to his house, and I'd never been inside.

The door of the trailer opened. Jonathan stepped out onto a wooden porch, mouth pursed in a frown.

"Evelyn? What's up? I wasn't expecting you."

"I know. I just came by to chat for a minute. And to bring you some cookies." I held up the bag.

He crossed his arms and his frown grew. Then Diggy hopped out of the car, leaped past me, and tore up the porch steps to Jonathan.

"Diggy! Bad manners!"

That's when a miracle happened right in front of my eyes. Diggy's tail was wagging so fast, I could hardly see it. Jonathan's frown morphed into a smile that covered his whole face and made his eyes glow. He fell to his knees. In all the years I'd known him, I'd never seen that expression on his face. And I'd never seen Diggy approach anybody with that kind of enthusiasm.

I quietly walked to the porch, purse and bag in hand.

"Such a handsome boy," Jonathan murmured and buried his hands in Diggy's long fur; then he looked up at me. "What's his name? How long have you had him?"

"His name is Diggy because he likes to dig holes. I got him from a rescue organization a year ago when he was just a pup. Someone had dropped him and his mother along the side of the road and his mother got hit. She didn't survive. A Good Samaritan stopped and found Diggy crying. He was in pretty bad shape." I stopped at the bottom of the stairs. "They called me, knowing I used to do dog rescues. They were desperate to find a place to foster him. The poor little guy. He cried for a long time."

Jonathan buried his face in Diggy's fur. I thought I heard him say, "You understand, don't you, buddy?" When he finally stood, he grinned at me. "Okay. You can come in."

I handed him the bag and thanked God under my breath for giving me the idea to bring Diggy along . . . and for the miracle I'd just witnessed.

When I stepped inside the trailer, I was pleasantly surprised. For some reason, I thought the place would be a pigsty, but it was immaculate. *So much for not judging someone, Evelyn.*

"Sit down." Jonathan pointed at a worn, but clean couch along one wall. "The furniture isn't much, but it works. Got it from a veteran's organization." He went to the kitchen and Diggy followed, close on his heels. Jonathan placed the bag of cookies carefully on the counter, as if it held treasure. "I was about to have a cup of coffee. You want one?"

"Yes, please." That would give me time to figure out how to approach the topic of Kirk's murder.

I sat on the couch. Diggy stayed at Jonathan's side. After Jonathan poured the coffee in mismatched mugs, he smiled down at the dog. Diggy's feathered tail gently wagged.

Jonathan came back to the living area and handed me a mug. "Here you go."

"Thank you." I settled back.

Jonathan sat on another couch across from me, Diggy at his feet. Jonathan patted the seat next to him and the dog jumped up and put his head in Jonathan's lap.

"I've never seen him act like this before," I marveled. "He's always been so unattached. Unemotional. That's why I could never adopt him out. He just didn't take to anyone."

"Sounds like me, in a way." Jonathan's soft smile and warm glance swept over the dog then rested on me.

The seed of a thought dropped into my mind, but I didn't have time to pursue it before he spoke.

"Listen, I'm sorry I fell apart yesterday. Seeing Kirk dead like that gave me flash-backs."

"I understand."

"Why have you come?"

His directness startled me, and I shifted nervously. "Please don't get upset with me, but I want to ask you some questions. I want to solve Kirk's murder."

His head jerked. "Why in the world would you want to do that?"

I took a deep breath. "Because I want to protect you."

"You want to protect me? So, you feel responsible for me?" His eyes glinted. "Obligated? Because of George?"

Diggy shifted on the couch.

A flare of anger made my cheeks burn. "Don't accuse me of things, Jonathan. You don't know me at all, and that's not because I haven't tried. Yes, how George felt about you is important, but I want to do this because *I* care for you."

Jonathan sagged against the back of the couch. "I'm sorry. I overreact easily."

"I get it, but can you please stop rejecting me and accept the fact that I want to be your friend?"

"Okay." His mouth lifted on one side. "George used to say that you could be spunky sometimes. That was the exact word he used."

George *had* said that. The memory made my anger fade, and I grinned. "Very true, and if you want to avoid another episode of my spunkiness, be nice and talk to me."

Jonathan nodded. "Yes, ma'am."

"I want to prove you aren't guilty. But before I can do that, I need your assurance that you aren't. You aren't, are you?"

His blue eyes, so much like George's, suddenly snapped with emotion, but I wasn't sure what kind.

"No, I'm not guilty. But the cops aren't going to see it that way once they find out my connection with Kirk."

"You two had an altercation, I heard?"

"We did. And I hit him first. Gave him a shiner."

"You want to tell me why?"

His mouth puckered. "No."

"O–kay. So . . . you were friends when you were young?"

"I thought so until . . . there was something that happened between us. I don't want to talk about it. If I'd known he was going to be at the church that day, I would never have showed up. I didn't want to hit him again."

"Oh my." I wasn't sure what else to say.

"That's an understatement. So, you can see why the cops think I did it. I had good reason, which they will discover in due time, if they don't already know." He leaned forward. "I assure you, Evelyn, I'm a lot of things, but not a killer."

I believed him. Hopefully I wasn't being naive, but I didn't think so.

"Are you sure you won't tell me what happened between the two of you?"

"Look, I don't want to be rude, but no."

I stood, knowing he meant what he said. "Okay. I won't keep you then. I have a bunch of stuff to do today." I took my mug to the sink then picked up my purse and went to the door.

Diggy didn't move until Jonathan stood. Then he hopped off the couch and sat next to the gangly man, ignoring me.

The thought that had been a seed in my mind earlier suddenly bloomed, and I made a decision. "Would you like to keep Diggy, at least temporarily? Maybe foster him, if you can't keep him? He's taken a real shine to you."

Jonathan's face lit. "You'd leave your dog here for me?"

I smiled. "He's never really been mine. Like I said before, he's never taken to anyone until now."

Jonathan scratched the dog's head. "So, you're looking for a home for him?"

"I am, but it's impossible to adopt out a dog who avoids connecting with people."

"Can I . . . I mean . . . am I eligible to adopt him?"

"Nothing would make me happier. In fact, taking him away from you at this point seems just plain wrong. It's like he was just waiting for you. I can bring you some dog food."

Jonathan blinked rapidly. "You don't have to bring food. I'll go buy something. Tell me what. The very best."

I suggested a brand, my heart filled to bursting. "All right. He's housebroken, of course. He loves car rides, but you can't leave him in a hot car. He's okay on the leash, but I suspect he'll stick close by you. If you have any questions, you can call me."

"I . . . I don't know how to thank you." He

wiped his eyes with the back of his hand.

"You don't have to. Your joy, and Diggy's, is enough for me. And if you'd like, later on, I could look into getting Diggy trained and licensed as an emotional support dog for you. I don't know if it's possible, but I have some people I could ask. Then you could take him with you to events and in public places."

"I don't go many places, but I'll think about it." Jonathan walked me to the door. Then another miracle happened. He hugged me. It was awkward, and he backed away quickly, but it was a hug, nonetheless.

As I walked to my car, I realized this was another indication that I was ready to move on. George and I used to find great joy in putting dogs and people together. That feeling had returned like a long-lost friend and, for the first time, it wasn't accompanied by grief. I really was healing.

On Wednesday night, notebook tucked in my purse, I headed out to church, determined to find out everything I could about the morning of the murder. Although the crime would be the topic in many whispered conversations, actually talking to people outright would be difficult. How could I explain why I was asking questions?

When I stepped into the large foyer of the church, Pastor Mark saw me, stopped his current conversation, and zigzagged through the crowd to get to me.

"Evelyn, how are you doing?"

"I'm doing well, considering."

"Yesterday morning was terrible. None of us wants to use the fellowship hall." The pastor's expression was grim.

"Yeah. It'll be hard to go down there, at least for a while."

"It's a good thing renovation plans were already in the works."

"It is!"

"Particularly for you, I imagine."

I nodded. "Pastor, how well did you know Kirk?"

A grimace flashed over Pastor Mark's face, but it was quickly replaced by an expression of pastoral sadness. "He's only been here at the church for a few months. Unlike a lot of our parishioners, I didn't grow up around here, so I didn't know him when he was young."

"I was kind of surprised that no one upstairs in the church heard anything when he was killed."

"I've thought that, myself. But I was on the phone, and we have music going on in the background. Plus, the insulation is pretty good since the basement level is where the kids have children's church."

One of the deacons approached. "Pastor, we need to discuss something before Bible study begins."

Pastor Mark patted my arm. "Why don't you call Carrie and make an appointment to see me. We can discuss it all, and I can pray with you."

"Okay, that would be wonderful." Apparently, he thought I was discussing Kirk because I needed the outlet. I was sorry to have inadvertently misled him. Pastor Mark was a kind man. After George died, the pastor had been my steadfast supporter, always available whenever I needed prayer or an ear to listen. I didn't like the fact that I had to consider him a suspect. My gut said he had nothing to do with the murder, but I suspected he knew more about Kirk than he was letting on.

I couldn't locate Carrie, but I managed to find Velma, which wasn't difficult, because she was looking for me.

She marched toward me like a drill sergeant. I felt like saluting when she halted in front of me. "I don't know what we're going to do about the Tuesday lunch program. Pastor won't discuss it right now. He says it's too soon. Next week we'll look into finding another venue until the fellowship hall is redone, because people will associate it with murder." She harrumphed. "People need to grow up. Build a bridge. Bad things happen. We should just go on."

"Well, I'm sure the pastor will do what's

best," I murmured. "Murder is hard to deal with."

She shrugged. "I suppose. Are you going to take charge of the program?"

"The lunch program? Me?"

"That's what I asked."

"I have no intention or desire to do so. I just want to help."

"Fine." She started to turn away, but I tapped her shoulder and she faced me again.

"Do you have any thoughts about what happened?"

"What do you mean?"

"Kirk's murder."

She looked over her glasses at me. "What an odd question. You were there, weren't you?"

"I guess what I mean is, do you have any thoughts about why someone would murder him?"

"I can't imagine why you'd even want to know that. But in my opinion, he probably deserved it. He was a bossy know-it-all."

I thought about the pot calling the kettle black, but I wisely didn't voice my opinion. "How long had you known him?"

"Long enough to know that I never liked him, which is most of his life. And then he left his wife and three children and came back here. He should have stayed away. Especially from Hazel Prescott."

He'd left his wife and kids. That was food

for thought. "You knew Hazel well?"

"She was my best friend. We cooked together. And now she's dead. Because of him. And that spoiled airhead, Carrie." Velma's nostrils flared.

"You think they killed her?" I asked.

"Not directly. But there's more than one way to kill someone."

Velma's gaze wandered across the room then back to me. "Well, since you don't have much to offer in the way of the lunch program, I need to talk to some other people before the study begins. Are we done?"

"I suppose."

I watched her walk away. So, Kirk had left his family, and Velma thought he, along with Carrie, had contributed to Hazel's death. I made some mental notes then looked around for Carrie. She was in a corner of the room with a group of ladies. I approached them, hoping to pull her aside.

"So, you're not going to help with the missions fund-raiser this year?" The church pianist eyed Carrie with raised brows.

"No. That's why I'm giving you guys Aunt Hazel's recipe."

"Wow, you've never given anyone that recipe before." A young blond, bouncing a baby on her hip, glanced from woman to woman.

Every year the women of the church hosted an Italian dinner to raise money for the missionaries we supported. Hazel's eggplant Parmesan was one of the favorite offerings.

"With Aunt Hazel's passing, I have all of her recipes. I want to share this, especially since I can't help this year. I've got a lot going on, plus I just discovered I can't have nightshades."

The pianist frowned. "What in the world are nightshades?"

"Things like tomatoes, potatoes, and peppers, right?" The young blond looked at Carrie. "The allergy is more common than people think."

"Yes. That's it." Carrie took a step backward. "I gotta go. I'll email the recipe to the group."

She whirled around and walked away, moving so fast I had to scurry to keep up with her. "Carrie? Can I talk to you for a minute?"

She shot me a glance over her shoulder. "Can it wait, Evelyn? I have some things to do before the service."

I nodded. "I'll catch you after the study then."

Vernon entered the building, but he was accompanied by his wife as well as four little kids, who were all babbling at the same time. His wife was frowning, and a scowl darkened his face. This wouldn't be a good time to talk to him.

Danny strode into the foyer a few steps behind Vernon. I felt flustered thinking about what my friends had said the night before, as well as my own feelings. I tried to duck into the sanctuary before he saw me, but I was too late. He came barreling toward me.

"Evelyn! I've been researching computers for you, and I have some ideas."

"That's great." I forced myself to smile.

"You okay?"

I shrugged. "I just feel weird."

His mouth fell open. "Oh! How insensitive of me. Again. Of course. This is the first time you've been back to the church since the, uh, unfortunate event."

He had no idea the real reason for my awkwardness.

Danny nodded toward the sanctuary. "Want to head inside? I could use a Bible study partner. I'm pretty sure, knowing you, that you studied hard for this week. I didn't so much. But if I sit next to you, maybe I can look over your shoulder and see your answers, just in case anyone calls on me." He grinned. "Although I'm pretty sure God frowns on cheating."

His good humor was catching. I laughed. "If I share willingly, and there's no grade involved, I doubt it's cheating."

"Good. Let's do it."

A few minutes later, I was seated in the sanctuary, Danny on my right. As hard as I tried, I couldn't concentrate on a thing the pastor was saying. First, having Danny in such close proximity proved that my friends were right. I did find him attractive — something I'd have to deal with one way or another because though he seemed to want to maintain our relationship, it might be just friendship he had in mind.

I also kept turning Kirk's murder over in my head. Like, why had the pastor made a face when I mentioned Kirk's name? And what had happened between Kirk and Jonathan?

I opened my notebook to pretend to take notes and thumbed to the page where I'd written my list of suspects, but I didn't realize Danny was looking until he tapped the page.

"What's that," he whispered. "And why is my name on there?"

I felt a blush cover my whole face. I flipped past the page so quickly, it tore.

"I'll tell you afterward," I whispered back.

When the study ended, people cleared out quickly, but Danny didn't move.

He pointed at my now closed notebook. "Well? If I didn't know better, you've written a list of suspects for Kirk's murder. My first clue? The page is titled 'suspects.' "

That would teach me to neatly title the pages in my notebook.

"Well," I imitated him. "You *don't* know bet-

ter, because it *is* a list of suspects for Kirk's murder."

"No kidding! And I'm on it?" He scratched his chin. "I guess I can see why. I was there at the church and — wait!" He scrunched his face into a frown, moved closer, and whispered. "*Why* are you making a list of suspects?"

"Because I want to solve this murder," I whispered back.

"Really?" He blinked like a toad in a hailstorm. "Why?"

"Because of Jonathan. He's not guilty, but the police think he is. I want to help clear his name."

"Seriously?"

"Seriously."

One of the church deacons approached us. "Hey, Danny. We have a computer question. Can you come and talk to us for a minute?" He pointed to a group of men in the corner of the room.

Danny nodded and smiled at the man. "Sure thing. Be there in a minute."

The deacon turned and left.

Danny looked back at me, a grin pulling on the corner of his lips. "I don't know whether I think you're totally awesome or crazy. Or both."

"How about awesomely crazy," I muttered.

He stood, laughing. "I'm amazed I can know someone as long as I've known you and be totally surprised by your actions."

"That's not necessarily a good thing."

"And it's not necessarily a bad thing either." He winked. "We still on for Friday?"

"Yes."

"Good!" He leaned down close to my ear, eyes twinkling. "By the way, I didn't do it." He walked away, chuckling.

I felt sheepish but amused at the same time.

I looked around for Carrie. She was in an intense conversation with Vernon. He walked away, and she began tidying up the sanctuary with a pale face.

I made a beeline for her. "Are you okay?"

She blinked. "I'm fine. You need something?"

"The pastor wants me to make an appointment to see him this week for a little bit of counseling after finding Kirk." I hoped mentioning the topic would open Carrie up for conversation.

She swallowed, and tears filled her eyes. "Such an awful thing." She blinked several times. "I don't know what the rest of the pastor's week looks like. I'll check before I leave tonight. Is there any particular time that's good for you?"

"Afternoons. I have work to do around the farm in the morning, when it's cooler."

"I'll text you, okay?"

"That would be great. You and Kirk were cousins, right?"

She backed up a step. "Why are you asking?"

I racked my brain for a good answer and finally shrugged. "I guess it's part of my personal therapy for working through this whole thing. Sometimes helps to know more about the person who died." A stretch of the truth, perhaps, but not too far from reality.

"Yes, he was my cousin, I'm sad to say."

"I heard he left his family and came back here. He was staying with your aunt Hazel?"

"He was. She passed away shortly after he came back. He shouldn't have come."

I blinked at her, not sure what to say next.

"Sorry. That was totally inappropriate. But he wasn't a nice man. He should have stayed with his family. His kids needed him." She backed away from me. "I have some things to tidy up, and I'll check those dates for you. I'll let you know."

"Sounds good." I wanted to ask more questions, but she walked away before I could think of anything else to say.

I looked around for Vernon, but he'd disappeared. Danny was still tied up with the men in the corner. I managed to slip out of the building without him noticing. I didn't feel like doing any more explaining. Not yet, anyway.

As I walked to my car, I thought about what I knew. Carrie had disliked Kirk. He had left his wife and kids. Did that somehow play into his murder? Velma didn't like Kirk, that was obvious. And she seemed resentful toward him *and* Carrie. And finally, how did Vernon fit into the picture? He was here the morning Kirk was murdered. And why were he and Carrie in a heated discussion?

I drove toward home, knowing two things for sure. Kirk wasn't well liked, and I'd just begun to scratch the surface of why he'd died.

FOUR

On Thursday morning, I woke to BonBon's face resting on my pillow, two inches from mine. No stomach hopping. Her brown eyes sought mine. She put a paw on my arm, and I would have sworn she was trying to ask me a question.

Finally, it dawned on me what was going on. I scratched her head. "You miss Diggy, don't you? I wish I could explain to you what happened. Then you would be happy like he is." Her tail slowly thumped on the mattress.

I stretched and swung my legs over the edge of the bed. "You guys hungry?"

The other two dogs jumped up, tails wagging furiously.

"All right, let's go."

I let them all out the back door, following my usual routine, gathering eggs, cuddling with Henry, and checking my herbs. When we returned to the house, I checked my to-do list on my cell phone. I had a haircut at noon. Carrie had confirmed an appointment with

Pastor Mark at three today. I had a few more things to prepare for the farmers' market. I also wanted to experiment with a recipe for elderberry syrup. I'd need honey from Penny for that, and it would be a good excuse to visit her. I wanted to talk.

I sent her a text message, asking if I could stop by to get some after I finished my chores. She said yes, accompanied by a little bee emoji.

After I fed the dogs, I made myself some oatmeal for breakfast and added a dollop of homemade yogurt, along with some berries and honey. I also made some of my newly excellent coffee. Then I settled down in my chair to eat and do my devotions. After I was done, I flipped my notebook open to my suspect list.

I smoothed the torn page and studied their names. Given the state of the kitchen at the church that morning, Kirk's murder hadn't been planned. It looked like a fit of emotion, perhaps temper. And now that I thought about it, I wasn't sure exactly what had killed Kirk. There was blood, probably from the gash in his head, and a big pot on the floor. Had someone bashed his head with that?

Hopefully, when I met with Pastor Mark, I could eliminate him from my suspect list. I needed to look into why Velma and Carrie were so resentful about Kirk's return and the effect he had on Hazel.

My gaze stopped at Jonathan's name. I wanted to know why he and Kirk fought. I had to convince him to talk to me, and I needed an excuse to stop by his house again. I glanced across the room and noticed Diggy's empty dog bed. That was it! I'd gather all Diggy's things and take them to the trailer after I met with the pastor. I'd also make a stop at the Coffee Perk and pick up some sweets.

Penny must have been watching for me. She opened the screen door holding her little dog, Ju Ju, the dachsie. "Come on in! It's so good to see you."

She put Ju Ju down, and the little dog greeted me with enthusiasm. Penny pointed at her kitchen counter where five jars of golden honey glinted in the light. "Here's some of the best. You'll have to tell me how the elderberry syrup turns out."

I paid her for the honey. "You'll get a bottle from the first batch."

"That would be super. Have a seat. You want anything to drink?" She pointed toward her cozy little living area.

"No, thank you."

I sat on the couch. Penny sat across from me in a comfy chair with Ju Ju in her lap.

"You ready for the farmers' market this Saturday?" she asked.

"I have to make more tea bags later on

today. And wrap some soap." I grinned at her. "Hey, guess what? I can now make a cup of coffee to rival Morgan's."

"No! Really?" Penny giggled. "How?"

"With my new french press that I bought from her."

"I never thought I'd see the day. I need to drop by soon so you can prove it to me."

We smiled at each other. Being with her was like being with a much-loved younger sister.

She eyed me. "You're wearing bright colors. I can count on one hand the times I've seen that."

I looked down at my red blouse. "I was in a good mood, I guess. And I'm going to get my hair cut this afternoon."

"No kidding! No more sewing shears?"

"No more sewing shears."

"Have you heard about your laptop?"

I nodded. "Danny says it's dead. I have to get a new one. He's taking me shopping on Friday afternoon to pick one out."

Penny gasped. "No kidding? He's taking you to buy one?"

"Yes. But I don't think it's that big a deal."

"Seriously, Evelyn, sometimes you really are naive. You do realize that Danny could just get you a laptop, set it up, and sell it to you. He does that for other people. I've never heard of him taking someone to the store to pick one out."

"I suppose."

She raised her brows. "Maybe Danny the bachelor is finally falling for someone."

"Exactly why I'm not thinking about it. Because what if he's not, and I fall for him?"

Penny leaned forward, her hands clasped on her knees. "So, you're not closed to the idea?"

I shook my head and wrapped my arms around a throw pillow. "No, I guess I'm not. But Danny and I have been casual friends for so long, it's hard to see him as more. What if we're all reading the situation wrong and I misinterpret things and embarrass myself. Besides, I just never thought about dating again. I loved George so much. How could anyone else fill that place?"

"No one else should, right? New people in our lives fill new roles."

"Good point." I leaned back, kicked off my shoes, and curled up on the couch. "My feelings are so mixed. I'm probably overthinking everything."

"I truly understand." Her eyes glinted with tears.

"I know you do." I felt tears in my eyes as well.

"Well! Enough emotion!" She clapped her hands. "I have something to add to your information collection. I'm not sure what it means, though."

"Anything is good at this point. I'm at a

total loss."

She chuckled. "Okay, I was talking to Betty, the postmistress."

"The Oak Grove font of information."

"Yes. And she said that she remembered like fifteen years ago, when Carrie and Vernon were in their early twenties, they were pretty tight. They hung together with a small group of friends. Then one of their friends suddenly died, and Carrie and Vernon never hung around together again. And Carrie became what she is now. Sort of a loner."

I scratched my head. "I seem to recall something about that, now that you mention it. I wasn't part of much in the community at that point. George and I were just building up our farm, and I didn't know many people."

"I can't imagine how it has anything to do with Kirk," Penny said, "but it is information about Carrie and Vernon, so, if nothing else, you just get to know your suspects."

"Everything is fair game at this point. Besides, I saw the two of them having an intense conversation last night at church."

"Interesting." Penny stroked Ju Ju's silky fur. "Have you talked to Jonathan?"

"Yes. And I don't think he had anything to do with Kirk's death. But he still won't tell me why the two of them didn't get along. I'm going to stop by and see him again." I smiled. "You won't believe this, but Diggy fell in love with Jonathan. I left him there yesterday."

Her eyes widened. "No kidding! The dog who won't attach to anyone?"

"Yes." I told her how Jonathan and Diggy had immediately bonded. "Sometimes dogs can sense brokenness in people. I've heard stories, but I've never seen it with my own eyes."

"That's fantastic! They are amazing creatures." Penny hugged Ju Ju and smiled. "It's like you were just holding the dog for his real purpose in life."

"Just like people. We all have a purpose, and we wait for God to reveal it."

"More than one purpose, I suspect," she said.

"He never reveals it all at once, does He?"

"Keeps us seeking Him."

"That it does."

I arrived on time for my hair appointment at the local Kut, Kurl, and Kolor. Sammie Joe had cut my hair in the past, and she greeted me with a hug when I walked in.

"Evelyn! I wondered if I'd ever see you again." She ran her fingers through my hair. "None too soon, I'd say."

Two other stylists and their clients looked up at me.

"I've been cutting it myself with sewing scissors. It looks rather ragged."

"Yes, it does." She patted the back of a hair

wash chair. "You sit yourself down here so I can wash it."

She lathered shampoo into my hair with a firm hand. I closed my eyes and relaxed.

"I heard you found Kirk Philips dead in the fellowship hall of your church," Sammie Jo said after she'd finished the shampoo and rinsed my hair.

Conversation in the salon stopped.

"Yes, I did."

"I'm so sorry that happened to you. But I'm not totally surprised about Kirk."

"Why ever not?" I looked up at her.

"He wasn't nice." Sammie motioned for me to sit up. She wrapped my hair with a towel and pointed at her workstation.

"I know he was pretty bossy," I said as I stood.

"He married my best friend. She said he abused her. Had affairs. Then he walked out on her. Left her with three kids."

"Wow."

"She had proof. She was taking him to the cleaners."

A stylist with a short blond bob snorted. "Men like that deserve it!"

"That's putting it mildly," Sammie Jo said. "If she had proof, he would've been paying out the nose, that's for sure."

"Loser," another customer murmured. "Running home like a baby instead of taking it like a man. I heard he'd come to stay with his aunt. Hazel something?"

"Hazel Prescott." Sammie Jo wrapped a hair-cutting cape around me. "She was best friends with that woman at your church. The one who's so bossy?"

"Velma Johnson?"

"That's her. Surprised she has friends, but the two of them were really close."

"How close was Kirk to his aunt?" I asked.

"I'm not really sure," Sammie Joe said. "I just think it's weird she died after he showed up."

"I heard that the murderer is that odd fellow who used to wander the streets," another stylist said.

I clenched my fists in my lap.

Sammie Jo cleared her throat and grimaced. "Sorry, Evelyn."

"What'd I say wrong?" the other stylist asked.

"That guy is related to Evelyn by marriage, right, honey?"

I nodded. "His name is Jonathan. He has PTSD. He's a veteran. I don't believe he killed Kirk. He's not capable."

"I'm sorry," the other stylist said. "Really. I didn't know."

"It's okay." But it wasn't. Word was getting around. And Jonathan was guilty of murder in people's minds.

Silence fell on the salon for a few minutes. Sammie Jo snipped away, and clumps of my hair fell around her feet.

She paused, scissors in the air, and I looked up at her.

"You know what's really odd?" she asked in a soft voice.

"What?"

"I just remembered. Jonathan used to date my best friend. Before she married Kirk."

As I left the hair dresser, I got a text from Harper. She said she had some information for me. She was going to be at the Coffee Perk, doing a little bit of work on her laptop, if I could stop by.

I agreed, especially since I had already planned to buy goodies for Jonathan, hoping it would help him open up to me. I had some time before I met with Pastor Mark.

The Perk was bustling with customers when I walked in. Harper sat at a corner table with her laptop, a muffin, and a cup of coffee. The tables around her were filled with customers. She looked up and waved. I nodded and stepped in line to wait.

"That haircut looks amazing," Morgan said when I reached the counter. "And you're wearing a bright color."

"Thank you, and yes, I am." My gaze settled on some blueberry muffins behind the glass counter. "I'd like three of those."

"Two for Jonathan?"

"You know me too well."

"And coffee?" Morgan asked.

"Yes. Today I'd like one of those fancy ones. A cafe mocha latte."

"Well, that's a switch for you."

"I feel like something different today. Besides, my new french press makes fabulous regular coffee. I don't need to buy it anymore."

"That's great, but still. A new haircut. A bright shirt. A different drink. This wouldn't have anything to do with going computer shopping with Danny Kaplan, would it?"

A blush crept over my cheeks. "How do you know that? Have you been talking to Penny?"

Morgan laughed. "No. I didn't even know that she knows. Besides, she never gives up a confidence. No, I heard it from the horse's mouth."

"Danny told you?"

"He did." She scurried around, making my drink. "He was here, finishing work on my system. He mentioned that yours had died and he was taking you to get another one."

"It's just business," I protested.

"Right." Morgan put a lid on my coffee. "I'm sure he takes all his clients out on a Friday afternoon to buy a computer."

I was pretty sure my cheeks were as bright as my shirt as she set my coffee in front of me.

"Sorry." Morgan smiled. "It's just that we all watched you suffer after George's death.

And we want you to enjoy your life."

I paid her for my drink and muffins.

She handed me some change. "If that means Danny, that would be good. Or anyone else, for that matter. But Danny is a good guy."

"That's one point I can't argue with."

I joined Harper at her table before Morgan could say anything else I wasn't ready to hear.

"Your hair looks great!" Harper said.

"Thank you. What are you up to?"

"I came here intending to drink coffee and start planning for the coming school year. I have some new ideas, but I got distracted by ads for estate sales."

I smiled. "We all need to go antiquing together sometime."

Her eyes lit. "That's a great idea! But meanwhile, you have a mystery to solve, and I have some information for you."

"Good!" I pulled a muffin from my bag and took a sip of my coffee and sighed. "Delicious."

"I'll talk while you indulge." Harper grinned. "Jo and I were eating out last night at the sub place, and Velma happened to walk in. Jo invited her to sit with us."

"Oh dear," I murmured.

Harper chuckled. "Jo is a kind woman. Anyway, Velma ranted on and on about Kirk and the lunch program going down the tubes, and so on and so forth. Then she got on the topic of Hazel. Apparently, she and Hazel were friends from way back."

"I've heard that."

"Velma never really stopped for a breath, so she was hard to follow, but from what I gleaned, she really resented the fact that Hazel died. She said it was because of selfish young people. A woman Hazel's age should enjoy her life, not be saddled with a mental case niece and greedy thief of a nephew who deserved to be murdered." Harper leaned over the table and lowered her voice. "The discourse continued, and I can't remember it all, but she did say something about Carrie and drugs. That it was the best-kept secret in town, but it should come out now."

"Carrie and drugs?" I whispered.

"Yes. Hazel told Velma in confidence about something that had happened years ago. As soon as Velma realized she'd let that slip, she stopped talking about it and veered off into talking about how Kirk killed Hazel by nagging her for money. Worse, Carrie has already cleaned out Hazel's house, sold stuff, and put the house on the market. Frankly, I've never seen Velma so upset."

"Wow. Now that's interesting. I'm not sure what it means, but it's interesting."

Two women sitting at a table next to us stood and, after a glance at us, left.

"Okay, there's more I discovered from Louise when I stopped by the library."

"Oh?"

"Yes. Kirk's wife was very close to Vernon's wife at one time. I forget her name, but they were like best friends. I don't know if they've kept in touch, but it's another fact for your arsenal."

"Wow. The joys of a small town. Everyone seems to be related to everyone else, if not by blood then by a relationship of some sort."

"Everyone knows everyone. And this gives Vernon motive, at least a little bit."

I took another sip of my latte. "Well, it does if Vernon's wife knew about Kirk abusing his wife, and if Vernon's wife told Vernon, and if Vernon cared enough about it to do something drastic. That's a lot of ifs."

Harper sighed.

As they say in the movies, the plot thickens.

I stepped into the church reception area for my appointment with Pastor Mark, feeling lighter with my new haircut. Carrie sat behind the desk, on the phone.

"I'll pick the car up tonight at five thirty," she said into the receiver. Then she hung up. "Hello, Evelyn. Pastor Mark is waiting for you." She waved toward the pastor's partially open office door.

"Okay, thank you."

Pastor Mark looked up from his desk as I stepped into the room.

"Hello, Evelyn! Shut the door behind you

and have a seat."

I did. I loved the soothing blues and browns of his office. I'd spent a lot of time here after George died. I would walk in filled with grief and leave with hope. This man could not possibly be the murderer.

Pastor Mark walked around his desk and sat in another chair near me. "So, are you doing okay?"

"I am, considering I found a dead person two days ago."

"And worse, in a place like this church, which should represent good things and the presence of Jesus and the Holy Spirit, not death and destruction."

I nodded. "Yes. There is that."

"Fortunately, we were already going to overhaul the whole fellowship hall anyway, and I'm grateful we have someone knowledgeable in the congregation. Vernon Benson is our general contractor."

"I know Vernon. He was here the morning Kirk was killed, right?"

"Yes, I guess he was. His wife, Beth, showed up for a little while as well. She's his business manager, and we were discussing the finances of the redo."

Another suspect for my list.

The pastor knit his brows. "Why do you ask?"

I shrugged, not sure how to answer without lying.

"Evelyn." Pastor Mark leaned forward. "I've been thinking about the questions you asked me last night, and I wondered . . . have you become a sleuth? Like your friends?"

I blinked like an owl at him. "How do you know about them?"

His eyes twinkled. "One of my pastor friends has a parishioner named Penny something or other who was involved in something like this."

I felt slightly dismayed. "Do you guys get together and talk about the people in your churches?"

He reached over and patted my arm. "Not like you're thinking. Only when something happens that's highly unusual, and never anything shared in confidence. You have to admit, a group of women solving crimes is unusual."

"We're not horrible people," I protested.

"Not at all. In fact, I'd say you care more deeply than most. So, am I right? Are you trying to solve the crime?"

"Yes. I am. To keep Jonathan from being arrested."

The pastor's eyes filled with unexpected tears. "Ahh, Jonathan. I keep trying to reach him. So far, he avoids me. Unfortunately, I know the PTSD symptoms well. I struggled myself after a turn in the military, until I invited the Lord into my life." His gaze snapped back to me. "You're sure Jonathan didn't do this?"

"I am." I crossed my legs.

"Are you feeling stress from finding Kirk? That's originally why I wanted to meet with you."

"Yes, but not because he was dead. Because of Jonathan. And all the repercussions."

"I would have thought finding a dead man would be extremely disturbing."

"It was, but I don't think about it. My desire to clear Jonathan makes that easier. Besides, this isn't my first murder. I helped Penny after she found Rocky Dickerson shot to death."

"I remember that incident. You've seen two murder scenes. That's two more than most people ever see." The pastor leaned back. "So, how can I help you? Besides assure you that I didn't kill Kirk?"

"You can tell me things that might help me."

"All right, Miss Marple, I will as long as it doesn't betray a confidence. And, by the way, I've already told the police anything you could possibly ask."

"That's fine."

"The truth is, everyone here at the church that morning had the opportunity to kill him. I was in my office. I was on the phone quite a bit, so I probably have an alibi. Carrie was alone in reception, as well as making copies and doing whatever it is that she does. Danny was working on our computers, and he was in and out. Like I said, Vernon and Beth were here earlier that morning. Depending on the time of death, either one of them could have done it. Velma was . . . being Velma." He chuckled.

"When I mentioned Kirk last night, you made a funny face. Why is that?"

Pastor Mark's cheeks puffed as he considered my words. "Frankly, I found him challenging to deal with. I suspected his motives weren't good. He offended a lot of people. I was torn between loving him as a pastor and asking him to leave the church because he caused so much turmoil behind the scenes. He told me he was having marriage problems and wanted to sort them out, but as I got to know him, I could see that he wasn't interested in doing that at all. I hate to say this, but he had a devilish mean streak."

"Why did you let him temporarily take charge of the lunch program then?"

He shrugged. "I guess that was me hoping if he had something productive to do, he'd settle down. It's a weak point of mine, unfortunately. I go the extra mile with people because I want so badly for them to come to the Lord."

I smiled. "You love people."

"That I do."

"So, did you overhear anyone arguing with Kirk that morning?"

"Velma and Kirk were in a heated conversation in the reception area at one point."

"Do you know what that was about?"

"The lunch program." He lowered his brows. "She tends to have heated conversations with a lot of people."

My feelings must have shown on my face.

"Yes, I know she's bossy. I'm praying that she can grow and learn to be kinder. Of course, that could be me and my weakness for rehabilitating people again."

I took a deep breath, knowing I was going to step on touchy ground. "I heard something this morning that I'm hesitant to mention. I know you probably can't say anything even if you are aware of it, but it might be useful to you as a pastor, if nothing else. Someone told me something about Carrie and drugs and the death of her friend."

Pastor Mark inhaled. "You're right. I won't talk about that. Just remember that people often do things in the past that they regret. Hopefully those things can be left there and won't bring repercussions into the present."

"Good point." That was probably more of a confirmation than he thought it was.

"Anything else?"

I sighed. "I can't even imagine what it would be like to be a cop and have to dig up dirt on people all the time. This can be a little too eye-opening."

Pastor Mark's face darkened for a minute.

"I hope more than anything that the person who killed Kirk is not a member of my staff."

"Or anyone we know, for that matter." Unfortunately, I didn't see any other possibility. I uncrossed my legs and pulled my purse into my lap. "Thank you for talking with me today."

He leaned toward me. "Before you go, please remember, Evelyn, even though you *think* you're okay after finding Kirk, it might catch up with you. Right now you have a goal — helping Jonathan — that's keeping your attention away from what you saw. Just be aware and don't be surprised if the memory suddenly barges back into your mind. Sort of a PTSD kind of thing, like me and Jonathan."

"Okay."

We stood. He walked back around his desk and dropped onto his chair then he fixed me with a stern glare. "I also want you to be careful. I know you. Once you set your mind on something, you do it to the best of your ability, and you don't stop. But murderers play for keeps."

"I'll be careful," I promised, even as I felt a chill come over me.

I left his office. Carrie was nowhere to be seen. I headed down the hallway toward the foyer and found her in an intense conversation with Velma.

"Why are you giving away Hazel's recipes?" Velma poked Carrie in the shoulder.

"Because they're mine."

"I helped her develop all of those."

"Your name isn't on them. Besides, I only gave away one of them. I can't help with the dinner this year, so I'm giving them the recipe."

"You're shirking your church duties," Velma snapped. "And you have no right to give that recipe to anyone."

"I have every right. I'm Aunt Hazel's beneficiary."

Velma pointed her finger at Carrie. "You are now that Kirk is dead."

Carrie stepped backward. "He wasn't in her will."

"No, but he was trying to get money from her. She told me so. And she also promised that I'd get her recipes. I'd planned to write a cookbook with both our names on it."

I cleared my throat.

They turned to face me. Carrie's face was white as copy paper. She swung on her heel and ran through the foyer and out the building.

"You!" Velma headed for me and walked right into my space.

I backed up. "Me? What did I do?"

"You've been talking about me. That's gossip." She jabbed her long pointer finger at me. I stepped backward so she wouldn't poke me in the shoulder like she had Carrie.

I shook my head. "I don't think so."

"You were in the Coffee Perk talking about me."

Oh dear. Someone must have overheard me and Harper discussing the mystery.

"I'm collecting clues, not gossiping. I'm trying to solve the mystery of who killed Kirk."

She clucked her tongue. "Of all the arrogant people. That's what police are for. I've heard about you and your friends . . . Wait one moment. You think I did it?" She edged closer to me again. "You have nerve. Especially since you're related to the man who is the real murderer."

"Jonathan didn't do it, of that I'm sure. But at any rate, I'm sorry I offended you, even if I didn't mean to."

"Wait until the pastor hears about this." She brushed past me, hitting my arm with hers, grumbling under her breath.

I headed for the front door again, in a hurry to leave the church. If Velma was the murderer, she now knew that I was investigating.

After learning what I had at the hairdresser, I knew without a doubt that I had to convince Jonathan to tell me everything about him and Kirk. I'd already gathered up all of Diggy's belongings, so I drove straight to his house. When I got there, Jonathan opened the door and stepped onto the porch, Diggy next to him. I got out of the truck.

"This is a surprise," Jonathan said.

"I know." I began to pull stuff from the passenger seat. "I thought I'd drop by with Diggy's toys and his bed."

Jonathan strolled over to help me.

"I brought a snack too." I waved the bag at him. "I was hoping for a cup of coffee to go with it." Not that I wanted more coffee, but it would be a good reason to stay.

"I recognize that bag. It's from that coffee shop you like. I guess I'll have to say yes. Stuff from there is always good."

His pleasant attitude and welcoming demeanor surprised me. I'd truly underestimated the power of Diggy.

We carried everything inside. Diggy sniffed me for a moment then followed Jonathan to the kitchen.

"I just made a pot." He filled two mugs, walked over, and handed one to me. I dropped onto my seat on the couch and he sat across from me, Diggy at his feet.

"So everything is going well with the pup?" I asked.

"Yes." His eyes glowed. "Thank you so much."

I smiled. "I'm glad Diggy has finally found a home and person he loves. Everyone should love and be loved."

Jonathan nodded. "You have to be able to accept the love. Hard for me."

"A dog is often easier than a person. Not as many expectations."

"That's the truth. People are pretty complicated. And they can hurt you."

"Especially when you lose them."

A cloud passed over his face. He sipped his coffee then leaned back. Diggy jumped up on the couch and put his head in Jonathan's lap.

"You ever think about getting married again?" he asked.

I choked. "That was out of the blue."

"Sorry. But I just wondered. It's been a while since George died."

I decided to be totally honest with him, since I was about to ask him to be totally honest with me. "For a long time, I thought I never would. George was the love of my life. But recently I've wondered if God has something more for me. I . . . I think I'm starting to get a bit lonely." I surprised myself with my admission, but it was true.

Jonathan nodded thoughtfully. "I think about it sometimes. I had a fiancée once. Broke my heart."

"I know," I said softly. "I heard about her. She's the one who married Kirk?"

His face darkened, and his lips narrowed. I thought he might yell at me, but instead, he rested his hand on Diggy's head and relaxed.

"I suppose if you're determined to try to solve this mystery, I should tell you what happened between me and Kirk. Why I gave him a black eye."

"That might be a good idea."

He put his coffee cup on the end table. "Bottom line, he took my fiancée. Married her and moved to St. Louis. They had kids."

"I'm so sorry, Jonathan. Why did she choose him?"

"She couldn't stand the thought that I was signing up to be in the Marines. Said I had to make a choice between her and the service. I got mad and signed the papers."

"Not fair of her."

"No, I guess not. But I always suffered guilt for the decision. You can see how it all turned out. She was probably right. And when I was recovering in the hospital after the bomb blast, she started writing to me." His face twitched. "She told me that Kirk had started cheating on her. I read those letters over and over again. They made me so angry."

"That wasn't fair of her to write to you like that after what she did to you. She should have gone to other people for the help she needed, not you."

His eyes flashed.

I put my hand out. "Don't be mad. You know it's true."

Jonathan dug his hand into Diggy's fur. "You're right. She shouldn't have. At any rate, she kept in touch. Not too long ago, she kicked him out, and he came back here. He knew she'd contacted me, and he started throwing it in my face. Saying it was all my fault. Insinuating there was something between me and her, which there wasn't." He swallowed hard. "She has kids. Three of them."

I waited for him to regain his composure.

"Sorry, Evelyn. This is very emotional for me. Anyway, he said he was going to do something. He wasn't about to go to court and have to pay her child support. I was scared for her. I told him he was worse than an animal. What man doesn't care for his kids? He goaded me until I hit him."

"You need to tell Agent Waters about this. They already know you and Kirk argued."

"Of course they do. Everyone knows everyone's business around here. And I'm sure they already know many of these details as well. I won't go back to the sheriff's office. I refuse."

"Have they questioned you again?"

"That agent person came by here a couple of times, but I told her nothing. When the sheriff came by once, I hid in the bedroom. I'm not talking to that man. He's another one who goads me until I react."

"You still need to tell Agent Waters the truth. What you have to say could help the investigation."

"I doubt it. It'll probably just make me look guiltier. People always suspect someone who is homeless and mental."

"You're no longer homeless. And you're not mental. Just troubled, but you're getting better. You finally let me into your house — twice."

That earned me a tiny smile.

"Agent Waters is smart, Jonathan. The fact that you haven't been arrested is probably her influence. Besides, what have you got to lose?"

He jumped up and paced the floor, Diggy at his heels. At least he wasn't yanking at his hair.

"I could arrange for her to be at my house. You could talk to her with me there."

He stopped and sighed. I thought he was going to refuse, but he didn't. "I guess you're right. I have nothing to lose. Except everything." His laugh sounded almost like crying. "I'll be there. Just tell me when."

When I got home, I called Agent Waters first thing and briefly explained the situation and asked if she'd come to my house.

"I want him to be in a safe place when he talks."

"Safe place?" she echoed.

"Like, not at the sheriff's office. That brings out the worst in him."

I thought I heard her laugh. "It brings out the worst in a lot of people."

She was silent for a moment, and I wondered if she'd refuse.

"Well, normally I wouldn't agree to something like this with a suspect, but I suppose in this case, I will."

"I also have some things I've learned that might be of interest to you as well."

"All right. That's fine."

We agreed on a time. Then I let Jonathan know. I hoped he wouldn't change his mind.

I worked the rest of the afternoon on product for the farmers' market. I wrapped soap in different shades of gingham fabric and tied the bundles with ribbon to match. I stuffed tea bags and made up packets of herbs and herb blends.

The scent of the herbs inspired me, and I decided to do some cooking. I made a big pot of spaghetti sauce, using basil, oregano, thyme, and parsley. The scent of the fresh herbs helped me ignore the part of my brain that wanted to remember Kirk's blood mixed with tomato sauce.

I also made onion-thyme jam, and, spur of the moment, I mixed up some pesto.

Later that evening, when the spaghetti sauce was done and cooled, I spooned it into wide-necked jars to freeze. I kept one jar in the fridge so I could eat it during the week. The rest I stuck in the freezer, which had been depressingly empty for a long time. Now I had something to serve company.

I admired the pretty jars before I shut the door. *Evelyn, I do believe life is finally moving on.*

FIVE

On Friday morning, I walked Agent Waters to my formal living room. The dogs followed us, happy to see her again.

"Would you like some coffee or ice water or anything?" I asked.

"No, thank you."

BonBon jumped up to sit next to her, and Agent Waters smiled.

"That little dog loves everyone." I perched on my chair, across the room from her. "She'll be glad to see Diggy today."

"Is that your fourth dog? I thought there was one missing."

I told her about Diggy's response to Jonathan.

"Dogs can do miraculous things," she said.

"They can." I settled into my chair. "Would you like me to tell you what I've discovered while we wait for Jonathan?"

She sighed and pulled out her notebook and pretty wood pen. "I'm not keen about you and your friends sleuthing, but go ahead.

Spill it. And remember, this is not my permission to go solving mysteries. I won't be responsible for your safety."

"So you said. And I understand." I told her everything I'd learned so far, ticking each item off with my fingers.

"I hope that helps," I said when I was done. I glanced at my watch. "Jonathan will be here soon."

She leaned toward me. "Just because I agreed to this, doesn't mean he's not a suspect."

"I know. And I also know if you thought he was guilty, you'd arrest him."

We both heard the muffler of his old car coming up the driveway. The dogs stood at attention. BonBon jumped from her lap and led the rest of them to the front door.

I stared at the agent. "Will you please be kind?"

She half-smiled. "I'm not going to knock him to the ground and handcuff him, if that's what worries you."

I headed for the front door, opened it, and waited for Jonathan.

"I almost didn't come," he muttered as he stepped inside with Diggy by his side. "It's been a bad day."

BonBon wailed in greeting.

"Maybe now BonBon will realize what's going on. She's missed Diggy." I looked into Jonathan's eyes. "What's wrong?"

"Someone broke into my trailer while I was out earlier today. And now I'm talking to this agent today. I'll probably be arrested. If I am, I want you to take care of Diggy for me. You can have all my money."

"She's not here to arrest you."

He grunted and followed me to the living room, Diggy and BonBon at his heels, rough-housing. In the doorway, he shifted from foot to foot, tapping his fingers on his thigh. He wouldn't meet Agent Waters's gaze.

"Please sit down, hon." I waved toward the room. "You want some coffee?"

He shook his head as he dropped onto a chair. "I just want to get this over with."

Diggy stopped playing and sat next to Jonathan. BonBon pressed up against the bigger dog.

Agent Waters nodded a greeting at him. "I overheard that conversation. I'm not here to arrest you. What happened at your trailer?"

Jonathan shrugged. "Not sure, but things were messed up. I didn't have time to dig through everything to see if something was gone. But the air inside . . . was different. Not that I expect anyone to believe me."

"I don't disbelieve you. If you want me to come by and look around, I will. Just let me know." Her gentle tone surprised me. "Evelyn says you want to explain the issues between you and Kirk?"

Jonathan glanced at me and shrugged.

"Don't know if it'll help anything. In my experience, people don't believe what comes from people like me. Especially cops."

She rested her hand on the notebook on her lap, fancy wooden pen in her fingers. "Anything I can learn right now will help me. And I hope I don't fall into the same category of those other cops in your experience."

Jonathan finally met Agent Waters's eyes. "We'll see, I guess." He explained about Kirk, his fiancée, and the letters, stuttering a bit. He tapped his fingers wildly on the arm of the chair until Diggy rested his nose on his thigh. Jonathan put his hand on the dog's head.

"I shouldn't have hit him," Jonathan said when he was done. "I should have just walked away. Instead, I let him egg me on, talking about how evil she was, and I was afraid for her."

"Some people are mean like that," Agent Waters murmured.

Jonathan crossed his arms. "So, are you going to arrest me?"

"No." She shut her notebook. "You're still a suspect, of course, but not the only one."

Jonathan visibly relaxed. He left shortly after that with two jars of my frozen spaghetti sauce. Agent Waters and I chatted in my front yard for a few minutes then I sent her on her way with some soap and tea blends.

When I went back inside the house, Bon-

Bon followed me down the hall to the kitchen, walking quietly at my side.

"I hope you understand now, little girl." I picked her up and kissed her head. "Diggy has a job to do. We'll have to see about getting you another friend to play with."

After lunch I began to obsessively clean my house, scrubbing walls and dusting furniture, keeping myself busy until it was time to get ready to go out with Danny. I even vacuumed the furniture. While I plumped the living room sofa cushions, I found Agent Waters's wood-barreled pen.

"Oh dear." I held the pen up to the dogs, who had been watching my odd behavior. "She must be frantic."

I called her and left a message, telling her when I'd be home and the best times on the weekend to get the pen. She texted me back and thanked me, and said it might be Saturday evening, but more than likely Monday before she could get by, but she was glad I'd found it.

After I finished making my house unnaturally clean, I began to ready myself for the computer-buying outing by going through my closet and drawers. After fifteen minutes, every garment I owned was piled on my bed.

That's when I had to admit to myself that I liked Danny. A lot.

Feeling like a teenager, I tore through the

pile, picking up garment after garment then tossing them aside. On one hand, I wanted to look my best. On the other, I wanted to avoid fixing myself up, so I didn't look like this was a date. But what if it was a date? *But what if it's not?*

I finally decided to go for middle of the road. Not too dressy. Not too drab. My best jeans, sandals with heels and a belt to match, and a pretty blue knit shirt. Of course, I did choose my favorite shirt. The one that my friends said brought out my eye color and made my skin glow.

When Danny's truck appeared in my driveway, I was perched in the front room of my house, purse in my lap, biting my lip. I jumped up and jogged for the front door. We reached it at the same time, and I swung it open.

Danny looked me up and down. "You look great. Nice shirt." His blue, short-sleeved dress shirt was almost the identical color of mine.

"Great minds and all." I locked my door.

As we headed for his truck, all my nervousness left.

He grinned at me. "You ready to pick out your computer?"

I grinned back. "Excited and ready to learn."

"Well, you couldn't pick a better teacher than me, if I do say so myself. I know computers. And on top of all that, I'm humble."

"Okay, Mr. Humble Computer Guy. You've got your work cut out for you. I'm woefully ignorant."

Two hours later, after visiting several stores that sold all sorts of computers and related accessories, I was back in Danny's truck, holding a box containing my shiny new laptop, plus a bag of software.

"You want to put that on the floor? Get it out of your way?"

"Nope." I patted it and sighed in satisfaction. "I want to hold it all in my lap for a little while. I feel like a kid at Christmas."

"I'm glad I could help with that."

We drove in pleasant silence for a few miles. I looked down at my bagged purchases and realized I had a long evening in front of me getting everything in working order. I wasn't sure how much help Danny would give me, and I didn't know if I should tell him I felt out of my element setting it all up in a timely fashion.

He reached over and tapped the box. "Don't worry. I'll help you get everything done so you can use it tomorrow at the farmers' market."

"Are you reading my mind? I was just wondering if I would be able to get it done in time."

"I'm not a mind reader, I'm a face reader. In both my lines of work, it's helpful to look beyond people's words and try to understand how they feel. Because people don't always say what they really mean. Or else they say nothing at all."

"And I guess my face was saying, 'Evelyn, you don't even know how to start a new computer.' "

He chuckled. "That's about the size of it."

"I would very much appreciate your help. And in return, I'll fix you dinner."

"Now that's a deal!"

Back at my house, I invited him into the kitchen. Since I'd already made spaghetti sauce, I thought I'd just throw it on some noodles and fix a salad. I poured a jar of sauce into a pan and was carrying it to the stove when the pan slipped from my grasp and fell to the floor. A puddle of sauce spread under my feet. Suddenly the memory of Kirk, dead on the floor of the church kitchen, blood mingled with tomato sauce, exploded from my memory. I went rigid.

"Evelyn?" Danny's voice sounded a little distant.

He touched my arm.

"I'm sorry. I just had a flashback of Kirk dead in the fellowship hall. It's the spaghetti sauce with the pot on the floor. Pastor Mark warned me that might happen."

"Come here and sit down." He guided me to a kitchen chair. "I'll clean it up."

"You don't have to."

He pounded his fists lightly on his chest like Tarzan. "Me, man. Let me be manly and rescue you."

That made me smile and relax a bit. "Go for it."

"That's better."

He grabbed more paper towels than he needed. I bit my lip when he soaked them until they dripped. He kept talking, waving his arms and dribbling water all over the counters and floor. His actions were so contrary to his exacting appearance and precise actions at work, I wanted to laugh. This side of him was unexpected and oddly charming.

Watching him work distracted me from the memory of Kirk's murder. What's more, this was confirmation that I was truly smitten.

"Pastor Mark was right, by the way," Danny said from the floor where he smeared sauce all over the place. "Those kinds of flashbacks can happen."

"He says that my desire to solve this mystery for Jonathan's sake might have kept me from facing the reality of finding a dead person."

"Could be."

We chatted about other things as he cleaned. He managed to get most of the sauce up, using the better part of a roll of towels. There was sauce along the edge of the counters and in corners, but I'd clean that up later.

He shoved dirty towels in the trash can. I looked him up and down. His clothes had stayed amazingly immaculate.

He put his hands on his hips. "I'm guessing spaghetti is off the menu."

"You guess right," I said. "How about grilled cheese sandwiches? I could make them with fresh pesto."

"That sounds perfect."

Danny helped me while I made dinner. Or rather, he made a mess while I worked. But we laughed like schoolchildren. I hadn't enjoyed myself so much in a long time. When we were done eating, we set to work on the computer.

He talked me through everything he was doing.

"You weren't exaggerating earlier. You are a good teacher."

"And you're an avid learner. We're a great combo."

We got the machine set up and running. While I watched, he installed an updated version of my inventory software. Then he installed the software I'd purchased and the information from my backup drive.

When we were finished, I rubbed my fingers over the top of the laptop screen. "So pretty."

"Say, I have a good idea," he said. "How about in honor of Fred's passing, we give this one a name too."

"What a good idea." I studied the laptop. "I think she's a girl."

"A girl." Danny scratched his chin. "Didn't you mention once that your middle name was unusual?"

"I did! Fiona. After my great-grandmother." I giggled, pleasantly surprised he would not only suggest something so fanciful as naming my computer, but that he remembered what I'd said about my middle name.

"Fiona is a great name. It suits you and this new machine."

"Fiona it is!"

We grinned at each other. Our gazes locked. I felt a jolt of something I hadn't felt for any man except George for years.

Danny reached over and stroked a piece of my hair from my face. "Your haircut looks nice, by the way." He dropped his arm and winked. "And your hair would look nice, even if you decided to do blue streaks."

I blushed.

"Now." He crossed his arms. "I have one more topic to address."

"What's that?"

"You solving this murder."

"Please don't lecture me."

I squinted at him. He laughed and patted my shoulder.

"I have no plans to do so. I suspect even if I did lecture you, it would do no good."

"It wouldn't."

"I can't deny that I'm concerned for your safety, but I'm also curious. I thought maybe we could discuss the whole thing. I'd like to know what you've discovered. Plus, maybe you talking about it will make patterns appear that you hadn't noticed before."

"Really?"

"Really."

Six

On Saturday, I set up my stall in my usual spot at the farmers' market. I was in a bit of a tranquil fog. I'd enjoyed my evening with Danny and felt like a teenager who'd been on her first date. And now I was doing one of my favorite activities — selling products at the farmers' market.

As I got things up and running, I ran into a glitch with a program on my computer and sent a quick text to Danny asking him what to do. He texted back immediately with instructions. My mistake, so I felt slightly foolish, but also felt warm that he'd responded so quickly. Then he asked me when I'd be home. I told him.

All the early birds came first, so the morning passed quickly. During a lull in the crowd, I chatted quietly with an elderly woman named May who had a table next to me. She made quilted items, including bags, and she had a new assortment. One of them was large, with big interior and exterior pockets.

Perfect for carrying a laptop, especially when traveling.

"I want one, but I can't decide which color."

May smiled. "I have extras in boxes under my table, so you have time to decide."

"That sounds good. I want one for my new laptop." Then I asked her if she'd watch my table for a second while I took a bathroom break.

I headed for the ladies' room and heard footsteps behind me. "Evelyn, wait."

I turned. Vernon's wife, Beth, hurried toward me.

"I need to talk to you."

"Okay." I was surprised to see her without her kids.

"I'm not going to beat around the bush." She glared at me. "You're trying to solve this murder."

"I am." Word of my sleuthing was spreading like wildfire. I suspected Velma was behind it.

"You'd better not be spreading rumors about my husband."

"I'm just collecting information so I can keep my cousin, Jonathan, from going to jail."

"My husband isn't guilty. He didn't touch Kirk. Yeah, he probably wanted to. The guy threatened everyone. But Vernon didn't hurt him."

"What did Kirk threaten Vernon about?"

Her face hardened. "None of your business. Just leave us alone. We'll sue you if you keep it up."

Vernon appeared in the distance, dragging whiney children and calling for Beth.

"Bad things happen to nosy people," she snapped, and whirled on her heel before I could say a word.

I returned to my stall, heart pounding harder than normal. Beth had defended Vernon's innocence, but she hadn't said a word about her own. And she'd threatened me. That made her suspect number one on my list.

A couple hours later a group of women from my church headed for my stall. Carrie was with them. She paused at May's table, looking at all the beautiful bags and purses.

"Someone said you had some salve for sale," a young mom said when they reached my table. She held out her hands, which were dry and rough. "Washing my hands after dealing with poopy diapers."

I smiled. "I'm out of the salve. It all sold quickly, but I have a sample, so you can try it. I have more to sell at the house. You're welcome to come by and get some." I scooped out a small blob and pressed it into her palm.

She rubbed it in. "Mmmm. That smells heavenly."

The other women crowded around, asking for samples.

Then Carrie approached with a large blue-and-tan quilted bag in her arms. She'd bought one like I had looked at, which made me want one even more.

"I'd like to try some of that salve stuff," she said.

I scooped some out for her.

She rubbed her hands and sniffed. "It is nice. I might have to buy some."

"Come by the house. I have extra jars." I pointed to her bag. "I'm going to buy one of those, I think. It'll hold a lot of stuff."

She nodded. "Great for traveling too."

The women picked through all the other things I had on display, including cooking herbs.

Carrie glanced through the tea and picked up a plastic bag of my sleepy tea. "Is this good?"

"I think so." I smiled. "I use it sometimes when I've had a stressful day."

She flipped through bags of herbs. "Vernon and Velma say you're trying to solve the mystery of who killed Kirk. Both of them are really mad."

"Yes, I know. And, yes. I'm trying to." No sense in denying it at this point.

"Do you suspect anyone?"

I shrugged. "Not sure yet."

"Velma hated him." Carrie looked at me.

"I gathered that."

"Vernon . . ."

I waited.

"Well, Kirk was threatening Vernon."

"Really?"

She nodded.

"About what?"

She wet her lips. "I can't say."

"All right."

She fingered a package of my relaxation tea bags. "I'll take this."

I took her money and handed her the change.

"Thanks, Evelyn." She walked briskly up the aisle to join the rest of the women. At least she hadn't gotten defensive and yelled at me. But I hoped I hadn't just talked to a murderer.

A couple hours later, before I packed up my stuff to head home, I bought my laptop bag from May. I picked a bright one with oranges and purples and pinks, which reminded me of a summer flower bed. And it wasn't anything like my usual style.

"That one is my favorite," May said. "Are you going on a trip?"

"No. I have a new laptop, and I want a bag to put it in and to carry other stuff, like my Bible and notebook."

"That's a great idea. That lady who just bought one said she's taking hers on a vacation."

I paid for my bag. "Really?"

"Yes. It would be perfect for a plane ride.

The straps are long enough to sling over your shoulder."

"They certainly are."

As I began packing up my product, I wondered if Agent Waters knew that Carrie was planning a trip.

I arrived home after the farmers' market and began unpacking my truck, carrying some of the boxes to my storage area in my barn workshop and some to the house. I left my purse and my new quilted bag on my kitchen counter. All the while, I thought about Kirk's murder. All four of my suspects knew I was trying to solve the mystery. That made me uneasy. Velma had lectured me and jabbed at me with her bony finger. She didn't like Kirk. She called him a thief. Was he stealing money from Hazel, and Velma found out? Vernon's wife, Beth, threatened me at the farmers' market. Apparently, Vernon had a reason to kill Kirk, but I didn't know why. Carrie might be planning a vacation — to escape arrest? To leave for good?

I debated about calling Agent Waters and telling her everything I knew, including Carrie's plans, but decided not to. I'd sound like a tattletale. Besides, she'd be by soon enough to get her pen. I could fill her in then.

But then I continued to ponder as I walked back and forth, putting things away. I realized I suspected Carrie over everyone else. Not only was she planning to leave, there was the fact that she wouldn't help with the Italian dinner this year. Was she avoiding spaghetti sauce like I was because she'd seen Kirk's blood mingling with tomato sauce on the fellowship hall floor? And she'd developed a sudden sensitivity to nightshades, which included tomatoes. She'd bought some relaxation tea. Did she need help sleeping? A guilty conscience would do that.

But why? What reason would she have to kill Kirk? I supposed if he were threatening Vernon, he could also be threatening Carrie. But about what? Something about drugs?

I decided I'd better call Agent Waters after all. I hefted the final box of stuff from my truck to take it to the house when I heard a car coming up my driveway. I turned. I didn't recognize the vehicle. But when it drew closer, my stomach tightened. Carrie was behind the wheel. I debated making a run for the house, but I debated too long.

Carrie got out of her car wearing a denim jacket that was too warm for the day. "I came by to get some salve." She shifted her hands nervously in the pockets of the jacket. "You said you had extra here. I might be going away. I want to take some."

"Did you get a new car?" I asked.

"Yes." Her face softened. "I've always wanted a new car. Aunt Hazel never approved. She always said used was better."

"It's pretty. Would you like me to get you some salve?" If I could get into the house, I could make a phone call without her seeing me.

She sighed. "You know, don't you?"

"I know . . . uh, what do you mean? What do I know?" I backed toward my front door.

She stepped closer. "You know I killed Kirk." She fiddled with something in her pocket. "I was hoping you didn't."

"I didn't know for sure, but I suspected." My scalp prickled with fear.

The dogs barked frantically from the house. How I wished I'd let them out.

"I . . . I don't want to go to jail."

"Did you mean to kill him? Did you plan it out?"

She sighed. "No. I pushed him. He fell against the kitchen island, and when he was on the floor, I just took one of the big pots and hit him. I was so angry."

"Why?"

"He killed my aunt Hazel, for one thing."

"I thought she died of natural causes. Like a stroke or something."

"It was a stroke, but it was his fault. After his wife kicked him out, he quit his job and came home. He told Aunt Hazel if she didn't give him some money, he'd tell everyone the truth about me. That's the other reason I was so angry."

I felt confused. "What truth?"

"About me killing my best friend. My best friend was killed in a car accident. She was using drugs that I gave to her. Drugs I got from Vernon."

"Vernon gave you drugs?" I remembered the two of them in their intense conversation at church, but I had a hard time imagining straitlaced Vernon doing anything like that.

"We were going through a rebellious stage. The three of us were partying that night. She'd never done any drugs before. Then we let her drive home. Alone." A couple tears flowed down Carrie's face. "We both stopped using that day, we felt so guilty. I wanted to tell the truth a long time ago, but Vernon wouldn't let me. Especially after he 'came to Jesus.' He didn't want it getting out. Said it would ruin his reputation. I did confess to my aunt Hazel. At some point, she must have told Kirk. Maybe she thought he could help me or something. That was a stupid thing to do. She should have known he wasn't trustworthy." She hiccupped.

"Did Kirk try to get money from Vernon as well?"

Carrie nodded. "He did. Threatened to take down his reputation and then his business."

"Did Vernon know you killed Kirk?"

"He guessed." She shuffled her sandaled feet in the grass.

"I'm sorry you've had to bear this guilt all these years."

She grunted. "After Aunt Hazel died, Kirk demanded I give him money from her estate. I wasn't going to give it up. I took care of Aunt Hazel all my life. I earned that money. And now, I'm going to go away and take it all with me."

"And do what? Don't you think they'll find you?"

She shrugged. "They don't even think I'm guilty."

"I wouldn't be too sure about that," I said. "Besides, you just bought a new car."

"I'll come back to it, I'm sure. As long as you're out of the picture, they won't know anything."

Fear squeezed my stomach.

"I'm going to have to do something because you know." She pulled a plastic bag containing a pen knife from her left pocket. "This belongs to Jonathan. I'm going to leave it here, and they'll think he killed you."

I gasped. "You're the one who broke into his house?"

She nodded.

"Are you kidding me?" I wanted to knock her down. "You would frame an innocent man who has suffered so much?"

"I don't want to go to prison."

"Do you have a gun in your other pocket?"

"Yes. It was Aunt Hazel's."

I heard a car turn into my drive and felt a spike of hope. "They'll eventually figure out it was you."

"I don't think so."

The car rounded the last curve in my driveway and headed into view. I still couldn't see who it was. Carrie was so focused on me, she hadn't yet heard it.

"What else can I do?" she whined.

"Turn yourself in."

"I don't want to go to jail," she wailed.

I had to keep her from doing something really stupid . . . like shooting me. "Maybe you won't have to. There's a difference between accidentally killing someone in the heat of the moment and shooting someone in cold blood. Like me. Here. Now."

The vehicle came close enough that I could see who was driving. I watched over Carrie's shoulder. Agent Waters's car!

Carrie followed my gaze and gasped. "Who is that?"

"Agent Waters."

Carrie began to pull the gun from her pocket.

"Don't do it. If you shoot me, she might shoot you. In fact, if you even pull that out of your pocket, at best you'll end up body slammed, face-first on the ground."

Carrie's face drooped, and she removed her hand from her pocket. "I probably couldn't have done it anyway."

Agent Waters parked and slowly climbed from her car where she stood, shielded by the door. "You okay, Evelyn?"

"Yes. I think Carrie wants to turn herself in for Kirk's death. She has a gun in her pocket."

"Carrie, get down on the ground now!" Agent Waters screamed.

The desperation in Carrie's eyes made me wonder if she would go for the weapon again, but she didn't. Instead she dropped to her knees and began to sob.

Agent Waters began to walk toward us, gun drawn. "All the way on the ground, Carrie. Flat on your stomach. Hands behind your head."

Carrie obeyed. "Forgive me, Evelyn. Oh God, please forgive me."

"I do," I said. "And I know that He does too."

Agent Waters approached slowly. After she'd handcuffed Carrie, she looked at me. "Guess it was a good thing I decided to pick up my pen today."

"I guess so." My knees felt like buckling.

"Go sit down, Evelyn," she ordered. "You look like you're going to pass out. I don't want to have to pick you up."

As I sat on the steps of my front porch, watching Agent Waters handcuff Carrie and stick her in the back of the car, Danny's truck appeared in my driveway.

The agent stood at attention, hand over her holster again. "Grand Central for such an isolated place. You know who that is?"

"It's Danny. It's fine." I stood, inordinately glad to see him.

He skidded to a stop, opened his door, and bounded toward me. "What's going on? Are you okay?"

"Yes. Why are you here?"

"I came to look at your computer. You said you'd had trouble with the software, remember? What happened here?" He waved his hands wildly in the air. I'd never seen him so discombobulated.

"Carrie killed Kirk. She knew I was near to figuring it all out and she came to confront me. Actually, she wanted to kill me."

He gasped. His gaze took in every inch of me. "No blood, thank God! Did she hurt you? Are you okay?"

"She didn't hurt me. Just scared me, but now I feel sorry for her. I'm not sure she would have done it. She was just desperate."

"Desperate people can do desperate things." He shot Carrie a narrow glance as Agent Waters talked into her radio. "She actually killed Kirk? That's hard to believe. She's always been so quiet."

"Yes . . . well, I'm not sure. It depends on whether he fell first and that killed him, or if it happened when she clobbered him with a pot."

"Clobbered him?"

"That's what she said."

"That's what I mean by desperation." He grabbed my shoulders and gently shook me. "You could have been killed."

I'd never seen him so emotional. Before I could say a word, he leaned down and pressed his lips on mine. Then he stepped backward with a deep breath.

All I could do was blink at him in wonder.

"I'm sorry, Evelyn. That was not the way I intended to kiss you for the first time. I wanted to ask your permission, for one thing. And I wanted it to be romantic. By candlelight or something. But this made me realize I've wasted too much time already. I like you. Well, more than like you." He paused. "I think I'm falling in love with you. Or maybe I love you already."

"Wow."

He frowned for a minute then he laughed. "I'm not sure how to interpret that."

"I guess it means I feel the same way."

We stared into each other's eyes.

"Excuse me." Agent Waters appeared in the periphery of my eyesight and cleared her throat.

We turned to face her.

"I hate to interrupt this, er, touchingly emotional moment, but if you can spare me just a minute, Evelyn, I believe I have a murderer in my car. I need a statement." The twinkle in her eyes belied the sarcasm in her words.

"That's fine."

"I'll wait on the porch," Danny said. "Then we'll continue this conversation."

Agent Waters laughed and rolled her eyes. "I've never heard what I just witnessed between the two of you called 'conversation.'" She made quotes in the air with her fingers. "But, hey, whatever works for you."

Morgan called for an emergency meeting of the book club on Sunday afternoon so I could fill everyone in on the details of Carrie's arrest. When I walked in, I knew I was in for a major interrogation.

Jo patted the chair next to her. "You did it. You solved the mystery."

I shrugged. "Yes and no. The murderer came to me."

"Because you asked the right questions," Morgan said.

The door opened, and Jeanine walked in with a plate of cookies. "Your favorite, Evelyn! A celebration for your success."

"Thank you."

Penny and Harper followed close on Jeanine's heels. Penny had a big heart-shaped foil balloon from the grocery store in her hand. It said, "Way to go!" in big bold letters.

"I need coffee!" Harper grabbed a mug. "I helped in the church nursery this morning."

Penny handed me the balloon and studied

me with narrowed eyes. "Your eyes are sparkling."

I raised my brow. "You've never seen them sparkle before?"

"Not with that kind of color on your cheeks. In fact, I'm not trying to be offensive, but you look ten years younger."

"I guess that's a compliment." I grinned.

Everyone stared at me.

Penny suddenly inhaled. "This isn't just because you solved the mystery. He kissed you, didn't he?"

"What!" Morgan exclaimed. "You mean, Danny?"

"Did he? Seriously?" Harper leaned toward me, chin in hands.

Jeanine clapped her hands. "Does this mean you have a wedding cake in your future? If so, I want to make it!"

"Do tell." Jo smiled.

I looked at the faces of my dear friends. "Yes, he did kiss me. We're officially dating. And I have no idea if a wedding cake is in my future, but if that happens, you guys will be the first to know. And, Jeanine, you'll make the cake for sure. And yes, he drove me to and from church. And yes, he held my hand. And kissed me goodbye." I smiled happily, thinking about the way the skin around his green eyes crinkled when he grinned and the way he'd stroked my hair before he left my house.

High-fives ensued.

"So, back to why we're meeting today," Morgan said. "Tell us everything about the mystery."

"I saw Carrie at the farmers' market, and that's what gave me the final pieces that put her on top of the suspect list. As I unpacked my truck after I got home, I added it all together, and it made sense. She had a sudden nightshade intolerance and gave her aunt's recipe to the women at church for the yearly Italian food fund-raiser. Remember how she was always bragging about the eggplant Parmesan, but she kept it a state secret? I believe she could no longer stand looking at spaghetti sauce." I explained my own flashback in my kitchen Friday night.

"Then I found out that she had been selling all her aunt's belongings and the house, and she was planning a trip. She bought a large quilted travel bag and said she was planning on taking a trip.

"She acted funny when she bought some of my sleepy tea, like she was having trouble sleeping. I knew it had to have something to do with the past and maybe with the rumors I'd heard about her and drugs, but I just couldn't figure out what."

Penny clasped her hands around her coffee cup. "When she showed up at your house, was she intending to kill you too?"

"I think she wanted to. She had a gun. And

she'd planned to frame Jonathan." I explained about the penknife.

"That's a lot smarter than people gave her credit for," Jo said. "I guess I was right about there being more to her than meets the eye."

I nodded. "You were. And thank God she did all that talking, like she needed to come clean, and kept talking, because Agent Waters came by to pick up a pen she'd left at my house." I explained about the special gift from her brother.

"Yes, thank God," Jo said.

"Why did Carrie kill Kirk?" Penny asked. "We want details."

I explained everything Carrie had told me about her friend's death, tying in all the things I'd learned around town, Kirk threatening Carrie and trying to extort money from her, and about Vernon as well. And finally the things that Jonathan had told me.

"So Vernon used to do drugs too?" Jo asked.

"Mr. Perfect?" Morgan added.

"Yes, he did. But that accident changed both of them. And I think he felt so guilty, he was acting like the impossibly perfect Christian," I said.

"Makes sense," Harper said.

"That's why he was getting so grumpy lately," Morgan murmured.

"Did Beth know?" Penny asked.

"I'd say probably. I don't know for sure. But I do know that Kirk threatened Vernon.

To be honest, at first I thought Beth had killed Kirk — to protect Vernon." I told them about our confrontation at the farmers' market. "And I also suspected Velma. She got pretty threatening with me when I ran into her at church. But I think she was just upset because she felt Hazel died because of Carrie and Kirk. Then, to add insult to injury, Carrie had taken all the recipes Hazel and Velma had worked on together."

"So all's well that ends well, to coin a phrase," Jo said.

"I guess you could say that." I grinned at each of my friends, so grateful for them and for life.

Morgan raised her coffee cup. "To solving mysteries!"

We all raised ours and said in unison, "To solving mysteries!"

ABOUT THE AUTHOR

Candice Prentice is the author of eight books. She lives in the semi-suburbs of Maryland with her husband. When she's not writing, she quilts and sews. She loves to scour the web, books, old newspapers, and old magazines for cool, obscure historical facts. She's also a bit of a health nut. Visit her website and blog at www.candiceprentice .com.

■ ■ ■ ■

NUTS FOR COFFEE

BY DARLENE FRANKLIN

■ ■ ■ ■

Thanks to Elma Brooks, Carrie Moore Gould, Paula Shreckhise, Vicky Burkhart Sluiter, Jasmine Augustine, and Tammy Cordery for letting me borrow their names for use in this story.

For everything in the world — the lust of the flesh, the lust of the eyes, and the pride of life — comes not from the Father but from the world.

1 JOHN 2:16 NIV

ONE

"Which one shall I open next?" I looked over the array of gifts spread across a large round table covered with a lovely linen tablecloth at the Coffee Perk. Morgan Butler and my other friends from the book club had outdone themselves to help me celebrate my seventy-fifth birthday, which also coincided with our Tuesday night meeting.

Birthdays often depressed me, since the Lord never blessed me with a husband or children of my own. So I was touched when church folk as well as a few friends from out of town also showed up.

However, I'll admit I was a little miffed when no one came from Goring's Boring Mill, the place where I had worked until last Christmas. I had come to love the machines and how they drilled such precise holes through almost everything. But the younger generation was gradually taking over, and I decided it was time to quit even the ten hours a week I'd been putting in since my retirement. They still might make it. The office didn't close until six, which was when the party had started.

I reached for a gaily decorated bag, as lovely a creation as the kind I liked to craft. Beautiful calligraphy read "To Jo Anderson." I flipped it over to see who had given the gift, but it wasn't signed.

"Somebody's not playing fair." I held up the blank card. "Who gave this to me?" I kept close track of every gift and giver. Otherwise I'd miss a thank-you card.

"Not me." The answer came from several directions at once. I kept an eye out while I weighed the bag in my hands. It was heavy, perhaps a bottle of some sort.

It was a 24-ounce carton of cinnamon-hazelnut coffee creamer. "Someone's been paying attention." In fact, it was even my favorite brand. I subscribed to a "flavor of the month" coffee creamer club from Off the Top Creamery, and their Hazelnut Delight was my favorite. "Morgan, is this your doing?"

Morgan chuckled. "No, but I'm sure I'm not the only one who knows how nuts you are about it."

Before I offered it to the group, I checked the label to see if it used real or artificial flavorings. I knew for certain that another member of our book club, Harper Daggett, was allergic to nuts. Others might be as well.

I slipped on my glasses and peered at the fine print on the back of the carton.

"Is something wrong?" Evelyn Kliff asked. It was good to see her back to her old self. She'd had a rough time after her husband's death.

I speculated whether Evelyn was the giver, but she had no reason to lie about it. "I was checking to see if the company uses real nuts. They use real cinnamon, but the hazelnut flavor is artificial. It should be safe for everyone." Amazing how chemicals could trick the mind.

"If someone has an allergy, it's still safest not to drink it. You never know." Sherri Wexel's worried behavior made Ma Berenstein's care look like a bear on a rampage. She'd come by invitation because we'd known each other all our lives, but we weren't close.

"Pass it around," Penny Parson said. I was glad to see she could make it to the party since she had spent the day at an animal rights rally. "I want to see this creamer you told everyone you wanted."

Everyone laughed, me the loudest. I had already received several gift certificates for Off the Top Creamery to help feed my addiction.

"No one willing to own up to giving me this gift?" I repeated. This time I made a point of looking at each person individually. I saw a flicker of — something — but I couldn't pin it down.

The doorbell jingled. "Sorry we're late," Monica Mayne cheerfully called. She had arrived with her husband. I looked around her for her father, my former boss, Dave Goring. Disappointed again.

Conversation around the table halted until they joined us.

Monica seized upon the hazelnut creamer. "Oh, this is my favorite. You don't mind if I have some, do you?"

"No, of course not." What else could I say? My lips twitched a little bit as I said, "If you're worried about your nut allergy, it's safe. I already checked."

"I know that." Monica poured in a more than generous amount without stirring. "We use the same brand in the office. I'm sure you remember that."

I liked Monica, loved her, in fact. I had been the family "aunt" after her mother died. But I wasn't blind to the bad taste she left in many people's mouths. Her last remark caused the hairs on my arms to bristle. I had still been at the top of my game when I quit work altogether.

"Sorry we're late. We're having issues with the computer." Bruce Mayne, Monica's affable husband, spoke up.

"Oh dear." From what I'd heard, the office had gone downhill since I left.

"Please open our present next." Monica handed it to me over the stack of gifts, disregarding everyone who had been there earlier. "We can't stay long. Bruce has to take me to the repair shop to pick up my car."

Bruce, a high school football hero who retained his athletic physique but hadn't matured into the glory he'd imagined for himself, bent over and embraced me. I never had been able to resist that smile. He said, "Congratulations on reaching the three-quarter-century mark! The office just hasn't been the same since you left."

Maybe not, but he wasn't too disappointed. Both Bruce and Monica's brother, Chad, were eager to take over management of the company. Monica only worked there part-time. She ran her own cosmetics business.

I pushed the unkind thoughts away. "Are the others coming? Is there an emergency tonight?" I looked around Monica, but neither her brother, Chad, nor Dave had magically appeared.

Monica frowned. "They should be right behind us. Bruce, please get me a second cup of coffee. You don't mind, do you, Morgan?"

My book club ladies liked Monica less than I did. They thought she took advantage of me. But, goodhearted as usual, Morgan provided a refill. To no one's surprise, Monica poured creamer into the second cup as well.

I heard a few gasps. My brand-new carton was a third gone.

Monica tapped the surface of the coffee and nodded. "Just right." She set down the cup. "I can't wait for you to see our present."

I had decided to give in and open her present when Dave Goring at last arrived. I set the gift down again.

Bruce took the carton from Monica's hands. "That's enough, dear. I don't believe the birthday girl has poured any yet."

I hadn't — I already had a fancy drink and had planned to take the creamer home and enjoy it over several days

Monica tossed a "sorry" in my direction. Dave caught my eye when he sat down. He shrugged. I knew his assessment of his son-in-law: a so-so head for business, not good in management, an amiable salesman. But he was an adequate engineer and a top-rank husband who adored his Monica beyond reason. He made a perfect public face for the sales force.

Monica's older brother, Chad Goring, hadn't come. I had already received his card with an enclosed check. Bruce had his father's business sense but lacked his genuine warmth, although he could fake it well enough. With Bruce as his partner, Goring's Boring Mill should continue into a successful future after Dave's retirement. Which made the current rumors disconcerting.

Monica's gift lay in front of me, so she wasn't responsible for the creamer either. I set aside her gift without commenting — she could wait at least one turn. I chose a package wrapped in shiny lavender, the color that I associated with Evelyn. It suited her personality, always giving of herself. I would repurpose the paper later. Inside a thin box I found lovely vellum envelopes with lavender paper, stenciled with the outlines of the Long's Peak in Colorado. Absolutely beautiful. I couldn't wait to use it.

Monica began to make unsettled noises. When I glanced at her, she was in genuine distress. Her face had reddened and swollen slightly, and she was coughing. It looked like anaphylactic shock. "The creamer," Dave said. He hadn't heard our earlier discussion.

I shook my head. "It's artificially flavored."

Before Bruce could dig out Monica's EpiPen, Monica's symptoms had subsided. The scary signs disappeared almost as quickly as they had arisen, and she breathed normally. "I believe it was a false alarm," Dave said, relieved. "It's happened before."

"You should still see a doctor," Harper said.

Monica brought the cup to her mouth, flashing a naughty grin. Then she grew sober and set the mug back on the table.

I had put her off long enough.

I read the card. "From Bruce and Monica and all your friends at Goring's Boring Mill."

The charming greeting card featured at least a dozen signatures. I was blessed to have friends from my old office who would remember my birthday, and I knew it.

The wrapping was professional. Expensive, quality paper with clean folds and minimum tape. When I looked closer on the surface, I noticed tiny silver diamonds that created the illusion of silver. I pointed it out to my friends. "A perfect paper for a seventy-fifth birthday." I hardly wanted to disturb it.

"Open it already," Jeanine Gransbury said. "I'll take care of the paper." Our town baker was getting the wrapping paper ready for me to take home. She had made my favorite cake, a pineapple upside-down cake, for the occasion.

I slowly separated paper from tape so I could reuse it. "I was just thinking how you like fancy paper, Dave. You used to compare it to advertising — the right paper set the mood, created anticipation, and most importantly, made it memorable. And this paper suits your adage."

He smiled indulgently.

I tugged the last tape free and carefully unfolded the paper. Inside I found a simple stamp kit, with a small booklet of decoration suggestions. "I can't wait to use it."

"There's something more," Bruce said.

Underneath the box I found a registration confirmation for a craft convention in Topeka next month.

"How lovely! Tell everyone thanks." Later, I would send each signee a separate thank-you note.

Bruce's cell rang as if on cue, and they left.

I didn't give the Maynes more than a passing thought until close to my bedtime.

Dave Goring called. "Jo, I'm glad you're there. I thought you would want to know." His voice broke.

"What's wrong?" I asked, sharply.

"Monica is dead. The anaphylactic shock returned when she tried to drink the rest of the coffee."

"But that's impossible. There weren't any nuts in —"

"There must have been." His ragged voice cut off my denial.

I held my breath in shock. "I'm so sorry." My words sounded foolish.

He paused to gain composure. "The police are asking questions about the coffee creamer."

Two

"I'll be right over," I said.

"That's not necessary," Dave said.

I didn't pay attention to his protest. Dave Goring was the most even-keeled man I had ever met, but the death of his daughter was bound to shake him. I'd helped my friend through many tough times in the past, and I saw no reason to stop just because I no longer received a paycheck.

I called the pastor of my church — he would start the prayer chain and get the ladies' group involved in providing meals and helping around the house — before I headed out. I was greatly concerned about the circumstances of Monica's death. I couldn't help but feel guilty. Questions circled my mind as I gathered my purse and got into my car.

Dave and both his children lived within three miles of each other, in one of the higher-income-bracket neighborhoods. I had visited Dave's home, an older split-level that was popular back in the sixties, the most often. It resurrected my dreams of raising a family in a place just like it before my fiancé, Harrison, had died in Vietnam.

Tonight I was headed to the Maynes' home. Monica and Bruce spent to the limit on a four-bedroom, three-bath house with a sweeping driveway and a pool in the backyard. Dave had bailed them out of financial difficulty at least three times over the years, but they had never downscaled.

The sheriff's car had parked in front of the house, so I pulled in behind Dave's car.

Deputy Barney Long opened the door when I knocked. "Miss Anderson, we were just coming to see you."

"Happy birthday, Jo," Sheriff Hayden called. He couldn't have been happy to have yet another member of the book club involved in another mystery, so I appreciated his olive branch.

The deputy effectively blocked me from entering. Dave tapped him on the shoulder. "She's my guest. Please let her in."

Hayden returned to the front room, one of those open spaces with a large vaulted ceiling that Monica had adored. Bruce sat in there. I wondered if he should have a lawyer present, but I shook the thought away. In the other direction I saw their housekeeper in the kitchen. I was glad to see her.

Dave drew my attention away. "Why don't

you join me in Monica's office, and I'll rustle up some decent decaf coffee."

There was a time neither one of us considered decaf worth drinking. How age changed a person. "I should be serving you," I protested when he pulled out my chair.

His fleeting smile was sadder than ever. "You're doing me a favor. You're my escape. I know we Gorings need to stick together, but I'm too distraught to deal with my juniors tonight."

"We all grieve in our own ways."

"It's more than that. I'm not sure I buy Bruce's show of grief. Their marriage had been showing signs of strain recently."

"Oh my." That would have broken Dave's heart almost as badly as Monica's death had.

Monica kept a coffeemaker that fixed individual cups of coffee by her desk. Dave whipped up a cup for both of us. He didn't say much as we drank. "May I ask for your help?" he finally said.

"Anything," I promised.

"Could you hunt down Monica's business contacts for her cosmetics company and let them know what's happened? Anyone Bruce might not know. She kept that part of her life separate from the rest of us, but you're good at digging out information." He handed me a business card. "Here is the office address and phone number, in case you need it."

I looked down at Monica's smiling face —

stunning, when she had her makeup on — and felt again the pang of her loss. A *Mesmerizing Beauty,* as she had named her company.

Ever since social media hit it big, people have been more widely known than ever before, and yet more alone than ever. "I bet I can find the information you're looking for if I ferret around."

"That's great. I'm afraid I don't know her password." Dave looked around, helpless.

"I should be able to figure it out," I assured him.

Someone knocked on the door. It was Chad. "Dad, can we talk?"

Dave stood, "Sure, Son," he said. Before they shut the door, he looked back at me. "Please talk to me before you leave."

I studied my surroundings. I had only been inside Monica's home office a few times, but I would have recognized it anywhere. The computer was her favorite color, mauve. An 11 x 14 portrait of her and Bruce with their son, Burke, when he graduated from high school, hung on the wall. Abstract prints that looked like her favorite eye makeup colors also hung along the wall. No calendar. She probably computerized her datebook.

I turned on the computer and tried a password. As I had guessed, she hadn't changed it: Enjolie020180 — her middle name and date of birth. I had warned her it could be easily hacked, but she ignored common sense. Her birthday was January 2, and she thought reversing the day and the month in the European style and using zeroes made it infallible.

It took less time than I'd expected to send news of her passing to her contacts. She had kept the information well organized, and I could easily identify which were personal and which were business.

The hour was growing late, and I wondered if I was still capable of the all-nighters I had pulled when Dave's wife died. Monica had a comfortable couch by the desk, ready to receive guests. I could curl up there and rest a few minutes if I felt the need.

It didn't take long to locate her staff members. It was barely nine — not too late to call. I got in touch with her senior officers, told them what I knew, and left it to them to handle what happened at her office tomorrow.

Next, I checked to see if I could access her account at the family business from this computer. She and I had shared responsibility for company perks such as coffee, snacks, vending machines, even parties. I'll admit I was curious to see how she had changed things after I left.

I spotted Off the Top Creamery among the vendors, the same company that ran my flavor-of-the-month subscription. Hazelnut was the office favorite flavor as well. Monica had increased the budget for creamer to an unreasonable amount, in my opinion. I was about to scroll to the next page when I spotted something unusual. The last delivery had been today at eleven minutes after four. The only items delivered were three 24-ounce cartons of hazelnut creamer. It was a strange order, especially since I knew the company truck routinely delivered to Oak Grove on Mondays — and because Goring's usual orders were taken from the company's economical line and not the high-priced luxury line.

Had someone put in a rush order just for my birthday? It had cost an additional fifty dollars to deliver the three cartons, which by themselves cost thirty dollars plus sales tax. I whistled. Someone wanted that creamer badly. I hoped it wasn't for my sake.

If I went to the office, I could learn more. The business might be closed tomorrow, but maybe not. They could continue for a few days without onsite management, and the company couldn't afford to shut down for long. Or I could visit employees in their homes. Monica had addresses and phone numbers for each one. I was surprised by the turnover since I'd left, about twenty-five percent by the look of it. There was a new female sales rep, a first for the company. I wondered what Monica had thought about that.

Curious about this Paula Shreckhise, I clicked through the links to the employee directory. I was surprised to discover she was a shapely blond in her early twenties, the kind who could cause problems in a workplace without meaning to. That was a pity; both Chad and Bruce were at a vulnerable age.

I felt guilty for the direction my thoughts had taken. Bruce had always seemed completely devoted to Monica, even if all wasn't well in paradise, as Dave had suggested. I'd keep my ears open for hints of what the problems could have been.

I couldn't shake the feeling that my birthday had something to do with Monica's death. I studied what the computer could tell me about the delivery. Several lines were left blank, such as who had ordered the creamer, which struck me as odd. Had someone tried to hide their identity?

I debated about looking further. I reminded myself that Dave had given me complete access. Perhaps he intended me to look into more than Monica's contacts. I plunged ahead.

Goring's Boring Mill had turned a consistent profit for three decades. Dave had refused to expand; he feared the company would be subject to the principle that a person rises to the level of their incompetence. He figured it was better to be small and consistently profitable than to expand

and get into trouble.

Chad had different ideas. Over time, he wore his father down. After all, the company would be his to run someday — his and Bruce's. During my final months, they had added a machine that was capable of creating different piercing widths. Perhaps the new sales rep had been brought on board to reach new clients.

Sigh. Sales had been erratic, and the machine was underutilized. The company must be cash short, so the expensive creamer perplexed me even more.

I peeked at Monica's photo albums. She'd scanned a few older snaps, including several of her and me together. I teared up at the sight of me with my arm around the motherless teenage girl. *Oh Monica.* The grief I had been repressing swelled up.

The door behind me opened, and I jumped. It was Dave. "I'm heading home and wondered if you were ready to leave."

"My car. I'm so sorry." It was almost eleven. I should have been in the living room with the others, offering my moral support. Instead, I had been indulging the sleuthing bug I had caught along with the other members of my book club over the past few months.

"We're glad you could come. I appreciate the help. Phone calls can be overwhelming." Dave was struggling to stay in control, and my heart went out to him. I would make things easier for him if at all possible.

He held my sweater for me, and we headed into the cool night. Days still got warm in September, but cooled off more quickly after sunset. I pulled my car out first because I was blocking his vehicle, and headed home alone.

I decided to set aside some of the creamer in case the police asked for a sample. I wanted to be sure to keep some for myself, so I poured a couple of ounces into a clean jar and put the carton back in my fridge.

When I picked up the jar, it rattled faintly. Dread settled in my stomach as I tilted the jar so that the heavier-than-liquid bits would slide to the side where I could see them. What I saw made my heart pound with fear.

A clump of chopped nuts settled on the bottom of the jar. There were nuts in my creamer after all, and there was a good chance Monica had died because of it.

THREE

I left a message on the sheriff's answering machine and headed for bed. What a strange, weird birthday. The best of times and the worst of times, as Dickens described it.

I barely got my necessary eight hours of sleep before Sheriff Hayden knocked at my door. As soon as he came in, he demanded to see the creamer. "You should have brought this with you last night."

I refused to be badgered. "You didn't ask me to."

He frowned at me as he took out his note-pad.

Here it comes.

"I need to ask you a few questions."

"Why don't you take a seat?" Many people commented on my ergonomic chairs. I had discovered their comfort at work, and it was a feature I valued when I delved deep into one of my paper-craft projects. I had added personal touches to make the office chairs look more homey.

The sheriff didn't pay any attention to his seat. He settled in and pulled a pen from his pocket.

My throat went dry. I wished I had thought to offer coffee.

"When and where did you get that creamer?" He looked at me.

"It was a present. Yesterday was my birthday, and people know hazelnut is my favorite flavor."

His pen scratched across the paper. "Who gave it to you?"

"I don't know." I shrugged. "It came in a pretty bag but without any card. I always send thank-you notes, so I double-checked."

He looked at me with suspicion, as if I had lost the card on purpose. "Are you absolutely certain?"

Why would I lie? "I'll be sorting through everything this morning and putting it away. If I discover something I missed, I'll call."

I didn't tell him what I had learned about Goring's purchase of creamer. I didn't know if it meant anything, and I didn't want to give Dave any unnecessary stress.

He nodded. "Who offered Mrs. Mayne the creamer?"

"No one." I shook my head. "She arrived late. She helped herself to the creamer as soon as she sat down."

He closed his book. "Can you think of anything else to tell me?"

I considered. I had learned several suggestive things last night, but nothing concrete. "No."

After I gave him the jar of creamer, he showed himself out, and I set to work going through my gifts. I liked to keep things organized. I added the lovely lavender stationery to my supplies. I might use it for the thank-you notes. I'd love an excuse to use my purple pen.

I added the gift certificates to my account with the creamer company. I would call them later. If I didn't take care of my gifts now, they would quickly devolve into clutter. I had several nice things, but I was especially fond of the stamp set from my former fellow workers. I placed it inside my box of paper-craft supplies.

I rubbed my hands together and prepared to get to work on the wrapping paper. First, I cleared the table. Wrapping a present gave me even more pleasure than purchasing one. Harper called them works of art.

When making my paper crafts, I purchased some supplies, but most often I used recycled gift wrap. My birthday gifts had provided me with an artist's palette of paper to recycle, from flowers and metallic colors to animals and star bursts. I flattened the sheets, ran a warm iron over them to reduce wrinkles, then lightly folded them to put into my supply box for future use.

The process had left me with birthday cards and my list of gifts and givers. I looked inside every card and on the backs, on and under the back flap of every envelope, turned every gift tag over. I didn't find anything new.

I decided to use some cards with cute kittens for my thank-you notes. The new stationery was better suited for long, newsy letters.

The front doorbell rang. I was surprised to see Harper Daggett. "Morgan found this at the shop after the party and asked me to bring it by." She handed me another birthday card. "Besides, we heard about Monica's death. I know you're close to the family."

Pain raced through my veins as I thought about the young woman who had been like a daughter. "Come in, please. You're just in time. I was about to write my thank-you notes."

She picked up one of my cat cards and said, "This is cute."

"Thanks. Would you like some tea?" I asked. "I have peppermint. I believe that's your favorite."

"Sounds lovely." She pointed to my coffee-maker sitting on the edge of the counter. "You usually offer coffee."

The thought made me shudder. "I don't know if I'll be ready for a cup of coffee until Monica's murder is cleared up."

"Murder?" Harper said. "I thought it was an accident."

"Somebody added chopped hazelnuts to the carton. I found them when I poured out some of the creamer to keep for myself, before I gave it to the sheriff."

The teakettle whistled, and I poured boiling water into our mugs then fixed a tray with sweeteners of various kinds, including some of Penny's honey. I took my tea black.

Harper took a small sip of tea. It was clear she had something on her mind, but she'd get there in her own time.

"It was pretty awful to have Monica die on your birthday, you being so close to the family and all."

I shook my head. "At my age, birthday celebrations last for a week. The choir sang happy birthday to me when we rehearsed. They'll probably have cake for me in my Sunday school class, and the office has invited me to come in for their monthly birthday party." I would need to check on that. It was scheduled for Friday, but it might be canceled because of Monica's death. "When I piece all the parties together, I've had quite an event."

I sobered. "But of course, I'm saddened by Monica's death. When I went to the Mayne house last night, I found pictures of the two of us together. It reminded me of how close we were at one time." I reached for a tissue and dabbed at my eyes.

"I'm sure she still appreciated you." Harper

drank her tea then stirred a bit of honey into it.

We sat in companionable silence for a few minutes. Then she spoke. "I'm scared. Someone put nuts into that creamer intentionally. I can't help but think they meant to trigger a reaction. What if I had drunk it instead of Monica?" She shivered in spite of the hot tea and the warm room.

I went stone cold. "You just put my deepest fear into words. Someone sent that creamer disguised as a gift, but meaning to do harm. And that makes me angry." I grabbed another tissue as tears fully formed behind my eyelids. "But it's not a very foolproof plan. I might not have opened it at the party, and nothing would have happened."

Harper smiled sadly. "That's even sadder to me. Whoever did it knew you well and used your kindness against Monica. You would never get a gift like that and not offer to share it with everyone there."

"If someone knew me that well, they would probably also know you would be unlikely to drink it, just to be on the safe side —"

"That's assuming it was someone also well acquainted with our book club."

"I think they were targeting Monica." The truth crystallized in my mind while I finished my tea. I took out a new notebook to organize my thoughts. I chose a red binder with pink loose-leaf paper and a bloodred pen to write.

No other color would fit the subject of murder better.

Harper smiled indulgently.

I smiled back. "What's funny?"

She tapped on my notebook. "You even color coordinate your murder notes."

"That's how I work." On the first page I wrote "Monica's Death" in large red letters taking up two lines, underscored, with exclamation points. I looked at it again and crossed out *death,* substituting it with *murder.*

Harper drew in her breath. "Murder. Are you sure?"

I nodded. "Look at what we've established." I wrote the facts down as I mentioned them. "Number one. Anyone who knew me well enough to know my favorite creamer brand would also know I would share it at my party."

"Number two. Anyone who knows you, that is, our book club, would know you were unlikely to drink it so you were safe."

Harper nodded, with me so far.

"Number three. Anyone who knew Monica would know she would drink it, and in abundance." I thought about it some more. "And they knew she would be at my party. The question is —"

"Who knows you, me, and Monica that well?" Harper said.

"And who had opportunity," I said. "Another case for the book club."

FOUR

"I'll call an emergency meeting of the book club tonight," Harper offered. I hugged her for understanding. She was like the daughter I'd never had, like Monica, only more so — we had more in common than I'd ever shared with the murder victim.

She helped me load the dishwasher and put the tea things away. "Is there anything else I can do to help?" she asked when we were finished.

I shook my head. "No. I was getting ready to write thank-you notes, and those have to be personal."

Harper smiled. "Your letters are works of art. I've kept every card I've received from you. I tell people you should write a book on the lost art of letter writing."

I laughed. I doubted anyone would be interested. I did keep a journal, but that was private between me and God.

Harper looked around the house. "You've got a basket of ironing in the laundry room.

If you don't mind, I'll do that and keep you company for a little bit longer."

I gave up protesting. Harper was determined to find something to do. "Thanks. I'll work on the thank-you notes." I did enjoy her company.

I worked on my project for half an hour but gave up when I had to tear up my first note two times. I put away my supplies. "I can't do this. The Bible talks about a time for everything, and apparently this isn't my time to write."

"Why don't we play a game of Scrabble?" Harper knew it was my favorite board game.

"I don't want to impose on you. You only came to drop off the birthday card."

Her look reminded me she had more than one reason for her visit. "No problem. Consider it another birthday present."

Put that way, I couldn't refuse. After a spirited game — one seven-word triumph by me, but Harper won — we decided to head to the Coffee Perk for an early lunch.

Morgan greeted us from behind the register. "Jo, Harper! What a surprise." She came around the counter and hugged me. "I'm so sorry about Monica's death."

Harper and I exchanged looks. "You don't know the half of it."

Our usual table was taken, but I was just as glad. I didn't want to sit in the same chair and stare at the door, waiting for Monica to walk back in.

Morgan met us at the table. She brought a cup of Americano coffee for each of us and took out an order pad. "Let me take your order, and then you can talk. Do you want any of the creamers for your coffee today, Jo?"

I didn't know if I would ever drink hazelnut again, or even almond. "I'll take French Vanilla," I decided. As long as I was in a coffee shop, I would indulge. I could drink ordinary coffee at home.

The shop got busy after she took our order. When she brought our food, she said, "Don't leave before you speak to me."

We assured her we wouldn't. I munched on the pimento cheese sandwiches that Morgan made especially for me. Every now and then she made sliced cucumber and I pretended I was in an English tea shop.

Morgan rejoined us about five minutes later. In a low voice, she said, "How are you doing today, Jo? What an awful way for your birthday to end."

Harper and I bent forward to keep our conversation as private as possible. We filled her in on what had happened last night and the conclusions we had reached this morning. "I could use the help of the book club. Can we schedule an extra meeting here tonight?"

"Of course." Morgan sounded a bit too

enthusiastic. Murder had overtaken our fairly ordinary lives this past year. "Is there anything I can do?"

There was no reason to hold back. "Yes. As far I know, Off the Top Creamery is the only supplier of that brand of coffee creamer. Do you know if anyone else carries it?" Even if someone at Goring's had special ordered creamer to arrive on my birthday, I wanted to check for other possible sources.

"Not that I know of, but I'll check." Morgan left to deal with other customers.

Harper and I were about to leave when Penny came in, calling for a cup of her favorite. When she spotted us, she headed straight for our table and took a seat.

Her eyes sparked with agitation. "Sheriff Hayden came by to see me this morning. Right after he spoke with you, from what I gather."

I blinked. "What did he want?"

"He asked me about the spat I had with Monica. Remember that time I picketed against her new cosmetic line? I mean, in what world is it okay to harm an animal just so a person's eyes are safe? Doesn't that rabbit need to see as well? There are so many other ways to test for side effects . . ."

I supported Penny's opinions in theory, but she could go on and on. I interrupted. "Did he accuse you of anything? Did you call for a lawyer?"

She tossed her head. "He stopped just short of it. Gave me the standard 'don't leave town anytime soon' line. I told him I have plans to go to a rally next week. And he told me I couldn't go. The temerity of the man!"

The worst thing was, Hayden's theory made a kind of twisted sense. Penny had made fierce accusations about Monica in a public setting. It was suggestive as to motive, but nothing else made sense. "If he's looking for people who disliked Monica, there are plenty of people ahead of you."

Penny said, "I disapprove of how she runs her operation. But I would never kill someone. That's just common sense. How could someone who's committed her life to ending animal cruelty ever murder a human being?"

Exactly. Penny didn't have a strong motive, but we still needed to provide the sheriff with other suspects in case he fixated on her.

Penny continued her story. "He didn't believe me when I told him I spent the day at an animal rights rally in the next county over yesterday. I didn't get back until late afternoon."

I didn't point out that she had opportunity to doctor the creamer before she left.

I cleared my throat. "I'm looking into it." I told the ladies about my plans to spend a few hours at the office at my earliest opportunity. "I hope I can pick up some gossip. There's a new woman on staff I want to meet."

"You'd best be careful," Harper said.

"Don't take any risks on my account," Penny said.

"I won't." I told Penny about the proposed meeting that night, and the three of us went our separate ways.

I contacted the new office manager at Goring's to ask about coming to the office. She said that the business would stay open but allow employees time to go to the viewing. They would close during the funeral, of course. We agreed that I would come in the next morning.

My mail arrived, with a few late cards, some with cash or gift cards, which reminded me I hadn't yet started on my thank-you notes. I glanced at the clock. If everything went well, I had just about enough time to get them done.

When I counted, I realized I had more gifts than kitten cards. I liked to send everyone the same stationery, with a few personal flourishes. The local stationery store held a nice collection. I almost headed out with one of my gift cards.

Not a good idea. My mind wanted to trick me into avoiding a task that normally brought me pleasure. Why was I procrastinating? Then it hit me. I was afraid people would expect me to mention Monica. I decided to keep my notes short and to the point.

I had just enough kitten cards for the

members of the book club and the folks at Goring's who had contributed to my gift. I'd start with those.

First up, Sherri Wexel, who was working at the office as a temp. She had also come to my party with a personal gift. I had felt strangely pleased that she would come, since we had never been that close. *I so appreciate your attendance at my party yesterday. . . . Thank you for the lovely pens.*

Each card for the folks at Goring's reminded me of the loss they had endured. I remembered some of them had disagreements with Monica. I'd better get to the office before every friend became a suspect.

The thought that any one of my comrades had a reason to kill Monica made the note cards difficult. They took longer than usual to write, and I didn't finish them all. I sighed. My contemporaries advised me to accept the gradual reduction of sharpness that came with age — easier said than done.

I took a brief nap, reheated frozen lasagna I had placed in the freezer on Sunday, and added a small salad before heading over to the coffee shop.

The sight of all my friends brought tears to my eyes. "Thanks for coming tonight. I feel like this week has been all about me." I wiped at my eyes. "And now . . ."

"And now it's time for us to pitch in and help you, the way you've been helping us over the past few months," Evelyn said briskly. "We've been considering how we might help."

Bless them. I had come armed with some ideas of my own, but their proactive thinking reminded me of all the reasons why I loved these women.

Evelyn and Jeanine pointed at each other. "We figured we'd work on the nuts angle. I'm going to experiment in the kitchen," Jeanine said. "How could someone get nuts into the container, how much time it might take, how much noise they would make. Also how to best prepare the nuts. The practical nuts-and-bolts of the murder."

We went silent for a few moments. *Murder* was such a final word.

A thought dawned on me. "If it helps, I still have the carton."

Jeanine looked at me in surprise. "I thought you turned it over to the sheriff."

I shook my head. "I poured the creamer into a jar."

"I'll stop by after the meeting to pick it up."

"And I'm going to the library. I want to learn more about nut allergies," Evelyn said.

"Can you think of anything else? Someone needs to speak with the folks at Goring's, but you're doing that," Harper said.

No one said anything while we considered other options.

"We should all go to the viewing," Evelyn said, finally breaking the silence. "To pay our respects, of course. But we might also pick up on some gossip."

Everyone nodded in assent.

The meeting broke up after that. Morgan and Harper stopped me before I left. "Be careful when you go to the office," Harper said.

Were they afraid for me? The possibility made me shiver. It would be a sad day when I was afraid to go to my old office. Of course, the circumstances were already sad.

I shook away the worry. "I'm visiting old friends and looking through computer records, which Dave authorized me to do. Nothing will happen to me."

I felt as confident as my words — I only hoped I didn't have cause to regret them.

FIVE

I arrived at the office of Goring's Boring Mill early Thursday morning. Elma Brooks, the lady who had taken over as office manager after my retirement, was there to greet me.

Elma had left full-time motherhood when her children entered high school. By the time she'd come to Goring's, they were in college, but they were the highlight of her life. She looked like the grandmother she now was, one young enough to play with them.

I searched my memories. When I had left, her daughter was expecting her first child. "Do you have any pictures of your new grandbaby?"

Her phone held more pictures than I actually cared to see, but I could see how she had fallen in love with the pink-faced baby girl with a shock of black hair. A familiar pang that I would never know the joy of grandchildren ran across my heart. Dave's grandson, Burke, was the closest I would experience.

Eventually the show-and-tell ended, and Elma took me on a tour of the office, showing me a few changes. "Mr. Goring said to give you full run of the place. Is there anything I can help you with?"

I only wanted to tell her as much as was necessary. "I don't know yet. I'll set up shop in Monica's office, if you don't mind. Dave wants me to go through her business contacts and clear up any unfinished business."

Sherri Wexel had arrived to take over the receptionist's desk when I went to the front, where Monica's space was located. I thanked Elma for her help, and she followed me into Monica's office.

Even though Monica only spent a few hours a week at her father's company, it spoke to her personality. I closed my eyes, trying to pinpoint the differences since I had last seen it. Her desk and file cabinets stood in the same place. The same soft caramel sweater she wore whenever she ventured into the plant hung in the closet.

Elma's mouth turned down. "Ever since we've had an additional person in management, things have gone downhill."

I welcomed the gossip. Elma was the last person directly hired by Dave, and she had a good sense of office politics. "How so?"

"The new boring mill isn't attracting business. He underestimated the potential market."

She didn't have to identify who "he" was: Chad Goring, in his first major decision as Dave's heir.

Elma listed the expectations and disappointments as if she were an expert in the boring process. I suppressed a grin. She couldn't have explained the difference between turning and boring before starting to work for the company.

"And his hiring decisions have been just as disastrous," she said. "He had his mind on a different kind of business when he hired his new sales rep. Even giving her the benefit of the doubt, she's too young to have enough experience to handle the job well. People look for a salesperson with experience before they buy."

"I saw her photo when I looked at Monica's computer the other night," I said. "She had an unusual name. Paula something." I hoped she had more going for her than her looks. I trusted Elma to know. Sweet, pleasant-looking if not beautiful, Elma was a good judge of character.

"Paula Shreckhise," Elma said. "I spoke with the boss — Dave — about my reservations." She sighed.

"What did he say?" I asked.

"I would guess he wasn't thrilled either, but he said to be patient. She could learn what she didn't know, and she had contacts among the people we hoped would bring us their projects. But I still think she was more interested in selling something else."

It was unlike Elma to be so catty, but I didn't remark on it. Perhaps she sensed my need to learn everything I could about current office politics.

Elma shook her head, a snowy-white cap, the color some brunettes get in their fifties. "First thing, she set her cap for the boss, but he saw straight through her. Then she split her attention between Chad and Bruce. Bruce has always been faithful to Monica, a beautiful thing in this day and age, but — Oh dear." She stopped speaking.

I put an arm around her. "I suspected as much." I hesitated. "How far did things go between Bruce and Paula? Do you know?"

Elma's face fell. "I don't know exactly, but the last time Monica was here, I heard her talking to a divorce lawyer."

That would have dealt a horrible blow to Dave. He had always taken such comfort in his daughter's steady marriage, and he doted on Burke, who was in his second year at Yale. Chad's determined bachelorhood distressed him.

"Have arrangements been made for Burke to come home?" I should've offered to make those arrangements the other night.

"He's coming in this weekend, in time for the funeral." She glanced through the blinds. "The staff is coming in. Can I help you with anything else?"

I reeled in my mind, which was flying in a dozen directions. "Perhaps give them the okay to speak freely with me. I'm especially interested in a special order of hazelnut creamer that was placed the same day as the party. I couldn't see who ordered it."

"I was surprised when they delivered it." Elma scratched her head. "I was going to check into it later, but then everything happened."

I followed her out the door in search of a cup of coffee. A fresh pot was brewing in the break room. Sherri came in while I was checking the refrigerator for creamers. "I see you're making yourself at home."

"A cup of coffee helps get me started," I said. "They used to keep creamers in small cups for individual consumption. Do they still have those?"

"They've found it more cost-effective to buy it by the carton. We've got quite a variety, including that hazelnut you like." Her face colored, an unpleasant match for her strawberry-blond hair.

"I'll take the cocoa flavor." The word *hazelnut* still made me shiver.

"Mocha." She shook her head. "I've never acquired a taste for it. I like coffee, and I like chocolate, but not together." She poured a cup of coffee for herself without adding anything and sat down on a padded chair that looked like it had been in the office ever since it opened — the ergonomic chairs didn't get past the offices. That reminded me that Monica had wanted to remodel the break room, which made me sad all over again.

I took advantage of the opportunity to chat with Sherri. She had a newcomer's perspective on the company, so she might see things a different way.

"I'm sure Dave, Mr. Goring, that is, appreciates your help during this time."

Sherri sniffed. "I hope he does. It's hard to tell. I've been working here since you left, but they're still paying me through a temp agency."

"I thought that was your preference. You expressed an interest in being able to go on trips and take care of family."

I felt a twinge of guilt. Dave had asked my opinion before hiring her. Yes, she and I had had personal differences, but that wasn't the reason I was hesitant to recommend Dave hire her. Her work ethic was the problem. She tended to forsake a project in midstream. She'd done that to me in the past. And she stayed home at the first sniffle, only to recover and go out on other business later. She'd been that way in high school, and she hadn't changed much, from what I could tell.

"I thought it was what I wanted." She took a sip of her coffee. "But I'm needed here, Jo. Things have changed since you left, from what I hear. You described Goring's as such a happy place to work, but the air's thick with tension. And I'll tell you what — Monica was at the center of it."

Six

Sherri brushed off her skirt. "I'd better get back to the front."

As glad as I was for her newfound dedication to the job, I hoped she had more insight to share. I'd have to catch her again later.

Back in Monica's office, I was struck by the sense that something had changed. I sat in the chair facing her desk, closed my eyes again, and tried to remember. The furniture hadn't changed or been moved around. It must be the accessories.

I spotted a few things as soon as I opened my eyes. Mother Teresa's poem, "Do It Anyway," had disappeared, replaced by a shorter sentiment: "Yesterday is not ours to recover, but tomorrow is ours to win or lose." An interesting statement, given Goring's current state of affairs.

She'd also added a black-and-white print of city streets that might have been Paris. I didn't remember it, but it looked like an advertisement for her cosmetics business.

All her personal photographs had disappeared. Knowing Monica the way I did, I suspected she had weighed the competition and found herself wanting. She had taken care of herself, but she wasn't born with a model's face. Working with a younger, attractive sales rep — and having her husband make a bit of a fool of himself with her — must have been hard. I shook my head. Poor Monica.

Next up: figuring out more about the creamer timeline. All I had so far was the day and time it was delivered.

It seemed unlikely that Monica would have ordered it, certainly not that much. She had been conscientious about spending company money on personal affairs, even more so after her own business took off. Had someone asked her to do it?

I looked through her files, looking for references to the creamer, but didn't find anything. I decided to check her physical file. The dawn of the computer age had only multiplied the amount of paper generated in her office. She kept the files for break room supplies in her desk drawer. Nothing. Perhaps the petty cash box? I took it out of the drawer, placed it on the desk, and checked the side drawer for keys.

While searching, I uncovered a sheet torn off a message pad. She had been taking notes at a meeting. She had circled one of the notes. "Order more hazelnut creamer for Jo's birthday as well as extra for the office."

The smoking gun! Unfortunately, she hadn't dated the note or indicated who was at the meeting.

I grabbed my notebook again and wrote down the note. I needed to develop a list of topics to bring up when I met with other employees. I'd heard they were bringing in pizza for lunch, and I intended to take advantage of the captive audience.

The invoice for the shipment lay exactly where it should. I dialed the creamery and identified myself. The agent remembered me. "Miss Anderson, how may we help you?"

Their personal touch had made me a loyal customer. "I'm calling on behalf of Goring's Boring Mill. I'm helping out where I can since Monica Mayne died."

"Oh Miss Anderson, we heard! Everyone over here feels dreadful about her death. I heard it happened on your birthday. How awful for you. Do you know the details about her services?"

I told her the name of the funeral home. It sounded like she didn't know Monica's death was due to the nuts in the creamer. I didn't want to tell her, but I had to. I explained the details. "I honestly don't think anyone at your plant was responsible, but I'm hoping you can help me trace what happened with the creamer."

A sharp intake of breath before she said, "Of course. Anything I can do to help."

"I have an invoice number for creamer that was special ordered sometime in the past few days. I'd like to know who ordered it, when they ordered it, time and day, what they ordered, who packed it, who delivered it, when it was dropped off."

I laughed at myself. "I'm sorry, I'm bombarding you with questions. I'm trying to piece together what happened with it. Is there any chance I could speak with the delivery person?"

"I'll ask him to give you a call when he comes back in from his deliveries. Now let me check on the information I have about your situation. The creamer was ordered at 11:47 on Tuesday morning by Mrs. Mayne." She tapped a few more keys. "We delivered it at 4:11 on the same day." I already knew that, but I was glad for the confirmation. "The deliveryman went out after he returned from his other deliveries, since she had indicated it was a matter of some urgency. A Mrs. Wexel signed for it."

I thanked her and hung up, considering what I had learned. Ordering something at the last minute was out of character for any of the Gorings. They were more likely to apologize sweetly and buy me something extra nice to make up for it. But now my birthday had become an excuse for murder, and that made me angry.

The deliveryman called me a few minutes later, but I didn't learn anything useful. I had assumed the creamer had been doctored at the office — how else would they know which carton had nuts in it? I already knew they'd had only two hours to get it done, since my party had started at six.

But when did the carton get to the party? It wasn't there when I arrived at the Coffee Perk. I'd oohed and aahed over the pretty decorations and only glanced at the gift table. I didn't want anyone to think I was eager to open them. I tried to remember details from the night. When we started eating, customers stopped by to wish me well. A couple of employees from Goring's, including Elma, came in and wished me well, then left. I didn't pay close attention to the gift table again until a few members of the church choir stopped by, about twenty past six. The bag with the creamer had made its appearance by then.

Did Elma know anything about it? How should I phrase such a delicate question? I didn't believe she had killed Monica, but she might have been asked to deliver the murder weapon.

My phone buzzed. It was Elma. "I just thought of something you should know. I brought the present to your party. Oh dear, the police are going to find my fingerprints on it. I hope they don't suspect me."

I certainly didn't. "I can't think why they would. Who asked you to bring it?"

Her volume dropped. "I don't know. I found the bag on my desk, with a note to bring it to your party."

I heard a faint click on the line and wondered if anyone was listening in. "I'll come see you." I disconnected and walked to the back of the office, where Elma had a corner space. People called out greetings and questions as I passed by. My friendship with the Gorings and the Maynes was well known. Every employee expressed a desire to help. I didn't detect a false note among them.

The glass walls in Elma's office allowed her to watch everything that was going on, but I appreciated it when she closed the blinds for our conversation. As I took my seat, I said, "I find myself wondering about listening ears."

Elma shivered enough to shake her small frame. "The heavy atmosphere is making everyone in the office uncomfortable. If there's anything we can do to clear things up, we want to help."

"That's good to hear." *Everyone except for the responsible party,* an inner voice reminded me. "You said someone asked you to bring the present to my party?"

"Yes, it appeared on my desk with a note. It was unsigned. I kept it." She opened her top drawer and extracted papers held together by a clip. "Here it is." She used a pen to tease it off the paperclip to avoid creating more fingerprints.

Please bring this to Jo Anderson's birthday party at the Coffee Perk after six this evening. I brought out my notebook. "Do you remember when you saw it on your desk?" I held my pen poised over the page.

"About fifteen minutes before I left, about quarter to six. And before you ask, it stayed in my sight from the time I saw it on my desk until I put it on the table at the party."

I added a note at the appropriate timestamp in my notes. But unless I could figure out who had left the note, I'd hit another dead end. "Do you recognize the handwriting? Or do you have samples to compare it to?"

"No, I don't recognize it. But I can put together samples of handwriting from almost everyone." She tapped her pen on her forehead. "Not that I'm a handwriting expert."

"Neither am I, but we might notice something. I don't need it to hold up in a court of law. I only want to find the next step in the chain."

A couple of the samples we found looked like possibilities — Jasmine Derry and Tammy Cord. When we questioned them, Jasmine admitted she had wrapped the carton after she found a note on her desk — also unsigned, of course.

That was suggestive. Jasmine excelled at gift-wrapping. I had employed her help in getting ready for company parties. Whoever recruited her help probably knew that.

She saw the note at quarter past five, and she set about the task immediately. "I hope you liked it. It wasn't easy to package."

I made appreciative noises. "When did you leave it on Elma's desk?"

She made quick mental calculations. "About twenty minutes to six. Elma was out of the office for a few minutes. I noticed the time because I signed back onto the phone when I was done."

I jotted down the information.

Jasmine said, "I was surprised to see the carton on my desk. I had just seen it in the refrigerator in the break room during my break."

That got my attention. "And when was that?"

Jasmine glanced at Elma hesitantly. "At 4:30."

"Write down 4:25," Elma said. "I know you slip in early," she said to Jasmine. She faced me again. "I saw the cartons there earlier myself. A note was hanging on one of them."

"That's right," Tammy said. "It read, 'Do not touch. For Jo Anderson's birthday.' "

"It was gone when I went back to clean the break room about five," Jasmine said. "I noticed because someone had spilled a little creamer on the floor, and I checked the refrigerator after I cleaned it."

I felt a tingle when I wrote down 5:00 on the timeline.

"By the time I finished cleaning up and got back to my desk, the carton was waiting for me," Jasmine said.

"How long was your break?" Her answer would help define the window of opportunity.

"Our breaks are ten minutes." Jasmine squirmed a little uncomfortably. She'd always had a little trouble following a rigid time schedule.

Elma cleared her throat. "Don't lie. You won't get into trouble today for taking an extra-long break. It might teach you to stop doing it in the future." She tapped her computer keys. "This is what I have. You left for your break at 4:27. You used the facilities after you took your break and didn't make it back to your desk until 4:50."

Ouch. Elma was responsible for employee conduct, but that kind of minute accounting could grind a person down.

"It wasn't my fault I was late," Jasmine protested. "Tammy got caught up in a phone call and came in for our break late."

"You logged back in at 4:50."

I made a note of the time while I considered the implications. Most likely, someone had doctored the creamer between the end of Jasmine's break at 4:50 and the time she came back to clean the kitchen at five.

Ten minutes to account for. Just ten minutes. That shouldn't be so difficult, should it?

SEVEN

I felt good about establishing the timeline, but so far, I'd ignored the human factor. Who had a reason to want Monica dead? The question made me squirm. I'd hoped an office rumor might arise about an unknown subject that would make things easier. So far, that hadn't happened.

Except for Bruce's interest in the new sales rep. I needed to make Paula Shreckhise's acquaintance. The day's office calendar suggested she might be in her office and alone.

Before I headed in her direction, I refreshed my makeup. I felt a little silly. Why bother gilding my withered skin? Even when I was her age, I wasn't beauty pageant material. But someone like Paula probably placed importance on appearance. I didn't want her to dismiss me before she heard me out.

Once I was satisfied I had done everything possible, I headed in the direction of the offices closest to the manufacturing plant.

I caught my first sight of Paula through

half-open blinds and slowed down. She was as lovely as her picture suggested. Her smile, warm and welcoming, could probably be heard on the phone. She was at least fifteen years younger than Monica, possibly more — twenty-five years old at the most, which seemed terribly young for such a responsible position. I reminded myself that everyone seemed young to me these days. In a business still dominated by men, she might be the perfect choice.

I reminded myself I wasn't here to judge her job qualifications. I wanted to learn if her allure had reached beyond Goring's customers to the management. I squared my shoulders and headed for her door, which she opened before I could knock.

"I noticed you debating about whether to come in. I've heard so many wonderful things about you, Miss Anderson."

I felt myself smiling in return, liking her immediately. She had genuine warmth. Perhaps she wasn't a schemer after all. Perhaps she was just someone available, vulnerable to Bruce's charm. Because Bruce was the Harrison Ford of our small company.

Sturdier, more business-styled versions of the chairs I had in my home ranged around Paula's desk. A picture of her and what I presumed was her family hung opposite a print of Degas's dancers.

We exchanged personal details, while I

435

reeled in my initial positive reaction. I reminded myself that sales had not improved in spite of her hiring and rumors flew about her and Bruce.

"They say you were employed here for most of your adult life, that you were like a part of the Goring family. You don't know how that encouraged me. I was afraid people might be jealous of me. But Mr. Goring — Dave Goring, that is — has gone out of his way to make me feel welcome."

"That sounds like him." How could I get her to open up about any possible tension? I briefly hoped there was no tension, that it was all in my imagination. But Monica was dead, and someone had wanted her gone badly enough to add nuts to her — my — coffee creamer.

The quickest route was to reveal something I had shared with very few people. Was it necessary, I pondered? If not for the sake of the woman in front of me who might have gotten in over her head, then for Monica's sake, I must.

"You heard right. I began working at Goring's Boring Mill when I was a young woman." I ran my tongue across my lips, gathering courage to continue. "Harrison, my fiancé, had died in Vietnam. I mourned him, and I never found another that was his match."

Paula made sympathetic noises, which was

one reason why I didn't mention the old pain very often.

I rushed forward. "Except for Dave Goring." There, I had made my admission. "I admired him from afar, because he was happily married. I am ashamed to say that we almost crossed the line when he and his wife had a rough patch early in their marriage. I have always thanked God that they reconciled before Dave and I did something we would both regret. But oh, I knew the temptation."

Paula flushed. "Has someone been making catty remarks about me? I can't help the looks I was born with. What do you do when the boss comes on to you? Even in these days, a woman can lose her job."

Sexual harassment — illegal, of course. I hated to think it had happened. Dave would have been horrified. Or maybe not. Maybe he would remember how close we had been.

I continued with my story. "I only meant I know how easily it can happen. You're a vibrant young woman. Bruce is handsome and charming, a good man. In the office, it's easy to forget he's married. If he let his eyes stray, it's natural he would be drawn to you." People who liked and respected each other could easily cross the line into the forbidden.

"As long as you put it that way." Paula took out her calendar as if checking something. "It started when Mr. Mayne invited me to a business luncheon to explain my job. After a couple of months, we worked on a project together. We went out a few nights and our talk drifted into personal matters. We went on business trips together and —" She colored, and I filled in the rest.

I made sympathetic noises, while my heart churned. Had Monica or Dave noticed the warning signs?

"Was Bruce" — I forced the words past my throat — "unhappy in his marriage?"

She shifted in her chair. "I'm not sure if I should be telling you all of this. I always knew what I had with Bruce was temporary. No matter what tensions he was having with Monica, he would never have left her."

"I believe you," I said. "I won't repeat anything you say to me." I felt compelled to add, "unless it has a bearing on Monica's murder."

"It's so awful." Paula's face crumpled. "Bruce only said they had grown apart. Their son had kept them together, but now that he was gone, and she had her own business, they hardly saw each other anymore."

It was a common enough tale, but it usually led to divorce, not murder. "That's sad."

"He's had a terrible year. He's felt pushed out at work. They expect us to find customers who need the new machine, but there aren't that many. I brought in one big deal, which made me their best sales rep this year. That reflected badly on him. Between problems at work and problems at home, I was his safe place." She plumped herself a bit, as if she were pleased with the situation.

Paula fell silent for a few seconds. "Not to speak ill of the dead, but Monica seemed to engender ill will wherever she went. She treated the staff here like they were her personal servants. She even asked me to come to a sales meeting to model her cosmetics! She didn't offer to pay me anything. She told me to think of it as doing my boss a favor."

I sighed. That did sound like the Monica I had known and loved anyway.

"I've heard of at least one customer she drove away a few years ago. I almost brought their business back, but when they saw Monica in the office, they walked out again." I could see that failure hadn't set well with Paula.

"Was that the Gould Company by any chance?" I asked. Darren Gould had been at Monica's throat ever since she dropped him in college to marry Bruce.

"As a matter of fact, yes."

So that old feud continued. Surely, that had nothing to do with Monica's death. "When did that happen?" I asked.

"About ten days ago. I talked them into coming back on Tuesday morning, since Monica always spent the day in her office."

My heart sped up for a second, but he had

been there in the morning, before the creamer had even been delivered.

I didn't learn anything else enlightening from Paula, so I excused myself and headed back to Monica's office. I had decided it felt like a monk's cell, isolating her from the people she should have been closest to. That had been the story of Monica's life, building self-fortresses that cut herself off from her support systems. She had suffered more than Chad from the death of her mother. And Dave had thrown himself into his work, leaving his daughter without an anchor when she was most vulnerable.

It was clear Paula didn't like Monica and saw herself as Bruce's ally. Enough to murder for him?

Monica had always rubbed the staff the wrong way, but we had all accepted it in the boss's daughter. As I'd noted before, however, there'd been about a twenty-five percent turnover in staffing since I left. Were the new hires less forgiving, more supportive of either of the younger managers, Chad or Bruce?

At least Dave hadn't come up as a source of tension. That would have broken me entirely. It was difficult enough to consider his son-in-law as the murderer, but I didn't see I had much choice.

I made a note to check on whether or not Monica had been seeking a divorce. Paula didn't think Bruce wanted one. I'd keep my ears open. If all else failed, I would check in with our gossip-prone postmistress.

Maybe the name of Monica's lawyer would show up on her computer. She didn't have a date planner — I had already checked. Few people did in this electronic age, relying on their gadgets to keep them on track.

Monica's phone was in Bruce's possession. I envisioned a call from her divorce lawyer, to confirm an appointment she'd made before she died, and winced. I wish I had a way to get it away from him.

Her office record made mention of an appointment with Richard Booker, one of Oak Grove's premier divorce lawyers. That was highly suggestive.

I took out my notebook and drew a heavy line below the timeline. Who did I know with a possible reason to want Monica Mayne dead?

Sherri Wexel. Her name wasn't too hard to write, but I hoped I didn't include her out of pure spite. She disliked Monica, but so did a lot of people.

Penny Parson. I wrote my friend's name down, crossed it out, and wrote it again. She did have a motive, she had opportunity, but she couldn't have known anything about the creamer at the office. Could she?

Paula Shreckhise. I had liked her in spite of myself, but I almost would prefer for her to be the guilty party.

She had mentioned a feud with Darren Gould. I didn't know if a decades-old grievance was a motive for murder, but I added his name to the list.

At last, the two names I felt loyalty to. Who I prayed weren't responsible.

Bruce Mayne.

Chad Goring.

I almost closed the book. I wanted to. Those two were bad enough.

But in fairness, I needed to add a final name: Dave Goring. I scribbled his name on the page and slammed the cover shut before I was tempted to rip it out.

Timeline:

11:47 Order placed by Monica

4:11 Order delivered — receipt signed by Sherri

4:25 Unopened carton still in refrigerator, with label about my birthday

4:47 Carton still untouched when employees left break room

4:50 Jasmine signed back on the phone

5:00 Carton not in refrigerator when Jasmine returned to clean break room

5:15 Carton appeared on Jasmine's desk asking her to wrap it

5:40 Jasmine left the wrapped carton on Elma's desk with a note

5:45 Elma discovered the present and the

note to take it to my party
6:20 The present was on the gift table.
Elma left it there before 6:20

EIGHT

After the busy week I'd had, I slept a bit later than usual on Friday, so I was a little surprised by my early morning visitors.

Jeanine and Evelyn had arrived, bearing gifts. I smelled yeasty scents of cinnamon and hazelnuts, with an overlay of coffee.

"I'm hoping you haven't had breakfast yet," Jeanine said. "I chopped up so many hazelnuts, I had to find ways to use them. This is a variation on my cinnamon roll recipe, with hazelnuts instead of pecans."

We took seats around the kitchen table. Jeanine's cinnamon rolls were spectacular, and I couldn't wait to try them with hazelnuts. A single bite sent me into seventh heaven.

"I called the funeral home this morning." Evelyn was wearing a pale green Hensley sweater that suited her perfectly. "They're having a viewing this evening."

I nodded.

"We're eager to tell you what we learned," Jeanine added.

The sweet hazelnut spread turned to gravel in my mouth. I chewed it thoroughly and swallowed before speaking. "Tell me."

"I'll start." Evelyn squared her shoulders. "It was scary to learn how few nuts it takes to cause a severe anaphylactic reaction. I also learned more about what happens when a person has an allergic reaction. Chemicals in our bodies try to kill the protein in the nuts, and that in turn releases a deadly reaction."

I interrupted before she gave a complete lecture. "So how many nuts does it take?"

Her eyes gleamed. "As little as a hundredth of a peanut. I expect it would be similar with a hazelnut, although I couldn't find that exact information."

I gasped, staring at the nut-covered roll on my plate, suddenly grateful for my allergy-free life.

"Two nuts would be overkill." I sank into my cushions farther. "They could have added some of those crushed nuts that come in packages." I wondered how many people could die from a single three-ounce pouch of crushed pecans as I stared at the nut-studded rolls.

Jeanine covered the rolls. The talk had dampened all of our appetites.

Evelyn consulted her notes. "There are fifteen grams of protein for every three and a half ounces of peanuts. That's seventy nuts, more or less, which is theoretically enough to kill thousands of people. A teaspoon would be enough to have killed everyone in the room that night." She glanced up. "If everyone had an allergy, of course."

Somebody had not only killed Monica, but recklessly endangered who knew how many other people who also had an allergy. I turned my attention to Jeanine next. "Did you figure out how they got the nuts into the creamer?"

"Yes." She brought out the container, now flattened and dried. "If you look here" — she pointed to the corners of the carton where they met at the bottom — "you can see tiny markings on it, as if someone pried it open carefully."

I put on my glasses and studied it carefully. The markings were barely visible, like the markings on an origami sheet. They were triangular — two sides that came to a point. Definitely not there originally. "Do you have any idea how they got there?" I asked.

"Not exactly. Something like this, perhaps." Jeanine reached into her bag for an implement that looked like a mini-pie server, the right size for a small wheel of cheese. "I don't think the person necessarily intended to open the carton. He — or she — only wanted to add a small amount of ground nuts into the creamer, so they slipped something like this under the edges."

I was beginning to worry. By tampering with the carton, had we erased any evidence?

"When I saw the marks, I also spotted this." She pulled out a sealed baggie with one-sided tape in it. On it I saw tiny sprinkles of white stuff. When I sniffed it, I could still smell hazelnut.

I considered. "It wouldn't have taken all that long, but to do this, someone needed privacy." The ten minutes in my timeline was just about long enough, but who at Goring's could be confident that they would not be uninterrupted for that long?

Someone spilled creamer on the floor. I remembered what Jasmine had told me and gasped.

"What is it?" Evelyn asked.

I explained what I had learned about the timeline and how Jasmine had noticed spilled creamer on the floor. All fingers pointed back to someone at Goring's as the killer.

"You'd best be careful," Jeanine said.

"They can't like you asking questions," Evelyn added.

Should I tell them about my list of suspects? Of course, although I felt horrible that Penny was on the list. "Although I don't see any way Penny would have been at Goring's late Tuesday afternoon. Logically, she's eliminated."

Jeanine wrinkled her eyebrows. "That's good."

"I'm surprised to see Sherri's name on your list." Evelyn tut-tutted. "She's been helping out at the soup kitchen on Tuesday evenings, since I've made the book club a regular appointment on my calendar."

"But she was at work . . ." My voice trailed away. Or was she? Was I certain Sherri hadn't left early? I'd have to check my records. "I'll look into it. She did stop by my birthday party, of course."

They asked who Darren Gould was, and I explained. "I'm looking for a way to connect with him. Do you have any ideas?"

We thought about asking a golfer to help us track him down — I knew his company had sponsored some events at the local golf club. But the simplest approach was to contact him directly. We knew each other vaguely, in the way people know each other in a small town.

We returned to our discussion of the viewing. We decided it was best to arrive separately. If we came as a group, the very people we hoped to speak with might clam up.

My friends left, and I cleaned up from breakfast. A glance at the clock reminded me it was time to call Morgan.

"Coffee Perk, where the brew is always the way you like it."

I loved to hear Morgan's voice. She always sounded so happy.

"It's Jo. I'm calling about the creamer. Have you found out anything more?" The line clicked. I always forgot to ask if it was a good time.

Morgan came back in a few seconds. "Do you mind if I call you back? Say, in three to five minutes?"

"Sure."

I was looking through my stationery for more notecards to finish my thank-you notes when she called back. "I got someone else to take over the register so we could talk without interruption. I learned quite a bit. Most companies carry a hazelnut flavor. Several are naturally flavored. The creams from Off the Top are mostly artificially flavored, and they process it themselves. They had a patent for their cinnamon hazelnut. They expressed their regret about what happened."

I listened to the undertones. "Tell me, are you trying a new supplier?"

Morgan laughed. "You know me too well, Jo. Another company offers a better deal on regular milk, not creamers. I ordered a few bottles to try them out." She sighed. "Even if I didn't like Off the Top's products and services, I almost feel like I have to keep using them. They say they've lost a few customers. Rumors are spreading."

My ears perked up at that. Was there a chance that someone had gone through this whole charade to create trouble for the creamer manufacturer? It seemed so unlikely.

We said our goodbyes, and I considered

what I had learned that morning. Someone had poured a small amount of ground hazelnuts into the carton by using a triangular-shaped utensil. That person must have known how little was needed. I would have dumped in at least a tablespoon to be sure it would spread through the entire carton.

How I wished my only purpose in going to tonight's viewing was to pay my respects to Monica. I didn't want to have to play detective.

A light bulb went off. Perhaps the funeral parlor would allow me to come in early. Everyone knew I was a close friend of the family. Perhaps I could add something to Monica's final trousseau. I knew just what. She had given me an exquisite turquoise and amber bracelet that I would never wear. I would return the gift, with love.

I wrapped the bracelet in tissue but started to cry when I tried to stand. I set down the bracelet and let the tears fall.

NINE

The short cry relieved grief I had buried deep, ever since her mother passed on. Now that Monica was also dead, I found myself missing them both.

If I felt that way, I couldn't imagine how the family felt. I popped on my reading glasses in the hope of dislodging the rose-colored lenses my mind kept between me and my suspects. No matter what else we learned, the strongest motives and opportunities kept pointing back to the Gorings, either the family or the company. I needed to confirm alibis for those vital ten minutes and find out where Darren Gould was, if I could. He was a long shot, but he only needed a couple of minutes, a tiny tool, and a small amount of crushed nuts.

Before I did any of that, I wanted to say a proper goodbye to Monica. I called the funeral home and explained what I wanted. They said the cosmetician would be working on Monica that afternoon, but she should finish by two o'clock. They agreed that I could come in after two. I had no desire to interrupt the cosmetician in her duties, so I aimed for quarter past the hour.

I settled at my desk and wrote most of the remaining thank-you notes. I used my last stamp on the last envelope. So many people had given me gifts that I had run out of supplies. I needed to spend some serious time thanking God for a lifetime of friends.

As I climbed into my Toyota, I wondered if I was wrong to keep looking into the murder. Was I so busy focusing on Monica's death that I was overlooking all the wonderful gifts God had given me — including my long friendship with the Gorings?

That thought took over as I pulled into the funeral parlor. I was definitely thankful for the opportunity to come at this time, without observers. I always found my feelings to be a very private affair. I had overcome the loss of my beloved Harrison, and later let go of a man I had no claim to, by shutting off emotions, but at times like this my habits caught up with me.

Tears welled behind my eyes. I allowed them to fall. Later I would need a clear head. Let them think of me as having a stiff upper lip. I didn't care. I would grieve Monica, and the lost possibilities, right now.

The funeral director met me at the door and showed me straight into the room where

Monica's viewing would be held. A table with a lot of family photos took pride of place. I recognized several of them — next to her mother on Mother's Day, her wedding, Burke's christening.

A few tears trickled down my cheeks, and I pulled out the first tissue from the packet I carried in my purse. Now she and her mother were celebrating their reunion in heaven and offering up prayers for the boys they left behind, I was sure.

I was pleased to find the casket was open. I'd been a little concerned about her appearance after the deadly reaction to the nuts, but Monica looked lovely. The cosmetician had done a beautiful job, and the bracelet I brought matched her clothes perfectly.

I briefly wondered who had chosen the dress. It suited Monica's tastes exactly, with its muted autumn colors highlighted by the artful makeup. I hoped they had used Monica's own makeup, since that was her career. All in all, she was as beautiful as a dead person could be. It was almost too bad she couldn't be a guest at her own funeral.

Once again tears threatened. I took a seat on the front row and read the obituary. It always felt wrong when someone younger than me died since I still lived. This time was no different. She was born on January 2, 1980. I remembered reading a newspaper article about the first baby born in town in the New Year only a few months before I began working at Goring's Boring Mill. I could still remember her baby picture on her father's desk the day I was hired. The business had just started to take off, but he bragged more about his children than his success.

She hadn't quite made it to her fortieth birthday. I swallowed a teary laugh. She might like it that way, left forever young. She had once told me she would refuse to celebrate the day when it came. Where she was now, it didn't matter anymore.

Oh Monica. The tears came now. I reached for a tissue and wiped my eyes, removing mascara and eye shadow in a single swipe, then cried some more. I had been there about fifteen minutes when the funeral director came in. "I'm sorry to bother you, but Mr. Mayne is here with his sister to make some final arrangements."

Bruce's sister — Vicky, that was her name. She had probably chosen the clothes for Monica. She lived in the next county over, so I didn't see her very often, but I knew she and Monica were close.

I slipped into the restroom to sponge off my face. Bruce and Vicky were standing in the parlor doorway when I came out. Bruce came forward with an extended hand. "The director told me you were here. I'm not surprised. You always were a good friend, Jo."

His shoulders sagged, and he looked as though he couldn't bear the weight.

I prepared to leave, but Bruce grabbed my hand. "Please, stay a moment longer. I don't want to be with a lot of strangers, and we're practically family."

Guilt struck me. I hadn't spoken with Bruce except for a few words on Tuesday night. I sank onto the chair again, suddenly wishing I had dressed differently, but I hadn't expected to see anyone.

They stopped at the casket first. "They did a good job with the makeup," Vicky observed.

Bruce shook his head — no amount of makeup could make up for his loss. He bent over abruptly. "What is this?"

Perhaps the funeral director hadn't told him. "Monica gave me that beautiful bracelet. I was hoping she could wear it."

"What a lovely thought." Vicky studied the bracelet more closely. "And it matches the dress perfectly, as if we were thinking the same thing."

God often works that way. The thought rippled through my mind, but I didn't voice it. Bruce might not appreciate religious truisms in his grief.

"I didn't deserve her." Bruce's words came out between moans. "I was so lucky to win the hand of the beautiful Miss Monica Goring, and we were so happy. But then we got complacent, and we lost our way after Burke left home."

"And then you met Paula Shreckhise," I said before I could stop myself.

His eyes cleared for a moment. "And then I met Paula." His face crumpled.

Vicky took his arm. "Let's sit down." She glared at me. "You presume too much."

I hadn't known Bruce as a boy, but he looked like a lost child at that moment, and my heart went out to him. "What happened, Bruce?" Part of me was genuinely concerned for the hurting man. Part of me, God forgive me, wanted to challenge his devotion to Monica.

Bruce looked to his sister for help. She studied me for a hard minute. "Dave Goring trusts you with his life. And I trust Dave Goring." The fierceness of the gaze suggested she would tear me limb from limb if I betrayed that trust.

Unfortunately, fulfilling my duty to Dave might mean hurting those around him. As much as I disliked the process, it would be wrong to let a murderer go free. *The truth will set you free.* I thought back on my near fling with Dave. "I'm not here to judge you, Bruce, but talking about it might help free you."

Vicky gave her brother a tissue to wipe his face. "I'll leave you two alone."

Bruce reached for his sister. "Please stay. You can talk freely in front of Jo."

Perhaps we were all hesitating to speak ill

of the dead. I would break the ice. "I loved Monica like the daughter I never had, but she could be difficult."

"You can say that again," Vicky said.

Bruce's head shot up then he slumped again. His eyes were as red-rimmed as mine. I could only hope our shared grief would make it easier for him to speak freely.

"Tell her," he said to Vicky.

Here I'd thought Monica and Vicky were close, but the undertones suggested something else. "Didn't you and Monica get along?"

"We were close, once." Vicky's chuckle was forced. "But she changed. After she began to build her own company, she seemed to resent Bruce's lack of drive. Like he should leave his job in her father's company and start one of his own. She wanted him to go big or go home."

Bruce picked up the story. "She set out lavish dishes whenever my family came to visit. We live in a house far bigger than we needed for the three of us." Bruce stood and poured himself a glass of ice water from the pitcher on a nearby table. "At first, I hoped we would fill it with children, but God only blessed us with one. After that —"

I could guess. "She learned she couldn't have any more children."

He nodded. "I suggested we move into a smaller house. I thought it might help us turn a new leaf."

"And Monica flatly refused," I said.

"If she couldn't be successful at having children, she would become the best hostess in all of Kansas," Vicky said.

From time to time Monica had been featured in home and living sections of local publications. She'd hung the photo shoots in her office. She also held up Burke's success, as a high school athlete and a student at Cal Tech, as evidence of her success as a mother. Bruce had remained at her side, proud of her success and content with his supporting position within the Goring family business.

She'd had the perfect family, but she wanted more. "She always wanted to be the best at everything," I said. "I always thought that's what drove her into the cosmetics field."

Vicky frowned. " 'Why don't you do more to help yourself?' she would ask me before beginning her sales pitch. I liked her stuff, in fact I use it. But when she kept pushing me, I was tempted to change."

That sounded like Monica. "No wonder she didn't like Paula. Monica was an attractive woman, but Paula was in a different league, and not just because she was younger. Her face is pretty enough for television, as they used to say in my day."

That brought a smile to Bruce's face. "Even before she put makeup on."

Not the most tactful thing he could have said.

Bruce finished the water, put his glass back on the table, and sat down again. "Monica didn't mind my position at Goring's at first. She was excited about the roll-out of the new machine. I had a lot to do with developing the patents and so forth."

He really was a good engineer.

"But then when sales didn't perform as expected, she turned her back on me just when Paula and I had to make it work." His hands shook where they dangled between his legs. "Paula made me feel important again."

It was the oldest tale in the book, sad but true. "I'm so sorry."

"Monica was always after me to pester her father for more responsibility, to suggest he make me his partner. I work for the man. I respect him. But the business rightly belongs to Chad."

I doubted he meant what he said. "She didn't see it that way."

"She thought I should be partner, taking her place in the family business." He shook his head. "That's part of the reason I suggested the new machine. I hoped it would make her proud of me again."

And when they failed — oh dear. The longer I listened to Bruce, the more I wondered why things hadn't come to a head earlier.

"You might as well tell her everything," Vicky said.

I leaned forward. There was more?

TEN

"I heard Monica was thinking about divorce." I wanted to spare him the embarrassment of mentioning it.

Bruce's eyes flashed. "She told me, but I was hoping she might change her mind." He looked to his sister again, and she nodded her head ever so slightly.

That seemed unlikely. Little could turn Monica aside from a path once she had set her mind on it.

"What is it, Bruce?" I asked softly. Harper told me I was like a sweet neighbor lady who invited confidences and imparted wisdom. If it was true — and I had my doubts — this was the time to make him comfortable and invite his innermost secrets.

"Paula is pregnant."

My eyes tried to close, to shut out the news, but I forced them open. Pregnancy outside of wedlock was never the best, and given Monica's difficulties with childbearing, it would bring extra pain to bear.

Why did Bruce think the news might change Monica's mind?

"I knew it was a long shot. In this day and age, Paula would probably raise her child on her own. Leave the company, of course." His ears colored. "Or perhaps I should."

Or abortion. I hoped not, for both moral and personal reasons.

"But — suppose she were willing to give the child up for adoption? Perhaps Monica would have considered adopting the child with me. We might have made a new start. She'd always said no to adoption before, but I hoped, maybe, if it was my child . . ." His shrugging shoulders radiated longing. "Now I'll never know."

Monica wasn't the only one who wanted more children. Bruce had dealt with his pain by volunteering at every sport Burke participated in and being active in PTA.

Since Burke had left for college, Bruce hadn't figured out where to channel his energy. I'd heard he wanted to teach Sunday school, but Monica had nixed the idea.

I could understand Bruce wanting to adopt the baby, but I didn't think Monica would have agreed. If he'd asked her, and she refused him, would he have been angry enough for murder? I hated the thought.

"I spent the last few hours of Monica's life telling Vicky and my parents about the situation. I barely got back in time for your party."

462

I perked up. "When did you see your family?"

"Tuesday afternoon." He waved his hand.

"He ate an early dinner with us," Vicky said.

"And when was that? As early as three? As late as five thirty?"

"I left about three thirty, when the day shift ended, and got back just in time for your party," Bruce said. "Why? Does it matter?"

I wouldn't tell him about my timetable, not yet. "What a day you had. Thanks for making the effort to come to my party."

"I was hoping we might get to talk, but Monica pulled me away, and then of course, she got sick."

It sounded like Bruce was in the clear.

He lifted his grief-ravaged face to mine. "Tell me, Jo. Who wanted to do this to my Monica? I know that book club of yours has gained a reputation for looking into murder. Can you help me?"

Vicky sat back in her chair and gave me a second look. "You don't have to ask. She's already investigating the murder, and you'll be glad to know you just provided your alibi."

He looked at me, shocked.

I nodded my head guiltily. "I don't want to suspect anyone."

"What have you learned?" he demanded.

I was wondering how to phrase my refusal when Vicky spoke. "She can't tell you, Bruce. You'd have a hard time keeping it a secret, and you might make it harder for her to question people." She smiled. "But I'm sure she'll keep your secrets safe unless they have a bearing on what happened to Monica."

He nodded.

"I have another question." I was relieved that Bruce had been exonerated, but he still knew valuable information. "Did Monica know about the baby?" If it was common knowledge, surely someone would have mentioned it at the office.

"I don't think so." His eyes, while still red, were clearing. "But I'm not sure."

"I understand." If that was true, then Bruce wouldn't have killed her for refusing to adopt Paula's baby. I stood and laid a hand on Bruce's shoulder. "I'm sorry to intrude on your mourning. I'll see you both tonight."

Vicky waved goodbye as I walked out.

This afternoon, I would set aside any thoughts of detecting. I wanted to look my best tonight — Monica deserved it. My hair salon was in the same strip mall as the small clothing shop I frequented, so I scheduled an appointment then shopped for a dress while I waited.

I owned a single black dress for such occasions, but I wanted something special for Monica. I also wanted to avoid anything that screamed "death," but that was still appropriate for a funeral. The tag on the dress I found described it as "violet paisley" but it contained swirls of black, gray, and white among the purple, with long, capped sleeves and a low waistline with slim hips. It did lovely things for my figure.

I locked it in its bag in my car trunk and headed inside the beauty parlor. Did I just want a shampoo and style? No, I wanted the full works — a manicure, haircut, and tint.

When I was choosing my fingernail color, I noticed the bottles were from Mesmerizing Beauty.

The beautician, Miriam Lee, noticed me studying the fingernail polish. "You like those? They're a real good deal."

I checked the price tag. The sales price was reduced to a shocking price. They had to be losing money.

"I'd like my nails done in this color." I chose a purplish pearl color that would coat my nails without looking like I had dipped my hand in a paint bucket. When she placed my hand in the softening solution, I said, "I'm surprised at the price. It seems like you must be losing money."

Miriam giggled lightly. "I'm making heaps of money on that. After the lawsuit, the company couldn't sell it anymore. Before they had to stop, Monica had a big sale, pennies on the dollar. I bought lots."

I shouldn't have asked. I had come here to relax.

"You want to add a tattoo?" Miriam asked.

"Flowers, maybe?"

Tiny lilacs seemed appropriate. But the nail polish had reminded me that Monica had lost heavily in her cosmetics company when she was found guilty of copying colors — and Sherri was a part of that lawsuit.

I waited while the color set and flipped through an old issue of *People* magazine, wanting to distract myself from the problems at hand. But the news of the latest celebrity scandal, when a famous couple broke up when he got her best friend pregnant, struck too close to home.

I couldn't avoid Monica, no matter what I did.

In spite of everything, I left the shop feeling pampered and refreshed. My feet felt as young as a teenager's, as if I could race down the street in high heels. It would be a snap in my sensible pumps.

After a few bites to eat at home — I didn't really feel hungry but knew better than to skip a meal — I settled in my chair. A bath sounded nice, but that would unravel my hairdo. Ditto, lying on a pillow. Besides, I didn't think I would sleep.

"How about Me?"

I knew that voice. Times I was fussed, I often turned to prayer. I went to my closet for a shawl I had crocheted years ago and draped it around my shoulders. The personal revival tent helped me to shut out distractions.

I chose an app on my phone to read aloud from the prophet Isaiah, taking comfort once again in the glorious news about the year of the Lord's favor.

Isaiah certainly had his share of difficulties in his life, as Monica had had — but the same God who had promised to comfort those who mourn, to give them the oil of joy instead of mourning, was alive today. I prayed that would start this evening. That the questions I asked would aid in the process of healing.

The phone rang a few minutes before I was prepared to leave. "I'd like to take you to the viewing tonight," Harper said.

I was about to decline when she barged ahead. "I know we decided to arrive separately, but I had a feeling that you could use help. These people are almost like family to you."

I changed my mind. Dear Harper. She realized how little I wanted to be alone this day.

ELEVEN

After I disconnected the phone call with Harper, I donned my lovely new dress and stepped onto the porch, ready to get into her car as soon as she arrived.

She complimented me on my dress and hair when I got in the car.

"Something's happened since the last time we spoke," I said.

She twisted in my direction and turned off the car. "Tell me about it. Get it off your chest to make room to carry more." She shook her head. "And here I thought you were having a quiet day at home."

I chuckled. "That's what I wanted, but it hasn't turned out that way." I told her about running into Bruce and his sister at the funeral home.

"So he's definitely cleared from suspicion?" Harper asked.

"As far as I can tell. And there's more." I explained about the sale on nail polish and the questions it raised about possible motives.

Harper scrunched her face. "Wasn't your old friend Sherri involved in that lawsuit?"

I nodded unhappily. "I had about eliminated her from suspicion."

"Now let me see those nails." Harper admired them. Hers were the same as always, simple and neat.

I turned back toward the windshield. "We'd best get going, or else we might miss someone." Although the viewing was a come and go affair, I wanted to arrive early and stay late to observe as much as possible.

If people let me be.

"You're right." Harper faced the steering wheel again. "You've had a busy day. Are you *feeling* all right?"

I sighed and shuddered, gentle laughter flowing from my soul. "I am doing very well. With friends like you, with the good Lord, my soul is always well."

"Very good. Let's go."

Evelyn was arranging delicacies for the night's guests when we walked in. She waved us over. "I asked the funeral director if he minded. People always linger over food. More likely to talk, I hope."

We finished our explanation as Bruce came in with his sister and other members of his family. Vicky made a point of introducing me to everyone and telling them I was as close as family to Monica.

I smiled and commented how glad I was that Bruce's family was there to support him.

Burke trailed in last. He waved when he saw me, and I relaxed. I had been concerned he might ignore me after his time away.

I studied the changes the year at college had made in Burke as I walked across the room. He had grown into his height, with his father's good looks and his grandfather's grace. He would be a lady-killer, if he wasn't already. He had avoided entanglements in high school. He also seemed more confident, a result, perhaps, of attending a school like Yale, where he was surrounded by the nation's best and brightest.

"Aunt Jo, Dad said you might be here." When he hugged me, I felt like I was touching Monica, and all those latent grandmotherly urges rose to the surface. "Look at you. College agrees with you."

Penny and Jeanine came in next, and I left Burke to chat with them. Morgan would come as soon as she'd closed up shop.

Penny commented on my nails, and I told my friends what I'd learned about the polish.

Jeanine flashed a grin at me. "I'm ahead of you. I remembered and went to the library. Louise will be doing some research for you. Here are the highlights." She handed me a sheet of paper. "You should know Sherri Wexel was a key witness in the trial. She even said, 'Monica Mayne deserves to die for what she did to the other cosmetic companies.' "

That sounded dire, but I also knew Sherri talked in hyperbole like that. Both she and Monica did. I wasn't surprised it had escalated in a courtroom, goaded on by a couple of lawyers.

"I'll run it out to the car," Harper suggested. "Let's split up," she said in a lower voice.

Very wise. We rotated around the room and outer area but quickly ran out of things to look at. I hoped more people would come. We didn't want to outstay our welcome. Where were Dave and Chad?

They arrived a couple of minutes before Morgan. Dave wore his mourning like an extra suit of clothes, but Chad looked more like he was a chimney stack, full of angry steam.

I preferred to attribute his anger to grief rather than to a more sinister motive. I understood that response to loss. When my only sister died five years ago, I channeled my pain into an attack on the medical profession that allowed someone so comparatively young to die.

But I was here to find out more. I headed Chad's direction, but Harper and Penny were already speaking with him. I found a quiet spot to observe.

Harper worked her magic, calming Chad

down. Dave made his way to me. He had aged ten years since I'd seen him earlier that week. My heart went out to him. "Wait here while I get you something to eat."

"That's not necessary." He took the seat I pointed out to him. A few people spoke to him, but his lack of response drove them away after a brief exchange. *Oh Dave.* He had shut down the same way after his wife had died.

I armed myself with cookies and coffee and took up the seat next to him.

He shook his head in refusal, but I wouldn't be denied. Dave was known for his sweet tooth. "Have you eaten today?"

"People bring food." He waved his hand.

"That's not what I asked. Are you eating it?"

"You know me too well." Dave studied the perfectly browned peanut butter cookie, crisscrossed with fork tines and sprinkled with sugar. "I'll pretend the peanut butter in the cookie is protein."

"That's the spirit."

He smiled wanly and chewed a bite. "Have you found the culprit yet?"

I glanced at him. I hadn't exactly told him what I was doing, had I?

"I know you, Jo, and your book club's reputation precedes you. Can we speak here, or should we arrange another time?"

My mouth twitched while I considered.

After all, Dave was on my official suspect list. "Tell me, what were you doing on Tuesday afternoon? Were you at the office?"

Understanding dawned on his face. "Of course! You suspect me!" He found the thought humorous. "I was in the plant. A machine malfunction. That's the reason I was late to your party. I never crossed the orange line at all."

He was referring to the connection between the plant and the offices.

"And I have a couple of foremen who can confirm that statement, if you have any doubts."

"You watch too much TV," I said. "But thank you."

He lowered his voice. "Whom else do you suspect?"

I had come here to talk, and Dave was chatty. I started with the easiest one. "What do you know about Darren Gould?"

"Gould?" Dave frowned in concentration. "The man who decided against giving us his business?"

"The man who had expressed great interest in the new boring drills — one of the reasons why you went ahead with production — and then didn't follow through." I didn't feel like I needed to pussyfoot around the problem.

"What about him?"

"I heard that your new sales rep — Paula Shreckhise — almost brought him back around, until he ran into Monica. Do you know anything about that?"

His face crumpled. "Oh Monica. I never understood how she could be so terrible at my business and so good at her own." He peered at me. "But as far as I know, Darren went elsewhere and Monica just shrugged it off."

That was like her, showing no consideration for the consequences of her actions on the family business.

He didn't speak for a moment. Instead, he let his eyes settle on his son and son-in-law. At the moment, they were speaking with minimal cordiality. The tension stretched taut across the room.

Dave nodded in that direction. "Both of them were highly upset. Bruce blamed himself for pushing for the new production, although we all voted for it. And Chad blamed Monica for losing Darren's business. When I expressed my doubts that either one could manage the company successfully after I'm gone, a ruckus broke out."

I didn't say anything. I didn't have to. I could see that Dave had shut himself off again.

I hated what Monica's death was doing to her father. "I'm saying we all had a reason to be" — I held back from saying *angry* — "disappointed with your daughter."

TWELVE

Dave ate the rest of the cookie in a single bite and drank the coffee. In a strangled voice, he said, "You'll excuse me while I mingle with the other guests, won't you?"

Helplessly, I watched him walk away.

I expressed my condolences to Chad, but asking him questions would be useless. He was slightly drunk and mostly belligerent. He moved toward Monica's casket, and I stayed close by. That maternal instinct made it hard to see him as a suspect. A few tears rolled down his cheek, which surprised me a little. The guy had been a tower of strength when his mother died, valiantly holding it together for his dad's sake. Maybe now I was seeing the lost boy who was neglected back then.

I put an arm around his shoulder. I didn't exactly draw him to me, but he didn't pull away either. "I lost my only sister a few years ago. It's a very lonely feeling."

"I remember." The words came out in a growl. "I didn't think I could miss her so much." His voice tightened on that last word.

"I know." Of the family, his loss seemed the least harsh — not a spouse, or a mother, or a child lost before her time — but he carried his grief the most publicly.

Or was it — guilt? As much as I hated to admit it, it could be.

I stayed for the length of the viewing, but my only other conversation of note was with Sherri. She came for a few minutes toward the end. I complimented her on her makeup, and then asked what brand of cosmetics she used.

"You're not going to trick me that way." She pointed at me. "I'm sure you've uncovered the lawsuit I helped file against Monica a few years ago." She lifted her chin. "I'm more than satisfied. I had my day in court and won enough money to keep me supplied in cosmetics for my lifetime."

"You are looking well." I rushed to ease the awkwardness then intensified it again immediately. "What were you doing at four-fifty on Tuesday?"

"I've heard about you and your timetables. You drove the staff crazy at times." She smiled indulgently. "Ten minutes to five. That was right after break. You can check the files, see when I logged back on the phone, and how frequent the calls were." She shook her head. "I didn't have time to sneak back into the break room and get at the cream."

I would check my computer tonight, but I couldn't speak with eyewitnesses until Monday.

Several employees from Goring's came in and a few others I thought had worked for Monica. I wouldn't trouble them unless all my current suspects were proven innocent. In my dreams, that still might happen.

One of Monica's employees came to me, a lovely young woman with a near-model's figure and a face made for a cosmetics commercial. "You're Jo Anderson, aren't you?" She made it sound like a privilege to meet me. She introduced herself as Paisley Poulson, Monica's second-in-command. "I've been wanting to get in touch with you. Mr. Mayne asked for my help in cleaning Monica's personal things out of her office. He said you might like a few of the items."

That was sweet of Bruce.

Since we were talking, I worked the conversation around to the question of the divorce lawyer. "I saw she had the phone number of a lawyer." I didn't mention his specialty. "Do you know if she'd made an appointment?"

She looked up sharply. "Do you mean the divorce lawyer?"

I nodded.

She glanced around to make sure no one was listening. "She had an appointment for this afternoon at two, but I don't know that she planned on keeping it. A part of her hoped she and Bruce might work things out in spite of everything."

For Bruce's sake, I hoped that would be good news. Of course, good news for Bruce might break Paula's heart. The truth that every action has an equal and opposite reaction applied to more than physics.

By the time the viewing ended, I headed to bed late, but I woke, refreshed, at my usual time. After my quiet time, I decided to take a long walk to clear my head and restore the balance I had lost over the past week. I brought the last of my note cards with me as well as my steno pad. The post office and library lay along my route, so I might as well take care of business.

The postmistress asked me about Monica as soon as I walked in. I could tell she was fishing for more information but didn't have much to share herself, so I left. Louise Applewhite, the librarian, had the library to herself when I went in. Even so, she spoke in a cathedral-soft voice. "Jo Anderson, I've been waiting for you to come in. I did some research and printed out relevant articles about the lawsuit brought against Monica Mayne's cosmetics company. I heard you would be coming around."

Louise had filled a file folder with printouts. I offered to pay for them, but she waved me off. "It's my bit of public service. If I can help you piece together what happened, I'll be mighty proud." She set me up at a table where we could see the front door and sat beside me. "This way I can help other people when they come in."

I scanned the articles and quickly found the ones relevant to Sherri Wexel. She had invested heavily in a different company, hoping to sell cosmetics in a program similar to Avon. When Monica's new line of nail polish matched her supply at a slightly lower price, she lost the business. Because of her own shady dealings, Monica paid a high price in the cosmetics war, but Sherri recouped all the investment she had lost and more.

Come to think of it, Sherri had returned to work shortly after the trial. I wondered if Monica had offered her an olive branch. Did Sherri have a motive to murder her? Not really.

Nevertheless, I wanted to check her alibi. I called the lady in charge of the soup kitchen and asked if I could be of help over the next couple of weeks.

She accepted my offer graciously if with a trace of surprise. I never refused a request for help, but I rarely volunteered.

I plunged in. "I heard Sherri Wexel has been helping out."

"Yes, she's been quite a regular. She was so excited about your birthday party the last time she was here."

My heart sped up. "Was that on Tuesday

night?" I asked.

"Yes, although she couldn't get here until after five. Still, her help was greatly appreciated."

She didn't show up until after five, which still left her as a suspect. "I'm sure there are a lot of things to do."

"She mainly put away groceries that night. She had gone shopping for us and stayed just long enough to get it organized."

I walked back home and did something I had promised myself I would never do. I used a back door I had created to get into the computer records at Goring's. Dave probably wouldn't mind — he had given me a free pass the other day — but he didn't know about this.

And I wouldn't ask until I had some definitive answers.

First of all, I wanted to check the time clock records. Sherri had clocked out at half-past four, which put her out of the picture. She wasn't the sort to stay late without being paid. Dave, Chad, and Paula were all at work at the time, but the time clocks didn't indicate where they were on-site.

Dave had installed security cameras after a bout with internal espionage a decade ago. They kept recordings for at least a month. Unfortunately, there were no cameras in the break room. Dave figured his employees should have at least one place they could let their hair down. But they might reveal other helpful details outside of the break room.

Production had broken down shortly after lunch. Dave didn't leave the plant, staying in place to make calls and monitor the situation.

Chad ran back and forth through the orange door that separated the offices and the plant a few times. One of those times he came back with a man I believed was Darren Gould. So he was at Goring's the afternoon of my birthday. Did he have any opportunity to tinker with the creamer? It seemed unlikely.

Darren examined the machine and poked into it. Was he there to repair it? I couldn't help wondering what they were talking about, since the recording was visual only. The machine wasn't yet working when he left.

A new file began with the shift change at three. Chad received a phone call and headed to his office. I held my breath, but the camera showed him returning to the plant before the creamer was delivered at 4:11. Neither Dave nor Chad left the plant again until after the machine had been fixed and they made their way to my party.

I wanted to check scanned documents, but Elma had added a password I didn't know. I went back to the petty cash spreadsheet. Gas, grocery store, stationery store, all perfectly ordinary. Nothing appeared out of place.

Perhaps the telephone records would tell me something. The company kept recordings of phone calls to monitor employee performance. I knew I was looking for a needle in a haystack. There were hundreds of phone calls on any given day, and my birthday was even worse, with the problems they had in the plant.

I started with the file from Tuesday morning. I had considered starting the search at the eleven o'clock mark, right before the order was called in, but perhaps an earlier call had prompted that decision. I scrolled back to begin at half-past nine.

I sped through the morning's calls. My birthday came up a few times, but I didn't hear anything about Monica or the creamer until she herself placed the order at the time my records already indicated.

THIRTEEN

In the end, I almost missed it. When Chad said, "The stuff's arrived," I thought he meant the parts needed to make repairs to the machine.

Then I heard the person he was speaking to, Paula Shreckhise, say, "Good."

A beat of silence.

"I'll settle things on this end," she said calmly.

"Thanks. I'll catch up with you later."

I chewed on their conversation for a while. It could be completely innocent — or they might have conspired to commit murder together. The timing made it suspicious.

When the rest of the calls didn't reveal any helpful information, I decided to visit the hardware store. I wanted to see if I could figure out what kind of instrument made the triangular marks on the creamer carton. The hardware store was the logical place to start, since Jeanine, our resident baker, was sure it hadn't been a kitchen utensil.

My years working at a manufacturing plant had made me more comfortable around hardware than I had been as a child, although I still wasn't familiar with equipment not directly related to a house or our industry. In other words, I would know the implement if I spotted it on the shelf, but without knowing the name, I wouldn't know how to begin searching for it on the web.

This particular store offered special items for women and children. I had occasionally purchased them for myself. This week, they were running a sale on garden tools, and I stopped to examine the miniature display of a house and garden. It was as detailed as a dollhouse, complete with plowed-up soil, a box of bulbs, and a tiny trowel. The shape of the trowel looked like a perfect match for what I was seeking.

My mind went into action. Did the store sell these miniature trowels as a novelty item?

They did. When I found it, the teensy tool was almost too small for me to grip the handle. It would take someone with delicate fingers that were still limber and young to be able to use it — like Paula. But I refused to commit my suspicions. I would ask Evelyn to bring the carton and see if the pattern matched. I called her up, and she agreed to meet me at the Coffee Perk for lunch.

I brought the trowel to the cash register. The clerk greeted me warmly — he had interned at Goring's for a few weeks while he was in high school. "Miss Anderson! I haven't seen you in here for a while."

A long time, in fact. As arthritis had taken hold, I turned more and more repairs over to others. "How are you doing, Ed?"

"I got married." His face was stamped with happiness. He rang up the purchase. "You're the second person this week to buy one of these things. They're not usually a hot ticket item."

I sucked in my breath quietly. "Oh really? And who was that?"

"You might know her. I heard she was working at Goring's. Young, blond, attractive —" He grinned. "I won't say any more. My wife wouldn't like it. I thought she had a young child at home, maybe."

I didn't disillusion him as I paid and left.

Evelyn brought Darren Gould to the Coffee Perk with her. "Look who called me," she said as she hugged me.

"I have information that I believe you will find helpful." Darren didn't elaborate until we took our seats and placed our orders.

I decided to wait until I heard what he had to say before I spilled my news.

"I was at Goring's on the day Monica died," he started without preamble. "I understand it was your birthday, by the way. Many happy returns and all that."

I nodded in appreciation.

"I heard you had decided against doing business with Goring's?" I dangled the question delicately.

He frowned. "I had a run-in with Monica. That's what I wanted to talk with you about."

Was everything I had learned today a falsehood?

"Paula Shreckhise called me and convinced me to take a second look. She more or less promised that she knew for certain Monica and Bruce would be out of the business within a short time. If I would come aboard with her and Chad now, I could get a really good deal."

He spread out a project bid printed on Goring stationery. The letterhead was genuine, but I was surprised I hadn't seen a copy of the proposal when I had gone through the company files.

I pulled it closer to examine it more thoroughly. The typeface was unmistakable, done on an old-fashioned typewriter in ten-point type. I could even guess which typewriter was used. The missing hump on the letter *h* reminded me of the machine I used when I first started working with Dave. Perhaps Paula had typed the proposal to keep it out of the official records?

Years ago, of course, before computers, I'd had to use a typewriter for all the paperwork. After we switched to computers, I still kept hard copies for my records.

Of course, I hadn't looked in everyone's personal files for paperwork that might not be in the computer. Perhaps I had searched the wrong office. "Did they give you any idea why they thought Monica and Bruce would be gone?"

"They hinted things were going poorly in the marriage. I thought they meant that if the couple divorced, Mr. Goring might fire his son-in-law. But then when Monica died —"

A chill ran down my spine, but we suspended discussion after Morgan brought out our meals. Darren didn't have anything else of significance to add, and I was glad when he said goodbye. I needed to speak with Evelyn alone about the carton.

"Do you have the carton with you?" I asked before I cleared off the table to get to work.

Evelyn lifted the large purse she carried with her and took out the carton. She opened it to the spot where she'd found the marks.

I showed her the miniature trowel I'd found.

"It looks like a match."

I agreed, but I couldn't figure out how to repeat the experiment. After a minute's thought, I called Morgan over.

"How can I help?" She leaned in, eyes widening when she saw the tiny trowel. "New developments?"

"I want to buy a carton that's exactly the same shape as my birthday present. The flavor doesn't matter, just the shape and size. And bring one of those yogurt parfaits while you're at it, please."

She looked puzzled, so I explained. "I'm going to try to repeat what the murderer did with the creamer."

Her face cleared. "I have just the right carton — almost out of date. I'll grab it."

Adrenaline surged through my veins while we waited.

Morgan sat down and pushed our dishes aside to make space for a towel. "In case the creamer spills. And I thought about trying something other than the yogurt granola. How about this?" She held up a small cup of ground coffee.

True to form, Morgan had come up with the perfect solution.

I knew I couldn't manipulate the experiment properly. "Evelyn, would you do the honors? My hands can't handle such delicate work."

She laughed. "I don't believe it. Look at all those beautiful paper crafts you do."

"You haven't seen my trash cans," I said. "I use large basic shapes and scissors and blades that fit my hand. That trowel is too small for me."

Evelyn dipped the trowel into the finely ground coffee. The aroma alone was enough to send me into a caffeine overdose, but she was focusing on her task. "It doesn't hold much." She let the coffee slide back into the cup. "Of course, we already figured out they only needed a tiny bit."

I obligingly tilted the carton over, so she could reach the folds at the bottom. Morgan reached out a hand to steady it, but I stopped her. "The murderer did it himself. Or herself."

Evelyn flashed a grin. "This shouldn't be too hard. I've had to dig the meat out of pecan shells before. This looks a lot simpler."

Nevertheless, we held our collective breath while she eased the trowel under the spot where the corners overlapped, and created a tiny opening. She scooped ground coffee onto her trowel and inserted it into the opening. A little bit spilled off the trowel, but most of it made it into the liquid.

She'd done it. Now we needed to see if the process had created the same mark as the ones on my birthday creamer.

"I'll pour it out. My hands can handle that much." My attempt at humor failed to get a laugh, we were all so apprehensive.

"Wait a minute." Morgan took the carton and shook it. A few driblets of milk spilled onto her hand, inconvenient but not suspicious. When she tilted the carton and we looked at the bottom, the opening was invisible unless you looked for it. She opened the top and poured a small amount in each of our cups. "I'm curious as to whether we can taste the coffee."

I was able to, detecting a trace of bitterness in the slightly sour milk. I swished it around in my mouth, separating the bitter aftertaste from the souring milk. When I finished, I spit it back into the cup. I noticed with humor the others did too.

Morgan poured the contents of the carton into my empty water glass then handed the carton to Evelyn.

I decided to trust the rest of the process to Evelyn. As soon as she opened the carton, a quarter-inch triangular shape was immediately apparent, in almost exactly the same place as on the original.

The marks looked identical, but I wanted to check. "This is my wheelhouse," I said.

I placed a sheet of paper over the first carton and ran over it with the flat side of my pencil lead until the trowel shape appeared. I flipped the page over, lined it up at the same spot on the other carton, and repeated the movement. The images were an identical match.

"That's how it was done," Morgan said.

My mouth went dry. "Then I'm sure I know who did it. Not enough for a court of law, but I'm satisfied."

Morgan glanced around. We were the only ones in the store. She quickly crossed the room and locked the door.

The three of us discussed my reasoning and

decided it was sound. We also decided on what I must do next.

Someone knocked at the door and Morgan went to open it. She returned with Harper in tow.

"Everyone in the book club will be praying for you," Evelyn said.

"You're not going alone," Harper said. "I know we can't all go, but I insist you take me with you."

I agreed. I would be grateful for the backup.

Fourteen

Harper and I sat across the street from Dave Goring's house. He had often talked about moving out of the house he had shared with his wife and where he had raised their two children, especially now that he rattled around in it alone. Perhaps he had hoped grandchildren would fill the empty places. He kept waiting for Chad to settle down and give him more, in addition to Burke, but Chad had never had the opportunity.

Burke would need his grandfather now, more than ever. He might even get to enjoy a second grandchild, with Paula's baby, if he were willing.

"Having second thoughts?" Harper asked softly. "I know this can't be easy."

"Have you ever read the Lord Peter Wimsey books by Dorothy L. Sayers?"

"Vaguely." She shrugged. "Sounds like something I've seen on PBS."

I had enjoyed the mystery series myself. "Sayers was one of the British greats. She wrote at the same time as Agatha Christie and Margery Allingham. In one of her books — *Hangman's Holiday,* maybe — Lord Peter made himself attend the hanging of the suspect he had helped bring to justice." I shuddered. "I feel a little like Lord Peter did at that moment."

Harper slipped her hand over mine. "Dear Lord, You have led Jo to the truth. You're the source of all the comfort and wisdom that she needs right now."

The prayer helped. I unlocked my car door and climbed out. The lights were on inside, so I was pretty certain Dave was there. I didn't see any other cars, but that didn't guarantee he was alone.

Burke answered the door when we knocked, and I felt terrible. He was the last person I wanted to hear what we had come to share.

Especially when he greeted me with that warm smile and welcoming hug. "Aunt Jo, how good to see you. Dad went home with his family today. He wanted me to come, but I —" He colored a little bit.

"Burke asked if he could spend the evening with me instead," Dave said. "The Maynes seem intent on tearing up Monica's character. We want to mourn her in peace."

I was tempted to leave, but that wouldn't accomplish my purpose.

Dave spoke next. "Burke, why don't you make us some decaf coffee and bring some of those brownies."

As soon as Burke disappeared in the direction of the kitchen, Dave asked, "So tell me. Why are you here? Do you have news for me?"

I was gathering courage to answer when Harper spoke. "We do. We don't have police-level proof, but we are certain we know who killed your daughter."

My tongue clung to the roof of my mouth, refusing to let go. I waited too long.

"Oh God, please no." His face paled. "Please tell me it's not Chad."

I wanted to cry. "He had an accomplice." There, it was out. "Paula Shreckhise."

"Paula?" He was incredulous. "I was under the impression that she was, um, intimate with Bruce."

Harper and I exchanged glances. "That's very true. Both Paula and Bruce admitted it." I adjusted my glasses before continuing. "But she could have been involved with both men at once."

"Are you sure?" Dave asked. Clattering stainless steel followed a loud thump. Burke had knocked over an urn when he returned to the living room. "You know who killed my mom?" Grief tore his face apart.

Harper brought him over to the couch. The coffee service could wait.

"Yes, I do," I told Burke. "And yes, I'm sure," I told Dave.

"Burke, go to your room," Dave commanded.

Burke stared at his grandfather, and the same commanding steel-blue eyes glared at each other. "She's my mother, and I'm not a child. I deserve to know."

I remembered similar discussions when Dave's wife died, about how to explain her death to Monica and Chad. His children had been a lot younger than Burke was right now.

They both looked to me for support. I hurt inside as I said, "Dave, I think your grandson is old enough to hear the truth. Burke, I will warn you, it's not easy."

I could almost see porcupine quills sprout out of the young man's back. "You're never going to convince me that my father killed my mother." He said it defiantly, but there was genuine fear in his eyes.

Dave shook his head, unable to say the words.

My news would be more welcome to Burke than it had been to Dave. "It's not your father, Burke."

"Then who is it?"

I opened my mouth, but Dave waved me to silence. In a voice thick with pain, he said, "They're saying it's your uncle Chad. Together with the new sales rep at the company — Paula Shreckhise."

"What — how — ?" The questions sputtered at the end of Burke's tongue. "Why?"

That came out as a howl.

As one, they turned on me and Harper. "You'd better explain yourselves." If I hadn't seen Dave's mouth moving, I wouldn't have recognized his voice.

"I may not know forensics, but I know the company inside out, and I have tons of common sense," I said crisply. "And you told me you wanted me to check into it."

Dave nodded grudgingly. "I was hoping you would decide it was some crazy person from the creamery."

"So was I." I sighed. "I checked with them first, but it was never very likely. How could they be sure Monica would drink it? Unless they just wanted to play with people's lives on the chance that someone had a nut allergy and would drink it." I started to explain about the special delivery but changed my mind. "Let's look at the three staples of detection: means, motive, and opportunity. We just figured out the means this afternoon."

I pulled out the empty cartons, showing their matching marks. "This is the creamer I received as a present, the one with the nuts in it that led to Monica's death. Jeanine and Evelyn helped us figure out how they managed it."

Burke had picked up the second carton. "Where did this one come from?"

"We did that ourselves this afternoon." We explained about the coffee and the miniscule amount of nuts it would take to kill someone with an allergy.

"It took longer to figure out what kind of tool would make that mark. I went to the hardware store and discovered a miniature trowel, for use in tiny flowerpots. They mentioned they had sold another one just like it to Paula on my birthday." I placed the tool next to the cartons.

"That was leaving it awfully late."

"They must have decided on it at the last minute." Harper jumped in. "That's the only explanation. They didn't even order the creamer until the day of the party."

"It was ordered at thirteen minutes to noon and delivered at four eleven," I confirmed. "We know that whoever doctored it did it in the break room between ten minutes to five o'clock and five o'clock on Tuesday afternoon."

"It couldn't have been Chad," Dave protested. "He was with me in the plant all afternoon, until we left."

I slowly unpeeled the papers I had clipped together, gathering courage to continue. "When I searched the company's internal phone records, I discovered Chad called Paula and told her the package had arrived. She said she'd get to it right away.

"From that, it was easy enough to determine she had an opportunity during the ten-minute window when the creamer could be tampered with." I explained how I had arrived at that conclusion. "Paula didn't take any calls for that period. No one has reported seeing her. She had ample opportunity."

"But why?" Burke's voice wavered close to tears.

"Wait a few minutes." Dave's voice was grim. "While Jo was talking, I sent texts to everyone involved, asking them to meet us here. I want to hear their side of things."

Bruce arrived first. "Dad says you know who killed Monica?" He flung the question at Harper and me even before he sat down next to his son.

"It's Uncle Chad, Dad. Him and that Paula person," Burke said. He placed a tentative arm around his father's shoulders.

"What rumors are you spreading about me, Jo?" Chad had arrived through the back door, with Paula behind. "Here I thought I was your favorite."

Oh Chad. How I longed for those happy days when he was a boy in my kitchen, eating popsicles and drinking sweet tea.

"She says you killed your sister. Made a pretty convincing argument of it too." Dave's voice was frozen solid. "I thought you should have a chance to explain yourself before I contact the police."

Paula's face blanched, and Dave whirled in her direction. "But you actually did the deed. What did my family ever do to you?"

Shocked, Bruce stared at Paula, sitting knee to knee with Chad. Perhaps he had cared for her more deeply than we had realized.

Son and son-in-law stared at each other in silence, the greed and suspicion that had sprouted between them making speech almost impossible.

Chad broke the silence. "I still can't believe Dad wants to make you a full partner in the company. I have spent my entire career building up a company that was my father's dream. And you were about to get a full share just because you married Monica." Resentment dripped like acid from his speech.

I didn't move a muscle, but my mind raced. I hadn't expected him to admit to anything, let alone lay out his motive.

He turned on me next. "We would have been okay, if you hadn't come along. We hoped Paula's sob story would satisfy your curiosity."

Paula pulled away from Chad by an inch. "It was all your idea."

Burke slipped silently out of the room.

"Tell us the plan," I said. As long as they were in a talkative mood, maybe they would explain the whole story.

Paula's mouth thinned. "I met Chad at a sales convention. We clicked right away, and before long, he invited me to work at his company. He said if we played it right, he would inherit a good business, and I would live the high life." She edged a little farther away from him and turned her furor in his direction. "I should have seen through your claims as soon as I walked into the place, but I was intrigued by the new direction the company was taking. It looked like you were going places."

"Paula, keep quiet." Chad had finally come to his senses.

"Why should I? All I got from listening to you is a baby I don't want and a ticket to jail."

Bruce moaned and laid his head in his hands, and she turned her anger on him. "You don't have anything to worry about. It's not yours."

I seemed to be the only one paying attention to Burke's comings and goings. He had returned and taken a spot away from our circle. His shoulders slumped at Paula's words, but he recovered quickly. He caught my eye and held up his phone. Perhaps he had called the police.

"Tell me the rest," Dave demanded.

"Certainly, *Dad.*" Paula laid on the sarcasm. "That's what I expected to call you after Chad and I were married, although I'm beginning to doubt that would ever have happened." She stood and took a seat by the table. Chad reached for her, but she didn't respond to him.

She poured herself a cup of coffee. I forced

myself to be patient. Anything to keep her talking.

She obliged. "Chad told me he was an only son, but his father was going to split the company between him and his brother-in-law. He wanted me to help prevent that — by sabotaging sales and by creating marital tension. Either way, he figured the golden boy would lose." Her face twisted in an ugly smile. "I didn't mind. Monica was an awful person."

It made a terrible kind of sense.

Dave held out his hands to his son. "But why, Chad, why? You've always had everything you ever wanted."

Chad scowled. "Why did you want to give *him* half the company? I'm your flesh and blood!"

"Oh, my son." Dave looked so sad. "He's *family.* I would still have loved him even if he broke up with Monica."

"Why you —" Chad lunged forward. Burke jumped between them. He had never performed as bravely on the football field as he did between the men.

The front doorbell rang, and Harper returned with the sheriff.

EPILOGUE

Time passed while the officers sifted through everyone's stories. Eventually they escorted both Paula and Chad away in handcuffs. After that, Burke took his father home. They offered Harper a ride.

I prepared to leave, but Dave sent an imploring look in my direction. "Please stay. I have a few more questions."

"Of course." I settled back against the sofa.

"Why did they want to *kill* Monica? Their plans to discredit her and Bruce were working." He didn't quite meet my eyes. "I know that Monica was seeing a divorce attorney."

I cleared my throat. "Things changed. From what I've been told, she had cancelled that appointment. Do you remember Darren Gould? Paula and Chad tried to recruit him to work with them, but it backfired. Instead he went to Monica, and she realized what they were doing. She was willing to give Bruce another chance."

"In spite of Bruce and Paula —" He left

502

the question dangling.

I nodded. "It made me feel better about Monica." I sighed. "Paula learned about it. Her hopes were falling apart, and suddenly she was the woman scorned. And Chad was still desperate for the company. So they took a daft chance."

He nodded. Silently he slipped his favorite CD of classic rock into the player. The music washed over us in waves of despair, joy, hope. A reminder of a time when the world was in flux and everything seemed possible. At least we had been young and idealistic enough to think so.

When it finished, I sat forward. "I should go, Dave. I'm so sorry it had to end this way."

He leaned forward, hands open in invitation. "I don't hold you responsible. Please stay, Jo, for a little while."

I studied my old friend, so overcome by grief. I couldn't say no. "I'll stay, Dave. For as long as you need me."

ABOUT THE AUTHOR

Bestselling author **Darlene Franklin**'s greatest claim to fame is that she writes full-time from a nursing home. She lives in Oklahoma, near her son and his family, and continues her interests in playing the piano and singing, books, good fellowship, and reality TV in addition to writing. She is an active member of Oklahoma City Christian Fiction Writers, American Christian Fiction Writers, and the Christian Authors Network. She has written over fifty books and more than 250 devotionals. Her historical fiction ranges from the Revolutionary War to World War II, from Texas to Vermont. You can find Darlene online at www.darlenefranklinwrites.com.

IN HOT WATER

BY ELIZABETH LUDWIG

ONE

The last bell before the Thanksgiving break rang, a welcome trill after a week spent with anxious, fidgeting first graders ready for some time off. Sighing heavily, I leaned my head against the wall and listened to the thunder of footsteps fading down the hall.

" 'Bye, Miss Daggett. Have a good Thanksgiving."

I opened my eyes. Six-year-old Bailey Munroe stared up at me, a wide smile on her sweet, freckled face.

"Hey, Bailey." I lowered to my haunches, eye-to-eye with the girl. "What have you got planned for Thanksgiving? Anything special?"

Her eyes brightened, and the smile inched wider. "Grandma says Daddy is coming home."

I did my best to match Bailey's smile. Her father had spent the last two years in and out of drug rehab, but I knew that to a child, nothing mattered more than spending time with someone they loved. Thankfully, she had a stable home with her grandmother, but it hurt my heart to think that might not be true for long.

I composed my features carefully and took Bailey by the hands. "How is your grandma, sweetie? Is she feeling any better?"

Worry flickered in her blue eyes then disappeared. "She walks slower now. Grandma says that's just because her legs are old."

I nodded. "I'm sure that's all it is."

As we talked, Bailey's grandmother appeared at the door, out of breath from having hurried down the hall. "Miss Daggett? I'm so sorry I'm late."

"Hi, Mrs. Munroe." I stood to shake her hand. "I was just asking about you. How are you feeling?"

Her hand fluttered up to her chest, her gaze flicking to her granddaughter. "Better every day, isn't that right, Bailey Bug? Especially with this little one doing all my chores."

Bailey slipped her hand into her grandmother's and flashed another of her sweet smiles. "Grandma says I'm her little helper."

I smiled and tugged gently on one of her blond curls. "Aw, I bet you are a good helper."

She nodded and looked up at her grandmother. "Should we go, Gram? We need to pick up the turkey for dinner before Daddy comes."

My heart jumped to my throat at the hesitation I read in Mrs. Munroe's eyes. She hid it quickly and nodded down at her grand-daughter. "You're right, Bailey Bug. We should go." To me, she said, "Have a happy Thanksgiving, Miss Daggett. Will you be visiting family?"

I stifled a twinge in my chest. "Actually, I'll be staying in Oak Grove. I've only got one brother, and he lives . . . well . . . everywhere. Right now, he's in Portugal. But I'm hoping he'll be home for Christmas. We can spend some time together then."

She nodded and pressed Bailey's hand to her coat. "I hope it works out. Family is important, eh, Bailey Bug?"

Wishing them both goodbye, I watched as they made their way slowly down the hall. Poor Bailey. What would she do if her grand-mother's health made it impossible for her to continue caring for her? Where would she go? "Wow. What's with the heavy sigh?" Across the hall, Marty, my fellow teacher and mentor, directed a pointed glance at her watch. "It's three thirty on Friday. We're of-ficially on Thanksgiving break. Don't you know you're supposed to be in a *good* mood?"

I shrugged and forced a weak smile. "Just finishing up."

"I saw." All signs of teasing gone, Marty straightened and followed me back to my desk. "How is Mrs. Munroe doing?"

"She says she's doing better."

"But still no word on her surgery?"

I grimaced. Mrs. Munroe didn't have insurance, and no doctor would even consider heart surgery without it. "I couldn't bring myself to ask. If only . . ."

I lowered my gaze and let out another sigh.

Marty placed a light touch on my shoulder. "Hey, you can't save everyone."

"I know. But it would be nice if I could save one." I picked up a stack of paper and shoved it into my take-home bag.

"Whoa, whoa, what is all that?" Changing the subject deftly, Marty laid her hand on my wrist in mock horror. "Tell me you don't intend to work the entire time we're off?"

"Not the entire week." I pasted on a bright smile and shoved my hair behind my ear to keep it from falling in my face. "Some friends and I are going antiquing this weekend."

"Friends?"

She sounded almost too skeptical. I laughed and resumed stuffing my bag.

"I *do* have a social life, believe it or not. You probably know a few of my friends. Jo Anderson and Morgan Butler?"

She thought for a second and then nodded. "Oh, your book club pals."

"Yep. Penny and Evelyn are coming too. I haven't heard from Jeanine yet. She's been pretty busy planning her fund-raiser for a mission team to Haiti, so she may not be able to make it."

Marty smiled. "I'm glad you've got something planned. You work too hard."

Hearing the concern in her voice, I squeezed the leather handle on my bag and swallowed a sudden knot in my throat. "Well . . . what about you? You work hard too."

She shook her head before I could finish. "Uh-uh. Not the same thing. Not even close." She wagged her finger playfully in my face. "You and my brother are two of a kind, you know that?"

"Cam? I mean, Cameron?" Heat flooded my face and I felt my heart flutter. "I mean, Deputy Davis?"

She smiled wryly. "Yes, to all three."

She grabbed my bag and laid the strap over my shoulder, then shooed me toward the door. "It's good that you both love what you do, but for heaven's sake, you're only twenty-eight. It's okay to have a little fun sometimes."

"I have fun." Seeing the look on her face, I let the protest die on my lips. "Okay, okay."

She leaned her shoulder against the doorframe and stared at me sternly, her arms crossed over her chest. "Take the whole week off, you hear? I don't want to catch you here, not even once."

Saluting smartly, I laughed and then motioned toward the light switch. "Hit that on your way out?"

"Done. 'Bye!"

She waved me off, and I headed toward my car. My steps grew lighter as I neared. Fishing my keys from my pocket, I hit the unlock button then tossed my bag into the back seat. Maybe Marty was right. Maybe this break was just what I needed.

I reached for the driver's door, only to be stopped by a male voice shouting in my direction.

"Hey, your taillight's broken."

I looked around and spotted a familiar broad shape outlined against the afternoon sky. My mouth went dry. I swallowed hard and fumbled with my keys. "Um, what?"

Cam . . . Deputy Cam . . . Deputy Davis motioned toward my rear . . . my car rear . . . and smiled.

"Your taillight. It's broken. Looks like maybe you backed into something?"

"Uh . . ." I circled toward the back of the car and groaned at the large crack in my passenger-side taillight. "Oh yeah. I did it this morning backing out of my driveway." He didn't ask for more explanation than that, but I shrugged and gave one anyway. "Trash cans."

He smiled. "Want to climb in? I'll check to see if it's still working."

"Um, okay."

He wasn't in uniform, just jeans and a loose-fitting T-shirt, so this probably wasn't an official request. Still, I scrambled into the driver's seat, jammed the key into the ignition, then put my foot on the brake. In the rearview mirror, I saw him give a thumbs-up.

"You're okay. It's still working, but you'll probably want to get it looked at before too long." He lifted one sandy-brown eyebrow. "You're not planning any long road trips over Thanksgiving, are you?"

I climbed out onto the pavement and shoved my hands into my pockets. I had more sense than to think he was really interested. He barely knew me, and I only knew him slightly better because of Marty and the many conversations we'd shared. Still . . .

"No, not really. Just a little weekend trip with some friends."

"Oh. Well, that should be fine." Instead of turning for the building, he mimicked my stance and shoved one of his hands into his pockets. "So, you and Marty are pretty good friends, right? From school?" He jabbed his thumb toward the building.

I smiled, and a flush crept over his face.

"I mean, you teach here at the school with Marty?"

"That's right. Are you here to pick her up?"

He nodded. "I figured I'd better or she'd never leave. In case you haven't noticed, she's a workaholic."

"Oh really?" My grin turned teasing. "She said the same thing about you."

He gave a soft grunt and then stuck out his

hand. "I don't think we've ever been formally introduced. I'm Cam Davis."

"Yep." Embarrassment made my cheeks burn. "I mean, Marty's told me a lot about you." I took his hand, fighting hard not to let my fingers tremble. *Squeeze. Not hard. Just enough to show confidence.* "Harper Daggett."

"It's a pleasure, Harper." He let go and motioned toward the school again. "Anyway, I'd better get inside. Enjoy your Thanksgiving."

I wanted to say something witty — a light-hearted quip that made us both smile. Instead, I mumbled, "You too," and watched as he strolled up the steps to the school doors, light flashing off the glass as he let himself inside.

"Some social life." I scowled as the memory of my words to Marty zipped through my thoughts. Most nights, "social" meant a few minutes on Facebook before I fell, exhausted, into bed. I didn't have time for dating. But if I did . . .

This time, self-pity laced my melancholy sigh. If I had the time, Cameron Davis would certainly be someone with whom I would like to be social.

Two

A small bell jangled merrily as I pushed open the door to the Coffee Perk early the next morning. Except for Jo and Morgan, the place was empty, which suited me fine. I shuffled to the coffeepot, filled a cup, and slapped two bucks on the counter before angling toward the eclectic array of tables.

Morgan slipped the money into the cash register drawer then leaned on the high counter, her chin propped on her arms. "Hey there, sunshine. Rough morning?"

"Ugh." I took a sip from my cup then plopped into a chair. "Rough night. I hardly slept a wink."

"Are you serious?" Jo eyed my russet curls, which I had pulled into a messy ponytail that dangled down my back. "I would *not* look that good if I went all night with no sleep." She refilled her cup and joined me at the table. "What's bugging you?"

I took another sip of black coffee, hoping the unadulterated caffeine would give me a boost, then ran my hand over my face. "One of the kids at school. I couldn't get her out of my mind."

"The one with the sick grandmother?" Morgan rounded the counter and sat across from us at the table. "How is her grandmother doing?"

"Not good. I lay awake all night trying to think of ways we could help raise the money for her surgery."

"Come up with anything good?"

I frowned. "Not really. Bake sales and car washes only go so far."

"You know we'll help in any way we can," Jo said softly.

At seventy-five, she was the oldest of our group, and I often looked on her as the mother hen I never had. I reached out and covered her hand with mine. "Thanks, Jo."

"You know what I think?" Morgan went back to the counter, took one of my favorite orange scones out of the doughnut case, and set it down in front of me. "I think it's a good thing we're doing something fun this weekend."

"Me too." I glanced at the clock on the wall above the window. "Have we heard from Jeanine yet?"

Jo tucked a lock of silver hair behind her ear. "She's coming. Said she needed a break from baking. She and the others should be here in about twenty minutes or so."

"Good. Gives me time to enjoy this delicious scone." I brought it to my lips and took a sizeable bite, savoring the sweet, tangy orange icing melting on my tongue. "Holy cow, that's good." I grabbed a napkin and wiped a drop of icing from my chin. "Did Jeanine change the recipe?"

Morgan's lips curved in a secretive grin. "I'll never tell."

Jo gave a snort. "I will. It's orange essential oil. She added a drop to her icing."

"Jo!" Morgan gave her a teasing pat then turned her smile to me. "She's right though. Glad you like it."

"Oh man . . . orange and coffee bean. Heaven." I took another bite and followed it with a swallow from my cup.

The bell chimed again. Expecting Jeanine and the others, I looked up, nearly choking on my hot coffee when it was Cam, and not my friends, who walked in. This time, he *was* in uniform — dark blue pants and a matching shirt. Somehow, I managed to force the scalding liquid down my throat and smile.

"Good morning."

His hazel eyes brightened, or possibly it was my imagination that made it seem so. "Hey there."

He walked over to the table and motioned toward the scone. "That looks good."

"It is."

Silence. I cast a desperate look at Morgan.

519

She hopped to her feet.

"I'll get you one."

He smiled. "Thanks. To go, please, and a large coffee. Black."

I lifted my cup in salute. "Good choice."

"Um . . . I think I'll go help Morgan." Jo pushed out of her chair and offered it to him. "Would you like a seat?"

I held my breath while he hesitated and blew it out when he smiled. "Yeah, I would. Thanks." He paused, his hand on the back of the chair, and looked at me. "Do you mind?"

"Not at all." *No. Never.* Please *have a seat.* I shot a smile his way.

He settled in the chair, his arms resting easily on the tabletop. "You're up early. First day of Thanksgiving break? I figured you'd sleep in."

"Normally, you'd be right, but my friends and I are going antiquing today."

He tilted his head. "Ah, the weekend trip. Where are you headed?"

"We figured we'd just hit the road, maybe go north, toward Reading and some of those smaller towns."

He nodded. "There's a lot of great little shops that way, especially if you stay off the interstate. Just be careful —"

He broke off, and I smiled. "Broken taillight?"

"Right." He blew out a breath then dropped his gaze to his hands. "Well, I'd better get a move on. Have fun on your trip."

"Thanks. We will."

He rose, but I stopped him before he left. "Uh, Deputy Davis?"

"Cam." He looked down at me and cleared his throat. "You can call me Cam."

"Thank you." I blushed and pointed to his cup. "You forgot your coffee."

An embarrassed smile twitched his lips, stopping my heart. "Oh gosh, thanks." Morgan returning, he grabbed his coffee and scone.

"See ya!"

Morgan and Jo waited until the door closed behind him before rushing to my side.

"What was that all about?" Morgan said.

Jo's laughter drowned her out. "Hunka, hunka."

"Jo!" I pressed my hands to my face. "Please."

"What? You don't think so?"

"I . . . maybe." I shook my head. "He was just being nice. I work with his sister."

Jo and Morgan shared a glance.

"Uh-huh. Okay." Morgan laid her hand over her chest. "Call me Cam."

"Stop it." I slapped her arm playfully and then stood as Jeanine stepped through the door, Evelyn and Penny on her heels.

"Okay, who's ready for some shopping?" Penny rubbed her hands together eagerly. Spotting the look on Jo and Morgan's faces, she stopped. "What?"

"Nothing." I grabbed a plastic to-go cup and pushed it into her hand. "Here. Grab some coffee and let's get on the road."

"Hand me one of those," Evelyn said, reaching around Penny for a cup. Jo frowned at her, but she shrugged and grabbed the coffeepot. "My coffeemaker broke this morning. I need something to get me going. I promise, no extra potty breaks."

Laughter echoed across the shop as we each grabbed something to tide us over until lunch. Morgan had brought in someone to run the shop while we were gone, so she took a little longer giving last-minute instructions before we piled into the Expedition Jeanine used to deliver her baked goods. Evelyn had spent most of the week researching sites, so she claimed the navigator's seat and pulled a list of estate sales and antique stores from her purse. Morgan and I were the youngest, so we climbed into the very back, while Penny and Jo sat in the middle.

Jeanine's seatbelt clicked firmly into place, and she shot a glance at us in the rearview mirror. "All right, girls. Let's hit the highway."

With strains of "Born to Be Wild" thrumming through my head, we swung out onto the road.

"Hey up there, where are we headed first?" Morgan called, cupping her hands to her mouth in exaggeration.

Jeanine laughed and glanced at Evelyn. "Well?"

"Pockets in Time," she said over her shoulder. She grinned and shook the page over her head. "It's a little place just north of here. After that, I thought we'd hit an estate sale."

"Sounds fun." Penny's head bobbed, and then she reached over the seat and tapped Jeanine on the shoulder. "Hey, how about some music?"

"As you wish, milady." Jeanine poked the button on the radio and soon, soft tunes floated through the car.

An hour later, we left the antique store with nothing in hand, but the estate sale we pulled up to looked promising. A crowd was already forming on the wide, circular driveway.

I climbed out of the vehicle and gave Morgan a poke in the ribs as I passed. "Last one inside buys lunch."

Morgan gave a snort of laughter but lagged behind to wait while Jeanine locked up the Ford. Lured by the many tables spilling out from the garage, I looped the strap to my wallet purse over my head and across my body and made a beeline toward the closest one. Items my grandmother used to call "tchotchkes" covered the table, but given the size of my quaint farmhouse, I quickly moved on.

Farther down the way, Penny had spotted a vintage kitchen table that would look perfect in her trailer. She had already begun bartering with the owner and only paused to wink playfully at me as I passed. Thinking of the limited space available in the SUV, I laughed and shook my head. Where on earth would we put it?

A large gentleman in suspenders and polished boots shouted for attention from the steps leading up to the old stone manor. "Hey, folks? There's lots more to see inside."

I sent one last glance over the tables. Granted, it was all beautiful, but I had no need for more sheets or kitchen linens. And I had enough dishes, pots, and pans to last me a lifetime.

Hoping to find something unique, I followed the man inside the house. The air was warmer in there, but it was also crowded and much darker. Heavy drapes masked the windows and made it hard to see. Maybe coming inside had been a mistake.

I frowned and edged toward one of the rooms off the main hall. It was a library or a study of some sort. A huge desk dominated most of the space, but behind it were rows of books and journals that packed the shelves from floor to ceiling.

"The girls would love this." I smiled and angled closer for a look at some of the titles. Most looked to be medical journals, but there were a few travel guides interspersed among them, which made me wonder about the occupation of the person who'd purchased them.

Higher up the shelf, a figurine of an owl caught my eye. I straightened for a better look. "Well, hello there."

The quirky little owl stood about five inches in height. Intrigued by his deep green color, I ran my finger over the smooth stone. Jade? What else could it be? I took the owl down from the shelf. In all honesty, the figurine could be considered nothing more than another tchotchke, but something about his wise little face charmed me. I turned the owl over and examined the back. It was in perfect condition, with no scratches or dings to mar the smooth finish.

I liked it, but where was the price tag? I flipped the owl over and found it on the bottom, a small pink sticker with *$50* scribbled in black ink.

I gave a low whistle. That was quite a chunk out of my shopping budget for the weekend. Still, I hadn't found anything else I liked, and anyway, I tended to pick things up, carry them around, and then put them back without buying, unless it was something that really spoke to me. Like this owl.

My mind made up, I turned to look for the owner and was pulled up short by a man in an argyle sweater glaring at me from the door. His scowl deepening, he jabbed his finger at the owl in my hand.

"That. Where did you get it?"

"I . . ." I shot a quick glance at the bookshelf behind me. "It was . . . I found it right over there."

He crossed his arms, his lips turning pale as he pressed them together. "I'm afraid there's been a mistake. You can't have that owl."

I eyed him curiously and then the little figurine nestled in my hand. "I'm sorry, are you the owner of the house?"

His face flushed, making his dark mustache look black against his reddened skin. "What does that matter?"

"Well, I just thought maybe we could negotiate —"

He cut me off before I could finish, his hand swiping through the air like a blade. "I said you can't have it. I'm sorry, young lady, but that owl isn't for sale!"

THREE

The man's face had flushed so red, he almost matched the crimson argyle print on his sweater. I hugged the owl closer as he stepped toward me, his hand extended. "Now, if you wouldn't mind giving me that owl?"

I eyed him warily. "I'm not sure I understand. It says it's for sale. There's a price tag on the bottom."

He crossed his arms and glared at me through narrowed eyelids. "All right, fine. I misspoke. The owl is for sale, but I already intended to buy it. I didn't see a price tag, so I went to find the owner of the house to inquire about it."

I resisted the urge to snort in triumph. If he'd been so interested, why would he have left the owl on the shelf?

From the corner of my eye, I saw Jo enter the room. I shot her a glance and she moved quickly to my side. "What's going on?"

I waved toward the gentleman in front of

me. "Apparently, we have a similar interest in owls."

The man flinched as I handed Jo the figurine and lifted his hands as though he feared we might drop it.

"Hmm. It's nice." Jo handed it back to me and leveled her gaze on the man. "Sorry, it looks like my friend here has dibs."

"Dibs?" His mouth worked, his lips gaping open and closed like a fish. "This is an estate sale, not a pawn shop. Besides, I saw the owl first."

Jo shrugged and made a balancing motion with her hands. "Estate sale . . . pawn shop . . . seems like kinda the same thing to me. And if you were interested in that owl, you shouldn't have walked away."

Intrigued by our conversation, several people had begun directing glances our way, including one woman with short dark hair who made no secret of edging toward us, her interest obvious. Jo ignored her and turned to me, as calm as ever. "You ready to go?"

"Uh, yeah." I shot one more glance at the man. His ears and face were still an angry red, but he kept his mouth clamped shut as we hurried past.

Outside and out of earshot, Jo turned to look at me. "Okay, what's with the owl? I mean, he's cute and all, but aside from that, what's so interesting about it?"

I replayed the scene of the man flinching

and lifting his hands protectively toward the owl in my head. "I have no idea, but judging by the way that guy acted, I think it might be an antique."

She frowned and looked at the owl again. "Did you see the lady with the dark hair? Honestly, I thought her eyes were going to fall out of her head."

"Yeah, I saw her." I glanced at the figurine squeezed in my hand. "I'm done shopping for now. I think I'll find the owner and pay for this thing and then head over to the SUV."

Jo nodded. "Okay, I'll round up the others."

I tipped my head toward her empty hands. "You didn't find anything?"

She gave a wry grin. "Just not my day, I suppose." She waved toward the garage. "I see Penny. I'll be right back."

I nodded and went to pay for my owl. The owner was an older man, so tall and thin he seemed to have outgrown his hair. What little remained was arranged in a comb-over that had me fighting not to stare.

"Excuse me." The man turned, and I held up the owl. "I'd like to pay for this."

"Of course." He flipped the owl over, squinted at the price tag, then handed it back to me with a smile. "That'll be fifty dollars."

I paid him and would have scurried outside if the dark-haired woman hadn't been standing directly behind me. She smiled as I turned and gave a nod to my newly purchased owl.

"Nice piece."

"Thank you?" I flashed her a quick smile before hurrying outside.

Penny had indeed elected to buy the table I'd seen her bartering over. When I got back to the Expedition, she and Morgan were tying it to the roof while Jeanine supervised.

"Umm . . ." I tilted my head and squinted up at them. "Is that safe?"

"Sure." Penny lifted one end of the rope. "I learned how to tie knots in Girl Scouts."

I smiled doubtfully. Wasn't knot tying for Boy Scouts? "You did?"

Penny winked and smiled down at me. "That's what I told Jeanine. Shh." She put her finger to her lips.

Jeanine shook her head in mock disgust. "Fine, but if that thing blows off halfway down the highway, don't blame me."

"There." Penny gave the rope a pat and then scrambled down to the ground. "All safe and secure. Don't worry. It's not going anywhere."

She wagged her finger at Jeanine as she climbed into the SUV. The rest of us followed after her and piled inside.

"We're a sight, anyway," Jeanine said, laughing as she backed out of the drive. "So, what about the rest of you? Find anything good?"

"Harper found an owl." Jo gestured to me.

"Tell them, Harper."

As the girls passed the owl from hand to hand, I shared the story of how I'd come to buy him.

Evelyn laughed and passed the owl back to me. "How's that saying go? To the victor go the spoils?"

"Just don't let it spoil your fun," Morgan said, leaning close for me to hear over the laughter and chatter.

I smiled and tucked the owl inside my purse. "Thanks."

We made one more stop before lunch. Evelyn added a silver teapot to our collection of finds, and Jo bought a stack of vintage books she planned on making into a lamp. Jeanine, however, was the most excited. She'd stumbled upon a collection of antique cookie cutters and didn't stop talking about them until we were seated at a long table inside a quaint little restaurant.

Morgan opened her menu with a flick of her wrist. "Well, I, for one, can't wait to try the cookies you make with those things. And speaking of cookies, I'm starving." She waved the waitress over and jabbed her finger onto a picture of a mouthwatering open-faced sandwich smothered in gravy. "This one. Quick."

We laughed and the waitress eyed the rest of us, her pencil hovering expectantly over her notepad. "That's today's special. Would anyone else like to try it?"

"Not me." I sent a teasing scowl at Morgan's slim waist. "Not all of us can afford the extra calories. I'll have the spinach salad with grilled chicken."

The others groaned and teased me about taking a break from my perpetual health food regimen, but I shook my head firmly, satisfied with the salad I'd chosen. "Oh, and Julie, is it?" I waved toward her nametag, and she nodded. "Julie, will you please ask the chef to leave out the nuts? I'm allergic."

In no time, we'd all placed our orders and were soon enjoying our food and chatting about where we'd stop next.

When we finished, Julie stepped to our table and waved our tickets in the air. "Okay, ladies. Whenever you're ready, give me a shout."

"Here you go." I took the owl out of my purse and set him next to me on the table before fishing out my wallet and handing her a twenty.

"Hey, that's cute." She took the money and pointed to the owl with the end of her pen. "Where did you get it?"

"An estate sale." I picked up the owl, which in my head I had dubbed Woodsy, and handed him to her for a closer look.

"It's gorgeous." She tapped the stone with her fingernail. "Is this jade?"

I smiled, but I was beginning to feel anxious

as people at some of the nearby tables turned to look at us, including a familiar woman with short, dark-brown hair. I swallowed nervously and looked up at Julie. "I'm not sure. It looks like it."

"My boyfriend loves jade. He's kind of an unofficial expert." She smiled and reached into the collar of her shirt and pulled out a small jade pendant. "He gave me this for my last birthday."

I leaned in for a closer look. "It's beautiful."

"Thanks." She replaced the necklace and smiled. "Your owl is really neat too."

"Thank you." I returned her smile and took Woodsy back. Once he was stuffed safely inside my purse, I let out a long breath. The others paid their bills, and after refilling our drinks, we headed out the door.

Evelyn pulled out her notes and snapped them open in excitement. "I can't wait to get to this next place. The pictures on their website are really fabulous. I bet we'll find lots of good stuff —"

Ahead of her, Jeanine stopped abruptly, and Evelyn crashed into her back with a loud "Oof."

"Jeanine, what are you — ?" Evelyn's mouth dropped open, and her hands fell to her sides, her notes dangling from her fingers.

"What?" Stepping around them to see what they were staring at, I skidded to a halt, my mouth falling open to match Evelyn's.

"The car." Penny's gaze bounced from the Ford to Jeanine. "It's . . ."

Jo's jaw firmed and she came to a stop, one hand on Penny's shoulder and the other on mine. "Someone's broken into the car."

FOUR

"Someone's *broken* into the car," I parroted, my brain struggling to process what we were seeing. The doors gaped open and a lot of our things were strewn over the sidewalk and into the parking lot, including our luggage. Finally, Penny gave a low snort of disgust and reached for her phone.

"Unbelievable. We were in there for what? An hour?" She jabbed the screen on her phone. "I'm calling the police."

The rest of us nodded numbly and listened while she gave the police our location and described what had happened.

"Is anything missing?" I whispered while Penny wrapped up. "Should we look?"

"My teapot!" Evelyn gave a quiet groan and took one step toward the vehicle, only to have her arm caught by Jeanine.

"Evelyn, no. Don't touch anything until the police get here."

She frowned, but nodded. Meanwhile, intrigued by what was happening, many of

535

the restaurant's patrons wandered outside, wagging their heads and whispering. One woman, bolder than the other people gathered around, strode toward me. I recognized the dark-haired woman from the estate sale immediately.

She tossed a glance at the Ford and then at me. "You're the lady who bought the little jade owl earlier today, right?"

"I . . . yes." I hugged my purse tighter to my side.

She tilted her head toward the SUV. "Is this your vehicle?"

"My friend's, yes."

She made a tsking sound and propped her hands on her hips. "I'm so sorry. Is anything missing?"

Jo inched to my side. "We don't know yet. We're waiting for the police to arrive so we can file a report."

"Good thinking." She eyed my purse. "I noticed you didn't lose your owl." When I lifted my eyebrows, she smiled and motioned toward the restaurant. "I saw you take it out in there."

"Oh. Yeah."

The woman flicked a business card from her purse, holding it between her index and middle fingers like a card shark. "I specialize in jade artwork. If you are ever interested in having the owl appraised, give me a call. I'd be glad to help. Free of charge, of course."

"Appraised?"

Jo lifted her chin. "Do you think it's valuable?"

The woman gave a sniff. "I really couldn't say without examining it closer. Some pieces can be worth a couple hundred dollars, especially if they're part of a collection. I'll be happy to check into it for you."

I took her card and stared at the name printed on the front. *Helen Gregoire.* Below her name was printed the words *Fine Art.*

"Thank you, Ms. —"

"Greg-wahr." She pronounced her name carefully, stretching the syllables. "Most people get it wrong."

"Greg-wahr. Got it."

I thanked her for the card and slipped it into my purse. Giving a wave, she turned on her heel and sauntered to a late-model silver Mercedes. Jo whistled softly.

"Nice car."

I nodded. Obviously she did well for herself.

"You know what?" I leaned closer to Jo and made a circling motion with my hand. "Somebody had to have seen something, wouldn't you think?"

"You want to ask around?" she said, her eyes twinkling.

I waved to my right. "I'll go this way, you go the other. We'll meet up at the car."

"Sounds like a plan."

She pulled her shoulders back and walked

cheerfully to the first onlooker. I chuckled under my breath. Jo wasn't above using her age to her advantage. With her silver hair and winsome grin, people often viewed her as completely benign. Truth be told, she was probably the sharpest among us.

I shook my head and approached the person closest to me. I didn't have the same advantages as Jo, but I *had* learned a thing or two working with children — namely, that people like to talk, if you let them.

I stepped up next to a forty-something woman with long red hair and tilted my head toward the SUV. "Looks like someone broke in."

She nodded. "I can hardly believe it. Things like that don't usually happen around here."

"You live around here?"

"I do. My daughter and I" — she placed her arm around a young girl with hair the same shade as hers — "were having lunch when someone said a white Ford had been broken into. I came out to check, but it's not mine." She motioned to a white vehicle on the other side of the parking lot.

"I'm glad it wasn't yours." I smiled and eased away to question the next couple. They too had merely been enjoying their lunch when the news of the break-in spread through the restaurant. By the third person, I sincerely hoped Jo was having better luck. How could so many people have been around yet not have seen a thing?

The windows. I grimaced as I looked back at the restaurant. The restaurant windows faced the street, not the parking lot, so even with a full house, no one would have been able to see what was going on. Still, I kept going until I met up with Jo. She shook her head and lifted her hands as she approached. Nothing.

A few feet away, Penny called to us, and I looked to where she pointed.

"Sheriff's here," Jo said, angling toward the others.

I followed, my heart rate picking up as Deputy Davis climbed from the patrol car. His gaze roamed the people gathered around, but catching sight of me, he headed in my direction.

"Hey, you okay?"

His concern instantly warmed my heart. "We're fine. How did you know . . . ?"

"Marty and I talked." He shrugged and gave a small shake of his head, as though talking about me with his sister was no big deal. "She told me about your book club, so when the call came in from a woman named Penny Parson, I figured it was your group." He motioned toward the SUV. "Wanna tell me what happened?"

"To be honest, we don't really know." I followed him to the Ford, where we were met by Jeanine, Evelyn, and the others. He took out a notepad and pen and wrote down our names, and then asked what we'd been doing when the vehicle was broken into.

"We were inside having lunch," I said. "When we came out, we found this."

He nodded. "Okay. Who does the vehicle belong to?"

"That would be me." Jeanine raised her hand.

"Have you had a chance to examine it?" he asked.

She shook her head. "We figured it would be best not to touch anything."

"Good thinking."

He scribbled a couple of things in the notepad then circled around to the back of the car and copied the plate number. I couldn't help it. I watched him while he worked, admiring the look of concentration on his face, the meticulous way he looked it all over . . . even the careful way he moved. When he finished, he came back to us and asked Jeanine to step closer.

"It looks like this is how they got in." He indicated a tiny hole punched in the door, just below the handle.

"That's it?" Jeanine lifted her eyebrows. "That little hole?"

"That's it. All told, it probably only took them a few seconds to get inside." He gestured toward the items on the sidewalk. "Any idea what they were looking for?"

Jeanine shook her head. "None. I mean, obviously, we'd been shopping." She pointed to the table still strapped to the top of the SUV. "I've heard of people breaking into cars around Christmastime, when people are making expensive purchases. Do you think that's what happened here?"

"I wouldn't rule it out." He held out his hand to the car. "Would you ladies mind taking a look to see if anything is missing?"

"Really?" Jo hesitated. "What about fingerprints?"

He shook his head. "Sorry, Ms. Anderson. Fingerprints are especially hard to lift from a vehicle since most of the surfaces are porous. Also, with this many people touching the surfaces —"

"It's not likely you would find anything," she finished for him.

"I'm afraid not."

She frowned and motioned the others forward. "Well, let's take a look."

Her books were scattered, but none were missing. Evelyn also found her silver teapot.

"My cookie cutters," Jeanine moaned, and held one of them up. It had obviously been stepped on. The others looked to be in no better shape.

"I'm so sorry, Jeanine." I crossed to her and slipped my arm around her shoulders. "Do you think maybe you can salvage a few of them?"

"Maybe." She shook her head sadly. "What a bummer."

"Were they valuable?" Deputy Davis asked.

Jeanine frowned. "Not really. I mean, to a collector like me, they may have been worth something, but they certainly weren't worth breaking into a car."

"Okay." He jotted down a couple of last notes and then indicated the people standing nearby. "If you ladies don't mind, I'm going to ask around, see if anybody witnessed anything."

"Good luck," Jo muttered, and followed it with a secret smile for me.

His gaze met mine, but I feigned ignorance and shrugged. When he walked away, I turned to Jo. "The table."

Jo glanced at the monstrosity strapped to the top of the Ford. "What about it?"

"It's practically a beacon," I said.

"Only if someone were actually looking for us." I stared at her unblinking, and she frowned. "You think someone was looking for us?"

"Nothing's missing. Why else would they break in and ransack the car?"

Jo crossed her arms. "Okay, so then what were they looking for?"

Both of our gazes fell to my purse. "Jo," I said, my pulse racing, "I think I need to find out more about this owl."

FIVE

While Jeanine and Penny drove to a nearby dealership to have the lock on the Expedition repaired, the rest of us headed toward a beautiful Victorian bed-and-breakfast Evelyn had stumbled upon when she was researching our trip. Since it was only a couple of blocks from the restaurant, we decided to walk, but we still arrived earlier than our scheduled reservation time. Marion Bonsel, our hostess, seemed undaunted by our premature appearance and handed us each a small envelope with a number printed on the front.

"All right then, here are your room assignments and the key code to the front door. If you'd like to go on up, the rooms are ready for you." A pretty smile tilted the corners of her mouth as she indicated a set of wide stairs hemmed by a gleaming mahogany newel post and railing. "While you're getting settled, I'll get a tea tray ready. I've got a homemade apple strudel cake cooling in the kitchen. Feel free to head down whenever you're ready and join me in the living room for a snack in front of the fire."

"Ooh, this is perfect weather for a cozy fire," Evelyn said.

Jo and I were sharing a room, so I followed her up the winding stairs until we reached the first bedroom.

"This is ours," I said, glancing at the number printed on the envelope Marion had given us. Our room was painted a dark blue and contained two full-size beds. At the foot of each bed was a carved wooden bench perfect for setting our suitcases on.

Jo laid her suitcase down and went to sit on the edge of one of the beds. "Okay, so let's get another look at that owl. Maybe we'll see something we didn't before."

I pulled Woodsy out then set my purse on the nightstand and joined Jo on the bed. "There's nothing special about him that I could see." I handed the owl to her.

"No maker's mark or that type of thing?"

"None that I noticed."

Jo rolled the owl over in her hand, examining it from top to bottom then frontways and back. "So odd," she said at last.

"Maybe I can find something on the internet." I took out my phone and typed "jade owl" in the search bar, but the links that came up were so numerous, I quickly gave up.

I frowned and bit my lip. I wasn't at a dead

end. The dark-haired woman from the estate sale had offered to appraise the owl for me. But something about her made me uncomfortable. My second choice was a lot less suspicious since it wasn't someone who'd been at the estate sale.

"Hey, Jo, do you remember Julie, the waitress at the restaurant where we stopped for lunch? She said her boyfriend was something of an expert on jade. Do you suppose we could talk to him?"

Jo's expression looked doubtful. "It wouldn't hurt, although her idea of an expert may be a little exaggerated."

"I suppose, but I think I'll give her a call anyway." Instead of replacing the owl in my purse, I wrapped him in a pair of socks and tucked him into my suitcase. That done, I dialed the number to the restaurant and waited while one of the other waitresses went to fetch Julie. She remembered me instantly once I mentioned the jade owl and said she would be glad to ask her boyfriend to take a look at it for me.

"Well?" Jo asked, leaning forward on the bed when I hung up. "Will he do it?"

"Yes." I held up my hand before she got excited. "But the earliest she said he could do it is tomorrow."

Her expression fell. "Oh."

I rubbed my hands together and stood. "Anyway, what do you say we head downstairs for some tea?"

"I'm ready." Jo hopped to her feet, as agile as a woman half her age, and headed for the stairs. "Hopefully, Jeanine and Penny won't be long. I'm almost ready for supper."

I laughed and glanced at my watch. "Jo, it's only four thirty."

She shook her head. "At my age, I've learned it's best not to wait."

The others were already gathered around the fire when we walked in. Marion motioned us toward a sweet little velvet love seat and handed us tea in delicate china cups as we passed.

Balancing my tea carefully, I perched on the edge of the love seat, trying to remember everything my mother had taught me about proper tea-drinking etiquette.

My gaze roamed over the papered walls and upward to the intricate crown molding. "Marion, your house is gorgeous."

"Thank you, Harper. It was my grandmother's house. I still remember coming here to play when I was a girl." She smiled and lifted a tiny pair of silver tongs from the tea tray. "Sugar?"

I shook my head, but Jo accepted two cubes and a splash of cream.

Evelyn lifted her plate. "Jo, you have to try this strudel cake. It's divine."

Jo needed no further coaxing, but I was a little more hesitant. "The cake does smell wonderful, Marion, but I'm very allergic to nuts."

She gave a nod to Evelyn. "No worries. Your friend here told me about your allergies when she made the reservations. Everything I'm serving this weekend is guaranteed nut-free."

"Really?" I smiled gratefully at Evelyn. "In that case, hand me the cake."

We laughed and chatted a bit while Marion dished up the pieces of cake for Jo and me. Taking my piece, I set down my tea and reached for one of the forks laid out neatly on the tray.

"Has anyone heard from Jeanine?"

Morgan nodded. "She said they would be about another thirty minutes. There was nothing the dealership could do about the hole in her door, but they said they could at least get it patched up until we get home."

"Good." I pushed my fork through my cake, my mouth already watering at the smell of apples and cinnamon. "Oh, by the way, would you girls mind if we stopped by that same restaurant in the morning? Julie, the lady who waited on us, is going to have her boyfriend take a look at Woodsy for me."

"Woodsy?" Evelyn frowned curiously. "You mean the owl?"

I gave an embarrassed shrug. "It seemed to make sense."

"Oh. Woodsy the Owl. I get it." Morgan slapped me on the arm, almost upsetting my cake. "That's cute."

"What's this about an owl?" Marion asked.

I explained about my estate sale find and why I wanted Julie's boyfriend to look at it. "According to Julie, he's somewhat of an expert," I finished.

"Well, I certainly hope he can tell you something about it," she said and then lifted the teapot. "Would anyone like some more tea?"

I glanced at my cup cooling on the coffee table and shook my head. Jo also shook her head, but nodded toward her plate of cake.

"Evelyn, you were absolutely right. This cake is delicious. Marion, would you mind sharing the recipe?"

She smiled and nodded. "I'd be happy to. In fact, it's a favorite with my guests, so I keep a few of the recipe cards printed up. I'll go and get them."

She left and I scooped up a bite. "Two for two in rave reviews. I guess I should try this cake."

Warm apples and butter melted over my tongue. I took another bite, savoring every bit of cinnamon and sweetness. "Oh my goodness, you girls were right. This stuff is —"

A tickle started at the back of my throat. I reached for my tea and took a sip. "Wow, that cake is fantastic."

"Right? I told you." Evelyn smacked her

lips together. "I'm going to make it for Thanksgiving dinner. My family will love it."

She continued talking, but I was more interested in the tickles intensifying on my tongue. In fact, they no longer felt like tickles. More like bee stings. I cleared my throat and instantly felt my face warm.

Morgan tilted her head, looking at me. "Harper, are you all right? Your face is a little red."

"I'm fine." I set the cake down and took another sip of tea. "I think some of that cake may have just gone down the wrong pipe."

She nodded and turned away, but Jo kept her gaze fastened on my face as I lowered my cup. Something was wrong. My tongue felt thick. My skin was itching. And then I knew.

I locked gazes with Jo. She stood.

"What? What is it? What do you need?"

"Jo," I managed, squeezing the words past a throat that felt much too tight. "Get my EpiPen."

Six

"Harper? Can you hear me?" There was a pause as someone jiggled my arm, and then, "C'mon, Harper. Open your eyes. Look at me."

Was that a man's voice? I dragged my eyes open, appalled at the shadowy circle of heads floating above me.

"There she is," Morgan said.

"Oh, thank goodness," Marion said.

Collective sighs rustled the air like leaves.

I blinked and licked my lips . . . my dry and somewhat *puffy* lips. "What . . . what happened?"

"You had an allergic reaction," Cam said.

Cam! It *was* a man's voice I'd heard. I hadn't imagined it. I stiffened as I realized I was not only on the floor, I was half-lying in his arms. I flinched and slid my hand to the carpet to push upright.

"Uh-uh." His hold on me tightened. "You're staying right where you are until I'm sure you're okay."

550

Behind him, Evelyn and Jo clung to each other, their gazes bouncing from me to Cam. One of them even said, "Aww." Both looked like they were scrolling through pictures of puppies on Facebook. I did an internal check, starting at my feet and working my way upward until I reached my thigh. "My leg hurths."

I felt him relax, and a contrite grin spread across his face. "That's probably my fault. I got a little carried away with the EpiPen."

"No, it wasn't your fault," Jo said, moving into my line of sight. "It was mine. It took me forever to find your pen. I'm so sorry, Harper." She sniffed and wiped a tear from her cheek.

"Ith okay, Jo." Ugh. Apparently, my tongue was as swollen as my lips.

Much as it thrilled me to be in Cam's arms, I felt a little ridiculous now that I could breathe again. I swallowed nervously and met his gaze. "I'm okay. I can thit up now."

He hesitated and then slipped his free hand to my cheek. His fingers lingered there for a moment then moved farther to support my head as he helped me get upright. "Let's get you into a chair."

A chair sounded good. I was feeling better, but my knees still wobbled like noodles. At this point, the last thing I wanted was to land on my face and further add to my embarrassment. I touched my bottom lip, which now felt only slightly smaller than a tennis ball, and grimaced. "Nuth."

His eyes twinkled as he helped me to sit. "What's that?"

"Nuts," Jo clarified. "She's allergic to them."

"I just don't understand it," Marion said, twisting her hands nervously. "I made sure not to add any to the cake. I even washed all of my dishes and cooking utensils."

"The oil maybe?" Evelyn said.

Marion shook her head. "I checked the label."

Ignoring the others, Cam leaned in to me, his hazel eyes wide. "Are you okay to move? We need to get you to a hospital and have you checked out."

"I called 911," Morgan said, patting her phone. "The ambulance should be here any minute."

I groaned. "An ambulance?" Relief crept in as I realized that already, the swelling had gone down enough for me to get my *s*'s back. "Is that really necessary?"

Cam gave a firm nod. "Absolutely. It's either that or I take you for a ride in my police car."

"A police car might be fun." Jo directed a firm glare at Cam. "But only if you use those lights."

"No lights," I said quickly and then tipped my head to whisper, "Let's just hope she doesn't remember the siren."

He chuckled softly, a pleasing sound in my ear.

"The ambulance is here," Evelyn called from the door.

My gaze locked with Cam's. "I *really* don't want an ambulance. Couldn't one of the girls take me?"

He studied me a moment and then lowered his head toward mine. "How about we let the paramedics check you out and see what they say?"

I nodded reluctantly. Ambulance rides were expensive, especially on a teacher's salary, but that wasn't what bothered me most. It was being forced to be the center of attention.

Jo looked at me, her brow creased with worry lines. "You're going to need your purse when you get to the hospital. I'll pick everything up and bring it down."

I blinked. "Pick what up? What do you mean?"

"Your purse was on the floor and everything was scattered around the nightstand and under the bed. That's what took me so long to find the EpiPen when you were having the reaction. I ended up grabbing the spare from your makeup bag."

I frowned in confusion. Could I have knocked it over when I left the room?

Morgan stepped forward to press her hand

to my shoulder. "We'll wait for Jeanine and meet you at the hospital."

"You don't have to," I said, my face warming. "I'm sure I'll be fine."

"Don't be silly. We're going. And we'll be praying for you," she said firmly.

I smiled and covered her hand with mine. "Thanks."

Evelyn ushered the paramedics inside and for the next several minutes, I waited while they took my information and checked my blood pressure.

A couple of minutes later Jo returned, her gaze perplexed as she held my purse out to me. "Here it is. How it ended up on the floor, I have no idea."

"Me either. I'm sure it was still on the nightstand when we left." I stared at it as though it might provide the answers. "Did you find everything? Maybe I should go look." I frowned and motioned for the paramedic to let me rise. Moving to my side, Cam quickly grabbed my elbow to steady me.

"Uh-uh," Morgan said, putting out her hand. "You need to get to the hospital. The rest of us will check for you."

"But —"

Cam shook his head. "No 'buts.' Do you have your wallet?"

I did a quick check and nodded. "It's here."

Though I didn't want to go to the hospital, I knew it would make everyone feel better knowing I'd been checked out by a doctor, so despite my misgivings, I let myself be loaded onto a gurney and rolled toward the door.

Marion followed behind us, her eyes misty. "I'm really so, so sorry. I just have no idea how this could have happened."

"Please don't worry about it, Marion," I said. "Accidents happen."

She looked only slightly less mortified as she nodded. The others gathered around for hugs before Jo shooed them away. "All right, that's enough. I'll call you when we get to the hospital."

Outside, Cam lingered next to the ambulance while the paramedics opened the doors. Meeting my gaze, he smiled at me. "Mind if I follow you to the hospital?"

"Really?" I blinked and gripped the blankets balled under my fists. "What about Sheriff Hayden? Won't he be mad if you're with me?"

He tapped the mic strapped to his shoulder. "If a call comes through, I'll answer it. Otherwise . . ." He cleared his throat and gave his collar a tug. "I'd like to make sure you're okay."

My heart thumped at the way his voice lowered. I felt my face warm, but I couldn't look away. "How did you even know what was going on?" I whispered.

"I was on my way here to give your friend a

copy of my report when the 911 call came in."

I smiled gratefully. "I'm starting to think you're my guardian angel."

He dropped his gaze, but his ears turned a little pink at the tips, and I knew he'd been flattered by my words.

"Are you ready, Miss Daggett?" one of the paramedics asked.

I nodded, bracing for the bump as they lifted me into the ambulance. At the hospital, the doctor confirmed what I already knew. I'd had an allergic reaction to nuts. Now, it was just a long wait until I could be cleared to go home. Jo volunteered to let the others know, and I settled back on the bed, content to let my weariness take over now that the excitement was past.

Hearing a knock, I turned my head, my eyes fluttering open.

Cam leaned into the room, a contrite grin on his face. "Sorry. I didn't mean to wake you."

"You didn't." I pushed up in the bed and laced my hands over my middle. "Another few minutes, you might have though." I ran my hand over my forehead. "Oh brother. I probably look a mess."

"You look great, especially considering what you've been through."

He eased toward my bedside, his long frame awkward in the tight space. Still, I appreciated his effort.

I smiled. "Thanks for staying. You really didn't have to."

He shrugged and pushed his hands into his pockets. "I'd be lying if I said I didn't want to." He looked around. "Where's your friend?"

"Jo? She went out to tell the others what's going on."

He nodded and motioned toward a chair. "Mind if I wait with you until she comes back?"

I lifted my hand and brushed self-consciously at my warm cheeks. "That's sweet. Thank you. I'd like that."

He lowered into the chair and leaned toward me, his elbows braced on his knees. "So, allergies, huh?"

I grimaced. "Yep. I've carried an EpiPen with me since I was a kid."

"A guy I grew up with did too. He always said it was more of a precaution, but I'm glad you had yours with you today."

"Me too." I blew out a shaky breath. "This was the first time I've ever had to use it. Of course, when you grow up with allergies, you kinda know which foods to steer clear of, which is why this caught me by surprise."

"I can imagine."

I pushed my hair behind my ear and looked at him curiously. "Was it because of your friend that you knew what to do?"

He shook his head. "That was part of my first-aid training. I take a refresher course every year."

"Lucky for me."

"For both of us." He averted his gaze. "Are you going to head on back to the bed-and-breakfast once you're released?"

"I think so. I don't want this to ruin our trip. The girls and I have been planning it for quite a while."

"You're lucky to have such good friends."

"I know." I ducked my head thinking of them. "They're all pretty special in their own way. I don't have a lot of family, so these girls mean a lot to me. I think what I love most is how we all get along, almost like sisters."

He chuckled. "Not my sister."

"I don't believe that for a minute. I've seen how your sister talks about you. She's pretty proud of you, you know."

His face reddened, but a wide smile stretched his lips. "To be honest, the feeling is mutual, but don't tell her I said so."

I made a locking motion over my mouth. There was rustling from the hall, and we both looked up as the doctor entered. To my disappointment, Cam stood.

"I'll wait outside."

"Okay."

He disappeared through the door, and I turned my attention to the doctor. When I was finally cleared to go home, Cam stood waiting in the lobby with Jo and the rest of our crew. They rushed to surround me, all of them talking at once about how worried they were — except for Jo, who hung back, an anxious frown on her face. I looked up over my shoulder at the nurse who'd wheeled me out.

"Thank you. One of my friends can push me out from here."

I handed the stack of paperwork they'd given me to Penny and then turned to Jeanine. "Would you mind bringing up the car? I know it's still early, but I'm tired. I'd really like to get back to the house and go to bed."

"Of course." She gave me one more hug and then fished her keys from her purse.

"I'll go with you," Evelyn said. "I don't want you walking through the parking lot alone."

Cam stepped forward, his hands on his hips. "I'll be glad to walk you, ladies."

They thanked him and headed for the door, their chatter echoing against the pale tiled floor. Instead of following them immediately, he pushed his hands into his pockets and flashed a quick smile at me.

"I'm glad you're okay."

"Me too. Thanks again for coming."

He nodded and lifted his hand to his brow in a sweet sort of semi-salute that melted my heart. Penny and Morgan's too, if their sighs were anything to judge by. While they watched him go, Jo eased to my side.

"Are you sure you're all right?"

"I'm fine. It was an accident, that's all."

She shook her head, her lips pressed tightly together. "I don't think so, Harper. This was no accident."

The look on her face wiped all other thoughts from my head. "What are you talking about?"

Her gaze swept the lobby, and then she leaned down over my wheelchair to whisper. "I checked the kitchen after you left. Like Marion said, there weren't any nuts in the coffee cake. I even checked the cupboards and the trash."

"But?" My heart hurried at the anger and fear I read in her eyes. "What did you find, Jo?"

She blew out a flustered breath, twin spots of color making her face ruddy. "There was a brownish powder all over the rim of the teakettle. At first, I didn't know what it was, so I tasted it to be sure. It was nuts, Harper. Someone ground them up and dumped them in the tea!"

SEVEN

Jo and I waited until we were back at the bed-and-breakfast to fill the others in on what she'd found. Like Jo, they were shocked and a little frightened by the discovery.

Morgan sat cross-legged on the floor while she listened, plucking in agitation at the pile on the rug in Jo's and my bedroom. Finally, she blew out a frustrated breath and threw her hands in the air. "I don't get it. Why would anyone want to do something like that on purpose?"

"And besides us, who else knows about your nut allergy?" Evelyn sat in the chair across from the bed, her foot tapping rapidly against the floor.

"Marion did, of course," Jo said. She pointed to Evelyn's foot. "So stop doing that or you're going to let her know we're awake."

Evelyn immediately froze, and Jo let out a quiet snort.

"But she had no way of knowing about the owl," I said quickly, shooting Jo a chiding glance. "I mean, we mentioned it to her, but she never saw it up close."

"Are you talking about the owl you bought at the estate sale?" Jeanine's gaze bounced from me to Jo. "What about it?"

I grabbed one of the pillows from my bed and hugged it to my chest. "I'm pretty sure that's what all this is about."

Their faces registered their confusion. Jo spoke up. "We're pretty sure someone intentionally put ground-up nuts in the tea so Harper would have an allergic reaction."

"What? Why?" The questions came from several directions at once.

"I think it was to create a diversion so someone could sneak up here to steal the owl out of my purse." Saying it out loud made the threat feel even more real. I swallowed a swell of fear and pushed on. "Except it wasn't in my purse. When we got here this afternoon, I moved it to my suitcase."

Penny sat on the window seat, her eyes wide. "Is it valuable?"

"I don't know. Jo and I are meeting with someone tomorrow to find out."

"Who?" Jeanine asked.

"Remember the girl who waited on us at lunch?"

"Julie," Jo said.

I nodded. "Her boyfriend is supposed to know quite a bit about jade."

Penny sucked in a sharp breath and laid

her hand over her chest. "Julie knew about your allergy. You told her when you ordered your salad. And she saw the owl."

"You think . . . ?" Morgan's gaze circled to each of us. "A waitress could use the money, right? And if that thing really is valuable . . . ?" Her eyebrows rose.

Jo lifted her hand. "Now, now. Let's not jump to conclusions." She turned to me. "Anyone in that restaurant could have seen the owl or heard you mention your allergy."

"That's true." Morgan scratched her head. "Wait. Why did you ask Julie's boyfriend to look at the owl? Didn't the dark-haired lady from the estate sale say she was an art dealer?"

Jo scowled. "Helen Greg-*wahr.*"

Morgan snapped her fingers. "That's her. Didn't I hear her say something about appraising it for free?"

I nodded. "She did, but something about her made me nervous."

"If she was at the restaurant, she would have heard you say you were allergic," Penny said.

Evelyn and Jeanine's heads nodded in agreement. Suddenly, the fact that my friends were as determined as I was to figure out who'd been behind the nuts in my tea gave me courage.

I fluttered my fingers toward the nightstand next to the bed. "Jeanine, would you look in there for some paper?"

She slid the drawer open, rummaged a bit, and pulled out a small, hotel-style notepad. "Here you go."

"Need a pen?" Evelyn dug one from her purse and handed it to me before sitting next to me on the bed.

Using the pillow like a desktop, I scribbled three names on the notepad — Julie, Marion, and Helen Gregoire.

Evelyn tapped the paper. "Don't forget Julie's boyfriend. If she recognized the owl's worth, there's nothing to say she didn't phone him."

"You're right." I didn't know his name, so I simply jotted "boyfriend" next to Julie. For several long seconds, no one spoke.

"Shouldn't we call the police?" Penny's voice startled us all. She looked at each of us, worry in her eyes. "I mean, Harper could have died. Shouldn't we report what happened?"

"And tell them what?" Jo tilted her head toward the notepad on my lap. "We still don't know if any of those people had anything to do with the nuts in Harper's tea."

"We can't even prove it was an intentional attack," Jeanine added.

Penny bit her lip, but she nodded. "So then, what do we do?"

A yawn stretched my lips. "For now, I say we get some sleep and think about this more in the morning."

"Sleep?" Evelyn's eyes widened in disbelief. "We're in Marion's house. What if she was the one who put the nuts in the tea?"

"She never left the room," Morgan said. "She couldn't have snuck up here to rummage through Harper's purse."

"That doesn't mean she couldn't have had an accomplice," Evelyn insisted.

Jo shook her head. "I was joking about her earlier. And even if Marion was involved, I doubt she'd try anything more tonight. Besides, I'm a light sleeper *and* I'm handy with a candlestick." She stood and picked up a wrought iron candlestick from the table next to the window. Wind whistled as she gave it a test swing. "See? Nobody's getting in here tonight."

"Good. That's settled." I pushed the pillow aside and swung my legs off the side of the bed to stretch. When no one moved to get up, I shooed them with my hands. "Go on. Everything will be fine. We'll see you all in the morning."

One by one, the girls reluctantly filed from the room. Jo set down the candlestick and locked the door behind them. Her eyebrows arched, she crossed her arms and rested her back against the door. "Well? Are you sure you're all right staying here tonight?"

"Marion didn't have anything to do with those nuts. Did you see how upset she was when the ambulance arrived? It'll be fine." I shook my head and stifled another yawn. "But those drugs they gave me at the hospital are really kicking in."

"Fine." She checked the lock again and then crossed to her own bed. "But I meant what I said. I really am a light sleeper. You'll be safe tonight if I have anything to say about it. Just try and get some rest."

We changed into our pajamas and climbed into bed. A second later, Jo snapped off the light. Despite what I'd said, I found it difficult to sleep. I stared at the ceiling, imagining all kinds of dangers lurking in the shadows.

Someone had tried to kill me. Or at the very least, they'd meant to hurt me. Neither thought sat well.

I flipped onto my side and stared at the zipper on my suitcase glistening in the moonlight streaming from the window.

Woodsy, I thought, sleep tugging at my eyelids at last, *I'm starting to wish I'd never bought you.*

EIGHT

Except for the slight pounding in my head left over from the drugs, I was none the worse for wear the next morning. Thankfully, Jo had no cause to use the candlestick in the middle of the night and rose early to slip downstairs for coffee. I followed along almost thirty minutes later, my stomach growling for lack of dinner. But there was no way I would risk breakfast after everything that happened. My stomach would have to wait.

I found Jo in the dining room, her Bible on the table in front of her and a steaming cup of coffee waiting at her elbow. She looked up as I entered. "Good morning."

"Morning." I nodded to her coffee. "Where did you get that?"

She pointed toward a silver urn on the buffet next to the table. Seeing my hesitation, she smiled. "Here."

Rising, she crossed to a paper bag next to the coffeepot and pulled out a Styrofoam cup, followed by a breakfast sandwich wrapped in paper. She put both in my hands with a smile. "Breakfast."

I looked at the food in my hands and then at her. "Are you kidding? Where did you get these?"

She hiked her thumb toward the door as she circled to her spot at the table. "There's a fast-food place just down the street. Marion told me about it."

"Marion —" I cut off as she entered carrying a platter of fluffy eggs.

"Oh, there you are. Good morning." She set the platter on a warming pan and turned to look at me. "How are you feeling?"

"Better, thanks." I eased over to sit next to Jo, suddenly very self-conscious of my pre-packaged biscuit.

Marion pointed to the bag Jo had left on the buffet. "I hope you don't mind. After what happened yesterday, I thought it would be wise not to risk another episode."

I looked at Jo. *Marion* had suggested getting my breakfast at the fast-food place? She gave a slight nod. Apparently, Jo thought her trustworthy. I laid my sandwich on the table and peeled the lid off of my coffee cup. Black, just the way I liked it. I couldn't help it — I took a sniff before putting the cup to my lips.

Marion bustled back toward the kitchen. "I'd better hurry and bring out the rest of your breakfast. I'm sure the others will be coming down soon."

"What was that about?" I whispered to Jo as she left.

"She was already working on breakfast when I came down," Jo whispered back. She tapped the corner of her Bible. "She found me in here reading, and we got to talking." She shook her head. "Call it intuition, Harper, but I don't think she had anything to do with putting the nuts in your tea."

I couldn't help but feel relieved. Jo had a sense about these things. More than likely, she was right about Marion.

But I still wasn't eating her eggs.

I unwrapped my sandwich and took a hungry bite. While I ate, Jo fixed herself a plate of eggs and fruit, along with a puffy homemade Danish that on any other day, I would have devoured.

"So, what's the plan for today?" I asked between bites.

Jo shrugged and carried her plate back to the table. "I'm not exactly sure. It's probably not a good idea for the whole lot of us to meet with Julie's boyfriend, not unless we want to scare him away."

"True." I reached for a napkin. "Well, what if they went back to the estate sale? Maybe talk to the homeowner to see if he knows anything about the guy we saw there yesterday."

Jo nodded. "That's good. And I could ask Penny or Evelyn to see what they can find out about Helen Gregoire."

I set my sandwich down. "You know, Jo, I've been wondering about something." I lowered my voice and kept one eye trained toward the door in case Marion returned. "Obviously, anyone could have seen us walking to the bed-and-breakfast after we left the restaurant yesterday, but Marion gave us all key codes to the front door. How was the person able to get into the house unless it was someone she knew?"

Jo's mouth drooped into a troubled frown. "That's a good question. We could ask her."

I thought for a second and then nodded. "Jo, does Marion know that we know the nuts were in the tea?"

"I don't think so." She unfolded her napkin and laid it in her lap, then shook her head. "No, I'm sure she doesn't. I didn't say anything to her."

"Good. Then let me do the talking."

Marion returned a moment later with platters of ham, bacon, and sausage. While she worked, she chatted pleasantly. "I can't tell you how happy I am that you're all right, Harper." She adjusted the heat on the warming pans and then placed silver tongs on each of the platters. "I've never known anyone with allergies. I have to say, I couldn't believe how quickly the reaction set in."

"Yeah. That's why I carry an EpiPen with me." I cleared my throat and began again.

"Say, Marion, about the key codes you gave us?"

"Yes?" She turned, wiping her hands on the checkered apron around her waist.

"I was just wondering, do you give those out to all your guests?" My thoughts whirled as I realized that anyone who'd stayed at the bed-and-breakfast could have used the codes to get in.

"I do." She propped her hands on her hips. "But I change them regularly. Why?"

I asked another question instead of answering hers. "And are the doors always locked?"

She smiled curiously. "Well, not during the day. We're a small town. Not a whole lot happens around here that would warrant keeping them locked all the time."

"Are you sure about that?" Jo muttered under her breath.

"Thank you, Marion," I said quickly, before she could ask about Jo's comment.

Thankfully, Penny and Evelyn made their way down the stairs, followed closely by Jeanine and Morgan. Marion busied herself showing them to breakfast — replenishing dishes and brewing coffee as fast as they could empty their plates and cups.

With breakfast finished, we all returned upstairs to fetch our bags. Though I trusted Jo's judgment about Marion, I was anxious to get underway. Because of the trouble I'd experienced, Marion waived the cost of my stay and walked with us to the door.

"Thank you all so much for coming," she said. "I'm so sorry for the scare."

Jeanine reached for the knob and would have stepped out onto the porch except for a large box blocking the entry.

"What's this?"

"Oh, let me get that." Marion eased past us and pushed the box aside with her foot. "FedEx must have delivered it late last night."

"Do you need help getting it inside?" Morgan said.

She waved away her offer with a smile. "Don't worry about it. I'm sure I can manage."

"We really don't mind," I said. "Why don't you let us help you move it into the hall?"

She hesitated a moment and then nodded. "Well, all right. If you wouldn't mind."

I shook my head, already reaching for one corner of the box when I saw something that froze me in my tracks. A large black-and-white shipping label was plastered to the top of the box.

And the name on the label . . . was Helen Gregoire.

NINE

For several long seconds, I simply stared at the label, my brain struggling to make sense of the information. Why in the world would Helen Gregoire have a package delivered here?

"Harper, are you all right?" I flinched as Marion laid her hand on my arm. She smiled at me curiously. "What's wrong?"

"I . . . uh . . ." I glanced over at Jo. "I think I should do one last pass of the room. Jo, would you mind helping me?"

She was so focused on folding a paper napkin and shoving it into her purse that she didn't look at me. "I checked it. Everything was out."

"Jo." I mentally urged her to lift her head while I turned to hide my face from Marion's view. "I think we should check it *again.*"

Finally, she lifted her gaze to mine. I widened my eyes.

Catching my meaning, she stammered, "O– Oh. Okay. Right."

Striding forward, I grabbed her arm and walked her inside.

"We'll be right down," I called to Jeanine and the others over my shoulder.

"Harper, what is going on?" Jo whispered.

"Not yet." I urged her to the stairs and then looked back to make sure we hadn't been followed. Satisfied, I blew out a breath. "The package on the porch? The shipping label was made out to Helen Gregoire."

"What!" Jo slapped her hand over her mouth then repeated more quietly, "What? Are you sure?"

"Positive."

"Why? How does she know Marion?"

"How should I know?" I motioned toward the counter where we had checked in. "Do you think she's a guest?"

Jo shook her head. "We would have seen her. Besides, what kind of guest gets mail delivered to a bed-and-breakfast?"

"Okay, then what's her relationship to Marion?"

Jo smoothed her hair behind her ear nervously. "Family, maybe? What was Marion's last name?"

It came to me in an instant. "Bonsel." I stared at Jo, as though the information would spark something I'd missed. She shook her head.

I scrambled for another possibility. "Maiden name?"

Jo nodded and wagged her finger. "That could be it. Maybe Marion's maiden name was Gregoire. But how will we know? Who can we ask?"

That answer *also* came instantly. Heat rushed to my face. "We could ask Cam."

"Deputy Davis." She nodded. "Should we tell the others?"

"Not until we leave. I don't want Marion to get suspicious."

She lowered her chin and pointed to her face. "Then I'd better head straight out to the car or she'll see it all over me."

I hid a smile. Jo was right. She'd never been able to hide what she was thinking. "Fine. Go. I'll get the others." I gave her a gentle push toward the door then followed her down the stairs.

Lowering her face, Jo marched out past the girls and Marion, and made a beeline for the car. Penny's table was still strapped to the top, the legs poking into the air like a peculiar pair of antlers.

"Oh. Here they are." Marion blinked quickly as Jo hurried by and then looked at me. "Everything okay?"

I smiled and lifted my hand in a casual wave. "All set."

Penny cocked her head to one side. "I thought you said — ?"

I grabbed her shoulders and turned her toward the truck. "Okay, let's go now, Penny.

We don't want to keep Marion any longer. Thanks again for letting us stay. You have a lovely place."

I led Penny from the porch as I talked, motioning for the others to follow. Too late, I realized that Evelyn had lagged behind.

"Uh-oh, we didn't move the box."

"Evelyn, no —" I couldn't finish. Both she and Marion were eyeing me with befuddlement. Heat flooded my cheeks. "I mean, you're right. I'll get it."

I managed a weak smile and put one foot on the steps, but Evelyn waved me away. "I can get it. No worries." She hefted the box and then tipped her head toward the door. "Marion, would you mind getting that?"

"Of course." She pushed the screen open and then stepped aside to let Evelyn pass. "Thank you so much. I have such a hard time lifting these days." She put her hand to her back and chuckled. "Old age, huh?"

"Oh, I hear you. Anyway, thanks again." Evelyn set the package down and then reached out to shake Marion's hand.

"It was my pleasure," she said, smiling warmly.

I held my breath while this went on and only blew it out when Evelyn made her way to the SUV.

"Evelyn, for pity's sake, get in here," Jo urged from the back seat.

"What? What's wrong?"

I took her arm and drew her toward the door. "I'll tell you inside. Now, buckle up."

"All right, what are we missing? What don't we know?" Jeanine said as she dropped the vehicle into Reverse. "Did something happen at breakfast?"

"Not breakfast. It was the box," I said.

Jo's head bobbed. "It had Helen Gregoire's name on it."

"The art dealer lady?" Morgan gripped the back of the seat and pulled herself forward. "Why?"

"That's what we need to find out." I locked gazes with Jeanine in the rearview mirror. "Is there a bookstore in this town? Or someplace where we could go to talk without being overheard?"

"I'm sure there is. Evelyn?"

"Got it." She took out her phone and began typing.

"In the meantime, you need to call Deputy Davis." Jo pointed to my phone and followed it with a stern look that said "no dawdling."

"We're calling the police?" Penny looked from Jo to me.

I shook my head. "No, no, it's nothing like that. We just thought he could help us figure out if there's a family connection between Marion and Helen."

Penny sighed with relief.

Evelyn held up her phone then looked at Jeanine. "Here's the bookstore. I already typed in the address. It should be just a couple of blocks."

While Jeanine drove, I looked up the number to the sheriff's office and prayed it would be Cam who answered while it rang.

"Sheriff's office."

I swallowed nervously. "Deputy Davis, please."

"Speaking."

Nerves of a different kind quivered in my stomach. "Uh . . . hi, Cam. This is Harper Daggett."

I heard rustling, followed by a clunk, and then the phone clicked from speaker to the handset. "Harper. Hi. What can I do for you?"

The rumbling of his voice in my ear suddenly made me feel shy. Or it could have been the five pairs of eyes fixed on me. Even Jeanine watched from the rearview mirror.

I licked my lips and dropped my gaze to the hangnail forming on my thumb. "Listen, I'm sorry to bother you at work."

"No, it's okay," he said quickly. He gave a low chuckle. "Slow day at the office."

I smiled at his lazy drawl. Honestly, the man could make me melt like butter on a warm biscuit.

Focus, Harper.

"Good. Glad to hear it." *Move on.* I tightened my grip on the phone. "I was calling about the . . . you know . . . my thing."

"Allergic reaction," Jo supplied from the

578

seat in front of me.

"Yes, my allergic reaction. Turns out, it may not have been an accident."

"What?" His voice hardened, became formal. "What do you mean?"

I explained about the nut residue Jo had found in the teapot, my purse, the owl, and Helen Gregoire and the shipping label that had appeared on Marion's doorstep with her name on it.

I looked at Jo expectantly. She nodded for me to continue.

"So, anyway," I finished, "one thing may not have anything at all to do with the other, but I was sort of hoping maybe you could help us find out what the connection is between Marion and Helen."

I bit my lip and waited. Either he would offer to help or he would think I was nuttier than Marion's tea.

"I'm glad you called," he said after a moment. "I'll do some checking and let you know what I find."

"Really?" My voice hitched with excitement, which quickly faded when I thought of his boss. "What about — ?"

"Don't say it."

Sheriff Hayden's name died in my throat.

"This is serious, Harper. Have you and your friends left the bed-and-breakfast?"

"Yes. We're . . . um . . . ." I hesitated to tell him we were going somewhere to talk. Sheriff

Hayden thought we were meddlesome. I didn't want Cam to feel the same way. I told him about the meeting with Julie and her boyfriend instead. "Julie thinks he might be able to tell me something about the owl."

"That's probably a good idea. Will you let me know what you find out?"

"Sure."

"And I'd like to get a look at that owl."

"I can send you a picture."

"Perfect." He gave me his cell phone number and then paused. "Harper, where are you and your friends headed next? Are you coming back to Oak Grove?"

"Actually, we're going to hang around here for a while."

"Okay, so long as your friends don't leave you alone. And you'll be careful about what you eat from here on out, right?"

"Of course."

"Good. Is this the number where I can reach you?"

"Yes. It's my cell phone."

I heard a clicking on the other end of the line. "Okay, well, I guess that's all for now."

Something told me he wanted to say more. I waited.

"Harper, I . . ."

My mouth went dry, which was odd since my palms were sweating like crazy. "Yeah?"

"Be careful, okay? I'd hate for anything to happen to you."

"Okay." *Okay?* I resisted the urge to smack my head. "Thanks for your help, Cam."

"You're welcome. Hey, Harper?"

I'd started to hang up. Hearing him call my name, I jerked the phone back to my ear. "Yeah?"

"I think I'll take a ride out that way, just to check on things. Maybe around lunch? If that's okay, I mean."

I smiled and repeated his words back to him. "Slow day?"

"Exactly."

I sucked in a breath. "That'll be fine. I'll call or text and let you know where we are."

"Okay. Talk to you later."

" 'Bye." I hit the END CALL button and sat back against the seat with a sigh.

Morgan broke the silence. "Wow. That sounded . . ." She swiped her hand across her brow.

"Uh-huh." I dropped the phone to my lap and covered my face with my hands. Honestly, what was happening to me where Cam Davis was concerned?

I had no answer. But deep down, I had to admit, I was really excited to see him.

TEN

Darcy's Book Bag was an out-of-the-way shop located on the far end of town with a fashion boutique on one side and a photo and frame shop on the other. The instant we walked through the door, we were enveloped in the soothing scent of coffee and new books. Chandeliers lit the main area, but there were also table lamps in cozy reading areas scattered throughout the store. Under normal circumstances, it was exactly the type of place we girls would hang out. Today, it was convenient and quiet, two things that ranked higher on the list than anything else.

I wasn't comfortable leaving Woodsy in the truck, so I rummaged through my suitcase and brought him in with me, though I had to have looked strange walking in with what looked like a pair of socks under my arm.

"I'll go get us some seats." Evelyn pointed toward a cluster of club chairs next to the window. "No one should disturb us over there."

"I'll go with you." Penny pulled a five-dollar bill from her purse and handed it to Jeanine. "Grab me some coffee?"

"Sure." She didn't ask what she wanted in it. Penny took her coffee black.

A teenager in a gray T-shirt and skinny jeans met us at the counter. Jet-black hair drooped over one eye, and he wore more eyeliner than I did, but he greeted us with a pleasant smile.

"Morning, ladies. What can I get for you?"

I pointed to the board. "I see an iced mocha up there. Any chance you can make it skinny?"

"Sure thing." He grabbed a cup and a marker. "Your name?"

"Harper."

He jotted it on the cup and turned to Jo. "And for you?"

"I'd like a large caramel frappe, please."

He nodded then took the rest of our orders. When the drinks came up, we wove our way to where Penny and Evelyn waited. Jeanine handed Penny her cup then dropped into the seat next to her and motioned toward the socks in my hand.

"Okay, so let's get another look at that owl."

"Here?" Jo laid her hand on my arm and glanced nervously around the shop. "What if someone sees?"

"Like who?" Jeanine's eyebrows rose. "There's no one here except him."

She pointed to the teenager who'd served

our coffee. He'd moved to sit behind the cash register and was now hunched over his phone, typing with his thumbs.

Jo grimaced. "Okay, fine, but one of us needs to keep an eye on the door."

"I'll do it. I can see it fine from here," Evelyn said.

Jo nodded, and I carefully unwrapped the owl then snapped a quick picture and texted it to Cam. That done, I set Woodsy on the table. We sat quietly studying it for several seconds, the only sound the occasional hiss of hot air being pushed through the ceiling ducts.

Morgan stroked her chin. "I don't get it. What's so special about him?"

"Maybe we should try looking online?" Jeanine picked up her phone.

Morgan patted my knee. "We'll see what we can find while you meet with Julie's boyfriend. Speaking of that, what time are you supposed to head for the restaurant?"

I looked at my watch. "Not for another hour. It's only ten thirty. Julie said he wouldn't get there until eleven thirty or twelve."

"You're not going by yourself, are you?" Penny tapped the floor nervously with her foot. "Deputy Davis said we shouldn't leave you alone."

"Actually . . ." Jo bit her lip. "Maybe it would be a good idea to wait until he can go with you. He said he was coming this way, didn't he?"

"He did." I pinched my bottom lip between my fingers. "I don't know, Jo. I wouldn't want Cam to think I was making this up just to spend time with him."

Penny snorted into her coffee cup. "I doubt that."

"What?"

Jeanine smiled and rested her hand on my arm. "Harper, in case you haven't realized it, that handsome young officer has a thing for you."

I glanced at Jo, who shrugged. "It's pretty obvious."

"Maybe to you." I searched their faces. They were all nodding. "Really?" It came out sounding more hopeful than I intended.

Jo jabbed her finger toward my phone. "Why not ask him to meet you at the restaurant?"

"Or I could do it." Morgan stretched out her hand, but I snatched the phone away before she could reach it, a move that inspired a round of giggles.

Tapping out the message, I hit SEND and then dropped the phone in my lap. "There. It's done. Now what?"

"Now we see if we can find anything online about jade owls," Jeanine said.

I held up my hand as the others took out

their phones. "Hold on a minute. What about Helen?"

"The art dealer?" Penny said. "I thought Deputy Davis was going to see what he could find out about her."

I nodded. "He is, but in the meantime, I sure would like to know a little more about her. Where does she work? What kind of social media presence does she have? Who are her friends?" I pointed to Morgan and Evelyn. "Is that something you two could work on?"

Both nodded.

"While they're doing that, Penny and I will see what we can find on the owl," Jeanine said.

"I'd appreciate it," I said, and turned to look at Jo. "That just leaves you and me. Want to go with me to the restaurant?"

"Of course."

"Do you need me to drive you?" Jeanine asked, pushing up from her chair.

I held up my hand and nodded toward the window at Jeanine's car. "Actually, I saw a sign for the bus stop just around the corner. It might be better if we take the bus so we don't telegraph where we are."

All eyes turned to Penny, who shrank into the cushions of her chair with a grin. "What? I told you the table wouldn't fall off."

Laughing, I reached for Woodsy and dropped him into my purse. Waving to Jo, I said, "We might as well get going. We'll be early, but I don't think it will matter if we sit at the restaurant while we're waiting for Julie's boyfriend to show up."

"That's probably a good idea. It'll take me a lot longer to get to the bus stop than it will you." She chuckled and pointed to my legs. Hers were much shorter by comparison.

"C'mon." I pushed out from the booth and headed for the door. It opened before I could grab it. Automatically, I backed up to let the person pass. He did, and never even looked up from his phone. My first instinct was to bemoan his lack of chivalry. After all, even if he didn't observe the custom of opening doors for a lady, Jo was quite a bit older than either of us.

My second instinct . . .

I grabbed Jo's arm as recognition took hold. Putting my finger to my lips, I pulled her away from the door and behind the closest bookshelf. I needn't have worried about quieting Jo. I knew by her wide gaze that she'd recognized the newcomer too.

It was the man in the argyle sweater from the estate sale.

Neither of us said a word as we edged our way to the counter. Pressing tightly to the bookshelf, I peeked around the corner for a better look. No doubt about it. I recognized the dark mustache and beady brown eyes. But what was he doing here?

Jo poked me in the ribs and leaned close to whisper. "What is he doing here?"

I might have laughed at the direction both of our thoughts had taken had I not been straining to hear what name the man would give to the teenager behind the counter.

"Small coffee." He pulled a bill from his wallet and slid it across the counter. The teenager took his money and a bell rang on the cash register as he totaled up the sale. He didn't ask for a name, just handed the man a cup.

"Harper? What is he doing?" Jo pressed closer. "Can you see him?"

"He's getting coffee," I whispered back.

"Are we sure it's him? The guy from the estate sale, I mean?"

She rose onto her tiptoes. As she did, her elbow dislodged one of the books. We saw it at the same moment. Both of us thrust out our hands to catch it. Both of us missed. Holding my breath, I watched in horror as it banged loudly to the floor.

ELEVEN

"Did he see us?" Sweat trickled from Jo's brow down the side of her face. Her hand shook as she wiped it away. "Is he looking this way?"

With memories of every horror movie I'd ever seen playing through my head, I risked a peek. I pulled back with a relieved sigh. "He's not looking this way. Even if he heard the book fall, I don't think he was paying attention."

Jo pressed her hand to her chest. "What about the girls? Should we tell them?"

I thought for a second then chanced another peek and shook my head. "He's just getting coffee. Besides, I don't think he saw anyone but you and me at the estate sale, right? And we don't even know if he's the one after the owl."

"No, but he was pretty mad at the estate sale."

True. We couldn't discount him just because Marion and Helen had a connection we couldn't explain. I reached for her arm. "All right. Let's go."

She resisted the pull of my hand. "Won't he see us?"

"He's picking out a magazine. His back is to the door. Now's our chance."

I sucked in a breath and held it as we squeezed out from behind the bookshelf and headed for the door.

The bell!

I cringed as it chimed. There was nothing for it. We kept walking, but I kept one eye trained on the man through the window as we scooted past. Jeanine had parked on the far side of the parking lot, toward the frame shop. My steps slowed as I spotted Penny's antlers.

"Oh no."

Jo stumbled and caught herself. "What?"

I pointed. There were several cars in the parking lot, but not enough to hide our estate sale monstrosity. So how come *he* hadn't seen it?

I looked back the way we'd come. He was on his phone. If he'd walked from the opposite direction, he could easily have missed it. Of course, it was silly to hope he'd be distracted twice.

I handed Woodsy to Jo and took out my phone. "I'll text Jeanine and the others and let them know he's there. Maybe they can keep an eye on him and tell us what he's up to."

"Good idea." She pushed Woodsy into her purse and clutched it tight. "I'll watch for the bus."

We were the only ones waiting when the bus pulled up. We climbed aboard and within a couple of minutes, we'd reached the restaurant. Julie waved to us as we entered. She was at another table, but she said something to her customers and then angled over to meet us at the door.

"Hey, there you are. I have a table ready for you." She pointed with her pen toward a booth at the back of the restaurant. "Will that be okay? I figured you'd want to sit somewhere quiet."

"That's perfect."

"Okay. Can I get you ladies something to drink while you're waiting? Iced tea, maybe?"

My nerves were already starting to feel the effects of too much caffeine. "Just water for me, thanks."

"Not me. I'll take a coffee, extra hot," Jo said, and then scooted on ahead of me toward the table Julie indicated.

While Julie went to get our beverages, I looked around the restaurant. It was busy for a Sunday, or maybe because of it. Some people were dressed in their finest and looked like they'd just come from church. Others looked like maybe they were heading for the lake.

I slid into the booth opposite Jo. From this angle, I had a clear view of the door. Somehow, that made me feel better. My phone pinged. I glanced at the screen. "It's Jeanine."

I scanned the message. "They've spotted the sweater guy. She's worried about following him. She thinks maybe he'll recognize the Ford."

Jo snorted. "You think? Tell her she shouldn't follow him anyway. It could be dangerous."

I typed out the message and hit SEND. Another ping. This time, it was Cam. He'd stopped for gas and was just a few minutes away. I set the phone down and let Jo know.

"Here you go, ladies." Julie placed our drinks on the table and tapped her order pad. "Let me know if you need anything else."

"Will do. Thanks again, Julie. We really appreciate your help."

"No problem." The bell rang at the cash register and she shrugged. "Oops. Gotta go."

Jo took a napkin and wiped the rim of her cup before taking a sip. "So, did Julie ever tell you what her boyfriend's name is?"

"Not yet. I forgot to ask."

"Hmm. Well, I hope he gets here soon. I sure would like to know why this owl is so special."

"You and me both."

I squinted as sunlight flashing off the door shone in my eyes. My heart skipped a beat when Cam stepped through. I raised my hand to catch his attention and then held my breath as he walked over.

He gave a nod to me and another to Jo. "Hey, Harper. Ms. Anderson."

"Call me Jo," she said and indicated the spot next to me with a tilt of her head. "Have a seat."

He shot me a glance and then settled into the booth. With his height and wide shoulders, it was a close fit. My skin tingled where his knee bumped mine.

"Any word yet from the boyfriend?" he said.

"Not yet." I licked my lips and prepared to motion for Julie. "Would you like something to drink?"

He laid his arms on the table. Instantly, I was reminded of the feel of them around my waist. "Nah. I'm good."

Julie had started over. He stopped her with a raised hand. She nodded and moved on to another customer.

"So, I have some news for you."

"About Helen?" Jo said.

"That's right. Gregoire is her professional name. Her real name is Clebum."

"Clebum?" Jo's nose crinkled. "What kind of name is that?"

"Apparently, one she didn't want to use professionally." I looked at Cam. "Any idea how she's connected to Marion?"

He nodded. "They're sisters. Marion is the older one."

"Sisters." Jo tapped her cup with her fingernail. On her face, I read the same suspicion I felt. If the owl really was valuable, Helen would have known, and Marion would have been compelled to help her.

"Do you know why Helen is having mail delivered to the bed-and-breakfast?" I asked.

He shrugged. "Sorry. I don't have an answer for that. Helen lives and works out of Wichita. Seems like any mail she has delivered would have gone there." His gaze jumped from me to Jo. "I assume one of you has the owl?"

"Right here." Jo dug it from her purse and laid it on the table. Of course, it was still wrapped in my socks. Suddenly, I wished I'd chosen to bring a pair other than the ones with kittens all over them. At least they were clean.

My cheeks flushed. I unwrapped Woodsy and then shoved the socks back to Jo. Cam didn't seem to notice. He picked up the owl and examined it from every side. After a moment, he put it down and directed his gaze to me.

"Interesting. He's a cute little guy. The picture didn't do him justice."

"Which is why she bought it in the first place," Jo said.

He leaned forward to clasp his hands on the table. "Have you talked to the owner at the estate sale about it?"

"Not yet. At the time, there was a little debate over who would buy it." I explained about the man in the argyle sweater. Cam's eyes narrowed as he listened.

"Seems like there's a lot of folks interested in that thing."

"I agree. That's why I'm hoping Julie's boyfriend can tell us something about it."

Jo's phone rang. She picked it up and looked at the screen.

"It's Jeanine."

I nodded. "Good. Maybe she knows something about the guy at the coffee shop."

While Jo took the call, I told Cam about seeing the man in the argyle sweater again this morning.

"It's possible he lives here, of course," I finished. "I mean, he was just getting a cup of coffee."

"Not just that." Jo put down the phone, her eyes wide. "After we left, Jeanine says the guy took a call that made him real agitated. He rushed out without waiting for his coffee."

My heart thumped. Though I suspected I already knew the answer, I still had to ask. "And? Did she see which way he was headed?"

"She did. She and the girls are following him." Jo looked at the door and then back at me. "Jeanine said . . . she thinks he's coming here."

Twelve

Our eyes shifted to the door, which was silly, since there was no way the man in the argyle sweater could make it to the restaurant so quickly. After several seconds, I blew out a breath and looked at Jo. "Is Jeanine sure this is where he's headed?"

"That's what she said." Her gaze fell to her phone. "I don't get it. Why do you suppose he's headed here in such a hurry?"

We fell silent as Julie strutted to the table, her eyes fastened firmly on Cam and her lips parted in a large smile. "Hey, handsome." She slid her gaze to me, her pen tapping lightly on her order pad. "Who's your friend?"

Something about the way she looked at him — like she was starving and he was a chocolate doughnut — set me on edge. I tightened my fingers around my water glass.

"Uh, Julie, this is Deputy Davis."

"Deputy, huh?" She looked over his uniform then slid the order pad into her apron pocket and stuck out her hand. "I'm Julie.

Pleasure to meet you, Deputy."

Cam started to rise, but Julie laid her hand on his shoulder and let it linger there. I hid a scowl. Didn't she have a boyfriend?

"No, no. Don't get up. I just came over to tell Harper that J. T. can't come by."

I blinked. "J. T.?"

"My boyfriend. He was supposed to get off work early, but his boss ended up holding him over. I'm really sorry. Do you want me to see if maybe he can meet with you this afternoon?"

Since I didn't have another option, I nodded. "I'd appreciate that. Thank you, Julie."

"No problem." Finally, she removed her hand from Cam's shoulder. "Nice meeting you."

His head bobbed. "You too."

Across the table, Jo shot me a grimace, which she quickly hid when Cam turned back to look at us.

I clasped my hands tightly around my glass. "I'm sorry, Cam. I shouldn't have asked you to come all this way."

His lips curved in a lazy smile that stopped my heart. "I'm glad you did. I kinda wanted to see how you were doing. All I needed was an excuse."

"Yep. That's my cue." Jo slapped her hands down on the table and then slid out of the booth. "I'm going outside to meet Jeanine and the girls." She caught Julie's eye and motioned to her cup. "One of these to go?"

"You got it," Julie said, "but we're out of lids."

"No problem. I'll take it without." She gave a nod to Cam and one to me. "You two take your time."

She bustled off without waiting for us to answer. I slid an embarrassed smile at him. "Sorry about that."

He shrugged. "It's okay."

Now that Jo was gone, I wondered if he'd shift to the other side of the booth. He turned, but it was toward me, and he made no move to get up.

"Listen, Harper, I . . ." He paused and lowered his gaze. "I really didn't like hearing that you thought someone was after you. It made me . . ." He curled his hands into fists. "Anyway, that's really why I decided to drive out. I'd like you to be careful while you're here. Oak Grove is pretty far, if I had to get to you in a hurry, I mean."

My mouth went dry. My brain was telling me that he was speaking as a police officer, but my heart? That wanted to believe something else.

"We won't do anything silly," I said, struggling to sound calm when my insides felt like Jell-O.

"I know you won't." He smiled. "You're not that type. Now, Marty?"

His face twisted in a mock grimace, and I

laughed. "You sure that's not just big brother talking?"

"Maybe." He smiled. "I have to admit, I'm a little protective where she's concerned."

"That's nice."

"Uh, she doesn't always think so."

"Well, maybe not all the time. I have a brother too. He can be the same way, when he's in the U.S., that is. Most of the time he's gallivanting around the world."

"Really? What does he do?"

I grabbed my straw and swirled it around in my water glass. "He's a writer for a travel magazine."

"Fun job."

I shrugged. "He's young and single. Right now, it's perfect for him. I just wish he came home a little more. You know . . . for holidays and stuff."

I swallowed hard at the thought of another Thanksgiving spent watching football and roasting a chicken because there was no way I could eat an entire turkey by myself.

"You miss him."

I glanced at Cam. He wasn't just making small talk. There was compassion in his eyes. And real interest, not the fake kind guys sometimes showed when they wanted a date but not much else.

I nodded slowly. "Yeah. I miss him. But I miss having a family more."

"Your parents are both gone?"

I lifted my chin. "Yeah. About six years ago. They died in a boating accident. I wasn't close to them."

I surprised myself by adding that last part. Maybe it was because I didn't want him to feel like he had to extend the accepted platitudes. Or maybe . . . I just wanted him to know about my not-so-pleasant past so he could run the other way if he wanted, before I got too invested. Cam just looked at me. Not in a judgy way. Just . . . curious.

"My family is kinda the opposite," he said. "We're close." He grunted. "Too close sometimes."

"There's no such thing," I said, before I could stop the words from coming out.

Instead of being offended, he smiled and nodded. "You're right. I only say that because Mom worries about me so much."

"You're a cop. Moms worry." My mouth! I would have slapped my hand over it to keep any more junk from spilling out, except that Cam laughed. Out loud. Like a belly laugh.

"You sound just like her."

My face heated, but I managed a small smile. "I'd like to meet her sometime."

Slowly the humor melted from his face, replaced with a seriousness that robbed my breath. "I'd like that too."

A bell rang. At the cash register, an impatient-looking customer scanned the restaurant. Where was Julie?

"Well, I should probably be going," Cam said.

I jerked my attention back to him. Though I hated for our time together to end, I couldn't exactly ask him to sit around chatting with me all afternoon. I nodded. "Me too. I'm sure the girls are waiting for me."

He slid out of the booth. I hesitated a moment and then followed him. Unfortunately, there was no graceful way to do it. I scooted like a seal until I reached the end of the bench. Cam put out his hand and helped me stand. It was a small touch, but the heat from it shot all the way up my arm. I pulled my hand away before it could reach my heart.

I smiled and tucked my hair behind my ear. "So, about the owl, I'll call you if I find out anything else."

"Okay. I'll do some checking too, see if there's anything I can dig up on my end."

"Thanks. Oh, and about Julie?"

"Yeah?"

"Should I let you know if she's able to set up another meeting with her boyfriend?"

"That'd be good."

I slid my hands into my pockets. Cam was standing close. I could smell his cologne. But he wasn't stepping away. In fact, it almost felt as though he were leaning in, like he wanted to hug me . . . or . . . maybe . . .

His gaze slipped down over my face and settled on my lips, making my mouth tingle.

"I should be going," he said, lower this time, and more pronounced, like he was trying to convince himself to leave.

I couldn't agree with him — didn't want to agree with him. I bit my lip and stayed quiet.

"So, Harper, when you get back to town?"

"Yeah?"

"I was thinking, maybe, if you aren't busy . . ."

It shocked me how badly I wanted him to finish his sentence. Butterflies fluttered in my stomach, and my palms itched.

A commotion started at the front of the restaurant, loud enough that both of us looked to see what was going on. Several people had left their tables and were gathered by the windows, craning to see out. But what were they looking at?

My scalp tingled with sudden awareness. Jo was outside. I moved toward the door, but Cam was faster. He grabbed my arm and pulled me behind him.

"Harper, wait. Let me check it out first."

"Check what out?" I looked at the people circled around. "What's going on?"

One man heard me and pointed. "There's a lady out there, lying on the sidewalk. I think she's just been mugged."

Thirteen

My heart leapt to my throat. "Jo's been mugged?"

"Harper, wait here. I'll check on her."

I heard Cam's words but couldn't heed them. I followed him through the door, hardly daring to breathe. Hardly daring to look for fear of what I might see . . .

With a little assistance from Cam, Jo climbed to her feet, a look of disgust written so plainly on her face, I expelled the breath in my lungs in a rush. She was just fine.

I hurried to her. "Jo, what happened? Are you all right?"

"Would you like to sit down?" Cam asked in the same instant. "How do you feel?"

Jo bent to brush herself off. "I'm perfectly fine."

"Are you sure?" Cam said. "What happened? Were you mugged? Did someone knock you down?"

"Knock me down?" Jo snorted and jammed her hands on her hips, her purse dangling from her arm. "I *fell* down. I tripped chasing after the guy who tried to steal my purse."

My eyes widened. "Jo! You didn't."

She nodded and bent to retrieve a smashed Styrofoam cup from the sidewalk. "I might have caught him too, if it weren't for this." She held the cup between two fingers and then dropped it in a nearby trashcan.

Cam held up a pen and notepad. "Okay, let's start at the beginning. What exactly happened?"

Jo smoothed her hand over her face. Now that the rush of adrenaline had begun to fade, her fingers started to shake. She looked around and motioned toward a bench under the restaurant window. "You know, maybe I will take a seat."

"Of course." Shoving the notepad into his pocket, Cam stepped toward her and took her elbow to help her to the bench.

The door to the restaurant flung open, and Julie rushed outside. Eyes wide, she looked from Jo, to Cam, to me. "What happened? Is everyone all right?"

"Everyone's fine, Julie," I said. "But my friend could use some water."

"Of course. I'll be right back." She ducked inside, and I turned my attention back to Jo.

"Tell us what happened."

She clutched her knees and sucked in a breath. "I was standing near the street watching for Jeanine when I saw a man rushing toward me." She pointed down the street to her right. "He was coming from that direction. Before I could even think, he shoved me and made a grab for my purse."

My heart thumped listening to her story. "What did you do?"

A twinkle in her eyes, she said, "I threw my coffee in his face. Extra hot. I bet he wasn't expecting that."

My gaze fell to the brown liquid pooling on the sidewalk. "So that's what you slipped on?"

She nodded. "I heard him howl and then he took off in that direction." She pointed across the parking lot toward a cluster of buildings and an alley running between. "I wasn't really trying to catch him. I just thought maybe I could see where he was going or what he was driving . . ."

I patted her shoulder while Cam wrote down everything she said. "Any chance you got a look at his face, Mrs. Anderson?"

She shook her head. "I'm afraid not. He was wearing some kind of mask. It looked like a skull."

Cam frowned and pulled out his phone. He typed something and then turned it for us to see. "Did it look like this?"

She tapped the screen in excitement. "That's it." She squinted and read the description. "A face shield?"

"Motorcyclists use them for protection from the weather," Cam said, sliding his phone back into his pocket.

"So does that mean the man who attacked Jo was riding a motorcycle?" I asked.

"It's possible." Cam reached for Jo's arm as she started to rise. "Are you all right, Mrs. Anderson? Would you like me to call you an ambulance?"

"There's no need. I'm fine," she said, and this time, I knew she meant it. The danger had passed and with it her sudden attack of the shakes.

I waved as a familiar Ford pulled into the parking lot. "There's Jeanine and the girls." I looked at Jo. "Will you be okay finishing up with Cam while I go fill them in on what's happened?"

"Of course." She eyed him a little cynically. "Do you have any more questions for me, Deputy?"

I shot Cam an apologetic glance. He would have his hands full now that Jo had gotten her vinegar back. I joined Jeanine and the others. The moment I finished explaining what had happened, they rushed to surround her. Thankfully, Cam had gotten all the information he needed and moved aside to meet me.

"Looks like she's going to be none the worse for wear."

I watched her with a wry grin and crossed my arms. Julie had returned with a cup of water, and between sips, Jo was reenacting everything that had happened, including the part where she threw the coffee at her assailant. "It would take more than a failed mugging to ruffle her feathers. She's one strong lady."

He agreed with a chuckle. "I'm going to ask around inside, see if anyone in there saw anything before I head down the street." He tipped his head toward the alley where Jo said the mugger had gone. "I doubt I'll find anything, but it might be worth a look."

"Thank you."

He nodded. "Will you and your friends be all right in the meantime?"

"I think so. This trip sure didn't end up the way we'd planned."

"Yeah. I'm sorry about that."

"It's okay." I paused and pushed my hands into my pockets. "Thanks for being here, Cam. I mean, I know it's your job, but I think we all feel a little better having you . . ."

Suddenly aware that I was rambling, I stopped and tugged nervously at a lock of my hair.

He smiled. "Be careful, okay? I'll call you this afternoon to see how everyone is doing."

"Thanks."

I drew a deep breath as he headed for the restaurant. When he was inside, I turned my attention back to Jo.

"I'm so glad you're all right," Penny said, running her hand over Jo's arm. "I don't think I would have had the presence of mind to react as quickly as you did."

"Me either," Evelyn agreed. "But Jo, you took such a risk. Why didn't you just let him have the purse?"

Jo reached inside and pulled out Woodsy. "I might have, if it weren't for this." She handed it to me with a grunt. "I think I'm done babysitting that thing. It's your turn."

I stared at the sock-wrapped statue in my hand. "You think this is what he was after? But how could that be? No one saw me give it to you. It had to have been a coincidence."

She grimaced and slipped the strap of her purse over her shoulder. "You're probably right. Either way, I'd say that thing is bad luck."

"Goodness . . . that owl. We have got to know more about it." Jeanine turned to me. "What did Julie's boyfriend have to say?"

"Nothing, I'm afraid. He got held up at work."

"Oh no." Morgan groaned and looked from me to Jo. "What are we going to do?"

"Well . . ." Jo lifted one shoulder in a shrug. "We could still talk to Marion's sister."

"Who?" Morgan and Jeanine asked in unison.

"Helen Gregoire," I said. "According to Cam, she's Marion's sister."

Penny's eyes grew wide. "You're kidding."

I shook my head. "Her real name is Helen

Clebum. Gregoire is her professional name."

"And speaking of her profession . . ." Morgan stepped forward. "It looks like her story about being an art dealer is true. We found all kinds of stuff online about her. The places she's worked all appear to be reputable businesses."

I frowned, thinking. "Okay. What about the owl?"

"That's another story," Jeanine said with a shake of her head. "Unfortunately, we just don't have any idea what we're looking for, so it was hard to narrow down our search."

Jo held up her phone. "So? Shall I give Marion a call?"

"I don't think we have any choice." I nodded toward her phone. "Call her. See if you can set something up for this afternoon, maybe around one?" I glanced at my watch. "That should give her a little over an hour."

We waited while Jo placed the call. When she finished, she hung up with a nod.

"We're all set. Marion said she'd get ahold of her sister and have her meet us at her place."

"Good. In the meantime, let's grab something to eat." Penny rubbed her stomach. "I'm starving."

"Me too, but maybe we find someplace new?" Evelyn hitched her thumb toward the door of the restaurant. "This place is starting to freak me out as much as that crazy owl."

Jeanine laughed and led the way toward her car. "I'm pretty sure I saw a diner just south of here. We can grab some sandwiches there."

Jeanine was right. In just a little over an hour, we'd eaten and were headed back toward Marion's bed-and-breakfast. This time, there was a sporty little compact car parked out front. Jo squeezed my hand.

"Are we sure about this?"

"Do you have another idea?"

She frowned and reached for the door handle. "Unfortunately, no. I wish I did."

"So do I," I muttered under my breath as I followed Jo and the others up the stairs.

Marion met us at the door, Helen at her elbow. Just Helen. No masked muggers or mysterious-looking henchmen. I let out a breath. Like the first time we'd met, Helen was perfect — every hair in place, her clothes and makeup flawless. She looked at me curiously, but with a sharpness in her gaze that made me think perhaps she didn't regard me with the same esteem. I smoothed my hand over my unruly curls.

"Please, come in," Marion said, holding the door wide. She motioned to Jo. "Your friend told us what happened. I can hardly believe it."

There was murmured agreement all around and then Marion slipped her arm around Helen. "Jo said you know my sister?"

"We met very briefly at an estate sale." I

stepped forward to shake Helen's hand. "Thank you for coming."

"Of course. I'm actually very glad to help. Marion said you have some questions about the owl you purchased?"

"I do. I'm hoping you might be able to shed some light on it."

Marion gestured toward the dining room. "Why don't we all come in here? There are enough chairs for everyone."

We moved that way and then Marion paused at the door. "Would anyone like something to drink?"

Helen smiled and shook her head. "Ever the hostess."

Seeing her tease her sister allayed a few of my fears. I took the chair opposite the one Helen chose and set Woodsy, still wrapped in my socks, on the table.

"The day I bought this, you said something about it being a fine piece," I said, jumping into the reason for our visit.

Around us, everyone quieted and turned their gazes to Helen. She folded her hands on the table, but instead of answering right away, she tapped her manicured fingernails lightly against the back of her other hand.

"Harper . . . may I call you that?"

I agreed with a tip of my head.

"Harper," she continued, "why don't you tell me everything that's happened since you bought that owl. I understand there was a mishap here at the B&B?"

My gaze skipped to Marion. "Yes, this does seem to be where it all started."

Drawing a breath, I relayed the details that had brought us to this point and then bumped Woodsy further onto the table.

"Needless to say, I thought it necessary that I learn what I could about this thing, which is why we called you."

"Interesting." Still, Helen made no move toward Woodsy. Her gaze flicked to Jo. "And today, you said someone tried to mug you?"

"That's correct."

"Did you have the owl with you at the time?"

Jo looked to me.

I nodded. "But there's no way anyone could have known —" I cut off, thinking of Julie and the quiet corner where she'd put us. Could it be?

I straightened and clasped my hands in my lap. "Do you know something about this owl?"

Helen's gaze measured me for several long seconds. Finally, she nodded. "I think perhaps I might."

She leaned forward, her jewel-toned lips forming a firm line. "Have you ever heard of Myanmar jadeite?"

I shook my head. "Jadeite. Is that different from regular jade?"

Her lips curved in a slight smile. "You could

say that. Jadeite deposits from the northern regions of Myanmar are touted as the highest quality in the world. It is very rare and very, very precious."

"How precious?" Morgan whispered.

Helen's gaze swung to her. "Depending on the buyer? A piece like the one Harper bought could be worth upward of three hundred thousand."

"Dollars?" Penny pinched her fingers over her mouth. "Oops. Sorry."

Helen shook her head. "Quite all right." She spread her hands on the table. "The truth is, the demand for jade in Asian countries has reached a frenzied height over the last decade. Finest jade, like what I suspect Harper's owl consists of, has increased to over three thousand dollars an ounce, making it far more valuable than gold."

"That's incredible," I said.

"That's not all." She sat back, calm except for the drumming of her nails against the tabletop. "Several years ago, a collection of jade figurines was stolen from a local museum. Now and then, pieces from the collection have shown up on the black market. I suspect . . ." She paused and directed her gaze to me. "I have reason to suspect that your owl may have been a part of it."

She held up one finger. "You must understand, this is pure speculation on my part. I've only seen photos of the collection. But if

I'm correct, you could have something very valuable on your hands."

My pulse climbed as she talked. "You would know if this was part of that collection if you saw it?"

She nodded slowly. "I think so."

My mind made up, I pushed the owl all the way across the table toward her. Our gazes met and held as she reached for it. While she unwrapped it from the socks, I held my breath, searching her face for clues to what she was thinking as she rolled it gently back and forth in her palm. Finally, she blew out a long breath, excitement making her eyes bright as she looked at me.

"I can't believe it."

"What?" Evelyn said. "Is it what you thought?"

Helen let out a small laugh then nodded in disbelief. "After all these years, I can hardly believe another piece has turned up, but there's no other explanation. I'm almost certain this owl is part of that missing collection!"

FOURTEEN

There was stunned silence around the table for several seconds following Helen's announcement, and then talk erupted from every direction at once. How did she know for sure the owl was part of the stolen collection? How had it ended up at the estate sale? If it was stolen from a museum, who did the owl belong to?

Finally, I held up my hand. "Wait. Everyone wait, please."

Slowly, the room quieted and I turned to Helen. "You said the collection was stolen from a museum?"

She nodded. "About ten years ago. I'm sure if you searched online you could find more information about it."

"So then, what do we do with the owl?" Morgan asked.

"We have to turn it over to the authorities," I said, before anyone else could speak.

Jo nodded. "She's right. They would be able to get it back to the right people."

"And assist you in claiming your reward," Helen said.

Silence fell as once again all eyes were trained on her.

"What do you mean, reward?" Jo said.

Helen shrugged. "Several years ago, there was a pretty hefty reward offered for information leading to the return of the stolen collection. I don't know about now, but surely the museum would offer something. That little owl is supposed to be the centerpiece."

Jo looked at me and then rose from the table. "I'm calling Deputy Davis."

She bustled from the room, and I shook my head, hardly able to process everything Helen had said. "So, that's why you were so interested when you saw me buy the owl at the estate sale?"

"Well, sort of. I admit, I didn't get a clear look at the owl, so I couldn't be sure."

"Hey, what about your mail?" Penny said.

Helen looked at her, blinking. "My what?"

"There was a box here for you. We saw it earlier today."

"Oh, that." Marion chuckled. "Helen has an apartment in Wichita, but sometimes, when she's purchasing a piece of art for herself, she doesn't want it sitting outside her door, so she has it delivered here." She pointed to a painting resting atop the buffet against the wall. "That is her latest find."

"It's beautiful," Jeanine said.

Helen inclined her head. "Thank you."

Jo returned and laid her phone on the table. "He's on his way. I tell you, this has got to be the wackiest case that man has ever heard."

"Well, I for one am glad it's over." Evelyn swiped her hand across her brow.

"Is it?" Jo raised her brow. "We still don't know who put the nuts in Harper's tea."

"Or who tried to steal the owl from Jo this afternoon," Penny added.

I nodded. "You're right. Until Cam gets here, I think we probably should do our best just to sit tight and hope nothing else happens."

Our nervous laughter was cut short by the ringing of my telephone. I looked at the display. "It's Julie. I told her to see about setting up another appointment with her boyfriend."

I took the phone, holding my palm over the mouthpiece until I'd slipped into the kitchen, away from the girls' excited chatter. "Hey, Julie."

"Harper?"

"Yes, it's me. Thanks for checking back with me."

"No problem. Listen, J. T. stopped by the restaurant just after you left. I hope you don't mind, but I sent him to the bed-and-breakfast so he could talk to you about your owl."

I blinked in confusion. "You sent him here? But how did you know where we'd gone?"

"Oh, I heard you all talking when I brought Jo her water. You're not mad, are you? I tried calling, but no one answered."

I glanced at the display screen. It did indicate a missed call. I swallowed and replaced the phone to my ear. "Listen, Julie, I'm really grateful for you getting ahold of your boyfriend, but there's really no need to send him out here. I actually found out what I needed to know from Marion's sister. Do you think maybe you could call him and tell him not to bother?"

"Oh. Well, I would, but it probably wouldn't do any good. He's probably already there. He left almost twenty minutes ago."

Already here? I crossed to the kitchen sink and leaned forward to peer out the window. "Julie, are you sure? I don't see any cars in the driveway. Maybe he got lost or something."

"I don't think so. J. T's pretty good with directions. If he shows up, would you mind sending him back to the restaurant?"

"Of course. I'm really sorry, Julie."

"Don't worry about it. I just wish we could've been more help."

Behind me, I heard the doorbell ring. "Oh wait. Someone's at the door. It must be J. T. Can you hold on a minute, and I'll go check."

"Sure."

I dropped the phone to my side and hurried down the hall. Marion was already at the door. I stopped her before she could actually open it. "Marion, I think that might be for me. Julie said J. T. is on his way over."

"Oh, well in that case, I'll let you get it." She smiled and ducked back into the dining room.

I reached for the knob and gave it a twist. "Hi, J. T. I'm so sorry . . ." I trailed off as I caught sight of the stranger standing on the doorstep. Only it wasn't a stranger.

"You." I stared at the man in the argyle sweater from the estate sale. "You're J. T.?"

His lips curled in a self-conscious grin. "Afraid so." He stepped forward and extended his hand. "We may have gotten off on the wrong foot. Please, allow me to introduce myself. I'm J. T. Miller, Julie's boyfriend."

Though he continued talking, his words passed straight over my head. I couldn't hear them. I was too busy staring at the coffee stains on his shirt.

Fifteen

J. T's gaze followed mine to the feathery brown stains on his shirt. Slowly, his smile faded. "Well, now, it's a shame you had to notice that."

He drew his other hand out from behind his back. In it was clutched a knife — the large, ugly kind I'd seen hunters use.

He put it to his lips. "Shh," he said, jabbing the tip back down the hall. "Turn around, and not one sound unless you want one of your friends to get hurt."

What else could I do? I could make a dash for it, but there was no way Jo could outrun him, and I couldn't leave her.

"Harper? Are you there?"

Julie! My gaze dropped to the phone still clutched in my hand. Had she heard what J. T. said? Maybe she would call for help.

J. T smiled, and he tilted his head toward the phone. "Go ahead. Answer her."

I brought the phone slowly to my ear. "Julie?"

"I'm here."

Her voice had a hollow quality to it, almost as if . . .

As if she were in the same room.

I swallowed hard as she stepped through the door behind J. T. Smiling, she wiggled her phone and then hit the END CALL button and shoved it into her jeans pocket.

I narrowed my eyes and pointed at her angrily. "You . . . you were the one who told J. T. about my nut allergy. You probably even ground up the nuts for him at the restaurant so he could put them in Marion's tea."

She shrugged. "It was a diversion. Nothing personal." She looked at J. T. "Where are they?"

He tipped his head toward the dining room. I stifled a groan as Jo stepped from there into the hall. "Harper? Who was at the door?"

Catching sight of the knife in J. T's hand, her eyes widened.

"Jo, get back!" I didn't have time for more. J. T. grabbed my arm and yanked me against his chest. With his knife at my throat, I didn't dare move.

"Where's the owl?" Julie said.

I marveled at the steadiness of her voice. She just as easily could have been asking if we wanted more tea.

Jo backed up and motioned toward the dining room. "It's in here."

"Move." J. T. thrust me forward so that we

eased into the dining room. I heard the chairs scrape back and one clattered to the floor as everyone huddled together against the far wall. I heard the questions, the startled cries, but I was too absorbed in the blade pinching the skin at my neck to actually make them out. Except for the knock on the front door. That sound kicked my pulse into overdrive.

"It's the cop," Julie said. "We have to let him in or he'll get suspicious."

When J. T. hesitated, she got angry. Reaching into the waistband of her pants, she pulled out a pistol and brandished it in his face. "We can't outrun him. Our only chance is to incapacitate him and lock the others up in a closet or something so we have time to get away."

"And we need a gun to do that? I thought you said no one would get hurt."

Julie sighed and rested her hand on her hip. "Fine. If you think you can take on the cop with just a knife, go right ahead." She motioned toward the door with the gun. "You saw him. He's six feet of solid muscle. He'll knock that knife out of your hand like that." She snapped her fingers to emphasize her point.

Finally, J. T. nodded, but he pressed the knife tighter to my throat. "Do it."

I couldn't move. With every breath the knife blade dug a little deeper. I took small, shallow breaths as I listened to Julie talking to

Cam. Behind me, I felt J. T. straining to hear, straining to pounce.

I couldn't let them do it. I couldn't let them lure Cam inside. There was no telling what might happen if I did.

I pulled my head forward, cringing when I felt the resistance of the knife. Across the room, I met Jo's gaze. Saw the pleading in her eyes. She knew. But she wouldn't stop me. Her lips moved, and I knew she was praying.

"Come on in, Deputy. We're all in the dining room."

Julie's voice was getting closer. It was now or never. I snapped my head back with as much force as I could muster. At the same time, I jammed my foot back and down, smashing onto J. T's instep. The shock loosened his hold on my neck. I swung to my left, away from the knife, but not far enough. White hot pain streaked across the right side of my throat. I doubled over and slapped my hands over the wound, nearly passing out as blood . . . my blood . . . seeped through my fingers.

Squeezing my eyes shut, I closed out the screams and the thud of crashing bodies and focused on drawing the next breath. And the next. Until it was quiet and all I could hear was the pounding of my own heart.

"Harper?"

Cam's voice floated to me from a distance.

"Harper, let me see."

He pulled me up by the shoulders then covered my hands with his.

"Let me see, Harper."

I managed a whimper and shook my head. Direct pressure. That's what I'd learned in first-aid class. Direct pressure to keep the blood . . .

"Harper, please. I have to see it."

His fingers were strong and insistent, pulling back on mine until I had to let go. I grabbed his arms instead and snapped my gaze to the hardened muscles of his jaw and kept it there. I couldn't look into his eyes while he probed. I was terrified of what I might see there. I felt my heart racing, but his pulse was wild too. I saw it in the ragged rhythm at the base of his throat above the collar of his white T-shirt. Suddenly, I felt his arms relax, and he blew out a breath.

"Thank God. Thank You, God." He pulled me close, cradling me against his chest with one hand while the other cupped the back of my head. "You're okay. It's a flesh wound, Harper. You're okay."

The tears came then, making it impossible for me to see. Around me, I heard more sniffles.

I pulled away from Cam's chest. "Was anybody hurt?"

A few feet away, J. T. was sprawled on the floor, unconscious and unmoving. Julie was also on the floor, but Morgan, Jeanine, Evelyn, and Penny all sat on top of her, holding her still as she grunted and moaned to be let up.

I blinked. "Where's Jo?"

"Right here." She stepped in from the hall with Marion and Helen close behind. "We waited until Julie's attention was focused on Cam, and then we rushed her from behind and knocked the gun away."

"And then the rest of us jumped on top of her," Penny said, sniffing as she wiped the tears from her cheeks.

"And Jo whacked J. T. with her purse," Morgan said. "Oh my goodness, Harper, you scared us to death."

"Are you sure you're okay?" Jeanine said. She too wiped tears from her cheeks.

I nodded. Cam was still holding me, though not as tightly as before. I gasped as I realized he had blood trickling from a rip in his sleeve and more from his knuckles.

"You're hurt."

He shook his head. "It's a scratch. I'm fine." He grabbed a handkerchief from his pocket and pressed it to my neck before looking to Jo. She hurried over and he eased me gently into her arms. "You got her, Jo?"

She nodded, both arms holding tightly to my waist. "I've got her."

He stepped toward J. T., who let out a low moan as Cam reached for his handcuffs and slapped them on his wrists. I watched, content to huddle against Jo as he read J. T. his rights then crossed to do the same with Julie.

"All this fuss because of one little owl," Jo muttered.

She was right; it hardly seemed possible. But at least now it was over and my friends were safe. I was safe. And so was Cam.

I shuddered as Cam dragged J. T. to his feet. Though our gazes only locked for a split second, I could read the revulsion and anger in his eyes before Cam jerked him away.

"It's going to be okay, Harper," Jo whispered, rubbing her hand lightly over my arm.

I blew out a breath and nodded. It *was* going to be okay. Now. But I still couldn't wait to get home. As far as estate sales were concerned, I'd done enough shopping to last me a lifetime.

Sixteen

The last bell of the day rang, sending a roomful of first graders scurrying for their coats.

"Bailey?" I rose from my desk and crooked a finger toward the little girl. "Would you mind staying for just a moment, please?"

A worried frown twisted her face. "Am I in trouble, Miss Daggett?"

"Not at all, sweetie. I just have a little surprise for you."

A knock sounded on the door and I glanced at my watch. Right on time.

"Come on in, Cam." I circled my desk and crouched down to look at Bailey eye-to-eye. "Bailey, I'd like you to meet my friend, Deputy Davis."

Her wide blue eyes traveled up and up as he joined me next to the desk.

"Hello, Bailey."

She grabbed one of her braids and twisted it around her finger. "Hello." Her gaze roamed Cam's uniform. "You're a police officer?"

He smiled. "That's right."

Once again, a light knock sounded on the door, and Bailey's grandmother stepped through. "Miss Daggett? You said you wanted to see me?"

"Hi, Mrs. Munroe. Thank you so much for stopping by." I crossed to the door and closed it behind her, then motioned toward the student desks. They were small, but we all fit, except for Cam, who was much too tall to squeeze into one. He pulled out a chair instead, his knees almost touching his chest as he hunkered down onto it.

I hid a smile. Cam had spent quite a bit of time in my classroom over the last couple of weeks. I made myself promise to buy him a regular-sized chair the next time he came to visit.

"So, what is all this about, Miss Daggett? I hope everything is okay in the classroom." Mrs. Munroe shot a worried glance at her granddaughter.

"Everything is fine, Mrs. Munroe. Bailey is one of my best students. I love having her. That's not why I asked you to come by."

Mrs. Munroe's face relaxed, and so did Bailey's. I looked at Cam. He pulled an envelope from his jacket pocket and gave it to me. "Are you sure about this?"

I nodded then took a deep breath and turned to Mrs. Munroe.

"I'm sure by now you've probably heard

about everything that happened to me over the Thanksgiving break."

She nodded and her eyes grew wide. "It was in the newspaper. Quite an adventure you had. I'm glad you made it through safely."

I looked at Cam and smiled. An adventure was one way to put it. He took my hand and gave it a squeeze, then just as quickly let go.

"I'm glad too, Mrs. Munroe," I said, turning my gaze back to her.

"Grandma showed me your picture," Bailey said. "What happened to the owl? Did you keep it?"

"No, I had to return it to the museum," I said. "You see, it didn't really belong to me."

Bailey's nose crinkled as she processed this information. I'm sure, in her mind, it would have been better to keep the owl, but then I couldn't have done this.

I held out the envelope to Mrs. Munroe. "I'd like you to have this."

She took the envelope and examined it curiously. "I don't understand."

"Please, just look inside," I urged.

Shrugging, she pulled back the flap and took out the letter tucked inside. I saw her eyes widen as she read, and the paper began to tremble. Finally, she lifted her hand to her mouth.

"What is it, Grandma?" Bailey leaned closer to see.

Her eyes brimming with tears, Mrs. Munroe

met my gaze. "This is your reward money. I can't accept it."

I shook my head. "It's already done. The curator said it would be a few days before the owl is authenticated and all the paperwork is finalized, but I've already given them instructions to write the check to you when you're ready to have your surgery."

Her tears fell freely then. I grabbed a box of tissues from my desk and handed them to her.

Bailey stood and began patting her grandmother's shoulder. "Is everything okay, Grandma?"

"Everything's fine, sweetheart," she said between sniffles. Struck by a sudden thought, she looked at me. "What about Bailey? I can't leave her."

"I already thought about that." I smiled and reached out to grasp Bailey's hand. "How would you like to come and stay with me while your grandmother recovers from her surgery?"

For a long moment, Bailey didn't answer. She looked to her grandmother, who nodded encouragingly.

"What about school?" she said at last.

"Well, Christmas is coming soon, but after that, I figure you'll just ride to class with me." I tipped my head to peer into her face. "What do you think?"

Uncertainty troubled her gaze. "Will my

grandma be better after her surgery?"

All three of us nodded, and slowly, a smile spread over her lips. "Okay, Miss Daggett."

I gasped as she leapt toward me, her small arms clinging to my neck. I squeezed back tightly as a shiver rolled through her thin body. Though she hadn't said much, this was one smart little girl. She knew what surgery meant for her grandmother. I blew out a happy sigh, fighting tears of my own as Bailey pulled back to hug her grandmother.

"We'll talk some more once you get your surgery scheduled," I said, rising along with Cam and Mrs. Munroe.

"And don't worry about your house," Cam said. "Some of the other deputies and I plan on keeping a close eye on it until you get back home."

She thanked me again then turned to Cam, who blushed and ducked his head under her lavish words. I couldn't help but smile as she and Bailey walked out, both of them chatting excitedly. I pressed my hand to my chest, my heart full.

"That was a good thing you did."

Cam was looking at me, his eyes shining with approval and . . . something else. I swallowed nervously.

"It was the right thing. That's all that matters."

He stepped closer, his hands claiming both of mine. "Are we still on for dinner tonight?"

I smiled. "You aren't sick of me? That's going to make three times this week."

He shook his head firmly. "Never."

I held my breath as his head dipped closer, but then he pulled back and looked at me, his hazel eyes twinkling. "Why do I get the feeling that dating you will never be boring?"

"Is that what we're doing? Dating, I mean?" I smiled teasingly, but my insides trembled while I waited for his answer.

"For now." His voice roughened as he slid both arms around me to pull me closer. "I'm pretty sure I'm going to want more. A lot more. If you'll have me."

"Oh, I'll have you, Deputy Davis," I said, tilting my head back and closing my eyes as his kiss melted over my mouth.

My heart thrilled as his kiss deepened. There was love in that touch, and a future full of promise. He offered both.

It was all I'd ever wanted.

ABOUT THE AUTHOR

Elizabeth Ludwig is an award-winning author who is an accomplished speaker and teacher, and often attends conferences and seminars where she lectures on editing for fiction writers, crafting effective novel proposals, and conducting successful editor/agent interviews. Along with her husband and two children, Elizabeth makes her home in the great state of Texas.

■ ■ ■ ■

Nutty as a
Fruitcake

BY JANICE THOMPSON

■ ■ ■ ■

ONE

"Seriously?" I argued aloud with the temperamental lock on my bakery door. "Again?" Three mornings in a row I'd struggled to get into my shop, but today's lower temperatures gave the task a sense of urgency. A shiver wriggled its way down my spine as I fought to turn the key one more time. When I heard the familiar *click,* I breathed a sigh of relief. "Finally."

The bell on the door jingled as I pushed it open. The familiar sound put me at ease right away. As I stepped into the warmth of the shop, the tantalizing scents of ginger, pumpkin, cinnamon, and brown sugar greeted me. I breathed in the aroma, all concerns about the lock erased in an instant. Other folks might need antianxiety meds on a day like today. Me? Just give me baked goods. Pumpkin bread, warm-from-the-oven blueberry scones, gooey mint chocolate chip brownies, a nutty slice of Italian cream cake — any of these could set things right in a hurry. And right now, I needed things to go right. With Christmas season upon me, the Mad Batter was in full swing.

I stumbled my way across the front of the shop and willed my eyes to adjust to the dark. They did not. My left knee rammed into a chair and it toppled over, hitting the tile floor with a *clang.* Before I could even let out a "Y'ouch!" my right elbow caught on the edge of the tall glass case that housed the pies. Well, terrific. I might not be able to see but I could certainly feel.

I rubbed my elbow, reached down to set the chair aright, then hobbled past a couple of small café tables. By the time I reached the light switch on the far side of the room, I felt as if I'd made my way through an obstacle course. Maybe I should go on one of those Ninja shows on TV. The layout of the Mad Batter was just as precarious as any of their courses, and I tackled it on a daily basis. Quite the feat. Without the cheering fans, of course. Someone should give me a medal.

I flipped the switch, flooding the front of the shop with light. By now, the pain in my elbow had subsided. Good thing, because I needed to be in tip-top shape today. With over a hundred fruitcakes on this week's schedule, even something as simple as a bad elbow or aching knee could really slow things down.

One hundred fruitcakes.

I could kick myself. Offering to raise funds

for a missions organization in Haiti was a noble effort, one I did not regret. But why had I gone with fruitcakes? Sure, the Christmas season was upon us. But cranberry scones would've been easier. Snowball cookies, even, or Santa-themed cookies and cupcakes. Why, oh why, had I settled on a complicated product that few people even enjoyed?

I leaned against the wall and rubbed my knee. As I did, my purse slipped off my shoulder and hit the floor, its contents tumbling out. Terrific. Just what I needed on an already crazy morning. I leaned down and tidied up the mess, then spoke the same words that saw me through most days at the shop: "Power through, Jeanine. You've got this." Of course, I usually gave myself that little pep talk much later in the day when my back ached from rolling out cookie dough or my wrists begged for mercy after piping buttercream for hours on end.

My gaze shifted to the glass cases at the front of the house. A sparse array of baked goods — mostly cupcakes, cookies, hand-pies, and the like — took up the bottom shelf space, but customers had stripped the top shelves bare of the muffins I'd baked yesterday morning. I'd need to restock, and soon. In three hours, this place would be filled with friends and loved ones from my small town of Oak Grove, eager for my special of the day — orange-cranberry muffins. I might also knock out a couple dozen oatmeal-cinnamon, along with the usual daily offerings — chocolate chip, blueberry, bran, and apple.

But first . . . coffee. I'd never make it through the baking process without that delicious Haitian blend I'd grown to love. I even preferred it to the house special at the Coffee Perk, though I would never tell Morgan that.

I gave the kitchen light switch a firm snap of the finger. If you didn't wriggle it just so, the lights would flicker. True to form, they blinked, went dark, then popped back on. "Work with me here," I urged them. The room stayed lit. I whispered up a prayer of thanks, walked to my tiny office at the back of the kitchen, and set my purse on the desk. I should probably check my ingredients for the fruitcakes, but that empty coffeepot kept calling my name, so I turned my attention to filling it.

Minutes later, with a cup of the steaming brew in hand, I surveyed my sparkling clean kitchen. I prided myself on neatness. In fact, I was even a little neurotic about it. My back ached just thinking about all the dishes I'd washed before leaving the store last night. But, it was part of the process. In a couple of hours this place would be a wreck once more. That beautiful Hobart 30-quart mixer — my pride and joy — would be sticky with batter, its blades coated in the gooey stuff. Muffin tins would be crusted over, countertops covered in crumbs, and kitchen sink stacked high with dirty mixing bowls, measuring cups, and utensils.

But only if I got to work.

I hefted a large bag of sugar from the storeroom and started mixing the ingredients for the orange-cranberry muffins. Once I got those out of the way, I could turn my attention to the apple. They took a little longer to bake, thanks to the moisture from the fruit.

About halfway into the process, my assistant, Natalie, entered the kitchen, singing a familiar worship song at the top of her lungs. As always, she'd pulled her mop of dark curls into a twisted bun. I had to give it to her. Natalie had the best attitude around. If the glass was half full to others, it was three-quarters full to this twentysomething. I rarely saw the girl without her classic smile. And that silly snort of hers . . . the one that came out whenever she laughed? Priceless.

"G'morning!" Her cheerful voice sounded as she bounded toward the office to set her purse down.

"Good morning to you too." I couldn't help but notice the snow on her coat collar. "Did you drive in or walk?"

"Walked." She threw her arms open and turned in a circle and snow flew everywhere. "I just love it. Don't you?"

"Ugh. No. I'm not a fan of all this snow."

"Oh, I am." Natalie's eyes sparkled as she

pulled off her coat and tossed it over the back of a chair. "I love everything about the Christmas season, and working here has only added to my passion. All those sweet Christmas treats, pumpkin coffee, peppermint tea . . . it's all so wonderful."

"You're so easy to please, Natalie."

"Am I?" She looked my way, perhaps wondering if I was making fun of her.

"You are. Everything about you is easy and sweet."

"I think that's the nicest compliment anyone's ever paid me, Jeanine." She walked my way and threw her arms around me for a hug. "Thank you for that."

"You're welcome. Now, I guess we'd better get to work or the customers won't have any of those sweet treats you were referring to. I want to get the muffins out of the way so I can deal with —"

"Snowball cookies?"

"No."

"Christmas ornament cookies?"

"No."

"Peppermint bark cheesecake?"

"No, Natalie. Fruitcakes."

Her smile tilted downward into a frown. "Oh right. Fruitcakes." She reached for an apron and fidgeted with the ties.

I did my best to sound cheerful in my response to her lack of zeal. "Like I said yesterday, you don't have to help. You can take care of the usual stuff while I handle the fruitcakes. This whole thing is for a missions fund-raiser, totally my own deal, not yours to worry about."

"I like missions. I just don't like," her nose wrinkled as she said, "fruitcake." Natalie finished tying her apron and gave me a little shrug. "Well, not much, anyway."

"I know, I know." I'd heard all about it yesterday.

She lit into a story about a friend of hers who'd apparently broken a tooth eating a fruitcake; then she switched gears and told an over-the-top tale of another friend who'd ended up in the ER because of a candied fruit allergy. By the time she finished, I was nearly ready to give up on the idea myself.

Then she smiled that terrific, gracious smile of hers. "Of course I'll help you with the fruitcakes, Jeanine. A baker doesn't have to love everything she bakes. I can't stand pumpkin muffins and I make those all the time, so I don't suppose it would hurt me to make a fruitcake or two."

"Or a hundred." I offered a strained smile. "And I had no idea you hated pumpkin, just FYI."

She shrugged. "I'm not a fan. What can I say?"

She'd already said enough. Natalie had agreed to help me with the fruitcakes. To-gether, we would knock them out and the children in Haiti would benefit from our labors. Somehow, knowing that made me look forward to the task. Almost, anyway.

By the time our first customers jingled the bell on the front door of the shop, we were ready for them. Cases were filled with warm muffins, their various scents merging together to form a wonderful cacophony of aromas. I'd fired up both coffeemakers, offering customers the Haitian blend and the Coffee Perk's blend as well.

Thinking of the coffee shop reminded me that I needed to give my good friend Morgan a call. When things slowed down, I headed to my office to do just that. She answered on the third ring with her usual jovial, "It's a good morning at the Coffee Perk. How can we help you?"

"Well, you could start by telling me if you prefer cranberry muffins or blueberry," I countered. "I'll stop by in a couple of hours to drop off today's order."

"Well, hello to you too, Jeanine." She laughed. "I guess we'll go with cranberry, since it's the Christmas season and all. Oh, and bring more of those pumpkin ones too. They're going like hotcakes. And then the usual sugar cookies and snowballs. You know what folks like."

"Right."

I must've paused too long because she came back with, "You okay over there?"

"Yeah. Actually, just talking myself down from the ledge before I fall off."

"What do you mean?"

I shifted the phone to my other ear. "I can't believe I have to turn out a hundred fruitcakes this week on top of my usual orders, that's all. I must've been nuts to think I could pull it off."

"Make that a hundred and seventeen," she countered. "We've taken in quite a few new orders over the past couple days."

"No way." I did my best not to groan aloud. "Seriously? Seventeen more? Are you sure?"

"Yep. And if I were you, I'd make even more. Folks who didn't order will still want to buy after the fact. You know how it is."

"Right." I paused to think it through. "Did all these people pay in advance?"

"Yep." She laughed. "Paid in cash, every one of 'em. That's what you wanted, right?"

"Actually, Matt was the one who suggested cash."

"Matt Kimball? The missionary?"

"Right. I met with him a couple weeks back. He said a lot of good-hearted people write checks that end up bouncing, so asking for cash was a way around that. I believe the words 'sadder but wiser' were used, if I remember correctly."

"Makes sense. But if you're in over your head with the baking, I can refund some of this money and tell folks you can't take on any more. I'm sure they'll understand."

I plopped into my office chair and leaned back. "You know me better than that, Morgan. I'll work around the clock if I have to. I'm just wondering how I'm going to put out all my usual product and still bake fruitcakes on the side."

"Natalie will help."

"Right. She's awesome in the kitchen, and I'm grateful for her help at the front counter, but I have to mix certain portions of the fruitcake batter myself."

"Why is that?"

"Because no one knows my secret family recipe, and I promised my great aunt Ida I'd never share it with anyone."

"Even Natalie?" Morgan sounded astounded.

"At least for now. I'll rethink that notion if I start to drown in batter."

"Wow. Must be some super-secret ingredient in there."

"If you only knew." I stifled a laugh. "Anyway, I'll tell Caroline to stop by the coffee shop on Friday to pick up what we've collected so far."

"Caroline Rogers?"

"Yes, don't you remember? She's the treasurer up at the church. I asked her to deposit the cash into the church's account, and then they're going to write one big check to Heart for Haiti. In fact, the church is adding another five hundred dollars to whatever we come up with. I thought that was very generous."

"Certainly is. As of today, you've got nearly three thousand dollars. One hundred and seventeen fruitcakes at twenty-five dollars a pop. That's a lotta dough." She laughed at her pun.

"I think you mean *batter.* But anyway, thank you for hanging onto it until Caroline gets there."

"It's in my safe, waiting for her arrival."

"Good."

"Don't you want me to hold back some of the money for ingredients?"

"No, that's my donation, along with my time and energy." I bit back another groan. If I'd known how much money I'd end up spending on candied fruit alone, I would've rethought my idea. "Anyway, it'll all work out. It always does."

"Especially where you're concerned, Jeanine. You're a miracle worker. I've never known anyone who can bake like you. You're a regular whiz-kid in the kitchen."

Her encouragement bolstered my confidence and almost made me feel as if I could actually pull this off. Almost.

"Thanks, Morgan. I'll stop by the coffee shop later this morning to drop off the muffins, but I don't know if I can make it to our usual book club gathering tonight. I'm going to be swamped."

"I'm sure the ladies will understand. But don't worry, Jeanine. If you get in over your head, we'll help. Of course, we'll probably have to help in the wee hours of the morning, but we won't leave you hanging. I really mean that. It's for a great cause. We'll get this done."

"I'm so grateful." I really meant that. As I hung up the phone, I drew in a deep breath, leaned back in my chair, and said, "By the time this is over, everyone in town will think I'm nutty as a fruitcake."

"Too late!" Natalie's voice rang out from the kitchen. "They already do!"

Two

The next couple days were a blur. Natalie and I somehow made it work at the bakery. I took care of the mixing, careful not to let her see the secret ingredient, and she took care of the baking, wrapping, and storing.

Beyond the Mad Batter, my life was in complete disarray. I couldn't remember the last time I'd done laundry. Or properly brushed my teeth, for that matter. At some point, I would have to take care of the coffee cups piled up in my kitchen sink at home, but they would have to wait. For now, I would eat, sleep, and breathe fruitcake. Ugh. Just the smell of all that candied fruit was making me sick.

When I awoke on Friday morning, I had no choice but to take some time for myself before heading into town. I started with the essentials: a hot shower, toothbrush, toothpaste, deodorant, and makeup. After showing up at work yesterday with messy hair and no makeup, my customers would be pleased to see me looking more like myself.

I walked the three blocks to the bakery, shivering all the way. If temperatures dropped much more, I'd have to give thought to driving to work. What I needed in my life — besides the obvious help with fruitcakes — was a handyman, someone who could take care of the broken bits and pieces in my life — jammed locks, wonky light switches, and so on.

I decided not to fret over those things right now. Instead, I opted to pray as I made my way down the dark, silent street. God knew all of my needs and would provide in His time.

Of course, the key jammed in the door. I still needed someone to look at that for me. My days were running together, each one feeling pretty much like the one before. When I finally made it inside, I went to work at once. I couldn't help but groan when I saw that we were running a little low on one particular ingredient, essential to the fruit-cakes. I'd have to figure it out . . . and fast.

Before I could give it much thought, my phone rang. Caroline Rogers's number greeted me. I answered with a rushed, "Hello?"

"Hey, Jeanine. How are the fruitcakes coming?"

I resisted the urge to groan and responded with a safe, "Fine. I've made over fifty so far.

Making progress."

"Awesome. I wanted to let you know that I'll finally be stopping by the Coffee Perk later this morning to pick up the fund-raiser monies. I called Morgan just now to let her know that I'll be by around eleven. She said she'll have it ready for me."

"Perfect. Thanks so much for doing this, Caroline. I really appreciate you. We all do."

"Are you kidding?" Her voice flooded with emotion. "I love this organization. Always have."

"Wish I had time to meet you for a cup of coffee, but I'm up to my eyeballs in baking."

She groaned. "I don't have time either. I've got a dentist appointment at eleven thirty. Root canal."

"Sorry to hear that."

"Me too. Rather unexpected. Anyway, I'll get the money to the church tonight before the annual Christmas party."

"Are you sure this is the best day for that?"

"You know me, Jeanine. I'm just like you. I keep going, no matter what."

"Right." I paused and let her words sink in. I wasn't the only workaholic in town. "Well, thanks again."

"You bet."

When I ended the call, I got back to work. Fortunately, Natalie arrived early and dove right in, taking care of the muffins, scones, and cookies and manning the cash register up front once the store opened.

When the crowd thinned, she joined me in the kitchen to help with the fruitcakes. I finally broached a difficult subject, one I'd been avoiding.

"Houston, we have a problem."

She glanced my way, eyes filled with concern. "This isn't Houston, but I'll do my best to help. What's up?"

"We're out of apricot nectar."

"Apricot nectar?" Natalie swiped at her bangs with the back of her hand. "What in the world do we need that for?"

"I, um . . ." I released a slow breath and whispered, "Please forgive me, Aunt Ida," before answering. "For the fruitcake."

"You've been putting apricot nectar in the fruitcake?"

I offered a hesitant nod.

"Really?" She clamped a hand to her mouth then pulled it away. "Is that your secret ingredient?"

"Maybe."

Her eyes widened. "I guess that explains why yours is so much sweeter than everyone else's. I've always wondered. Like I said, I'm not a fruitcake fan, but there's something about yours that's almost . . . tolerable."

"Gee, thanks." I laughed. "But whatever you do, please don't tell my aunt Ida I told you about the nectar."

"I didn't know you had an Aunt Ida, so I

think you're safe."

"She lives in Boise in a retirement home."

"Well then, you're doubly safe. I won't be visiting Idaho anytime soon." Natalie flashed a smile. "Now, tell me, how much do you need?"

"I have enough for another twenty or so, I think, which will put me at seventy-five fruitcakes made. But I need enough for another fifty after that. I'll give you the name of the supplier I used for the first go-round. Can you order more and tell them to get it here in a jiffy?"

"In this weather?" Natalie shook her head. "You think it'll arrive on time?"

She pointed to the kitchen window, and I glanced outside at the snow banked along the edges of the street.

"If not, I'll have to find a substitute." I paused to think that through. Sure, I could make do, right? Or maybe I could use a different nectar, merge it with the apricot to make it go further?

"Never mind ordering," I said after a moment's thought. "Just get me some apricot jam from the grocery and I'll create my own nectar out of it."

Natalie quirked a brow. "You sure?"

"Yeah. I'll thin it down with something to make it more nectar-like."

Natalie shrugged. "Okay. Anything else you need from the store? I'll go right now."

I put together a quick list then sent her on her way. With the kitchen to myself and the front end of the store void of customers, I finally settled into my groove with the fruit-cake prep. As I worked, I prayed for the children in Haiti. Tears came to my eyes as I thought about what a difference the monies I raised would make on their end. Maybe they could finally get those new bunk beds we'd been praying for. Or, perhaps that new stove. Wouldn't it be wonderful, to play a role in providing kitchen equipment for the orphanage?

Natalie arrived from the grocery store forty-five minutes later and encouraged me to take a break. She held up a bag and said, "I brought sandwiches from the deli."

"Just in time," I said. "And thank you for thinking of me."

"Hey, no one knows you like I do." She gave me a little wink and passed the bag my way. "Just let me take the jam back to the kitchen and I'll join you for a quick lunch."

"Emphasis on quick." I smiled and reached for the deli bag. When I opened it, I found a chicken salad sandwich inside, just the way I liked it, with lettuce and tomato. Natalie really did know me. I couldn't help but think of how amazing it felt to have someone her age in the shop, someone young enough to be my . . .

I wouldn't let myself think the word —

daughter. If I'd married. If I'd had a family . . . no, I wouldn't think about that, either. God had met every need of my heart and I had no complaints.

"How's that chicken salad look?" Natalie's voice was chipper as she took the seat across from me. "I got the —"

"Ham and cheddar," I said before she could get it out.

She laughed as she unwrapped her sandwich. "You know me pretty well too."

"Yep. Sure do." I took a little bite of my sandwich and sighed. "Man, this is perfect. Thanks again."

"You're welcome. By the way, I stopped by the coffee shop to pick up those empty trays from Monday's orders. Morgan said she'll be calling you later. Apparently, there was quite a run on those Santa cookies."

"Figures. 'Tis the season." I took another bite of my sandwich and heard my cell phone ring.

"Don't get it," Natalie encouraged me. "You can call them later."

I settled back in my chair and nodded. "Okay. I'll do that when things slow down."

I watched through the glass panel in the front door as a customer tried to wriggle the handle. She couldn't get it open, so I rose and walked to the door to open it for her.

The elderly Mrs. Bingham entered, leaning heavily on her cane. "You really need to get that fixed," she grumbled, gesturing to the door with her head. "It's a hazard. And for pity's sake, pull down that bell. It scares me to death every time I come in here."

"Oh, well, I —"

"And don't even get me started on the condition of your restroom. The last time I was here I couldn't get the hot water to run. Do you know how hard it is on these old joints of mine to wash my hands in cold water, especially in wintertime? I'm sure that's a health code violation, by the way. Someone could report you."

"You just have to jiggle the faucet handle a little," Natalie said. "There's a little trick to it. I can show you."

"I don't want you to show me. I want you to fix it."

"How can I help you, Mrs. Bingham?" I wiped crumbs from my lips and tried to look professional.

"I need a dozen of those snowball cookies. Stopped by Morgan's place and she's all out. It's a real nuisance to have to walk all the way here in the snow to get what I should've been able to purchase at her shop." Mrs. Bingham's expression softened. "But truth be told, I just can't resist those snowball cookies and neither can the ladies in my Bunco group, especially Jo Anderson. Have you ever seen that woman when there are sweets to be had? Maybe you'd better make that two dozen. They're as soft as butter, and I just love all that powdered sugar. Mmm."

"Right. Two dozen snowball cookies." I'd just started to head behind the glass case to fill her order when Natalie jumped up and offered to do it for me.

"Have a seat, Jeanine," she said with the wave of a hand then turned her attention to our crotchety customer. Before long she had Mrs. Bingham grinning and laughing. When the elderly woman left, Natalie rejoined me at the table.

"Thanks so much for doing that," I said. "You have a way with her."

"Hey, it's what you pay me to do, and I've decided that all of our customers, even the cranky ones, can be won over with sweetness."

"Well, you go above and beyond. Don't think I haven't noticed."

"No worries." Natalie took a nibble of her sandwich and washed it down with a swig of her soda. "But she's right. There are a lot of things around here that need fixing."

"I know."

"You should ask my dad to help."

"Your dad?" I reached for my napkin and wiped the mayonnaise from my lips. "He does handyman stuff?"

"When my mom was alive, he had a never-ending honey-do list. He stayed on top of it. I was always surprised to see how many different things he could do. Electrical. Plumbing. Carpentry. He's a whiz."

"Wow." I'd only met Peter Salyers a handful of times and would've guessed him to be more stockbroker than handyman. The handsome fifty-something dressed in nice suits and wore expensive shoes.

Not that I had time to think about such things. I was far too busy at the shop to be glancing in the direction of a handsome man. After that fiasco with my ex-fiancé years ago, I didn't need the drama of a fella in my life, anyway. I'd gotten by just fine without one, thank you very much.

Before I could respond, my cell phone rang again. "Wonder if it's the same person as before? It must be important."

She shrugged. "That's your call."

"Literally." I laughed and then bounded from my chair to the kitchen, where I'd left my cell phone on the large stainless-steel island.

"Jeanine?" The voice on the other end of the phone sounded tense. Wound up. "This is Caroline. Sorry to have to call again. Hope I'm not disturbing you."

"No, I'm just —"

"We've run into a problem."

"Oh?"

She paused. "I don't know how to tell you this, but when I got to the coffee shop to pick up the money, it was missing."

My heart skipped a beat. "Missing? There's got to be some mistake. Morgan said she'd leave it in her office for you to pick up."

"And that's exactly what she did. Only, somewhere between her taking it out of the safe and my arrival, the envelope disappeared."

I felt as if my knees might give way. I leaned against the wall to support myself. "Caroline, please tell me this is some sort of sick joke."

"I wish it was, Jeanine. All I can tell you is that the money you've been collecting for the past three weeks — all two thousand nine hundred and twenty-five dollars — is missing, and we have absolutely no idea who might have taken it."

THREE

When I closed up the shop at five, I headed to the Coffee Perk to meet with Morgan and Caroline. I could hardly keep my thoughts straight as I inched my way down the slippery sidewalk. Several of the locals passed by, including Louise Applewhite, town librarian. She stopped to ask me about her fruitcake order, and I did my best to make small talk, then excused myself. One of my book club ladies, Evelyn Kliff, happened by next. She couldn't seem to stop talking about a sale going on at the local dress shop. I managed to convince her that I needed to get to the coffee shop, and she waved goodbye and headed home.

A couple of minutes later I arrived at the coffee shop. I couldn't help but notice Cody, Morgan's new dishwasher, manning the cash register. Odd.

After offering a broad smile, Cody hollered out, "Welcome to the Coffee Perk," and I responded with a nod then took a couple of steps in his direction. "How can I help you, Ms. Gransbury?"

Hmm. I should probably order a cup of coffee. "Decaf, please. Large."

"Decaf?" He quirked a brow. "Haven't had many requests for that."

"I know, but I'm overcaffeinated right now. If I don't watch out, I'll be up all night, and I can't afford that. Four a.m. comes early."

"Gotcha."

He went to work on my order, and I paused to give him a second glance. I couldn't help but wonder about the young man. He couldn't be more than twenty-two, but had already covered most available skin space with tattoos of one kind or another. I didn't mean to stare, but who could blame me? He'd inked some sort of quote running up the length of his arm. I could only make out half of it as he turned back in my direction, coffee cup in hand.

"Until I see you again." His words cut through the stillness like a knife.

"Wh–what?"

"Until I see you again. That's what the tattoo on my arm says." He held it out to give me a closer view. "You were looking, right?"

"Oh, I . . . Sorry." Heat warmed my cheeks.

"It's okay. I wouldn't have gotten it if I didn't want people to look. No harm done." He flashed a warm smile and passed the cup of coffee my way. "This one's on the house, by the way."

"Thanks, Cody. And I'm sorry if I came across as nosy. It's all so intriguing to me." Clearly the tattoo commemorated someone he'd once held dear. A mother? Girlfriend? Child? I wanted to ask, but could only muster a quiet, "Did it hurt?"

"The tattoo?" His question led me to believe the pain went deeper than his skin.

"Yes."

He shrugged. "Only for a few hours. But the way I look at it, pain for a moment, memories for a lifetime." He lifted his arm and looked at the perfectly aligned script. For the first time, I noticed the lily at the end of it. "Miranda always loved lilies."

I offered a lame nod, but asked no questions. Maybe Morgan would offer some insight into who this Miranda-person was, but right now I'd better stop snooping and get back to the reason I came. I thanked Cody for the coffee and pointed myself toward the kitchen, where I found Morgan hard at work washing dishes.

"Well, this is odd," I observed. "Didn't you hire Cody to do dishes? Why is he working the cash register?"

She sighed. "He had some interest in learning, so I taught him the basics. Did he mess up your order?"

"No, he got it right. Even told me it was on the house." I gave her a little wink.

"Well, then he is following my instructions." She dried her hands on a dish towel. "Let's go into my office, okay? More privacy there."

"Sure."

Moments later we walked into her tiny office.

"Where's Caroline?" I shrugged off my jacket. "I thought she was meeting us."

"I think she's having a hard time recovering from that root canal," Morgan explained. "I could hardly make out what she was saying on the phone just now. So, it's just us."

"Okay." I took a seat and did my best to calm myself as my gaze shifted around the tiny office. "Explain what happened. Walk me through it, step by step."

Morgan pursed her lips. "Right. Well, this morning I got a call from Caroline saying she was on her way, so I went straight to the safe and pulled out the bag with the cash for the fruitcakes."

"What did you do with it?"

"I knew she would be walking through the door any minute, so I left it sitting on my desk. I closed my office door. Didn't think a thing about it, frankly. I was up to my eyeballs in customers."

"Anyone unusual?"

She paused. "I'm going to be really honest here and tell you that I can't remember who came in today. This place has been mobbed ever since we started selling Christmas-themed coffees."

"Did you walk into the office with Caroline to get the money?" I asked.

Morgan sighed and shook her head. "No. I was waiting on a customer. Just told her that the 'package' was on my desk. She walked in and came out with . . . well, nothing."

"And you hadn't seen anyone else go in there?" I queried. "Maybe someone pretending to go to the restroom? Something like that?"

"Like I said, I was drowning in customers. I suppose anything's possible."

Morgan paused, and I read the concern in her eyes.

"You have something on your mind?"

"Maybe." She shrugged. "I've always thought Caroline was a bit odd, that's all. Not judging a book by its cover, so please don't think that. But her rag-tag car; the old, worn clothing . . . I've worried that she's not able to take care of herself adequately."

"Right." I paused to think through Morgan's words. "Never really understood it. I mean, she has her own accounting firm and knows a great deal about money but lives so simply. And she's on staff at the church."

"I've always felt a little sorry for her. No husband to help fix that old clunker, no close friends to help with that dilapidated house. I don't know."

"Are you saying you suspect she might have

taken the money and claimed it was missing? Is that what you mean?"

"I don't know. But maybe it's time to contact the sheriff and get his input. He's going to need to know about this sooner or later."

"Ugh." The whole thing felt so uncomfortable enough already. "Do you think? I mean, it was just fund-raiser money, not anyone's livelihood."

"I have an idea. Let's get the ladies together for a pow-wow before we call in Sheriff Hayden. He's not the easiest person to work with."

"True." Morgan nodded.

"And who knows. Maybe one of the ladies will have some insight about what happened or what we should do. What do you think?"

"Sure."

Morgan placed the necessary calls and within half an hour our usual band of friends had congregated in the coffee shop. She put the CLOSED sign on the door, dismissed Cody for the day, and filled our coffee cups as we settled around our usual table, coffee cups in hand. I brought the ladies up to speed on our dilemma, and Evelyn gasped.

"Jeanine, that's awful! You've worked so hard selling those fruitcakes, and all for such a great cause. I feel just awful for you."

"Feel awful for the children at the orphanage in Haiti," I countered. "They're the ones who are going to lose out."

"Do you have any suspects?" Jo asked as she poured cream into her coffee.

I glanced Morgan's way to see if she would chime in, but she only shrugged. "The only person we're curious about at this point is Caroline."

Harper leaned back in her chair and took a sip of coffee, a worried look on her face. "She's always seemed like such an odd bird to me."

"How so?" I asked.

"Living all alone in that beat-up house on Elm Street, for one thing." Harper set her cup down. "Just think it's odd that so much money passes through her hands and she's seemingly, well . . ."

"Frugal?" Penny Parson spoke up.

Morgan shrugged. "Yeah, this is what I was trying to explain to Jeanine earlier, but I'm afraid I probably didn't get my point across. She handles finances for nearly everyone in town, so her firm must be doing well. Just seems like she doesn't spend much on herself, that's all."

"Maybe that's what she's planning to do with the three thousand dollars," Harper suggested.

I gasped. "You aren't seriously saying she took that money, are you? She's been my biggest help through all of this."

Jo shrugged. "She's the only person we

know for sure was in the office after Morgan removed the money from the safe. She walked in. She walked out. Money bag disappears."

"According to Caroline, it was the other way around," I countered. "She said that bag was already gone when she entered the room."

"She had the perfect reason for being in the room," Morgan said. "Being treasurer and all."

I shook my head. "Ladies, I know we've all become rather adept at crime-solving over the past few months, but let's not get ahead of ourselves. Caroline is a wonderful woman and a huge asset to the church and our community. She's never been anything but helpful and kind to me. So, before we make too many speculations or judge the way she chooses to live, let's remember to give her the benefit of the doubt."

"You go right ahead," Jo said. "I'm just leery, that's all."

"I, for one, think we need to involve law enforcement." Morgan reached for the phone. "This is the sort of thing that needs to be reported."

Harper nodded. "I agree. With no time to waste. But don't call Sheriff Hayden. Let me call Cam. He'll know what to do."

Jeanine agreed. Calling in Harper's new beau might be their best bet. The young deputy would take them seriously.

Harper reached for her cell phone and dialed, then put the call on speaker phone.

Deputy Davis seemed concerned when he heard the news. "Are you sure you didn't misplace it, Morgan? You've looked everywhere?"

"I've looked everywhere. And I know exactly where I put it. It just . . . vanished."

"Money doesn't just vanish," he responded. "I agree that it's probably been taken, not misplaced."

"But by whom?" Morgan asked.

"Right." Deputy Davis paused. "Tell you what, I'll stop by tomorrow morning and we'll visit. Will you be free around eight thirty, Morgan?"

"Sure. Maybe Jeanine can join us too." She looked my way, and I nodded. I didn't know how I'd manage time away from the shop during the morning rush, but I'd give it my best effort. The call came to an abrupt end when the deputy got another call.

"Well, there you go." Harper put her phone back in her pocket. "At least he knows now. We're not the only ones."

"Do I tell the public?" I asked. "Or do we wait?"

"I say wait." Jo leaned back in her chair and gave Morgan a pensive look. "If you tell people now, some might suspect you of stealing it."

"Good gravy." Morgan paled. "Surely not."

"Everyone in Oak Grove knows Morgan," I argued. "They would never suspect her."

"Either you suspect everyone or you suspect no one." Jo turned her gaze to me. "And, Jeanine, since you're the one who asked people to give, they will ultimately hold you responsible. You might want to prepare yourself for that."

Well, if that didn't make me feel worse, nothing would.

We wrapped up our meeting, and I paused to think through the events of the day. A lump rose in my throat when I thought about how much work I still had to do . . . and for what? I couldn't make up that three thousand dollars, not on my own. Still, I owed one hundred and seventeen people fruitcakes, and I wasn't one to go back on my word.

FOUR

The following morning my workday began as any other. I walked to the shop, slipping and sliding down the sidewalk, wrestled with the key in the door, and fidgeted with the light switch until the kitchen lit up. Then I slipped on my apron and dove right in. With Natalie's help I got the breakfast sweets ready. Fruitcakes would just have to wait.

At eight fifteen I left Natalie in charge and walked to the Coffee Perk to meet up with Morgan, Caroline, and Deputy Davis. I found Morgan in the kitchen. She glanced up as I entered.

"Hey, glad you made it. Did you see Caroline out there, by any chance?"

"No."

"I hated to bother her after that root canal, but I felt it was important she join us. I sure hope she makes it. She didn't show up at the party last night." Morgan gave me an inquisitive look. "For that matter, you didn't, either."

"Nope. Too many fruitcakes."

"We missed you."

"Thanks. I —"

"Good morning, ladies." A distinctly male voice rang out from behind me, and I turned to discover Deputy Davis had joined us. "Sorry to bother you on a Saturday morning. I know how busy you both are."

Before I could say "It's okay," Caroline dragged into the room. Her right cheek was swollen, and the bags under her eyes clued me in to the fact that she hadn't had much sleep.

"Whoa. Did you meet up with someone in a back alley?" the deputy asked.

She shook her head. "I wish. That would've been easier."

"That root canal must've been quite a doozie." Morgan dried her hands on a dish towel and then pulled off her apron. "You sure you're up for this?"

Caroline shrugged. "I feel awful, if you want the truth of it, but I'm here and I'll do my best to answer any questions the deputy feels like asking. I would've been here sooner, but my car is acting up."

"Again?" Morgan quirked a brow then led the way into her office where we all took a seat.

"Caroline, just tell us everything that happened." The deputy flipped open his laptop and started typing.

"There's not much to tell." She fidgeted

with her purse, which she'd set in her lap. "Morgan called to tell me the money was ready to be picked up. Said it was in her office. I got to the coffee shop, she offered me a free cup of coffee, and then pointed toward her office."

"You didn't go in the office with her, Morgan?" The deputy looked up from his laptop.

Morgan shook her head. "No. A customer came in right as we were headed back, so I just pointed her to the door and went to take care of him."

"And when you got to the office?" Deputy Davis directed his question to Caroline. "Then what?"

She shrugged. "I opened the door, walked inside, looked on the desk where Morgan said the envelope would be waiting . . . and saw nothing."

"So, you didn't pick up anything?"

"Of course not." Caroline's cheeks blazed red. "What are you asking?"

He raised his hand. "Just a typical line of questioning, no accusations. A lot of money has gone missing." He turned his attention to Morgan. "Did anyone else know the money bag was in there?"

She squirmed in her chair. "Not to my knowledge. And few people go into my office, anyway."

"Who all was in the building when the money went missing?"

Morgan paused, and her eyes narrowed to slits as she appeared to be thinking it through. "In the back of the house, you mean? Just me, a handful of customers up front, and Cody Watson, the new dishwasher."

"Cody Watson?" Deputy Davis wrote the name down. "Don't think I know that name."

"He's only in town for the holidays, staying with his aunt, Evelyn Kliff. Needed something to keep himself busy, and I needed the help."

"How well do you know Cody?"

Morgan shrugged. "Not very well, but as I said, he's Evelyn's nephew. I'm sure she'll be happy to vouch for him. He's a hard worker, even helping with the cash register when things are busy."

"The cash register?" The deputy's eyes narrowed to slits. "The dishwasher handles the money?"

"Yes." Morgan shrugged. "Just a couple of times. I'm training him to work the register when I'm too busy in the kitchen."

"I see."

The deputy turned to face me. "Jeanine, if you don't mind my asking, why is Morgan the one collecting the money for your Haiti fund-raiser if you're in charge?"

"Oh, that's easy," I responded. "She has a safe and I don't. If I'd invested in a safe like Morgan told me to do years ago, none of this would've happened."

"And you collected cash instead of checks because . . ."

"Well, that's kind of a long story." I did my best to explain, but he did not look convinced.

"All of this is for that Haiti group?" he asked. "Same guy who spoke in church a couple weeks back?"

"Yes. Matt Kimball," I explained. "Great young man. He's been in town for several weeks now, making the rounds from church to church to raise funds."

"And he's just one of many people who work for the ministry, right?"

"Right," I explained. "It's a large organization, with a board and everything."

"Just strikes me as odd that he asked for cash."

"Right." Morgan and I spoke in unison. In that moment, a wave of nausea passed over me. "Do you think that's why he asked me to collect cash, so he could steal it out from under me before it reached the church?"

Deputy Davis shrugged. "Stranger things have happened. But let's don't jump to conclusions. And even though this seems extreme, it is, after all, only three thousand dollars, not thirty thousand. We're not talking about a huge amount of money."

"Gee, thanks." I did my best not to roll my eyes. "Tell that to all the candied fruit I've chopped over the past few days."

"You know what I mean. If you're going to steal money, it's usually big money."

He continued to pepper us with questions but finally wrapped up about an hour into our meeting. A short time later, I left Morgan's office in a funk. As I passed by Cody in the kitchen, he flashed a smile and called out a cheerful "G'morning!" I responded with a smile. The deputy might consider him a suspect, but I still liked the kid. He didn't strike me as the suspicious type, in spite of his rough appearance. And he was my good friend's nephew, for Pete's sake.

When I got back to the bakery, Natalie was just wrapping up the breakfast rush. She met me in the kitchen to dive back into the fruitcake-making. I put her to work chopping fruit and busied myself creating apricot nectar from the jam she'd purchased. We took turns waiting on customers. About an hour into the process, the bell on the door jingled again.

"My turn to get it," I said as I turned toward the sink to wash my hands. Before I could complete the task, a strong male voice sounded from behind me.

"I hear you're needing a little work done around here."

I turned to discover Peter Salyers had entered the shop.

"Dad, you came!" Natalie let out a squeal and threw her arms around his neck. "Oops, didn't mean to get you all sticky. I'm chopping candied fruit."

"That would explain the smell." He chuckled.

"Actually, the smell is from that nectar Jeanine is making." Natalie gestured toward my work station then busied herself once again. Not that I planned to get back to work anytime soon, not with this handsome fellow standing in my kitchen. I always went a little weak in the knees when Peter came around. Today, however, the change in appearance really threw me. Instead of the usual suit and tie, he wore a plaid button-up and jeans. The handyman look was completed by a tool belt. The man was here to work, no doubt about it.

"Oh yes, I . . ." Man, I needed his help, but this felt awkward, at best.

He squared his shoulders, looking Hulk-like. "Natalie tells me you've got a problem with the light switch. Should I start there?"

"If you don't mind." I pointed him in the direction of the switch and demonstrated the glitch. Of course, it worked perfectly.

"I can see why you're worried." He gave me a little wink, those bright blue eyes of his twinkling with merriment. I found myself a little lost in them.

Until the lights went out.

"Bingo!" I pointed to the switch. "That's what it does. On one minute, off the next."

"Say no more. I'm sure it's just a loose wire. But just so you know, I'll have to shut off the electricity to your shop to work on the switches."

"Ack."

"Problem?"

"Well, let's see . . . I have six fruitcakes, four Italian cream cakes, forty-eight orange-cranberry muffins, and a tray of chocolate chip scones in my two commercial ovens back there." I pointed behind us. "If we shut off the electricity, I will lose the product and, consequently, any sales that might have come from that product. Other than that, no. I don't see any reason why you shouldn't shut me down for the day." I flashed a strained smile.

He tugged at his shirt collar. "I see. Well, maybe I could work on something else until you're done. I hear there's a plumbing issue?"

"Hot water handle on the faucet." I pointed to the ladies' room. "You might want to knock first."

He nodded then walked that way.

For whatever reason, my heart rate picked up as I watched him walk away. I could feel the heat in my cheeks as Natalie glanced my way.

"You okay, Jeanine?" she asked.

"Hmm? Oh sure. Just awfully hot in this kitchen today."

It sure was. And, with the addition of a certain handsome handyman, things had just gotten even hotter.

FIVE

The following Tuesday I headed to the coffee shop to meet up with the other ladies for our usual weekly book club gathering. Truth be told, I hadn't read a page of this month's book, a cozy mystery we'd all agreed on. There simply hadn't been time. Not that the other ladies would judge me. They knew what I was up against. And besides, I was right in the middle of a little mystery of my own right now, one that took precedence over a book.

In spite of my crazy schedule, I arrived early. Morgan offered a friendly wave and walked my way.

"Glad you're here before the others. There's something I wanted to share with you before the other ladies showed up." She dried her hands on a dish towel and gestured for me to follow her into the coffee shop's kitchen.

"Sure." I shrugged off my coat and slung it over the back of a chair at our usual table then followed behind her.

As I passed by the counter, the cash register

dinged, and I looked over to see Cody opening the drawer and emptying the money into
a night deposit bag. Morgan led the way,
chattering all the while about the weather.
When we reached the kitchen, she turned to
face me. In place of her usual smile, a frown
darkened her expression. If such a thing
could be judged from the creases between
her brows, Morgan was troubled by something.

"You okay?" I reached over and grabbed a
mint, unwrapped it, and popped it into my
mouth.

"Yeah." She shrugged. "Listen, I didn't
want to say anything publicly, but I want to
go on record as saying I take full responsibility for what happened to that money bag. It's
all my doing."

"You stole it?" I joked as I tossed the wrapper from the mint into the trash can.

"No, silly, but I put it out on the desk in
anticipation of Caroline's arrival. It was a
dumb move, a really dumb move, one I regret
with all my heart. I do hope you can forgive
me."

I leaned against the counter and examined
the concern in her expression. "Of course I
forgive you, Morgan. Could've happened to
any of us."

She nodded, and for the first time I noticed
a hint of tears in her eyes. "Thank you. That
means a lot. Sometimes I get so busy around

here that things fly under the radar." Morgan swiped at her eyes with the back of her hand. "Anyway, just so you know, I'm prepared to make it up to you. Or, rather, to the children in Haiti."

"What do you mean?"

"I mean, if that money doesn't turn up, I'm willing to give you the three thousand dollars myself."

I couldn't help but gasp aloud. "Morgan, no! Don't be silly. I could never take your money."

"It wouldn't be you taking it. It'd be Heart for Haiti. And they wouldn't be taking it, I would be offering. There's a difference."

"Well, sure, but . . ."

She paced the kitchen and fussed with the coffeemaker. "I've already prayed about it. It's the right thing to do. It was lost — or stolen — in my care. The buck stops here."

"If we were talking about a single buck, maybe," I countered. "But three thousand? No way could I let you do that."

"Like I said, I've already prayed about it. I have a little mad money account with about that much in it. It's yours — or, rather, the missions organization's — if Deputy Davis comes up empty in his investigation."

"I don't know what to say, Morgan."

"Say nothing. I don't want anyone to know. Promise?"

I offered a lame nod. "Okay, but only if

you're sure."

"Like I said, I've prayed about it. So don't fret. Just let me do this, okay? The idea that those kids in Haiti would have to suffer because I took my eyes off that money bag makes me feel sick inside."

I followed her back into the coffee shop, where I found Evelyn and Harper walking through the front door, deep in conversation. They approached Cody, who greeted his aunt with a hug and a smile. Minutes later, Jo and Penny arrived, books in hand.

As we gathered around our usual table, the ladies peppered me with questions about the missing cash, but I had no answers. Morgan didn't either.

"So Deputy Davis hasn't turned up anything at all?" Penny asked.

I shook my head and reached for my coffee cup. "Not a thing. He's just asked me to keep my eyes open for anything suspicious."

"I just don't understand it," Penny said. "I mean, what kind of person walks into the coffee shop office and swipes money meant for poor children in a third-world country?"

I caught a glimpse of Cody sweeping the area behind the counter. He never looked up, but my radar was sky-high as I observed his slow movements. Not that I could say anything with him hovering so close by. And I'd feel odd voicing my suspicions in front of Evelyn. They were family, after all.

"If we ever do find out, I hope they prosecute to the fullest extent of the law," Jo said, oblivious to my ponderings about Cody. "It's one thing to steal from folks who have money, but to take from children who have nothing? Children who need beds to sleep on? It's shameful, I tell you."

Cody disappeared into the kitchen then returned a moment later, no longer wearing his apron. "I've finished up, Morgan. Anything else before I go?"

Morgan glanced his way and smiled. "Nope. Enjoy your evening, Cody. See you bright and early tomorrow morning."

"Yep. See you back at the house, Aunt Evelyn." He gave us a quick wave then walked out the front door with a smile.

Jo's eyes narrowed to slits as she watched him walk down the sidewalk. "What is it with young people and tattoos?"

Before Evelyn could respond, a rap sounded at the front door. I looked over to discover Caroline standing on the other side. Morgan gestured for her to join us inside.

Caroline brushed the loose snow from her coat before stepping into the coffee shop. "Ladies, I'm so sorry to interrupt your book club, but this is awfully important."

"Are you still not feeling well?" Morgan asked. "I heard you got a nasty infection after that root canal."

"Right. Ugh." Caroline looked a bit wobbly. She dropped into a chair and leaned her elbows onto the table. "The dentist started me on an antibiotic, but I've been running a fever and everything. Timing couldn't be worse."

"Sounds awful." Harper shook her head. "I had a bad infection after an extracted wisdom tooth once. Took weeks to recover."

"Terrific." Caroline groaned. "Anyway, I've come with news, and it's not good."

"What's that?" I asked.

She pursed her lips, and for a moment I thought she might not respond at all. When she did speak, her words came out in a rush. "Matt Kimball was just fired from Heart for Haiti."

A collective gasp went up from our group and my heart skipped a beat. She had to be kidding.

"Our Matt Kimball?" I managed at last. The young missionary — who hailed from our great town — was loved by all. We'd just celebrated his recent engagement to a beautiful young woman. They were the perfect happy couple. This had to be some sort of mistake.

"But that's impossible," Evelyn said. "I've known him for years. His mother's a friend of mine. He's never been anything but wonderful."

"That's been my experience too," Jo added. "And I just love that fiancée of his. She's a real Haitian beauty."

"Things aren't always what they seem," Caroline countered. "They just let him go this morning. Some sort of scandal involving distribution of funds. Apparently, he has quite a long record of shorting the ministry."

Jo shook her head, and I noticed a hint of tears in her eyes. "If you can't trust a missionary, who can you trust?"

Caroline shrugged. "Nobody, I guess. Anyway, the board voted him out. It was unanimous." She turned to face me. "I just thought you'd want to know since all of this money you've collected was supposed to go through his hands. Pastor Johnson asked me to call you to let you know. We're all in shock, as you might imagine."

"So, now what?"

"Pastor Johnson is of the opinion that the money — if it turns up — should still go to the organization. They did the right thing by getting rid of Matt so quickly, and the ministry is still going strong. Their work in Haiti is really changing lives, and it's not fair to cheat the kids at the orphanage out of those new bunk beds just because one of the links in the chain happened to be crooked."

"I'll trust your judgment on this, Caroline."

"Thanks. And the church still plans to add an additional five hundred dollars."

I cast a glance in Morgan's direction and noticed she looked a bit pale. No doubt she was second-guessing herself, wishing she could take back the offer to replace the missing funds. I didn't blame her. In fact, I'd go a step further and insist she hang on to her money for now. The idea of passing any money to Heart for Haiti now sounded questionable, at best.

Still, as I thought about the children, as I thought about all of those bunk beds I'd hoped to provide, I felt a little sick inside. What could I do about all that now, especially with so many fruitcakes left to bake?

Right now, I just wanted to head home and climb under the covers and forget the whole thing.

Six

The following morning, Matt Kimball paid me a visit at the bakery with his fiancée, Phara, at his side. He arrived before any of the customers, barreling into the shop in such a frantic way that it frightened me. From the panicked look on his face, I could tell he wanted to talk. I felt so torn about it all. The passion in his voice as he spoke to me won me over, though, and before long he was standing in my kitchen watching me make fruitcakes while pouring out his heart. We'd left Phara at a table out front, showing off her new engagement ring to a couple of the customers.

Across the room, Natalie worked on muffins and scones. She glanced Matt's way every now and again, as if trying to gauge his emotional temperature. Or maybe she wanted to make sure I was okay. I couldn't be sure.

"You've got to believe me, Jeanine . . ." Matt paced from one end of the workspace to the other. "This is all a huge misunderstanding. Every penny I've raised for Heart for Haiti over the past few years has gone straight into the organization. Anything you've heard to the contrary is a lie."

"They why did they let you go?"

He clenched his fists. "I have to believe that Jim Anderson, the head of the board, has a personal vendetta against me. He's been angry ever since I suggested we move the organization away from the denomination we've been associated with for years, to reach a broader base of supporters. You'd be surprised at how limiting it can be if you're too tightly linked to a particular denomination."

"I see. So, he didn't care for the idea?"

"No, but the board saw it my way, and Heart for Haiti came out from under the umbrella of the church. That angered him — a lot."

"And he turned against you?"

"Yes. I believe he'd do anything to see me gone."

"Are you saying you've been set up?" I passed a cookie Matt's way and continued to work on fruitcakes.

Matt's expression tightened. "That's one way to put it. He was always jealous of my relationship with the other board members. I was set to move up the ladder, as it were, and Jim couldn't stand the notion that I'd been given more clout. So he found a way to turn people against me by making up this story about the money."

"Doesn't make a lot of sense, though," I argued. "This Jim person came up with the story of mismanaged funds just to make you look bad?"

"I'm saying he actually took off with the money, himself, and blamed me. That's what I'm saying."

I stopped working and looked Matt in the eyes. He looked truthful enough, if such a thing could be judged from the pained expression in his eyes.

"There's nothing I can do at this point, Matt, but pray that the truth comes to light."

He sighed, and for a moment I felt genuinely sorry for him. I remembered a time, back in sixth grade, when I'd been falsely accused of cheating on a test. I never managed to convince my teacher, Mrs. Kennedy, that she was wrong about me.

A shiver ran down my back as I realized how it felt to have others doubt your word.

"I hope it all ends well. I really do."

"Yes, and I hope your missing money is found." He shook his head. "At least they can't blame me for that."

"What do you mean?"

He shook his head, and the saddest expression came over his face. "Just saying, if I'd shown up that morning to pick up the money instead of Caroline, they might've tried to pin that on me too."

"Oh, I see. Well, it's probably for the best that you weren't at the coffee shop that day." I paused and debated whether or not to tell him that Morgan had offered to replace the missing funds. After a moment, I decided to keep that information to myself. "I'm sorry to cut this short, Matt, but I still have to finish up forty-plus fruitcakes by week's end. Folks still need to get what they paid for."

"Sad." He shook his head. "All the way around." He stuck out his hand. "I'll pray for you and you pray for me. Okay?"

I wiped my hands on my apron then shook his hand. "Okay." Seconds later, he was gone, and Natalie and I were left to the silence of the kitchen once again.

"It's okay," I said after a minute. "You can say what's on your mind."

"I'm just so confused." She paused and put both palms on the countertop. "Either that guy is the most skilled actor on the planet, or he's really telling the truth. But if he's telling the truth, then why are the hairs on my arms standing on end?" She held out her arm to show the proof.

I heard the front bell ring and saw Natalie's dad enter, dressed in his handyman attire once more. He gave me a nod.

"Sorry to interrupt. Mind if I work on that loose kitchen light switch today?"

"Will you need to turn off the power?" I asked.

"I've been thinking about that. Only to the switch for now, if that's okay." He flashed a smile so bright it almost caused me to forget about my troubles with missing money and Matt Kimball. Almost.

I got back to work on the fruitcakes and managed to keep going until lunchtime. Natalie went through her repertoire of Christmas carols, singing at the top of her lungs, as usual. As I settled at one of the tables up front with my lunch, Peter walked up. He pointed to the kitchen. "Got the light all fixed up." He squared his shoulders.

"Thank you so much, Peter." I smiled at him. "You've been a godsend. Truly."

"No trouble at all. Can I show you something?"

"Sure."

I followed behind him as he led the way to the front window. He pointed at the caulking along the edge. "I noticed your seals are coming loose. You're losing heat through these spots."

I did my best not to sigh aloud. "Poor old building."

"The windows need to be resealed, is all," he said. "Happy to take care of that for you tomorrow, if you like."

"Are you sure?" I was starting to feel bad about all the time and effort he was putting into making my shop a place I could be proud of.

"Very sure." He paused and gazed into my eyes with such intensity that I felt my cheeks grow warm. "I'm on Christmas break at work, and it's pretty boring over at my place. I mean, I can only watch so many romance movies before I finally snap."

"You watch romance movies?"

"Totally kidding about that."

"Gotcha. Well, again, I thank you. And please keep track of what I owe you for materials and your time."

He waved that notion away. "Nah. Just teach my girl all your baking tricks. I know it means a lot to her. Natalie's a whiz in the kitchen, and she'll go far with your input."

"Well, thank you. And, of course."

He pointed to the table I'd been sitting at. "Mind if I join you?" he asked.

Before I could say, "Don't mind a bit," he'd pulled out a chair and taken a seat.

"I might have enough ingredients to whip up another sandwich, if you like," I offered as I sat down across from him.

"No thanks. I had a big breakfast." He paused. "Sorry to bring up a sore subject, but Natalie told me about your fund-raiser. About the money going missing, I mean. I'm so sorry."

"Thanks. It's a bit . . . devastating." I took a nibble of my sandwich and leaned back in the chair, feeling more than a little self-conscious about eating in front of this guy.

"I'll bet." He reached over and patted my hand. "For the record, I think it's an amazing thing you're doing, raising funds for that missions organization."

"Thanks. I was so touched by Matt Kimball's presentation at the church a few weeks back. My heart went out to those kids, and I wanted to help."

"Matt Kimball?" His brow wrinkled. "The guy who was just here with his fiancée?"

"Yes."

"Heard all about him too. Watch out for him, Jeanine." Peter rested his hand on my arm, a gesture so sweet it caught me off-guard.

"I will. I feel awful about those funds going missing. I was just trying to help bring in some necessary money for the orphanage."

"I'm sure the kids would've appreciated that." A pause followed. "I've been thinking a lot about this. I hope you won't find this presumptuous, but I'd like to cover the cost of what you lost."

"Wh–what?" I could hardly believe my ears. "I can't let you do that. We're talking nearly three thousand dollars."

"I know how much it is. Natalie told me. I usually try to find a local charity to support each Christmas. This year I choose you." He paused and cleared his throat. "I mean, I choose the kids in Haiti."

"I truly don't know what to say."

"Don't say anything. Just tell me who to make the check out to."

I paused to think through my response. "To the church, I guess. They're adding five hundred dollars to any monies we bring in . . . and thank you."

"No, thank *you*. You've done a lot for my girl, Jeanine. From the time her mother died, she's needed a mother figure. You've been that, and more. You've taken her under your wing, taught her the ropes of your business, and inspired her to follow her dreams. What else could a father ask for?"

Before I could say anything, my cell phone rang. I glanced down to see Jo's number. "Sorry, but I need to take this."

"Sure." Peter rose and took a couple steps toward the kitchen. "I need to get going anyway."

I answered the call with a quick, "Hello?"

"Jeanine, I know you're busy." Jo's words sounded rushed, breathless. "But this is important."

"What is it?"

"I just happened to see Cody zoom by on a motorcycle. Have you ever noticed him on a motorcycle before?"

"No."

"Me either. Weird that one would suddenly appear, don't you think?"

"Oh, I don't know. People ride motorcycles all the time."

"True. Just raised a few suspicions, I guess. Maybe I'm overthinking things." Jo sighed. "Get back to work on those fruitcakes, girl."

"I will."

We ended the call, and I lost myself to my thoughts. Lots of people owned motorcycles. This certainly didn't make Cody any more suspect than before. Maybe he'd had it all along. Only one way to know for sure. I'd have to sneak it into the conversation next time I spoke to Evelyn.

SEVEN

Just after Peter left the bakery, Penny and Harper showed up.

"Heard you might need help with fruit-cakes." Harper held up an apron. "Thought maybe we could be of service."

"Seriously?"

"Yep." Penny held up an apron as well. "I'm not going to lie; baking is not my first love. But I can chop up fruit or put pans in the oven or whatever you need. I don't even mind doing dishes."

"You two are such good friends." I felt tears spring to my eyes. "I'm grateful for your help, and I know Natalie will appreciate it too. We've been going round the clock."

"Where do you stand?" Penny asked. "How many more do you have to bake?"

"I'm down to forty left to bake, approximately. I'd like to do a few extra, though."

"Sounds like we'd better get to it," Penny said.

"Yep." I rose from the table and led the way

to the kitchen, where Natalie was putting a tray of scones into the oven. After a quick explanation, she thanked the ladies and headed up to the front of the store to do some neglected housekeeping chores and to man the register.

I put the ladies to work measuring out the flour and sugar, but they seemed a bit distracted.

"I really like Natalie. She's so sweet," Penny said as she measured flour into a mixing bowl. "The more I get to know her, the more I like her." She added another cup of flour, then a confused look came over her face. "Was that three cups . . . or four?"

"I don't know. I wasn't paying attention." Harper shrugged as she measured sugar. "But I have noticed Natalie's dad. He's pretty sweet too, if you get my drift."

I glanced her way, suddenly feeling embarrassed.

"Not that I've noticed he's been hanging around or anything." A giggle followed as she continued to scoop sugar.

I turned away to hide the heat in my cheeks.

"He has been parked out front a lot," Harper said. "That's all I'm saying."

"Not that you've noticed," I echoed.

"Well, I can't help but notice that Lexus of his. That's a pretty fine vehicle."

"Yeah." Penny's eyes narrowed to slits as she looked my way. "What's going on there,

Jeanine? Anything you want to tell us?"

My cheeks felt a little warm as I responded, "Nothing's going on. He's a great guy."

"With gorgeous blue eyes," Penny said.

"And nice, broad shoulders," Harper added.

I dismissed them with a wave of my hand. "He's Natalie's dad, and he's grateful I've given her a job, that's all. He's on Christmas break right now and helping out with some things around the shop."

"You gave him a honey-do list, is that it?" Harper quirked a brow.

I swatted the air. "Enough already. He's just here to help . . . like you. That's what friends do."

"Yes." Harper grinned as she wiped her hands on her apron. "That's what friends do."

"But he does look really good in that plaid shirt," Penny said. "You have to admit."

"I don't have to admit anything." I fought the temptation to roll my eyes. "Now, are you here to work or to gossip about my love life?"

"Ooh, your love life?" Penny squealed. "Do tell."

I couldn't help it. I groaned. Loudly.

"Everything okay back there?" Natalie's voice sounded from the front of the shop.

"Yep," I hollered back. "These two are just a pain in the backside, and I'm not altogether sure they know what they're doing when it comes to measuring."

"Do I need to come back there and set them straight?" Natalie called out.

I shook my head. Not that she could see it.

We settled in and got to work. Truth be told, I had a lot of fun with my friends in the kitchen. Of course, none of them knew much about baking. But they gave it a lot of effort. Things went really well until Harper got distracted telling a story about something that happened at the library.

Penny sniffed the air. "Does anyone smell something burning?"

I jumped into action and checked the oven. Shoot. Three fruitcakes, burned to a crisp. I must've forgotten to set the timer. I pulled them out and set them aside. That was an expensive mistake, one I couldn't afford to make again.

We refocused and got back on track. Before long, nearly a dozen fruitcakes went into the oven. Maybe this task wouldn't be so overwhelming after all.

A few minutes after four, I heard the bell on the front door jingle and I listened in as Natalie greeted someone. I popped my head through the door to see that Caroline had entered the shop.

She saw me and gave a wave, so I walked over to greet her, leaving Harper and Penny to continue their work in the kitchen.

"Feeling any better?" I asked.

She nodded. "Not back to a hundred percent, but every day is a little better than the day before." She paused and glanced at my bakery cases. "Hey, this is an odd request, but I'm wondering if you have any day-old products you could give away or sell at a reduced price."

I paused to think through her request. "I usually sell out of most of the cookies and cupcakes, but I do have some muffins I was getting ready to toss. They're still good, but I don't sell them past the forty-eight-hour point."

"I'll be happy to take them off your hands. Just let me know how much."

"You can have them, Caroline." My heart went out to her at once. She must really be in bad shape financially to ask for outdated baked goods. Natalie and I worked with speed to load the muffins into a bag, then I threw in a couple of cookies for good measure. I passed the bag off to Caroline, who thanked me and headed out the front door.

"What was that all about?"

I turned to discover Harper standing behind me.

"Strangest thing. She asked for day-old food."

"Oh wow." Harper's eyes narrowed.

"Maybe she uses it to feed ducks at the park?" Natalie suggested. "I've heard of people doing that."

"In the middle of winter?" I shook my head.

"Don't think so. Besides, I got the feeling she was looking for quantity — the more, the better."

Penny joined us in the front of the shop. "You think she's up to something, Jeanine?"

"I don't know. Something about that conversation just felt . . . odd."

"I say we follow her." Harper quirked a brow. "See where she's going with all that stuff."

"I can't very well leave the shop," I argued. "We don't close for an hour."

"I'll watch the shop, Jeanine," Natalie said with the wave of a hand. "Don't worry about that."

I pulled off my apron and walked toward the door, suddenly feeling a little like a spy. "You coming with, ladies?"

Harper and Penny both nodded.

"You betcha," Penny said. She pulled off her apron. "Better hurry, though."

We grabbed our coats and slipped out the bakery door to the sidewalk. "There she is." Harper pointed to Caroline, who had managed to make good time. She was now three blocks to the north of us. We followed at a distance.

I shivered and wished I'd taken the time to put on my heavy coat.

As we reached the coffee shop, Morgan came outside to greet us. "What are you ladies up to?"

"Oh, nothing," Penny said. "Just on a spying mission."

"Really?" Morgan's eyes widened. "I'm coming with." She stuck her head inside and hollered out for Cody to man the register.

I did my best to keep my focus on Caroline, but it was getting harder, since she appeared to be walking at a faster pace.

"I can't keep up on this icy sidewalk," I grumbled. "This isn't worth breaking a hip over."

"Nothing is worth breaking a hip over," Morgan countered.

I glanced up to notice Jo and Evelyn standing in front of us by the dress shop window.

"Why are we talking about broken hips?" Jo asked.

"We're not really." Harper pointed to Caroline. "We're following a suspect."

"Caroline is a suspect?" Evelyn clamped a hand over her mouth then pulled it away. "What's she done?"

"She's asked for day-old baked goods," Penny explained.

Jo's thinly plucked brows arched. "And that's a crime? Seriously?"

"No. And she's not really a suspect," I explained.

"Jeanine gave her free food," Penny said. "So, we're worried she might be hungry."

"Oh my goodness." Evelyn looked stunned

by this notion. "She doesn't have money for food?"

"I don't know. I just know she asked for a reduced price on stale baked goods. I gave them to her."

"Poor thing." Evelyn's eyes reflected her concern.

We continued to follow Caroline down Main Street until she reached her home — an old, worn-down Victorian with a rotting porch. From behind the street sign, I watched as she made her way up the rickety stairs and walked into the house. I felt a little silly spying on my friend. Embarrassed, even.

Judging from the look on Jo's face, she felt awkward about our stealthy adventure too.

"Well, I guess that ends our sleuthing." Jo shrugged. "Which is fine with me. It's cold out here."

"I feel just awful for her," Harper said. "Maybe we should gather some food for her?"

"I would hate to embarrass her," I countered. "I want to pray about this, okay?"

"Sure."

We turned and walked back toward the bakery, the conversation growing quite animated as each woman speculated about Caroline's motives for wanting the free food.

A couple of minutes later, Caroline's older-model sedan whizzed by.

"Whoa, she's going someplace in a hurry," Harper said.

"Sure is." Now I was really puzzled. Nothing about this made sense. If Caroline was hungry, why not stay inside the warmth of her house to eat?

On the other hand, maybe her house wasn't warm. Maybe that's why she opted to get into the car, to ward off the cold.

My mind reeled with so many different thoughts as I walked back inside the warmth of my bakery. Was Caroline a thief? Had she stolen the money to care for her own needs, or was she simply a poor woman who barely had enough to eat? Right now, I couldn't be sure, but I would certainly find out.

EIGHT

On the day after we tracked Caroline to her house, I found my thoughts in a whirl. The money still hadn't been located, and Morgan was really pressing me to take the three thousand dollars from her. Then there was Peter, who had already handed me a check made out to the church. Should I give it to the pastor or just wait to see if the sheriff's department turned up any clues?

As I was pondering how to handle my dilemma, Deputy Davis stopped by. Before I could pepper him with questions, he shook his head. "Sorry, Jeanine. No word on the missing money. I'm just here to pick up the fruitcake I ordered."

"Ah." I bagged up a fruitcake and passed it his way. "So, nothing at all about the money?"

He shook his head. "This one really has me stymied. The more rocks I turn over, the more puzzled I become. I'm almost inclined to believe Morgan misplaced that bag."

"You think? Doesn't sound like her."

"She said herself that she's been busy with the Christmas rush. Crazy things happen when we're busy."

A familiar acrid scent filled the air, and I jumped to attention. "Oh no! I think the fruitcakes are burning!" I raced to the kitchen and opened the oven, but was happy to find that the burnt smell was coming from the oven's heating element, where a little of the batter had spilled over onto it. Whew. That was a close one.

Still, I couldn't help but wonder if Deputy Davis was right. Maybe, like me, Morgan was simply so distracted she couldn't keep up with everything. Maybe she'd dropped the bag behind the desk or something like that. I would stop by her place later and ask if I could give her office another look-see. Hopefully my suggestion to do so wouldn't hurt her feelings.

By noon I'd completed the fruitcake orders. Tomorrow I would bake an additional dozen or two, just in case people asked for more.

All day long customers came and went from the shop, picking up fruitcake after fruitcake. I was surprised when Cody entered the shop.

"Is my fruitcake ready?" he asked.

"Oh, I didn't realize you ordered one." I glanced over the list to make sure I hadn't omitted one.

"It's in my aunt's name, but it's really for me." He grinned. "I'm one of the few people on the planet who actually loves the stuff. And I've heard yours is extra special."

"More extra special than you know. I had to replace my secret ingredient with an extra-super-secret ingredient."

"The mind reels."

"Yep, but my lips are sealed. You'll have to let me know what you think." I reached for one of the wrapped fruitcakes and put it into a bag for him. "I'm grateful for your purchase."

He engaged me in conversation and, before long, at his prompting, I was following him to the door to look at his new motorcycle. We stepped out onto the sidewalk and I saw the bike, a beautiful blue-and-silver number, parked directly in front of my shop.

Cody's lips curled up in a relaxed smile. "What do you think of my new ride?"

I couldn't help but whistle as I gave the motorcycle a solid once-over. "Wow, nice. She's a beauty."

"Thanks. I've been walking all the way to the coffee shop every morning in the cold. Thought this might be a better option. There's actually a little more to it than that, but that's the story I'm telling everyone." He laughed.

I didn't know what to make of his explanation, so I just nodded and offered what I hoped would be a nonchalant smile. "Be safe on the roads, okay, Cody? They're pretty slick. I'm sure they're even more dangerous on two wheels than four."

"I will, but don't worry. I used to ride motorcycles all the time."

"You did?"

"Yep." His usual smile faded a bit. "I guess you could say I have a past. That's what my aunt would call it. I hope she doesn't think this transition back to a motorcycle is some sort of sign that I'm moving backward."

"Surely not."

"I just miss it, is all. I had to sell mine a couple years back. Nice to be back to where I'm most comfortable."

There were so many questions going through my mind: Where did you get the money? Why now? But I kept them to myself. He headed off to work, and I turned to walk back into my bakery. As I did, a familiar sedan buzzed by. Caroline. Where was she headed this time?

I didn't really have time to think about it. Natalie and I needed to whip up the batter for the extra fruitcakes. I found her tending the register. Within minutes another dozen customers flooded the place, many picking up fruitcakes, others purchasing snowball cookies, our special of the day.

Not that I had time to think about any of that. As I turned toward the kitchen, I heard Peter's familiar voice. "I'm going to take a crack at those windows today." He laughed.

"Maybe I'd better rephrase that. I'm not cracking your windows, I'm working on your seals." He shook his head. "That doesn't sound right either."

I couldn't help but laugh at the boyish expression on his face. "You're awesome, Peter," I said . . . and meant it. He really had been amazing over the past several days, hadn't he? I would miss him once the Christmas holiday season was behind us.

"Hey, I know!" The idea hit me suddenly, and I needed to voice it. "I know you didn't order a fruitcake, but I'll make one for you as a thank-you for all you've done."

His smile faded. "I hope you don't take this the wrong way, Jeanine, but I'm definitely not a fan of fruitcake."

"Hers isn't half-bad," Natalie called out from the counter.

"Gee, thanks," I hollered back and then shrugged. "Can't say I blame you. Anything else come to mind?"

Crinkles formed around the edges of those gorgeous blue eyes as a smile lit his face once again. "I never could turn down a good red velvet cake. I think it's the cream cheese icing that does me in . . . in a good way, I mean."

"Red velvet cake for the win, then." I winked then immediately regretted such a flirtatious move.

Ah, who cared. With such a handsome man

standing directly in front of me, it would be hard *not* to flirt.

Peter responded to my silliness with a nod and a quick, "Can't wait."

Just as I was heading to the kitchen, his mood seemed to shift. "Hey, before you get back to work, can we chat about something more serious? In the kitchen, maybe?"

"Sure." I shrugged and led the way to my workstation, which I'd left in a messy state. "What's up?"

"I didn't want to say this in front of your customers, but I wanted you to know that I've been doing a little checking on Matt Kimball."

"O–oh?"

"Yes. I don't know what it is about him, but something just doesn't feel right. I want you to be careful around him, Jeanine. Don't fall for any of his stories. I went straight to Pastor Johnson up at the church, and he's got plenty of reason to believe Matt is up to no good. From what he told me, the whole Heart for Haiti organization feels the same."

"Right." I shrugged. "There's got to be some truth to the rumors, though Matt did a convincing job with his story that he's being framed due to jealousy. He says one of the higher-ups in the organization is working overtime to get rid of him."

"That part is true, but I believe they have reason to want him gone. Legitimate reason,

I mean." He gave me a pensive look. "I just have a bad feeling about him and would hate to see you manipulated in any way. I care too much about you to see you hurt."

Whoa. Well, if that didn't take my breath away, nothing would.

Peter headed to the front of the shop to work on the windows, and I got back to work in my kitchen. My cheeks grew warm every time I remembered his words. "I care too much about you . . ."

Surely he meant that in the most generic sense, as a friend would care for a friend, as one human being would care for another.

Right?

NINE

A couple of days after my final customer picked up her fruitcake, I had more time to think clearly about the Heart for Haiti project. Because Peter — who had become a regular at the bakery — insisted, I drove up to the church to deliver his three-thousand-dollar check. Pastor Johnson was thrilled to see that someone had come to my rescue. He took the check and then invited me into his office for a chat about the latest scuttlebutt regarding Matt Kimball.

"I know that everyone is warning me to stay away from Matt," I said after I took a seat across from Pastor Johnson's desk. "But he's been to my shop a couple of times over the past week or so, pleading his case. He insists that he's been falsely accused. He's such a nice young man, and I really want to believe him. He tells a convincing story, that's for sure."

Pastor Johnson released a slow breath. "Sometimes it's so hard to know who to believe."

"The more he tells me, the more inclined I am to think he's been set up by others in the organization. He's even offered me names and details. Have you fleshed out his story? Maybe he's telling the truth."

"I'll admit I haven't given his story much credence." Pastor Johnson shrugged. "And here's why. Let's say he's right, and they're trying to set him up. How would it benefit a missions organization to create a scandal like that? Surely they wouldn't want the negative publicity."

The pastor's words made sense as I thought them through. "I hadn't thought about that."

"This whole thing has to be affecting their donations. I'm more inclined to think they want this to blow over quickly so that people like Peter Salyers" — he lifted Peter's check — "will continue to give and feel confident in doing so."

"Right. I guess that makes sense."

The worry lines around Pastor Johnson's eyes disappeared. "By the way, Peter came by the other day to visit about this very thing."

"Yes, I heard."

Pastor Johnson leaned forward and put his elbows on his desk as he peered into my eyes. "He's inclined to think Matt Kimball is trying to manipulate you."

"Yes." I did my best not to sigh aloud. "I heard that too."

"You've worked so hard to raise funds for those kids in Haiti, Jeanine." Pastor Johnson gave me a look filled with so much compassion that it brought tears to my eyes. "And we're so grateful. All of us. Please don't think that your hard work has gone unnoticed. Oak Grove is filled with fruitcakes, thanks to you."

I did my best not to laugh out loud at the image that presented.

"Well, you know what I mean." Pastor Johnson chuckled. "Anyway, I'm proud of you. You're such a giver."

"I never really thought about myself that way."

"Well, of course you are. Anyone who knows you would say the same. You've given to families in need. You've baked for church functions and not allowed us to pay you. You wanted to make a difference to those kids in Haiti, so you came up with a way to do so. You're always using your time, talents, and treasures to benefit others, and I, for one, think it's wonderful."

I paused to think through his flattering words. Giving of my time just came naturally, especially with so many legitimate needs in the world.

"Thank you," I managed after a few moments of reflection. "I would give even more, if I could."

"You're doing just fine." He smiled. "And God always makes up for the lack, doesn't

He? This time He used Peter Salyers. And I'm glad Peter made the donation to cover the money that went missing." He leaned back in his chair. "Speaking of which, any more leads on the missing cash?"

I shook my head. "No. Morgan and I tore up her office yesterday. Moved the furniture. Looked in every nook and cranny. She even opened the safe again, just to make sure she'd really taken the money out. Nothing. Absolutely nothing."

"And Deputy Davis hasn't made any progress in his investigation?"

I shook my head. "There were a ton of people in and out of her shop that day. Only a couple had access to her office."

"Like who?"

"Well, a young man who's been working for Morgan, for one."

"You mean Cody?" Pastor Johnson's eyes lit up as he spoke the name. "Great guy."

I decided not to voice any of my concerns about Cody aloud and simply opted for, "He seems nice."

"Who else had access?"

"Well, Caroline, of course." I shifted my position in the chair. "She's the only one who admits to entering the office."

Pastor Johnson sat up straight and gazed at me with greater intensity than before. "Are you saying that Caroline Rogers is a suspect? You think she might've stolen that money?"

"Well, I didn't say that, exactly."

"Good, because she's not at all the sort to steal from anyone, trust me."

He might feel that way, but I still wasn't convinced. "Pastor Johnson, what do you know about Caroline Rogers?"

A hint of a smile turned up the edges of his lips. "She's been our treasurer for years, of course, so I see her in the office a few hours each week."

"Right. And all is well in that department?"

He nodded. "Oh, she's done a fine job. She's great with numbers, that's for sure. Her firm is doing well."

"And she's trustworthy?" I asked.

Wrinkles formed between his brows. "What are you getting at, Jeanine? Surely you don't really doubt her integrity?"

I flinched at the word *integrity.* "No, not really. I'm just . . . nosy."

"Caroline Rogers is an amazing person. You know she spent several years of her life on the mission field, right?"

"She did?" This certainly took me by surprise. "When was that?"

"I believe she's been back home in the States less than ten years, ever since her mother's cancer journey. Before that, she worked in India in a home for children with significant disabilities. I've never known anyone with such a heart for missions. That's why she wanted to help you, of course, because she's been there, done that."

"I see." Now I felt like a heel for not getting to know her better. "Has she ever been married?"

The pastor smiled. "I believe she had a serious relationship — a fiancé — before she left for India. But in the end, she chose the children, not the man. Then, of course, she moved back to care for her mother, who had breast cancer. That's her mom's home she lives in."

"Oh wow." I paused to think through what he'd said. "Pretty run down."

"I've offered to help on many occasions, but you know how she is."

"I guess I don't, honestly."

"She sends most of her income to the children. Every time I offer to help her by sending men from the church to work on her house she gives me a speech about how the children's needs are greater than her own and how she wants to stay focused on them for the time being."

"Wow." I hardly knew what to say. Another little pause followed. "So, she still sends money to India? That's so admirable."

"Exactly." He nodded. "She does. Just a few weeks back she told me of a particular need regarding a plumbing issue at a children's home in Mumbai. I believe she single-handedly took care of making sure that need was met."

"Wow." It was the only word I could manage. Suddenly I felt awful for even suspecting Caroline in the first place.

TEN

The following Sunday I made my way into the sanctuary for the morning worship service. I sat in my usual place alongside Evelyn. My heart skipped a beat when Peter and Natalie joined us. Evelyn shot a funny gaze my way, and I did my best not to glare at her. Let her think what she wanted. Peter was just being nice.

Okay, so he did offer me a stick of gum, which I accepted. And he sang with gusto during the opening song, which I appreciated. And he even whispered a quiet "Amen!" when our music pastor announced that we would be hosting a Christmas Eve service later in the week.

I tried to shift my focus from Peter to the service, and before long I was fully engaged. The music portion was particularly emotional today. I always loved Christmas songs, especially the old hymns like "O Come, O Come, Emmanuel" and "Silent Night." On days like this, with snow banked along the front steps of the church and the congregation gathered in one accord around me, I could genuinely sense the spirit of Christmas. And it didn't hurt that the handsome fella standing next to me was singing a perfect tenor on every song.

Before the sermon, Pastor Johnson made several announcements. He told the congregation that I had turned in the monies from my fund-raiser. He didn't mention Peter by name, but did share that someone in the congregation had donated money to replace the three thousand dollars that had been stolen. This brought a round of applause from the parishioners. Then he surprised me even further by stating that yet another person had given three thousand dollars, bringing the total up to six thousand. Actually, six thousand five hundred, counting the church's contribution.

I could hardly believe my ears. Had Morgan gone ahead and given the three thousand dollars without telling me? Possibly. Or maybe someone else had done the deed? Perhaps I'd never know.

Focus, Jeanine. Focus.

The pastor's sermon hit me straight in the heart. He talked about Mary and Joseph being in an unfamiliar place for the birth of their baby. He shared that Jesus was born in a borrowed stable, far from family and friends. I wondered what it would feel like to be separated from my life here in Oak Grove.

I couldn't imagine giving up friends, family, familiarity, to live in a new place. Then again, that's exactly what Caroline Rogers had once done. She'd left all she knew to live in India. To work with children in need. Only someone with some serious courage could handle all of that. And surely someone who cared that much about children in a third-world country couldn't have stolen the money.

On the other hand, Matt Kimball supposedly cared about children in a third-world country, and he'd lost his job over poor financial dealings.

Focus, Jeanine. You're in church.

When the service came to an end, I whispered a prayer asking God to forgive me for my ridiculous level of distraction. Then I turned to Peter, realizing he was trying to get my attention.

"I'm sorry. What did you say?"

He smiled. "Oh, just wondered if you had any lunch plans. Natalie and I are going to that new Mexican restaurant on the highway."

"Don't say no, Jeanine." Natalie gave me a pleading look. "No baking today."

I smiled and said, "I would love to go. Thank you for asking."

Moments later we made our way into the foyer. I walked up to Pastor Johnson and asked who had donated the additional monies, but he simply shook his head.

"This person asked to be anonymous, Jeanine."

"Yes, but was it Morgan?" I whispered. "Because, if so, she'd already told me that she might do something like that. But only if the stolen money wasn't found."

"It wasn't Morgan." He grinned. "Now, go on and enjoy your day. Relax."

"Okay, okay."

I couldn't put it out of my mind, though, even when Jo walked up to me and went into a lengthy commentary on the sermon. My level of distraction went through the roof when I realized Cody was standing in the foyer, talking to one of the parishioners. I walked his way and he flashed a smile.

"Good morning."

"Good morning to you too. Did you enjoy the service?"

He nodded. "Yes. Very much. Reminded me of when I was a kid. My church back home in Texas was a lot like this one, especially at Christmastime."

Peter and Natalie joined us. I couldn't help but notice the grin on Natalie's face when she saw me talking to Cody.

"Gotta love a great Christmas service," she said.

"Oh, I do." Cody stared at her. Intently.

Oh my. Were these two infatuated, or what?

Before I knew what was happening, Peter had invited Cody to join us for lunch and we were all seated in a booth at El Palenque on the highway just outside of town. We ordered and then settled into a comfortable conversation. Peter spoke to Cody as if they were old friends, asking him questions about his childhood. I listened intently as the young man described a horrific accident that had taken the life of his sister.

"After my sister died, I felt like giving up." Cody's voice carried an edge of emotion. "Turned to drugs. Did all the wrong things." He pulled up the sleeve of his shirt and pointed to the tattoo on his arm. "Until I see you again." He then pointed at the inked flower. "My sister Miranda loved lilies."

"Oh, I get it now. I'm so sorry, Cody. I didn't realize it was your sister you'd lost." I reached over and rested my hand on his arm.

He nodded. "Three years ago. She was killed in a car accident, along with her husband. Not a lot of people know this, but she and Donny took me in after my mom died. In some ways, she was more like a mom to me. I guess that's what happens when you've got such a wide gap in ages."

"Oh, she was a lot older?"

"She was eleven when I was born. So, it just made sense after our parents . . ." His words drifted off. "Kind of a long story."

"Oh Cody." Natalie's eyes flooded with tears, and she gazed at him with such tenderness that my heart swelled with unexpected emotion.

"You've really been through it, haven't you?" Peter said.

"Yeah." A little shrug followed. "Deadbeat dad. Mom passed from cancer. Sister and brother-in-law killed in an accident." He sighed. "I guess some people would be shocked I'm still here, but I am."

"I, for one, am awfully glad." Natalie gave him a smile so sweet it almost broke the spell of the bad news he'd been giving us.

"Me too." He glanced Natalie's way. I allowed my gaze to follow his and watched as her cheeks flushed.

The waiter joined us and reached for his order pad. "You guys ready to order?"

"Hmm?" Cody's eyes never left Natalie's.

"We have a special on Queso Flameado," the waiter added. "Buy one, get the second one half off."

"What?" Cody's gaze remained fixed on Natalie, who glanced our way and offered a shy wave.

Okay, got it. These two were definitely interested in each other.

Peter must've noticed too.

"We'll take the special," he said then glanced my way. "Fajitas okay? We can share."

"Sure. I'd love to."

Sharing fajitas with this handsome man on a day when I didn't have to bake — or even

think about fruitcakes?
  You betcha.

ELEVEN

"Natalie, are you sure?"

I stared at my young coworker in shock. "Cody was the one who gave that three-thousand-dollar offering at church yesterday?"

She nodded. "He didn't mean to let it slip, but he did."

"Where did he get money like that?"

"Oh, he's got plenty of money," she explained. "After his sister and brother-in-law passed away, most of what they owned came to him. They had no children."

"I see. But are you sure about the three thousand dollars?"

"Mm-hmm. He called yesterday and we talked for hours."

"Really?" This was interesting.

"Yeah. We have a lot in common. I lost my mom too, you know."

"Right."

"We're both survivors and both focused on where the future will take us. Anyway, I don't even remember how it came up, but he started talking about how he couldn't stand the thought that the money had disappeared from the Coffee Perk. He said he felt terrible. He said he should've been keeping a better eye on the people coming and going from the coffee shop."

"But how could he know someone would steal the money?"

"He didn't. But he's just like that . . . protective." She smiled. "At least, that's my take on it." She started talking about all of Cody's amazing qualities, and before long I lost her altogether. The bell above the door jingled and a couple of customers came in. I waited on them and shooed Natalie back to the kitchen to finish the morning's cranberry scones.

Around ten o'clock, Peter arrived. He looked relaxed and happy as he entered the front of the shop.

"Well, good morning," I said. "Wasn't expecting you today."

"Oh?" The edges of his lips curled up in a delicious smile. "Haven't you figured out by now that I'm looking for an excuse to come see you every day?"

The idea had occurred to me, but only in passing.

"Figured you were a Good Samaritan," I countered. "Always rushing to my rescue."

"Well, there's that." He gazed at me with

such sweetness that my heart began to flutter. "But let's just say I don't frequent every shop in town offering to fix things. I've zeroed in on you."

If that didn't make my pulse quicken, nothing would.

A sudden influx of customers distracted me from the conversation. Peter turned toward the kitchen, saying something about looking at a squeaky floorboard. I turned my attention to Mrs. Bingham, who wanted two dozen snowball cookies. Again.

By midmorning I'd sold nearly every sweet treat in my case.

"Man." I stretched my back as Natalie entered the room. "Is every person in town hosting a party this week, or what?"

"Well, it is Christmas week," she responded. "Which reminds me . . ."

"Reminds you of what?"

"Do you have plans for Christmas Day?"

I shrugged. "Evelyn usually invites me over to hang out with her family. We haven't talked about it this year, but that's my norm."

Peter entered the room, hammer in hand. "Let's shake things up."

"Let me guess," I tried. "You want to come to my house to fix my broken screen door?"

"Didn't know your screen door was broken, but sure." He winked. "But not on Christmas Day."

"Actually, we were hoping you would come

730

to our place for Christmas dinner." Natalie leaned against the glass case. "I'm going to attempt to cook a ham and a couple of sides. I was hoping you would bring dessert and maybe some rolls."

"Seriously? You guys want me to spend Christmas with you?"

They both nodded, and my heart swelled with joy.

"Well then, I would love to. Should I bring a fruitcake for dessert?"

They both responded with an emphatic "No!" and I couldn't help but laugh.

"Okay, okay. Something else, then. I'll surprise you."

I tried to focus on my work over the next hour or so, but as Peter shifted in and out of the room singing Christmas tunes along with the radio, my level of distraction was through the roof. The crowd thinned around noon, and I took advantage of the opportunity to fix sandwiches for the three of us. We sat at a table in the front of the shop, but Natalie's phone rang as soon as she sat down.

"Ooh Cody!" She grabbed the phone and headed to the kitchen to speak to him in private.

I looked at Peter and smiled. "I wasn't born yesterday," I said as I reached for my sandwich. "I can see where that is headed."

"Definitely." Peter took a bite of his food and then leaned back in his chair. "I like the guy. He's been really open about his past, and I admire that. Sounds like he's pretty grounded at this stage in his life, which gives me hope that he'll be a good match for Natalie."

"I hope so." I lost myself to my thoughts for a moment before speaking again.

"You okay over there?" Peter asked after an awkward amount of time had passed.

"Yeah." I paused. "It's just . . . I feel like a terrible human being right now."

"What do you mean?"

"I honestly suspected Cody of stealing that money from Morgan's office."

"Oh." His eyes widened. "I see."

"I mean, if you think about it, he was a perfectly logical suspect. He had access. And, honestly? I thought he might have motive too."

"What sort of motive?" Peter took another bite of his sandwich and then a swig of his soda.

I shrugged. "It's goofy, I know, but I just figured a young man his age working as a dishwasher probably didn't make much money. Certainly not enough to buy a new motorcycle."

Peter wiped his mouth with his napkin and rested his hands on the table. "You thought he stole the money and used it to buy the bike?"

"Yes. And now I feel like a heel."

"No one could blame you, Jeanine. Like you said, he had access and he had the extreme disadvantage of being someone you barely knew."

"True."

"Sometimes . . ." Peter reached over and took my hand. "Sometimes if you really take the time to get to know someone, you find that you're awfully glad you did."

I gave his hand a little squeeze as I gazed into those gorgeous blue eyes. "Yes. Agreed."

"And sometimes, if you give someone a chance, you'll find that the very thing you've been hoping for is right in front of you."

I had no words to respond to such sweetness. Instead, I sat like a goober, staring into his eyes, until the bell above the door jingled and Jo walked in. She took one look at Peter and me holding hands and her eyes widened. I pulled my hand away and welcomed her as if nothing were out of the ordinary.

Peter took a couple more bites then grabbed the trash and disappeared into the kitchen.

"Inquiring minds want to know . . ." Jo grinned and leaned against the empty glass case. "What in the world is going on."

"I . . . well . . ." A little giggle followed. "You would think I was a teenager, Jo, that's how giddy I am right now."

She reached over and gave me a hug. "Well, if anyone deserves a bit of romance in her life, it's you, Jeanine. You're a peach, and he'll be lucky to have you."

I put my hand up. "Whoa, Nellie. Don't marry me off just yet. We're just at the hand-holding stage."

"Gotcha." She nodded. "Well, I didn't come in to coordinate your wedding. I just wanted to talk to you about that fruitcake I bought from you."

"Oh? What about it?"

"This fruitcake tastes a little . . . different, Jeanine." Her eyes narrowed to slits.

"From last year's?" I asked.

"No, from the one Harper bought. I had a slice of hers, and it was good, but the one I got is . . ." Her eyes took on a dreamy expression. "Absolutely yummy. I must learn your recipe."

"Oh, she'll never give out her recipe." Natalie hollered from the kitchen. "It's top secret, passed down from her great-great-something-or-another."

"Great Aunt Ida," I said. "And Natalie's right. I can't give away the recipe. But thanks for letting me know. I'll definitely be making more next year."

"Perfect. I'll order a dozen and give them as gifts." Jo walked toward the door and opened it. As she did so, a blast of cold air filled the room. "They're amazing!"

Peter joined me in the room once more. "Didn't mean to listen in, but what in the world did you put in that woman's fruitcake?

The nibble I took was normal."

"Right. Because it was from the first batch. See, I ran out of my secret ingredient and had to punt for the last fifty fruitcakes."

"Punt? You?" He laughed. "It's been my observation over the past few weeks that you're the most stick-to-the-recipe-type person I've ever met. You replaced the super-secret ingredient with another similar super-secret ingredient?"

I shrugged. "Sort of. I made my own nectar."

"You're a honeybee now?"

"No, silly." I couldn't help but laugh at the image that presented. "I combined a couple of ingredients to form a nectar. I took some preserves and watered them down with a bit of, well . . ." I stopped short of telling him.

"Another secret ingredient?"

"Yes." I nodded. "One that will remain secret."

He turned back toward the kitchen. With the wave of a hand, he hollered, "Well, whatever it is, buy it by the caseload."

Oh boy. That might be problematic. The first and only bottle of Jamaican rum had nearly run dry, and I wouldn't be caught dead buying another.

TWELVE

Less than an hour before closing time, Caroline entered the shop. As had become her custom, she asked for my outdated baked goods. I gathered as many items as I could from the back — things I'd set aside earlier this morning in anticipation of her visit. This had gotten to be quite the habit with her over the past week.

Still, I couldn't let this continue without speaking to her candidly. After giving her the bag of scones, cookies, and so on, I gestured for her to take a seat at one of the tables. I offered her a cup of the Haitian blend coffee and then joined her, finally working up the courage to voice the questions on my mind.

"Caroline, can I ask you something?" I gave my coffee a stir then stared into her tired green eyes.

"Sure, Jeanine." She took a sip of her coffee and leaned back in her seat, looking relaxed.

"You were a missionary?"

She dumped a packet of sweetener into her coffee and gave it a stir. "Of course. I thought you knew that."

I shook my head. "Only found out recently. What sort of work did you do?"

"I spent several years in India. Fell in love with the children. Most of them were disabled and so affectionate. They gave me lots of love. It would take me too long to tell you all that I did — everything from teaching in the school to working in the kitchen. You name it, I did it." Her eyes sparkled, and she seemed to radiate joy. "Best years of my life."

"From what I can gather, you still seem to put the needs of others before your own. Pastor Johnson says you're one of the most giving people he's ever known."

She nodded. "Psalm 82:3 is my life verse: 'Defend the weak and the fatherless; uphold the cause of the poor and the oppressed.' I have to do what I can when I can, even if it means a little sacrifice on my end."

"I think that's so admirable." Time to switch gears a little, to offer some advice. "I do hope you're taking care of yourself too, though. That's equally as important. If you don't take care of you, there won't be anything left to give others."

"Every personal need is met by the Lord, Jeanine." She reached over and patted my hand. "Don't fret over me. I always manage."

"I won't fret, but I am concerned. If you

need more baked goods, I'm here." I lowered my voice. "I'll give you whatever you need, so don't ever be afraid to ask. I would never forgive myself if I thought your cupboard was bare."

Her eyes widened, and she pulled her hand away. "Oh Jeanine! Is that what you think — that I'm actually eating these scones and muffins and such . . . myself?" When I nodded, she started laughing. "Oh honey. I'm sorry. I should've just come right out and told you. There's a family living under the overpass on the highway, just outside of town. I've been feeding them twice a day, noon and evening."

"What?"

She nodded. "They've been there for two weeks. In this cold. Can you imagine?"

I couldn't. The very idea broke my heart.

"They have two little ones — a toddler and a new baby. I've been trying to get food to them as much as I'm able," she explained. "And blankets too. And pillows."

"That's why you needed the baked goods?" I asked. "Why didn't you just tell me?"

She shrugged. "The Bible says we're not to let the right hand know what the left hand is doing."

"What do you mean?"

"I didn't want anyone to know I was feeding those folks because I don't want to draw attention to myself. And I know you — if I'd told you what I was up to, you would've offered me everything in your shop. Same with Julia up at the grocery store and Tom at the drugstore. Every donation has gone straight to that poor family."

"My goodness. How long have you been feeding them, Caroline?"

"Over a week. I would bake for them, myself, but I'm so busy with my work that there isn't time."

"Please don't think twice about asking me. I'm happy to donate."

"Awesome." Her lips curled down into a frown. "I can't help but worry about them in this weather. I offered to let them stay at my place, but so far they've turned down every offer."

"Well, God bless you for offering. And while we're at it, God bless you for everything you do for others. You're an amazing woman, Caroline Rogers."

"Thank you, Jeanine. I think you're pretty amazing too — baking all those fruitcakes, working so hard to make sure those kids in Haiti have beds to sleep on. That's pretty impressive." She rose and grabbed her bag of goodies. "Sorry to rush, but I need to get out to the overpass before the sun goes down. They'll be expecting me. And don't be surprised if you see them in church for the Christmas Eve service. I think I've almost got them talked into it."

"That would be wonderful. Reminds me of

Pastor Johnson's sermon about Mary and Joseph being in a strange place on the very first Christmas. Ironic."

"True. I hadn't thought about that." She paused. "Thanks again for the baked goods, Jeanine, and thanks for the coffee too."

Before I could say, "Would you like that cup of coffee to go?" she was out the door.

I wandered back to the kitchen deep in thought. Hearing that Caroline was feeding a homeless family certainly knocked her off the suspect list, didn't it? The more I thought about it, the more I realized Morgan must've simply misplaced the bag of money. Nothing else made sense.

When I got to the kitchen, I found Natalie washing dishes. She looked my way and swiped a loose hair from her forehead with the back of her hand. "Oh, hey, Jeanine."

"Hey to you. Thanks for doing those."

"It's what you pay me to do."

"Yes, but you go above and beyond, honey. You always have."

She laughed. "To be honest, I'm so happy not to be washing those sticky fruitcake pans, I'll happily wash anything else."

"I really put us through a lot with those fruitcakes, didn't I?" The question was more rhetorical than anything else. "You know, I've been pondering this question for weeks."

"What question?" Natalie asked and then

reached for a dish towel to dry the pan in her hands.

I grabbed a rag to wipe down my workstation. "Why I chose fruitcakes instead of something easier."

"Just tradition, right? Isn't it like some sort of unwritten rule that a bakery has to provide fruitcake at Christmastime, terrible or not?" She set the pan down on the drying rack and glanced my way, her eyes widening. "Not that yours is terrible, as I have already established."

I waved a hand in her direction to dismiss any concerns. "No worries about that, silly. But I think there's more to it than just providing it because it's Christmas. My great-aunt Ida was the best baker I've ever known. Her recipes were passed to my mother, who passed them to me. I have really distant memories of visiting Ida's home as a child and hovering in the kitchen while she baked. There was something so magical about all of that."

"Hey, I love hovering in the kitchen while you bake," Natalie said. "Just call me a kid at heart."

I couldn't help but smile at my young protégé. "Thank you. But I guess what I've figured out is there are a lot of life-lessons to be learned in the kitchen. I enjoyed listening to Ida tell stories about her life, about the people she was baking for, about how she struggled with arthritis but still managed to get out of bed every morning and do what needed to be done. About how her pipes burst after a big freeze, but a group of men from her church came to the rescue, fixing everything so she could keep on working."

"Wow."

"Right? I mean, I remember her baking, sure. And I got the recipes, so I was the designated family baker after she passed. But more than that, I got her. I got her laughter, her tone, her nuances, her jovial attitude. I was blessed to be able to share in all of that with her."

"And I with you." Natalie tossed a couple of dirty utensils into the sink and flashed a smile so warm it brought tears to my eyes. "I've learned a lot more than just recipes, Jeanine. You've been like a mom to me. You really have."

The most beautiful silence hung in the air over us. I would even call it holy.

In that moment, I knew what had to be done. I raised my finger, as if to say, "Give me a minute," then disappeared into my office.

With the tiny key from my desk drawer, I opened the top drawer of the filing cabinet and thumbed through the mess inside until I came to the right folder. When I pulled it out, a sense of childlike wonder flooded over me, a holy joy. I clutched the folder to my chest and made my way back into the kitchen. Natalie looked my way, creases forming between her brows.

"Whatcha got there?"

I gestured for her to join me at the workstation, where I opened the folder. "My great-aunt Ida's recipe file." I pressed it in her direction. "Which I'm giving to you."

"Wh–what?" Natalie's eyes widened, and for a moment I thought she'd gone speechless. "I . . . I . . . I . . ." She shook her head.

"It makes perfect sense, Natalie. I don't have a daughter to pass the recipes down to. You're the nearest and dearest thing I've got."

Her eyes flooded with tears right away. "That's the sweetest thing anyone's ever said to me, but are you sure there's not a cousin or a niece or something who might come out of the woodwork looking for this?" She clutched the folder to herself, as if daring someone to steal it away.

"Nope. Not a lot of gals in my family got the baking gene. Just me."

"But you still use these recipes, right? Don't give me your one and only, Jeanine. Who knows what might happen. The dog might chew it up."

"You don't have a dog."

"I might get one someday. You know?"

I couldn't help but laugh at the panic on her face. "You're right that I'll still need the recipes too, so here's the solution we can both live with. When things are slow at the bakery, take those recipes and create a file on the computer. It's probably better for both of us to have digital copies, anyway, in case something actually does happen to the hard copies."

"I . . . I will." Her eyes shifted to my office. "Things are kind of slow right now . . ."

"They sure are." I winked at her, and she bounded from the room. I hollered back to her, "Do you need the password for my computer?"

"Nope," she called back. "It's my dad's name."

I felt heat rise to my face. How she'd figured that out, I had no idea.

THIRTEEN

Things around Oak Grove really got exciting as Christmas week forged ahead. Seemed everyone in town decided to decorate this year. I'd never seen our little corner of the world looking so festive. I did my best to make the shop look and smell like Christmas by baking holiday favorites.

On Christmas Eve, I opened the shop as usual, but decided to shut down at noon so I could enjoy the Christmas Eve service at church. Peter, God bless him, was there with me every step of the way. So was Natalie. I could hardly wait for Christmas dinner at their home tomorrow. What fun we would have.

Peter.

As I thought about the man I'd grown so fond of, warm feelings of comfort swept over me. It'd been a long time since I'd felt that way, and I would enjoy it as much as I could. I couldn't stop thinking about an idea he'd presented, one that involved Hope for Haiti.

Maybe, by day's end, I could give him a solid yay or nay regarding that idea. Right now, I had to keep my eye on the bakery, which was teeming with people hungry for Christmas sweets.

As the final customers cleared out my cases, Peter manned one register and I took care of the other while Natalie worked to clean every square inch of the kitchen. By the time I put the CLOSED sign on the door, we were all exhausted. We collapsed around one of the tables, and I groaned because of the pain in my lower back.

"I can't believe I'm saying this, but I'm so glad to see Christmas end."

"Hey, it's just beginning." Peter's eyes twinkled as he looked my way.

"Well, you know what I mean. I've baked my last Christmas sweet treat." I wouldn't let him know until our dinner tomorrow that I'd made a yummy red velvet cheesecake, just for him.

Natalie glanced my way. "I hope you're saving a few of those snowballs for our get-together tomorrow."

"And I really love those orange-cranberry scones," Peter added.

"Oh, trust me, I've hidden away everything we'll need. And if you're interested in something now, there are extra cookies in the kitchen cupboard."

Natalie nodded and rose, then walked

toward the kitchen.

"Natalie, while you're up . . ."

She glanced my way.

"Would you put on another pot of coffee? I'm getting sleepy."

"Me too." Peter crossed his arms at his chest and rested his back against his chair. "Now that everyone's gone, I feel like I could crash."

"Sure." Natalie yawned. "Haitian blend?"

"Of course." I paused as the realization hit. "On the other hand, maybe we'd better not use up our stash if our only local connection is no longer working for Heart for Haiti."

"Oh, that's right." Natalie looked downcast all of a sudden. "But Matt did mention that he's got quite a stash at his house, so maybe he could part with a few bags."

"You talked to Matt about coffee?"

"Sure." She carried the plate with the cookies and scones to the table. "That morning I picked up the baking trays from the coffee shop. He and Phara were headed out to pick up her engagement ring. They just stopped by for a cup of coffee to go. We talked for a minute about the kids in Haiti, how much they're looking forward to the new bunk beds. And about the fruitcakes, of course. Then I told him how much we adore the Haitian blend. He seemed to like that news. He said it's his favorite too."

"Right." I paused, and something occurred

to me. "Wait, the day you picked up the trays at the Coffee Perk . . . wasn't that the same day the money went missing?"

She paused, and her eyes narrowed. "I guess."

"And your visit with Matt, did that take place before or after Caroline got there?"

Natalie shrugged and reached for a cookie. "Pretty sure she walked in when I was leaving. Why?"

"Just thinking."

"Did you still want me to make some coffee?" she asked.

"Sure."

Natalie disappeared into the kitchen, leaving me alone with Peter. Ordinarily that would excite me, but I found myself far too distracted to think of romance right now.

"A penny for your thoughts," Peter said.

"Hmm?" I glanced his way.

"Are you entertaining the notion that Matt took the cash and ran?"

"Maybe. But, why would he do that? I mean, the church was about to give him the money anyway, right? With an additional five hundred dollars, to boot."

"Right." Peter nodded.

"Doesn't make any sense that he would've taken it. On the other hand, the church had planned to give him a check to take back with him, made out to Heart for Haiti. Not cash."

"I see." His eyes clouded over. "Do you

think . . ."

I did my best not to overthink things. "I think he's going through a lot already. He's lost his job, his fiancée is returning to Haiti without him, and he's got half the town talking about him behind his back. I don't want to make things worse than they already are. You know?"

"Didn't know about the fiancée going back. That stinks."

"Sure does. Morgan just told me all about it. Phara's Haitian, so she has to go back sooner or later. I guess she's chosen sooner."

"Maybe she knows something we don't?"

"Or maybe she just has to get back home. You know?"

"Right. I'd be missing my family if I had to stay in a strange country."

In that moment, something occurred to me. I sprang from my seat and walked to the kitchen to grab my phone. I called Morgan and asked her to gather the ladies for a last-minute get-together.

"But it's Christmas Eve, Jeanine," she argued.

"I know, but this won't take long. Just call the ladies, please. I'm going to put in a call to Deputy Davis. Hopefully he can meet us there."

Morgan fussed a little more but agreed to call the ladies. I contacted the deputy, who was a little put off about the idea, but agreed to meet us ASAP at the Coffee Perk. Peter and Natalie insisted on going with me, of course. Less than twenty minutes later, we were all gathered around a table at the coffee shop, sipping on Morgan's house blend.

"What's this all about, Jeanine?" Jo asked. "I'm supposed to be prepping for Christmas dinner today."

"Me too," Evelyn said. "I left half-boiled eggs sitting in a pan on the stove. This had better be good."

"Oh, it's good, all right." I turned to Deputy Davis. "I've spent the last couple weeks racking my brain, trying to think of who might've stolen that three thousand dollars."

"We all have, Jeanine," Morgan said.

I nodded. "Right. But I haven't been able to let it go." A pause followed. "I thought maybe Morgan just misplaced the bag."

"But we tore my office up and it's not there," she explained.

"And I had my suspicions about Cody," I added.

"You suspected my nephew?" Evelyn's eyes widened. "Are you serious?"

I released a sigh. "Yes, and I'm sorry. He's an amazing young man. Clearly I know better now."

"To be honest, I had some concerns about him, myself," Deputy Davis added.

"Me too." Penny nodded. "But he's so

sweet. Kind of hard to suspect someone so nice."

"I just can't believe you all felt this way and didn't tell me." Evelyn shook her head. "I'm glad to hear he's won you over."

"He's a great guy." Peter rose and walked over to the coffee condiments area, where he dumped more creamer into his cup. "Some people just need a second chance."

"Right." I nodded. "And that left one suspect, Caroline Rogers. She was there at the scene of the crime. She had every opportunity to take the money and run. But, in the end, I ruled her out as well, which led me straight back to my original thought, that the money simply went missing."

"That much money rarely goes missing," Deputy Davis argued.

"Exactly." I stood and paced the room. "Which leads me to my final conclusion."

"Could you hurry, Jeanine?" Harper asked. "My to-do list at the house is huge. I don't even have my tree up yet."

"Okay, I'll hurry." I faced the group, put my hands on my hips, and blurted out the truth, as I knew it. "Matt Kimball stole the money."

"Wh–what?" Deputy Davis's head shot up. "Matt Kimball was in the coffee shop the day the money went missing?"

Natalie nodded. "He was. I came by to get the bakery trays, and Matt was here with his fiancée, getting a cup of coffee."

"Yes, but it's where they were going that grabbed my attention," I explained. "Natalie told me that Matt and Phara were headed out to pick up her engagement ring. When they showed up at the bakery days after the money went missing, she was sporting a fabulous diamond on her ring finger. In fact, she was showing it off to everyone she met."

"Oh right." Morgan nodded. "She showed it to me too."

"And me," Evelyn said. "Gorgeous ring."

"A very expensive ring for a man who made very little money, even when he had a job," I added.

"You're saying he stole that cash and used it to buy a ring for his fiancée?" Evelyn asked.

"Only one way to know for sure. There's only one jewelry store in town, right?"

Deputy Davis rose. "I'm on it." He reached for his phone and made the call. We all leaned in to listen to his end of the conversation with the jewelry store owner, Bob Wilson. Minutes later he set the phone down and looked our way. "Well, that was interesting. Bob remembers the couple. He said the ring he sold them was valued at over forty-five hundred dollars, but he let them have it for three."

"Bingo." I nodded.

"And . . ." The deputy smiled. "They paid in cash."

"Of course they did," I said. "The way I

look at it, Phara and Matt were working together. They saw a way to get money in their pockets and to get her out of the country."

Peter looked a bit confused by this explanation. "But you said she was headed back to Haiti without him, right?"

"My guess is, they're both on their way out of town . . . together. And I'm guessing they're waiting until today, when we're all in Christmas Eve service together, so that no one will be paying attention."

"They've got my attention now." Deputy Davis shoved his phone in his back pocket and headed for the door. He turned back to face me at the last moment. "Jeanine, thank you."

"For what?" I asked.

"For paying attention. And for caring enough about those kids to raise the money in the first place."

"Of course," I said with a wave of my hand. "Happy to be of service. Now, go catch those two, will you?"

He bounded out the door, and I reached for my cup of coffee, finally content this fiasco was behind us.

FOURTEEN

"Well, now this is a happy ending." Morgan rose from the table and walked to the coffeepot. "We know who took the money, and the culprits will soon be arrested."

"And I've given all one hundred seventeen fruitcakes to their rightful owners," I said, and then laughed.

"Yummy fruitcakes," Morgan added. "Still can't get over that flavor. Very tasty. Sure would like to know your secret ingredient."

"I'll go to my grave with it." I gave her a little wink then looked Natalie's way and put a finger to my lips.

She laughed. "I'm not telling."

"Hey, speaking of secrets, I heard one through the grapevine," Evelyn said. "Pastor Johnson told me that someone else gave three thousand dollars to Heart for Haiti."

I turned to face Evelyn. "Who was it?"

She shook her head. "He wouldn't tell me, but I have my suspicions." Her gaze shot to Morgan, whose cheeks flamed pink.

"No one around here can be trusted with a secret," Morgan said and then refilled her cup of coffee.

"You didn't have to do that, Morgan," I said. "After all, Peter and Cody already went above and beyond to make sure the kids had their bunk beds."

"Peter and Cody?" Morgan looked stunned as I spoke their names.

Peter stared at me, wide-eyed.

"Oops." I giggled. "Sorry. I wasn't supposed to tell anyone that. Have I mentioned I'm terrible with secrets?"

"Are you telling me that my nephew gave money too?" Evelyn asked. "If so, then I'm one proud aunt."

"He did," I explained. "But I think that was supposed to be top secret, as well."

"I know who not to share my most private conversations with." Penny looked my way and laughed. "But I'm glad God met the needs for the kids in Haiti. I really am."

"Sounds like He went above and beyond." Peter took a sip of his coffee.

"More than you know," Natalie said, and then smiled. "Are you going to tell them your idea, Dad?"

We all faced Peter, who looked a little overwhelmed with so many women staring him down.

"My company has a private jet," he explained. "I suggested to Pastor Johnson that we deliver the money in person."

"And by 'we' he means me," I said. "With Pastor Johnson too, of course. And Natalie."

"You're actually flying to Haiti?" Morgan shook her head. "Now I know my ears must be deceiving me."

"They're not." My heart swelled with joy. "We leave on Monday."

"Are you closing your shop?" Evelyn asked. "Mm-hmm."

"If anyone deserves a break, she does." Peter gave me an admiring look. "I've never seen anyone work so hard."

"Boy, that's the truth." Jo laughed. "I get tired just watching you, Jeanine."

I paused to think about her words. I was a hard worker, one of the hardest I knew. But all of those hours slaving over a hot oven were worth it, especially during the holiday season when I could see my customers' faces light up with joy.

Something else brought me joy as well. As I pondered the year's end, I reflected on the many changes this year had brought to our little group — some delightful, others bittersweet. Most of my friends had stumbled into new relationships, many finding love. Jo and Dave. Harper and Cam. Morgan and Dean. Evelyn and Danny. Even Natalie and Cody seemed to be heading in that direction. Of course, our dear Penny had lost the love of her life, but she managed to maintain a positive attitude, despite her loss. And who knows what could be in her future?

We ended our conversation, and Morgan closed up shop. Natalie met up with Cody for a walk, and Peter and I headed down the sidewalk toward my shop. I still needed to put a few things away before I could get away from the bakery for a few days. We stepped inside, and it felt a little chilly.

"Brr." I shivered. "Is that heater acting up again?"

"Want me to take a look at it?" Peter asked.

"Nope. Not today. Maybe after we get back from Haiti."

Haiti.

Would I really leave the bakery to head for Haiti in a few days? My mind reeled every time I thought about it. Still, as I pondered the smiles on the faces of those precious children, my heart flooded with joy.

Something else brought me joy too, and I couldn't keep my eyes off of him.

Peter slipped his arm around my waist and drew me close. "Just so you know, I'm here for the long haul, so you don't need to keep coming up with things for me to fix."

I laughed. "That's funny. You think this whole thing was a setup?"

He shrugged. "Well, if the shoe fits . . ."

We both laughed, and he pulled me even closer.

"Nothing could pry me away," he whispered

in my ear. "You won me over with your —"

"Snowball cookies?"

"No, but I love those too."

"My orange-cranberry scones?" I tried.

He shook his head. "No, Jeanine."

"My remarkable personality?"

This time he laughed. "Well, yes. That . . . and your amazing fruitcake."

I quirked a brow then gazed into those twinkling blue eyes. Was he making fun of me?

Peter placed a tiny kiss on my forehead. "But, if we're being perfectly honest — and I'm a firm believer in honesty — I'm partial to something else at the Mad Batter too."

"Oh?"

"Mm-hmm." His tiny kisses traveled from my forehead to my cheek. "Or should I say 'someone,' " he added. He tipped my chin with his hand and gazed at me with such intensity that I felt a little weak in the knees. "So, inquiring minds want to know . . . how do you feel about that notion?"

"Oh, I . . ." A childish giggle threatened to escape, but I pushed it down. What could I say, that I'd waited years for a man to speak words like this to me? That I'd poured myself into my work to stay busy so the loneliness wouldn't consume me? That I couldn't wait to fly off into the great beyond with this remarkable man?

In that moment, I decided to say nothing at

all. Instead, I threw my arms around his neck and planted a kiss on him that would tell Peter Salyers everything he needed to know . . . and more.

JEANINE'S HOMEMADE FRUITCAKE

4 cups pecans, finely chopped
1 3/4 cups candied pineapple, chopped
1 1/2 cups dried apricots, chopped
1 1/2 cups golden raisins
2 cups flour, divided
1 cup (2 sticks) butter, room temperature
1 cup brown sugar
5 eggs, room temperature
1 cup apricot nectar, divided (or substitute 1/2 cup apricot preserves mixed with 1/2 cup rum)
1/2 cup honey (or light corn syrup)
1/4 cup milk
1 1/2 teaspoons ground cinnamon
3/4 teaspoon baking powder
1/2 teaspoon salt
1/2 teaspoon allspice, ground

Grease and flour two loaf pans (5×9). Line bottoms with waxed paper; grease and flour the paper. Set aside. Combine pecans, pineapple, apricots, golden raisins, and 1/2 cup flour; set aside.

In a large bowl, mix butter and sugar until creamy; add room temperature eggs, one at a time. Beat well. Add 1/2 cup nectar, honey, and milk; beat well. Mixture should appear curdled in appearance.

Combine cinnamon, baking powder, salt, allspice, and remaining flour; add to the creamed mixture and mix well. Add pecan mixture; stir well.

Pour into prepared pans. Bake at 325 degrees for 1 1/2 hours or until a toothpick inserted in the center comes out clean. Cool for 10 minutes.

With a skewer, poke holes in the loaves. Spoon remaining nectar over loaves. Let stand for 10 minutes; remove from pans to a wire rack to cool completely. Wrap tightly and store in a cool place. Bring to room temperature and slice before serving.

Yield: 2 loaves.

JEANINE'S SNOWBALL COOKIES

Mix Together:
1 cup butter
1/2 cup powdered sugar
1 tsp vanilla

Sift Together (In Separate Bowl)
2 1/4 cups flour
1/4 tsp salt

Combine Ingredients
Mix well and add:
3/4 cup finely chopped nuts

Roll into 1″ balls. Place on parchment-lined baking sheet.

Bake 10 to 12 minutes at 400 degrees.

Roll in powdered sugar.
Cool.
Roll in powdered sugar again.

ABOUT THE AUTHOR

Janice Thompson, who lives in the Houston area, writes novels, nonfiction, magazine articles, and musical comedies for the stage. The mother of four married daughters, she is quickly adding grandchildren to the family mix.